The Harrowing

† FOR THE HOLY INNOCENTS †

THE HARROWING

A Novel

† † †

Jay Nelson

This is a work of fiction. Names, characters, organizations, places, and events are either the product of the author's imagination or are used fictitiously. May be disturbing to survivors of abuse and those easily scandalized, who should use care when reading.

All contents and cover art
Copyright © 2002 by Jay Nelson

First Edition: November, 2002

Website: www.theharrowing.com

All rights reserved by the author, including the right to reproduce this work or portions thereof in any form whatsoever. Limited permission is granted to use brief quotations in reviews.

ISBN 1-58898-815-5

CHAPTER ONE

1993: Good Friday, April 9

BRUNO NOLAN savagely flicked off the engine key and sat glowering in the shadow of the old brown sandstone cathedral, conscious of the solid weight of the pistol in his coat pocket. He punched the wheel as the engine in his battered old Beetle shuddered and finally died.

He didn't want to be there at all, damn it. But Kathy, his ex-wife, had been imperiously clear and nonnegotiable on his answering machine: "Your daughter will be serving for the first time ever at Midnight Mass this weekend. It would do Marie good to see her father there."

So here he was, breaking again the private vow he'd made decades ago. Back to Our Lady of Solitude, home of the parochial school he had so detested. He'd done his time in Soledad, as the kids had called it; yet, once again family duty had brought him back to this loathsome, decaying romanesque pile.

Hell, if ever he could use a drink, it was right now. But that was the point of coming here, instead, after all. If he was really going to stay sober, especially over Easter, then he had to get in touch with this "Higher Power" like they always were going on about at the meetings.

For him that meant facing again the God of his childhood, like it or not. No matter how Bruno might abhor and resent it, the Catholic Church still possessed a mortgage on his soul.

"Hell," he said aloud. He checked his grizzled beard in the mirror and straightened his black leather biker's jacket. At last he pulled out the Colt. "Lord, what would Mom say?" He cradled his dad's old .45 like a holy talisman, then decisively popped the clip and ejected the round from the chamber. As he was hiding the bullets under the seat, he paused, cursed again, and stuffed the weapon and ammo into separate pockets.

"Best I can do, Mom," he muttered, and got out of the Bug, pulling the coat closed over his middle-age paunch.

He strode around to the side, hopeful that he could sneak in unobserved past the chapel of Our Lady of Victory, grateful that his brother the priest was scheduled to be off with the bishop dealing with hordes of pilgrims up at the shrine at Ghost Springs. But as he rounded the corner of the western transept, he ran right into a dog collar anyway. Monsignor Malarkey himself, Old Man Malachy, eternal rector of the cathedral, was squeezing a young, chubby-cheeked girl in a school blazer to his chest.

Bruno bounced aside. The old priest's eyes opened wide with recognition behind his massive black frames but he didn't drop the girl. "Oh, there you go, lass." he said, giving her a big squeeze before gently placing her on the ground. He patted her head kindly. "Now, since you've been so helpful setting out the prayer books, you can go over to the rectory and ask Mrs. O'Leary for one of those yummy Easter treats she's been baking all morning." He smiled. "Yes, Gina, even though it's Good Friday. Tell her that you have my special dispensation."

"Thanks, Father Malachy!" the child chirped. Then with shy glances at Bruno through lenses even thicker than the priest's, the girl twirled and skipped off down the walk.

Malachy turned to face his former student, ducking and weaving, dukes up, wearing a big grin. "Eddie, my boy! What an unexpected delight! How goes the battle, lad?"

Bruno forced himself to remain calm, hands at his sides despite the itching of his palms. He smiled ruefully, "Don't do that anymore, uh, Father. Don't even go to bars. It's a different sort of struggle now." He swallowed hard and frowned even harder.

The old man straightened up and clapped him on the arm. "Well, that's progress, for sure. I'm glad to hear it, son." Bruno nodded but was obviously unwilling to share any more. "Listen, Bruno," Malachy said, finally remembering the name the boy he once taught to box now used, "if you ever need to talk to me about anything, please do. Call or just come by the rectory. I promise I won't tell your brother if you'd prefer."

"Yeah, thanks, Padre. I will. For sure." Bruno said uneasily. When hell freezes over, he thought. The priest gazed at him sadly, shrugged, and followed him inside.

☦ ☦ ☦

SKULKING later in the back of the transept with the rest of the sinners, Bruno wondered yet again why he had returned to the church of his youth. He hadn't set foot within since his daughter was baptized, even missing her First Holy Communion. Almost forty now, he'd rarely been inside any church at all in the three decades since he'd been a pudgy schoolboy called "Eddie."

His stout frame slumped forward in the hard wooden pew, forearms resting on the one ahead, rump on the seat-edge behind in the posture of those who've spent too much time there. Half-listening to old Malachy droning his way through the Way of the Cross, he felt strangely relieved, as if being there were a tacit admission of some unmentionable guilt.

In this cool-shadowed place, he felt the silent disapproval of all the women who had taught him about God: his long-dead mother and grandmother, the ever-spooky nuns, even the various images of Mary, the Mother of God, that now surrounded him. For behind him, the statue of Nuestra Señora de Victoria guarded her private chapel while the stern face of the mosaic of Our Lady of Solitude herself peered down in despair from the sanctuary's rear wall. Wreathed in tragedy, the black-draped crone stared in grim resignation over the solitary dagger that pierced her heart, as if she were personally disappointed in him. And somehow, deep inside, he still felt an old, hopeless longing to be approved by all of them. He sighed. No, that was for pious Father Mike, his little brother, perpetual do-gooder and suck-up, not him. His own cross was to forever fail them.

Malachy moved on to the next scene in the ancient drama. Bruno arose along with the rest, mostly retirees, genuflecting while the priest, gowned in a long white alb with a purple stole around his neck, recited, "The twelfth Station. Jesus dies on the cross." Bruno automatically murmured with the others, "We adore thee, O Christ, and we bless Thee, because by Thy holy cross Thou hast redeemed the world."

He knelt again while the cleric read the text for probably the millionth time in his life. Malachy recited as quickly and emotionlessly as if it were a shopping list. "For three hours has Jesus hung upon His transfixed hands; His blood has run in streams down His body and bedewed the ground..."

With the others he mumbled the response, "Grant that I may always love you, but do with me what you will." He ran his hand across his itching scalp, trying to ignore his whirling nausea. Well, if there was ever a proper time for desolation, then this lousy day called Good Friday was it: the one and only day of the year that even the bland modern Church tore off its feel-good shroud to revel again in images of primal gore. The medieval murk of despair was almost palpable.

Bruno's mind wandered. The clean crucifixion scene on the wall was sanitarily appropriate for such a comfortably middle-class congregation, unlike the carved Cristos, stained with bruises and bloody wounds rendered with horrible realism by the santeros. Though crudely sculpted by untrained peasants, their crucifixes still seemed excruciatingly accurate. The saint-carvers of the Southwest had known just how the blood would flow, having seen enough of it.

He knew that even as these urban Catholics heroically fought the boredom of the warm spring afternoon, others set themselves a sharper test of faith. Not just the devout clogging the road to the holy hole up north at Ghost Springs; the Penitente Brotherhoods were still rumored to be secretly performing their more realistic reenactments of the Passion with men kneeling on cactus pads, whipping themselves, maybe even a few hanging on splintery crosses up in the hills like in the old days. Or maybe not. Since the Bishop and senior clergy had officially joined them in today's public procession, perhaps their thirst for suffering had been set aside.

For Bruno just being there in church was sufficient penance and an old habit as well — after a lifetime of guilt it would not feel right doing anything else on this ill-named day. Even when they were kids, his mother would make him and his brother stay inside to say the rosary while kids from the public school up the street ran by outside laughing. Mike never seemed to mind, but to Eddie it was a real payment for his sins.

This dismal occasion wasn't much better. He gazed around the nearly empty church. The scattered faithful seemed no happier than he felt — not that anyone should when God died. Glad that he recognized none of their private torments on their eroded, careworn faces, he hoped it was mutual. His shameful past was enough of a blur that he couldn't be sure if he might have known any of them.

Bruno had sobered up after the divorce, even gotten into graduate school. Yet, a feeling grew that something was inexpressibly wrong with him, like there was a hidden volcano of insanity building pressure to erupt again.

His recovery from alcoholism, determined but not orthodox, had withered the previous fall due to a lack of faith in anything. He'd somehow stayed dry through the winter with the stoic determination of a sun-crazed anchorite, despite his former spouse's barbs and his patronizingly perfect brother. But hope had not been reborn with the spring, so here he was, once again tempting God.

"My God, my God, why hast Thou forsaken me?" he muttered into his hand covering his scruffy goatee as the stocky, stubble-haired priest paused in his reading and genuflected in silence to commemorate the final end of Jesus' long torment. Then Malachy stiffly rose, following a server carrying a cross down the aisle between two candle-bearers to the last Station, which would conclude the grim pageant.

Bruno felt his unease ebbing. Meanwhile the thin voices of the grandmothers croaked the hoary, heavyhearted song before the Mater Dolorosa. "At the cross her station keeping, stood the mournful mother weeping, close to Jesus to the last."

He rose again, feeling no deliverance but relieved that the dreary ceremony was ending. Tranced out the whole miserable day, he'd sat through the Sorrowful Mysteries of the Rosary and the reading of the Passion, watched as people kissed the painted wounds on the feet of the crucifix. Then at last the Stations of the Cross, and soon would follow the final act of today's morbid show — the Exposition of the Most Blessed Sacrament. Old Malachy would hoist the Host up in a many-rayed gilded monstrance for adoration, pass out Communion from the stash of already-sanctified wafers kept in La Victoria's chapel for the occasion and then clear out the place, leaving it as dark, forlorn and empty as Bruno felt himself to be.

Both altars in the sanctuary had already been denuded of all their finery. The golden tabernacle on the upper marble-topped counter where the holy bread was usually stashed would stand naked and empty, its thick metal doors unlocked and open. Both that and the newer altar below, a wooden table, would stay bare until the Resurrection was joyously announced to a sumptuously redecorated and packed house late Saturday night, when his daughter would serve as an acolyte.

Time for the Exposition finally arrived. The altar boys turned, squeaking up the aisle into the sanctuary, leaving the priest alone to complete the terminal Station.

Bruno hadn't noticed before how much one of the servers, a red-haired kid lugging one of the candlesticks, looked like he himself had at that age: short, chubby, freckled, and like Malachy, with the once-again fashionable crew cut. The boys wore modern garb — simple, loose, white robes with a soft rope around the middle, rather than the lacy surplices and long, many-buttoned cassocks of Eddie's day.

Finished at last, Malachy plodded into the sanctuary as the boys set down the cross and torches and waited before the altar. The tallest server helped the priest put on an embroidered gold cope, and the short, redheaded kid draped a white satin shawl over that. They then fetched the censer and incense boat, while the third one readied his hand-bell.

The priest mounted the steps, genuflected, and unlocked the sacred safe, taking out a large Host. Placing it in the center of the monstrance, he turned it around.

Grasping the gilt display stand with hands reverently wrapped in sacred satin, the priest solemnly blessed the congregation with it, as the altar boys rhythmically rang the bell and swung the censer, filling the air with sweet smoke.

Setting it carefully down, Malachy returned to the bottom step. The shorter boy hurried behind him to remove the shawl. As he backed up, his heel caught the incense boat, sending it clanging against the step, scattering beads of aromatic sap everywhere. Shocked, he dropped the cloth on the floor and nearly ran to fetch the container, his shoes squealing loudly through the startled church. Malachy wearily shook his head.

Bruno winced in commiseration. The incident was brief, if noisy. The chagrined kid's face was now more scarlet than his hair. Bruno's heart went out, for he'd screwed up enough himself, often enduring a throttling with a rosary or being cuffed about the head by Malachy or another priest as punishment.

"Damn," he thought, as the mortified child scurried into the back to refill the vessel, "I sure hope he doesn't take the poor kid up into the attic there above the sacristy."

"Christ!" Bruno grunted aloud, lurching forward off his seat like he'd been kicked in the gut, mind reeling in unexpected horror. The formless fear that had haunted him suddenly engulfed him in a wave of pure terror. He knew with abrupt and absolute certainty why he'd lost his faith as surely as a drowning man knows he is dying. Knew why a gun made him feel safer in church than God Himself ever did.

A whirlpool of images opened in his mind, and sucked him down. A tall man, looming behind him, urging him up steps. Kneeling in fear, his pants down around his ankles. A sharp pain in his ass, hands grabbing his shoulders hard. Hot breath stinking of wine, curses grunted in Latin. Finally, the sensation of drifting away, into a peaceful, white light.

But there was no such escape, not now.

Ashen-faced, he heaved himself up out of the pew, lurching for the side door while the priest calmly soldiered on, reverently filling the church with swirling clouds of fragrant smoke to honor the transcendent white cracker enthroned in gold.

Blinded by the radiance of the spring afternoon outside, Bruno retched until he was totally spent at the foot of the statue of St. Thomas the Doubter in the rose garden. But he could not expel the horrible vision.

The joyous birds sang on around him, as unmindful of his torment as the old ladies who warbled quite a different tune of adoration inside the dark church at his back.

CHAPTER TWO

Holy Saturday, April 10

LOST IN REVERIE, Monsignor Thomas DeLaval barely heard the light rapping on his office door. He unthinkingly held his breath, glancing up from the text he was concentrating on.

There it was again, furtive, barely audible: *tap*, pause, *tap-tap*, long pause, *tap* pause *tap* pause *tap*, more rapidly. Over his reading glasses, he spied a shadow on the carpet outside propel a small, folded slip of paper through the crack under the door. "What the hell?" he muttered, closing the thick, black, leather-bound book before him.

DeLaval lurched out of his chair quickly for such a stout man in his sixties. He ripped open the door but the mysterious messenger had vanished. The priest's baggy gray eyes peered distrustfully around, but the hall was vacant. The Catholic Complex, normally a quiet if busy place, was even more hushed than usual on this last morning of Holy Week, so expectant of Easter. Even the birds outside and the construction work on the new cathedral of Nuestra Señora de Victoria next door seemed reverently subdued.

DeLaval shook his round, balding head, grunting as he bent to pick up the paper. A prank surely, a silly joke from one of his colleagues before he left on vacation. Closing the door, he unfolded the note and a small square cut from the classified section of a newspaper fluttered softly to his feet. He cursed softly as he bent to pick it up — and froze. One of the tiny notices was circled in red, though the bold headline needed no additional emphasis. It stabbed into his memory with a spasm of sudden terror undiluted for having been dreaded for so many years.

"*REMEMBER FR. WILSON?*" it demanded. "*Info sought re: Fr. Philip P. Wilson, who served at St. Catherine's in Arkham 1956-7 by former student.*" There was a postal box number at the end, but his eyes suddenly couldn't focus.

"Oh hell!" he exclaimed with a nauseous surge of nameless apprehension. What kind of sick joke was this? He wanted to wad the damned thing up and simply throw it away. Even so, his stomach sank as he walked slowly back to the desk and sat down. He simply could not afford to dismiss it.

He stared reproachfully at the white piece of paper that had contained the clipping. Words were neatly lettered in red: "*THE TRAIL LEADS TO YOU. THE BOOK IS IN DANGER.*"

"I'll be damned," he growled, reaching protectively for the worn, leather-bound book. Next to its brass latch, it bore on its cover a worn gold-embossed version of the symbol on the wall he glared at absently while he brooded. There, the antique Cross of St. Peter Martyr held pride of place in all the many ornaments in his office. It was a thick, jet-black enameled cross with bejeweled gold end-caps, mounted on a pointy-ended oval plaque on which was carved the keys of heaven and hell crossed amid baroque clouds of glory. The crossbars were curiously small and wrapped around the joint was a sinuous golden letter 'S' that more than resembled a serpent.

DeLaval considered the possibilities. If this was a joke, it was getting less funny by the moment. Surely the clipping was no gag. Someone was out there sniffing around, trying to flush something out, maybe just one of Wilson's countless boys, angry at last. Alone, that could pose no personal threat to him.

But he had always known that anyone who guessed his secrets, connected to the Order or not, could betray him. He already had plenty of enemies, real and potential, like his perpetual nemesis Malachy, or perhaps that feebleminded bishop Chavez and his fawning chancellor, or even his so-called "friends" up there in Ghost Springs. Could one of them kill for his prize, even as himself once did?

Yet who knew about the "Book," that unholy Bible of blasphemy, the long-condemned *Codex de Arcanorum Diaboli*, and especially of its links to the murdered priest? And who among them could be so stupid as to think he would ever give it up for any reason? Might as well ask for the Cross itself.

Absurd though it was, this was no joke. Maybe, he thought uneasily, stroking the black-bound volume, it was some sort of blackmail scheme. But there were no demands, and for his own safety he dare not relinquish the *Codex* that Wilson had so unworthily inherited. The notations he'd added during his custody were small portions of the long list of the chosen and the damned, but quite enough to hang him in any court.

The paper also contained a short Latin phrase, *Deus Deus meus*, followed by a long column of numbers: *25:1-2,7; 12:5-15*; and so on, written in a tiny, precise hand. He shook his head in perplexity; first the Order's secret knock, and now a coded message from his seminary days long ago.

He rose and strode over to the center bookcase, scanning the wall of theology, and found his grandmother's huge Victorian, ornately-tooled Douay translation of the Bible, crammed in like an oversized afterthought.

DeLaval put the large tome on the desk and on impulse opened the liquor cabinet, his "tabernacle" as he often joked, behind his desk. He downed a quick shot of single-malt scotch, thought a moment, and then another. It was awfully damned early, but it was a long time until the solemn ceremonies of the night, and he definitely needed it. He refilled the glass, put the bottle away, and took a handful of antacid tablets. Plopping back down heavily in the plush chair, he reached for his pipe, and fired up his favorite Turkish blend. The furious puffing wreathed his head with fumes as he glared at the paper as if daring it to speak.

A little calmer, he unlatched the Bible, opening it to the Psalms. Soon he had it, Psalm 21, called of old "Deus Deus meus" from the opening line, "O God, my God, look upon me: why hast thou forsaken me?"

DeLaval swallowed hard and quickly went to work. The cipher was schoolboy simple but clever: the numbers referred to verse and word count, unrecognizable to most snoops.

He frowned, trying to concentrate on getting the word count right and avoid speculating. But that was difficult, and he had to make several tries. Finally, though, he had it.

The message read: *"Let all fear, for tribulation is very near. The council of the malignant hath besieged thee. They have numbered all, and they have stared upon thee, the reproach of men and the outcast of the people. Remove to a distance from the holy place: look towards defense."*

His hands trembled slightly. He read it again, but the meaning wouldn't change. The knot in his ample belly twisted hard and sank like a stone into the depths of his guts. So this is really it, he thought, at last, his personal Day of Judgment he had so long feared. Warning or threat, this was the end here.

Thank the Dread Lord he was ready to leave, having a long overdue vacation scheduled next week, but he didn't want to flee now, even for a short while. It was bad enough missing Olly's traditional post-Easter bash up in the mountains before the Feast. But to leave Alvarado for good now, just as he was at the point of formally reviving the Order? Only the Black Madonna was lacking, his efforts there having strangely failed.

"Damn it, it's not fair!" he grumbled.

Obviously, that had to be the reason. Someone was determined to keep him from taking his rightful place as the Magister of the Chapter, the head of the Black Order here in Alvarado. Whoever it was wanted him out of the way, coveting his place and knowing enough to actually threaten him.

Suddenly enraged, he balled the papers in his fist, dropped them in the ashtray and lit them. While the flames uncurled the blackening paper, he felt faint. The realization fully hit him. If anyone was checking into the life and death of Phil Wilson, he really must leave, and the sooner the better. Should he run even before the grand Mass at Midnight at which he was to be Master of Ceremonies, or was that just what his enemy wanted?

"'The wicked man fleeth, when no man pursueth,'" he growled and reached out to the phone as the flames flared and died, but hesitated, unsure whom he should call. If things truly were this desperate, why waste time going through such an elaborate charade unless he'd already been set up? If something was afoot so big that it threatened to jeopardize the *disciplina arcani* — the unbreakable discipline of the secret, it threatened all practitioners, not just him. A notice had been duly issued even if it was in a silly grammar school code: he was expected to react properly.

If the Great Council had indeed spoken against him, he would know. Hopefully just minutes before his death, and not through hours of torture as he had methodically administered to his old friend, but it would be clear. The Grand Master would never waste time on such frivolities as this.

Well, the hell with whoever it was, and whatever his agenda. Quickly as he could, the monsignor climbed up on the desk on his knees, and triggered the secret catch. The gold serpent creaked apart, freeing the ancient Cross from its tarnished silver mountings. Holding it as gently as he would a baby, he clambered back down off the desktop.

Staring at the venerable ebony symbol, he placed it reverently on the blotter next to the Book, and leaned on the desk. He dare not take his singular treasures with him, but where was a safe stash? Of course — the hidden repository that Wilson had used. Nobody alive knew about that, nobody who could hurt him, anyway. But how could he get to the vault undetected? Already the old cathedral was being primped for Easter.

As he plotted, there was another knock on the door, this time brisk, energetic and loud.

Startled, DeLaval froze, his heart pounding, mouth suddenly dry. The police? he thought wildly, as the world suddenly shrank around him. Not even time to kill himself. Like a vain fathead, he'd trusted in the collar over the gun and had long forsaken such violent precautions. There was only the Cross...

He picked it up. The door swung open, and a cheery male voice said, "Hola, padrino. What's happening?"

Damnation, he'd forgotten to lock the door. Shaking, DeLaval spun about, hiding the Cross behind him. A well-built young man in tight spandex climbing shorts and a purple armless tee-shirt stood in the opening, tote bag hanging from his shoulder. His black hair was very short, even shorter than old Malachy's, and a tiny gold ring glittered in one ear. He smiled under his pencil-thin mustache at the older man. "Hey, aren't you glad to see me?"

Smiling, DeLaval sighed hard. Ordinarily he'd be delighted and wouldn't have cared that it was in his office, but not now. Despite his sudden relief, not today.

"What are you doing here, Carlos?" he sputtered, sitting down. He stuffed the Cross deep into his old leather briefcase. "You haven't been scaling any steeples again, have you?"

"Why? Somebody missing a bell?" he laughed. "I've quit. Too risky nowadays to scale the cathedral with all that rotting stone. No, it's just our regular 'counseling' day." The youth pouted mockingly, "Or were you going to leave town without even a good-bye?" He threw himself down on the couch with his arms behind his head, long muscular legs propped upon the cushions. He smirked confidently at the older man, who glanced away, sorely aware of the teen's tanned, athletic body.

DeLaval quickly glanced out the door and shut it again, locking it with a sharp twist. He strode to the windows and closed the blinds. Turning around, he demanded, "Don't you ever knock? Did anyone see you come in?"

Carlos shrugged. "I came in the back way like I always do, so I don't think so. What do you care, anyway?"

"I don't have time to go into this, but you've got to leave. Right now," DeLaval insisted hotly. "I've got a million things to do before Mass tonight. I'm sorry. Really."

Carlos jumped up and coolly walked over to the monsignor, stopping mere inches from his face. "You seem awfully anxious, Father," he purred, toying with DeLaval's shirt buttons. "Sure you want me to go?"

The priest nodded, reddening, and jerked his hand away. "Just like that, you want to get rid of me?" Carlos demanded. "Why not let me stay and take care of your house while you're gone? Isn't there anything I can do for you while you're away? I need cash bad."

Inspiration suddenly shone on the monsignor. "Yes," DeLaval smiled darkly. "He placed his hand upon the black compendium. "Actually, there's something only you can do for me. But first, you must be silent and listen."

He had barely finished sealing the spell when there was another businesslike knock on the door. Heart leaping, he quickly rammed the Book into his briefcase beneath his desk.

"Father DeLaval, have you heard?" A tall, smiling man in a dark blue polo shirt and slacks exclaimed when DeLaval swung open the door. He waved a sheet of paper, "It's official! He's coming here! The Pope's coming..." He stopped dead in his tracks, noticing Carlos.

DeLaval breathed out hard, the thudding of his heart unspeakably loud. He forced himself to smile somehow.

"Why Michael, that's, that's wonderful news!" he grated.

Mike blushed, "Ah er, sorry, Monsignor. I didn't know you were, uh, busy."

"Come in, Mike, please. I want to hear all about it. Ah, we're done here, aren't we, Carlos?"

The teen gracefully rose, and drifted over to the door behind DeLaval. "Of course, Father Tom. Thanks for seeing me," he said dreamily. "I think I'll be going now."

The men stepped aside and the boy wandered into the hall. "Carlos," DeLaval called softly. "The exit's that way," he said, pointing towards the back.

Without a word, the young man headed towards the rear. DeLaval turned to face the younger priest. "Crazy kid's been climbing churches again," he began.

"Yeah, I heard," Father Mike Nolan said, embarrassment written across his open, well-shaped face. "We've all been warned to watch out for him. Sorry I interrupted your private counseling, of course, Father, but I was so excited by the news."

"Naturally, Mike, we all are! It's all right," DeLaval said and clapped him on the arm warmly. "Does Art know?"

"Uh, no. He's downtown getting ready for tonight."

"Well, don't you think somebody should tell him before the reporters get there?" the monsignor prodded gently.

"Absolutely, Father!" Mike grinned the smile that made many a high school girl sigh, and DeLaval himself more than once. It was even more attractive because the man honestly seemed completely unaware of his charm. "I'm on it!"

DeLaval steered him back through the door. Mike laughed, "Well, this will be some summer. Hey, anything I can do to help," he said as he was firmly pushed into the hall.

"Go tell His Excellency," DeLaval said, nodding and making agreeable shooing noises until he finally shut the door.

The old man leaned heavily on the thick panels until his heart stopped pounding. "Dread Lord of Hades," he sighed as sincerely as any prayer he'd ever said.

Opening his eyes, he saw the empty spot on the wall where the Cross no longer hung and knew that time was short. "If only I could avoid Mass. Better get out of here at least before somebody else comes," he mumbled, rubbing his chest. "Another damn shock like that might kill me."

He stumbled to the desk and grabbed the briefcase. Then, without even a last glance around at the life he was abandoning, he strode over to the door and softly opened it. He flicked off the light and shut the door. The lock clicked. Like a thief in the night, the monsignor crept down the hall and scurried away.

†

CHAPTER THREE

Easter Sunday, April 11

OUR LADY OF SOLITUDE overflowed with people for the grand celebration of Easter Midnight Mass. Rumors of the Pope's visit had rapidly spread, so not only were the usual corps of hardy believers come to witness the traditional climax of the church year at the witching hour, but many just curious. Even a television camera crew with blazing lights was stationed in a corner of the choir loft.

The floodlights made the atmosphere a bit too carnival-like for Mike. He loved the magical solemnity of the hoary ritual that usually surrounded the first announcement of the Resurrection. For in utter darkness, the bishop would kindle a sacred fire and from that light the magnificent paschal candle, a huge three-foot-tall consecrated pillar of pure white beeswax inset with wax nails. From its single flame, everyone's own small tapers would be lit, passing the light of faith around until the church was filled with a soft warm glow.

It was a moment of community when the idea of the Church as the Mystical Body of Christ actually made some sense to Mike. In some ways, it was better than Christmas.

But now the television's glare chased the mysterious darkness far away behind the arched vaults of the nave and the Mass had a strict schedule to keep. Despite his minor role, Mike was determined to keep a page ahead of everybody else so nothing would catch him by surprise.

His former teachers, the monsignors DeLaval and Malachy, were to be master of ceremonies and chaplain respectively. All should go splendidly though DeLaval was obviously distracted and in a black mood. However, it was Bishop Chavez' joyous giddiness that made everyone walk on tiptoes. This was dreaded even more than DeLaval's petulant sulks or

Malachy's temper, because when Chavez was most filled with the spirit was also when he was most dangerously prone to spontaneously stray from the script.

And of course, Mike had to keep an eye on his nieces, especially Marie. Her role tonight as torchbearer was even smaller than his, but it was her first time before the altar. From the glimpses he could steal, however, she was performing splendidly, with a quite-unexpected seriousness and dignity. However, the gravity of young maidens being easily disrupted, he was careful to try to avoid her and her cousin Beth's modestly downcast eyes, lest they all start giggling.

Still, just having her there filled his heart with pleasant gratitude. The lavish ritual flew by, and soon they were all seated in eager anticipation of the awaited announcement.

The bishop of Alvarado, Arturo Chavez, accepted his golden miter, flipped up the two small ribbons that hung behind with practiced ease and seated the bifurcated hat firmly upon his head. Taking the crook of office with a bow from Malachy, the Ordinary of the See of Alvarado paraded to the pulpit.

There he stood a moment, smiling. Silver-haired, tanned, and quite young and slim for a prelate, Chavez blessed the congregation with his famous welcoming smile. "My fellow clergy, faithful children, and all the people of this great community watching at home," he began, vestments glittering golden in the spotlight. "What marvelous news we have for you tonight." He took his time as the crowd stirred, adjusted the microphone on the pulpit and his designer eyeglasses while his episcopal ring scattered shards of light.

"Am I talking about the Resurrection? That Our Lord lives?" His grin grew even broader, if that were possible.

"Yes, of course," he said.

"But something almost as grand is going to happen soon right here in our community. It's so important, I'm going to forget about my usual sermon completely." He turned over his note cards decisively and the people murmured approval.

The bishop paused, relishing the moment. "I am happy to officially announce that His Holiness himself, our beloved Pope John Paul II, has most graciously agreed to visit our diocese during his trip to our country this coming August."

The entire populace gasped and rose to their feet cheering and applauding. Somebody even whistled, echoes ringing sharply throughout the nave. Mike almost laughed aloud himself, noticing that some of the elderly clergy seemed surprised as much by the impromptu outburst as by the Supreme Pontiff coming to their hometown.

He stood clapping with the rest. "Please," the bishop said with an even wider teeth-sparkling grin. "Please, calm down, hijos mios, calm. This has been in the works a long time — I first asked the Holy Father during my last visit to Rome, but it was only confirmed yesterday.

"We've much to do to prepare for the Pontiff and we will need the help of all the faithful. Sadly, although our new cathedral will not be finished in time, I hope that enough will be done so that His Holiness can personally dedicate it to La Victoria." He paused again for the clamor to diminish.

Mike smiled to himself to see the frown the chancellor, his old friend Robert Cruz, passed to a ruddy-faced Malachy, who shrugged happily in return. Meanwhile, DeLaval just glowered. Doubtless, the guys who really run the day-to-day show saw just another mountain of work.

"Be that as it may," Chavez declared, "this is a unique opportunity to show the world our great faith. Let us demonstrate that here; where the roots of our religion are oldest and deepest, we are most truly Catholic. Let's show His Holiness that our love for our Holy Mother the Church burns hotter than our finest green chiles!"

There was more laughter and excited applause. Chavez waited it out smiling. "As soon as the basic arrangements for his trip are worked out, I will let you know so we can begin our preparations," he said, pausing for a final spate of clapping. He took a deep breath. "Now then, my dear fellow Catholics of Alvarado, as part of this holy celebration, let us all rise and renew our baptismal vows." He raised his arms in the all-inclusive gesture he was loved for, and the people rose, ready to renew their allegiance to their church.

Most, anyway. As they recited the Nicene Creed, Bruno stood there with the rest. But he was rock-solid, lips tight and unyielding, glaring down at his hands clasped in front of him, saying nothing. He felt his ex-wife's curious glance, but he did not dare return Kathy's gaze. He was too angry at the church, at God, at himself, but it was his inexpressible shame that hurt the most.

So he silently did Catholic calisthenics on cue — stand, kneel, sit, repeat — and endured the remainder of the ceremony, trying not to think about the attic above the sacristy. He dared steal only glances of his daughter or at the mosaic of Our Lady of Solitude, still staring down in sympathy, lest he start weeping yet again.

Finally, though, it was time for Communion. Bruno hunkered far back in the pew as the rest of its occupants filed past him by on their way to receive the sacred wafers. He shifted, unobtrusively adjusting the holster in back. This time his trusty .45 was reassuringly fully-loaded and ready.

THE HARROWING 27

Even though he blocked the end of the pew, he wasn't about to move out of the way of the others. All too easy to get sucked along with the stream and there was no way in hell he was going to risk facing a priest, much less Jesus, in such a situation. "Easter duty" be damned: it was all he could do to force himself to sit there for the sake of his family.

So, fidgeting in his too-small suit, he apologetically blocked traffic, mumbling to the good people squeezing past his thick knees. Somehow he felt very young and unsure.

Despite the creepy business in the dark with the candles, thankfully alleviated by the floodlights, it had been a good show so far. The church glowed innocently with a jumble of Easter lilies, irises, and daffodils surrounding the twin altars with their fresh linens and many ivory candles. The servers had gracefully promenaded in wearing pure white tunics, scrubbed faces glowing, serenely bearing candlesticks while Mike beamed with proper avuncular pride from amidst the immaculate clergy, resplendent in their finest robes.

The rite had gone splendidly; his slim, redheaded daughter betraying no hesitation that Bruno could detect, nor missing a cue. The cathedral's parochial school choir's clear voices soared angelically through hymns so unfamiliar to the people that, blessedly, they did not dare join in.

But now Mass was nearly over, the lines of people waiting to take Holy Communion slowly shortening. This was always the most fascinating part of the ritual to Bruno. Who knew what secrets filled those souls behind visages kept so modestly bland as they consumed God in that most intimate moment?

As Mike might say, the eternal mystery of Communion remained. Certainly the outward form of the sacrament had mutated greatly in the years since the Second Vatican Council during Bruno and Mike's childhood had swept away the old Latin Mass, rigidly standardized for three hundred years with its emphasis on the utter transcendence of God.

In the old days, the priest kept his back to the people most of the time, facing the Almighty on their behalf, who was hidden in the gold-plated safe tucked beneath the crucifix. It was all the priest's show: aided by the acolytes, he alone recited the magic words in the dead language of the Cæsars that brought God down to Earth. The audience was there just to cheer him on and accept the fruits of his holy wizardry.

Nowadays, it was quite different. The priest faced the people who actively participated in the sacred meal across an altar like a big kitchen table. They brought up the bread and wine, read the Epistle and sometimes the Gospel. Nobody knelt for Communion anymore but queued up for a handout. They no longer gaped like starving chicks enticing the priest to throw in a Host.

The Eucharistic minister — rarely a priest, and often a woman anymore — would place the whole wheat disks into the grubby, outstretched paws of the common folk like they were grabbing an appetizer on the run. Then off they'd go back to their pews, munching Christ on the way, which still bothered Bruno. Hadn't the nuns said that chewing the Host was a sin?

Hosts were now a bit more like real bread than the cardboard-thin flavorless disks of the past. A person had to really munch these days to get one down. Sometimes they'd even be allowed a sip of the consecrated wine, too, which helped. However, it was now considered unnecessary to have servers stationed to field falling crumbs of Jesus' body with golden plates.

His memories all seemed so incredible now during this vibrant ceremony that he was having difficulty believing any of it. Yet it was still the same church, and whenever he closed his eyes, it came flooding back.

It had been a tricky business, holding the paten, a wooden-handled gold plate, beneath the chins of the kneeling communicants. It was especially difficult while walking backwards in a long cassock, trying not to trip as the priest crabbed quickly along the altar rail, dishing out the holy wafers directly onto the slimy tongues of the kneeling believers.

Bruno could clearly see it now in his mind, how he fumbled a catch that one spring morning. How he became so distracted by one old woman's tongue wriggling in her decaying mouth like some primeval purple slug that when the Host rolled off, he missed it. It floated as lightly as a dead leaf past the edge of his paten and inevitably down to the linoleum floor.

The rules said there then should follow a big embarrassing time-out. The priest had to stop, pick up the Host and eat it himself. Then he had to clean up the spot, leaving a holy rag there for further mystical scrubbing later. It was like the place was radioactive or something, and perhaps it was.

He had stared helplessly at his God upon the floor while the priest beside him angrily spat, "Damn it!" Never had he heard a holy father say such a thing. He was in trouble for sure.

Bruno blinked, returning to the present. He still could not recall the priest's face nor all that happened in the storage space behind the mournful mosaic on the rear wall. But it was real, somehow, as real as the sour taste in his mouth.

By now the dutiful had returned and were already refilling the pew from the other end. He dropped down the kneeler for his ex. Kathy knelt, her curly graying brown hair privately shrouding her as she engaged in spiritual rapport with her savior, head humbly bowed.

Bruno glanced away uneasily. He didn't belong here; much as some part of him still desperately craved it, he was more of an outcast than ever. But at least he now had an inkling, however hideous, of why.

By now the bustling clergy had polished up the communion dishes and Chavez bade them all rise for his final blessing. On the verge of tears, Bruno stood, but managed to smile as his radiant girl-child caught his eye as the procession flowed past.

He looked down again, shaking silently as the people around him fumbled about to leave. He felt a soft hand on his arm. It was Kathy, peering at him quizzically. He cleared his throat and forced a slight smile. "I'm okay," he whispered roughly. "Just proud?" she finished for him, her dark brown eyes welling slightly as she squeezed his hand. "Me too."

Not knowing what to say, he nodded.

Then they joined the flow of people on their way out, and stepped out of the church into a clear, but slightly chill spring night. The smiling ushers had swung open the heavy ironbound outer doors and the cool air swirled around them, redolent with fragrance from the cherry trees in the old town plaza below.

†

CHAPTER FOUR

BRUNO AND KATHY stepped out into the peace of midnight. The smooth stone face of the old cathedral was washed silver by the light of the new-risen gibbous moon. The great rose window above the portals glowed warmly over the plaza in the heart of old Alvarado.

As was usual, Chavez halted just outside to greet his exiting flock. The procession dissolved into a ragged reception line.

As they emerged, Bruno heard girlish squeals of delight above the murmur of the crowd. Beyond the knot of parishioners and clergy, Mike and the three servers stood on the small lawn. Marie and Beth had blown out their candles, handing them to the lanky boy who had carried the cross between them, and were jumping up and down hand in hand, laughing. While the adults watched indulgently, the kid wore a goofy grin like he had just been given a special honor by a pair of young goddesses. Perhaps he had, thought Bruno. Certainly, his daughter had never appeared so lovingly, achingly alive.

"We did it, we did it!" Marie shrilled as she spun herself into Bruno. "Whoa, girl," he said, laughing as he caught her. "Easy there, darling! Didn't your uncle warn you about the dangers of throwing up God?"

"Oh Dad, you're so naughty," she giggled, throwing her arms around him. He hugged back proudly, and then held her out at arm's length. Her luminescent beauty was flawless in the soft moonlight and the loose alb, bound at the waist, did not conceal that this twelve-year-old was becoming a woman. She smiled shyly and brushed her straight red hair back off her face. "I am unbelievably proud of you," Bruno said, "but you're growing up so fast."

She laughed again, kissed him on the cheek, and skipped off. "Now, Marie," Mike called as she raised her arms, "no handstands while wearing vestments!" She pouted for a moment then twirled away merrily with her longhaired companion. Bruno turned towards Kathy. "Well," he admitted. "You've done good. She's quite a fine young lady."

His ex-wife smiled proudly, if a little sadly, and took his arm. "We've done good," she said, emphasizing the "we." "But we could do a lot better, especially with her reading problems, if you'd show up and help more often. Maybe then you wouldn't be so surprised at how she's grown."

He nodded, unable to answer her criticism. He still owed her plenty of real amends, but her carping didn't help.

"Hey," he said, "I'm sorry I was late again with the payment. Tuition was due and the grant was even later than usual, so I —" Gently, she reached up and touched his lips. "You know that's not what I mean," she said softly. "You've missed so much by staying away. Marie needs a father, that's all. Your brother is closer to her than you are."

She saw the hurt in his eyes and hugged him. But her apology died stillborn, and her eyes widened angrily as she stepped back. "Bruno," Kathy hissed in a sharp, low whisper, "you didn't bring a gun to church, did you?"

Her former husband nodded red-faced, suddenly feeling totally stupid and aware that her voice had carried, though Mike was busy talking to an old couple. He could not tell her why. Apologizing seemed equally futile.

His former wife whispered icily, "Don't you even think of bringing it over to the house," and turned away, heels clicking sharply on the sidewalk.

Bruno turned towards his brother, still glad-handing the departing flock. "Hey, bro," he said when his turn finally came, "Good work. You taught Marie well."

Mike smiled feebly at the compliment. "She's a good kid. Better at it than we were at her age."

Bruno peered at him in mock amazement. "You're not thinking she might want to be ordained someday, are you?"

Mike laughed. "Well, if it was up to me...," he said and shrugged. "Maybe I should ask the Pope when he gets here.

"Anyway, Mike," he said, "You know I was no damn good. I couldn't even recite the Act of Contrition right, while you were made for this job."

Mike looked at him frankly and said, "Oh no, brother. You were the chosen one — until you threw it all away."

Before Bruno could retort Mike had turned and was already greeting a parishioner. Much calmer now, the girls had been listening, and his daughter tugged on his sleeve. "Dad? What did you mean, you couldn't even properly say the Act of Contrition?"

Bruno shook himself and chuckled uneasily. "Well, your uncle was so worried about going to hell if the Russians nuked us that he could rattle it off in thirty seconds, even before the air raid sirens stopped sounding. But I never got it right and was whacked more than once for saying it wrong. I thought it went something like 'Oh my God, I am hardly sorry for having defended me and we detest your just punishments, which aren't at all good —'" He was rudely interrupted by the noise of water pipes clearing their throats, and the sprinklers suddenly came on full all across the lawns around the church.

People shrieked, running for the sidewalks. Out of the corner of his eye, Bruno saw his brother hustle Marie over to the cement walk.

"Oh great," Mike said in disgust as he raised his arms, shedding water from his dalmatic. "I told the groundskeeper to be sure to disengage the automatic sprinkler system for this weekend. Look at us! We're soaked."

Bruno wiped the water off his face. He noticed Marie still clinging to Mike, and the wet linen clinging to her. Her blue-eyed gaze at her uncle contained something akin to adoration. "My hero," she said laughingly.

"Er, yes, well, that's okay," Mike stammered, stepping back, shaking water off his long stole. "I should have had a chasuble on — they were originally rain ponchos, after all. Isn't that right, Bruno? You're the historian."

Bruno was startled at the anger that rose in him. "Right as usual, padre," he said lightly and clapped him on the shoulder. "I think this is a good omen, don't you? Rain, anywhere in this desert is good — even up from the ground. It's a bloody miracle!"

"Yeah, I guess so," Mike grumbled. They looked around at the bedraggled group and chuckled. Marie, however, was beginning to shiver in her mother's ample arms.

"Hey, let's get you guys changed before you catch your death," said the ever-practical Kathy, as she bustled the girls towards the sacristy, shooting a final glare at her ex-husband. He turned to face Mike, but his younger brother had an odd expression. Ignoring Bruno and the milling crowd, he was staring upwards.

High above them came a slow grinding of stone on stone and a trickle of dust. Bruno glanced up too. The carved stone cross at the apex of the church between the towers tottered slightly in the gloom, an indistinct figure leaning against it.

Time seemed to telescope as Mike immediately turned, yelling, "Get down!" Bishop Chavez, still chatting with a little old lady, looked up astonished as the priest, arms outspread, wet stole flapping, leaped through the crowd upon him. The grandmother in black spun away into the mob. Mike and his bishop hit the wet flagstone pavement and rolled, knocking over even more startled parishioners and servers.

There was a terrible sound as the monolith gave way above. A falling scream — Bruno couldn't make out words — was drowned by a hard crash of stone smashing into flying bits against the pavement, and a softer, wetter thud, almost like a watermelon disintegrating into pulp.

Mike and the bishop stopped rolling. His left arm sprained, Mike lifted himself up gingerly and helped Chavez rise. "Are you okay?" Mike asked. His superior, pale and obviously shaken, waved him off. "Yes, yes, I'm fine. What happened? Is anyone hurt?"

Mike peered about. The old woman had landed amid a pile of deacons. She seemed dazed but undamaged. He moved forward, the stunned crowd parting before him. A shattered pile of stone, plastered white with over a century of pigeon droppings now occupied the spot where Chavez had stood by the door. A body was draped over it, blood dripping onto the rubble. Malachy was already there, feeling for the man's pulse.

The old priest grimly looked up at Mike and shook his head. He mumbled an absolution and made a sign of the cross over the corpse. "May God have mercy," he sighed and stood.

"Isn't that —" Mike began. Malachy nodded. "His name's Carlos. Troubled kid — climbed churches all over town — even the bell towers. I've caught him here several times."

"I saw him just this morning leaving Tom's office," Mike said. "Was he crushed?"

"No, I don't think so, son," Malachy replied. "See, he's on top of the cross, not under it. And look at what he's wearing

— climbing shoes and shorts. No, he was up there all right. The old sandstone must have finally given way." They both glanced up at the stump on the peak of the building between the never-completed steeples.

The sudden intrusion of a glaring light informed them that the TV crew had come to investigate the commotion. "Just what we need," Malachy said, shaking his head.

Mike turned, rubbing his sprained arm with a grimace, and nearly ran headfirst into the chancellor. Bob Cruz was holding his bleeding head, looking dazed, his normally sallow face pale behind his thick mustache. "Are you okay?" Mike asked. Cruz swayed, mumbling, "Not real sure." Mike helped him lie down on a dry spot, and put his satin dalmatic under his head.

Apart from a few bruises, no one else seemed injured. A flustered crowd still surrounded the bishop. Several clerics were brushing the dust off his vestments, and two seminarians held his miter and crosier, the top bent markedly to the side.

The camera's light held him as Chavez dramatically pushed his way through the ring of people surrounding the body. "Oh my Lord," he said. "What a terrible, terrible thing to happen, especially on this holy night. May God have mercy on this poor boy." He peered up at the cathedral.

"We knew this church was in disrepair," he said quietly, almost to himself. "But we never thought that it was in any way dangerous. God forgive me for taking so long to replace it." Tears streamed down his face as he crouched, tenderly touching the dead teen's hair in a final benediction.

The bishop stood to face the camera as a reporter elbowed his way through the mob towards him. Malachy turned to Mike. "You better get out there."

"What about Bob?" asked Mike. "He needs a doctor."

Malachy shrugged. "I'll stay with him until the ambulance gets here." Noting Mike gingerly holding his arm, he asked, "Can you stand facing the cameras? Go on, then. You're the savior of the hour; they'll want you to say something."

Mike's protests faded as his mentor gently but firmly led him into the glare of public attention.

Not far away, Bruno tore his eyes off the grisly tableau, looking up. There, on the other side of the body, Monsignor DeLaval pushed through the crowded clergy for a better view, smiling crookedly. Gray eyes glittering, he looked around sharply at his fellow priests, and noticed Bruno gaping at him from across the death scene. Grinning, the priest blew him a kiss, mouthed the word, "Boo!" and then quietly slipped away.

Bruno froze for several long minutes. He could not move, not even to reach his pistol. When at last he could, he ran as fast as his legs could carry him back to the safety of his car, away from the lights, noise, and death.

Meanwhile, DeLaval fled into the cathedral as the commotion grew behind him, clutching his robes. "Oh my God," he called out loudly, urgently coaxing the stragglers outside. "There's been an awful accident! Someone call an ambulance!"

He strode quickly towards the sacristy, peering carefully around him. He paused at the door, and with a quick glance, stepped instead across into the side chapel of the Virgin, securing the door behind him.

The room was silent and dark — but not empty. The presence light flickering dimly by the tabernacle and banks of votive candles revealed the small porcelain figurine of Nuestra Señora de Victoria standing defiant and ready for battle in her niche in the reredo above the small altar. Her diminutive size belied her importance as the spiritual heart of Alvarado.

Patroness of the conquistadors who brought her with them from Spain, La Victoria was a martial queen. She proudly wore a crown turreted like a castle on her black hair and a silver breastplate over her scarlet silk gown. With a silver sword and white shield bearing a crimson Maltese cross, she stood forever on watch against Moors and all other such enemies of the faith.

The statue's presence always made DeLaval nervous, but never like now. He told himself it meant his magic was working. It was daring to hide the *Codex* again in such a spot, but the boy's sacrifice, even if Mike's heroics made him miss Chavez and the others, would not be in vain; for now his restless spirit would further guard Wilson's secret stash. Had not his sorcery also drawn the very one who had revealed the vault to him? Doubtless that was a good omen, and surely DeLaval's bold effrontery would please his Dread Lord and Lady greatly.

The fat man cautiously felt around the rim of the altar, wary of alarm wires, and finally found the button in the small rosette that popped open the front panel. DeLaval writhed, pawing at his robes until he drew out first the Cross, and then the Book. He carefully tucked them into the small dark void and shut the vault, muttering a spell of protection.

He impudently smiled up at the delicate features of the doll-like statue, its glassy gaze ignoring him as always. "Now I can go. I gratefully return the *Codex* to the place where I first obtained it," he whispered. "Kindly guard it better for me than you did for dear old Xaphon."

He chuckled deeply and bowed. Then, still laughing, he turned. He tore off the vestments even as he left the chapel.

†

CHAPTER FIVE

MARIE yelled, "It's on, it's on!" as the *News at Noon* began. The adults lurched out of the patio chairs on the back porch and straggled into the front room. Bruno shooed the dogs away to crowd onto the sofa with Kathy and Marie. Mike went into the kitchen for more coffee, watching over the counter. Marie made loud shushing noises to get her elders to quiet down, and turned the sound up anyway.

"A joyous occasion turned tragic when the peace of Easter was shattered early this morning," the Anglo anchorman was saying. "A young man, nineteen-year-old Carlos Mondragon, fell to his death from atop Our Lady of Solitude Cathedral after Midnight Mass in what appears to have been a bizarre accident, though police have not yet ruled out suicide. Our own Conway Begay was there and joins us now from Plaza Vieja."

The screen split and also showed a dark Indian in a trim double-breasted suit and sunglasses standing on the plaza, the taped-off church and a scattering of tourists behind. "Conway, what's the story so far?" asked the anchor.

As the reporter repeated the basic facts, the screen showed anarchy — people moving about nervously in the dark, dodging out of the intense light as the cameraman forced his way through the crowd. There was a clear shot of the bishop kneeling over the corpse of Carlos, and then someone waved the camera back.

The camera followed fingers pointing up at the empty peak, then panning back down the Norman facade to the pile of bloody flesh and stone again. "Mondragon was apparently a disturbed youth, a rock climber well-known to the clergy for having scaled virtually every Catholic church in Alvarado," he concluded.

The tape cut to Malachy, still in his disheveled vestments, who added, "He was arrested for it several times but kept coming back, usually at night. Apparently Monsignor DeLaval thought counseling him might prove more effective." He shook his head. "God, what a tragedy."

Back to the newsroom again. "We couldn't locate Monsignor DeLaval for comment." The anchor continued, "The tragedy could have been much worse. The lawn sprinklers came on just moments before the collapse, forcing people away from the spot. But it was the quick action by Father Michael Nolan which miraculously..." His voice was drowned by the women squealing, "Mike! You're on now!" until Bruno forcibly dragged him out of the kitchen.

Mike's face, appearing somewhat shocked, filled the TV. "Thank God I heard the noise of the stone giving way just before it fell," he said modestly. "I sure didn't have time to think. I'm just grateful that I was able to move fast enough."

The family applauded, and it was Mike's turn to ask for quiet. The bishop, still without miter or skullcap, spoke into the camera, tears glistening, his face ashen in the glare. "— a horrible accident. I had no idea that this old church was in such awful shape. We will have it thoroughly inspected and repaired, if need be, before we conduct any more services here."

He paused for a question that the audience couldn't hear. "Yes," he said, "even though it will be torn down and replaced once the new cathedral is finished. The safety of all our people is an absolute priority to us." Bruno bit back a sarcastic remark that rose like sudden bile in his throat.

Chavez paused for another question. "No," he replied. "Tragic as this event was, I do not believe it will have any effect on His Holiness' visit. But that's still months away. We must first attend to the grieving of the family and friends of this most unfortunate young man."

There were more shots of the front of the church surrounded by yellow police tape and one of ambulance drivers loading the now-shrouded body. Then back to the reporters.

"What about it, Conway? Is the old church safe?"

"We don't know, Dan, but the city has refused to allow any more services to be held pending an examination by the building inspectors. And this at the church's busiest season."

The scene flashed to shots of the notice on the door, and then moved quickly on to a clip about the history of the cathedral. "...not the first unfortunate event in this church's checkered history," the voice-over said. "Poor construction, the theft of La Victoria, and even the flood of 1972 have all..."

Kathy switched off the set as the next story about the Pope's visit began. Bruno, standing behind Mike's chair, clapped his brother on the shoulders with both hands. "Father Fantastic!" he exclaimed with artificial heartiness. "Super-priest! Flies through the air and bowls bishops over with impunity!" Mike rolled his eyes heavenward and said, "Oh stop it. A boy died last night and I really don't feel like joking about it. Anyway, you're hurting my arm."

Instantly remorseful, Bruno apologized. "Sorry, bro. We're all very proud of what you did. Saving a life is not a little thing, you know. You couldn't have done anything for the kid — you'd have been crushed too." Mike nodded glumly.

"Anyway," his sibling declared, "you acted quickly and bravely. Come on, champ, let's get some grub."

Through the huge traditional Easter brunch of eggs, sausage, pastries, juice, and bits of chocolate bunny, Bruno's mood slowly sank. Though Kathy had said nothing more and he'd obeyed her injunction, he'd felt oddly detached, as if he was watching a movie of his family rather than being with them. For once, he didn't mind. Numbness, even sober, was good.

But coming back to this old stuccoed house where he'd spent his married life was a bit like returning to the church of his youth. Sad ghosts abounded here too.

Bruno toyed idly with a small pitcher of maple syrup while the women gathered up the dishes. During a lull in the conversation, he smirked, saying, "After the breakfast was over, he took the syrup and giving you thanks and praise, he poured the syrup, saying, 'Take ye and eat all of you, for these are my pancakes.'"

Mike frowned, leaning back to favor his arm, his clerical collar unbuttoned, white plastic tab sticking out of his black shirt pocket like a doctor's tongue depressor. "Eddie, must you?" he muttered.

Marie, bustling around the table in bright sundress and apron, calmly took the pitcher out of her father's hands and said in a voice pointedly like her mother's, "Oh Dad. Stop it. Why do you always have to make fun of everything?" Bruno shut up, abashed by the lack of even a token chuckle.

To fill the sudden, uncomfortable quiet, he said, "You know, Mike, it's been ages since you called me 'Eddie.' Not since we were both altar boys, really."

He realized too late that was a mistake. The whole sick pustule festering since Good Friday burst open again in his mind. Blithely unaware, Mike yawned hugely, got up, stretched, and patted his brother's shoulder.

"Been a long time, Buddy," he said cheerfully. "You know, I wasn't kidding last night when I said I thought you were the chosen one. When we were kids, I really did think you would be much more likely than me to become a priest. You really were my inspiration."

Bruno tried to shake the grotesque reflections out of his head. "Well that sure didn't last long, did it?"

"Yeah, but you were so gung ho," Mike said lightly. "Remember how you used to make us play Mass all the time?"

"This guy," he declared, "cut up old sheets to make play vestments and altar cloths. He'd use grape Kool-Aid for the wine and candy wafers for the Hosts and set up a big cardboard box for an altar. He even had a cigar box for a tabernacle and he'd punch me if I didn't genuflect in front of it properly."

"Did not," Bruno objected. "I never beat you up — for that, anyway."

"The heck you didn't," laughed Mike. Bruno felt his temper rising. "Well I'm sure I wasn't as bad as Malachy or Wilson," he said hotly. "I suppose you don't remember the times they choked us with a rosary or knuckled our heads. Be glad, daughter, that you weren't a server in the old days. Even the good priests could be right brutal bastards."

As his brother launched into his old tirade, Mike's eyes narrowed. His voice became softer, a sure sign he was becoming angry also. He put his hand again softly on Bruno's shoulder. "What's bugging you, big brother?" he inquired. "You've been acting weird. We were kids then and always pounding on each other. I meant nothing by it.

"You know it was a different world back then. Nobody thought twice if a priest paddled an altar boy or twisted an ear or two. Give it a rest already."

Bruno shook off his brother's hand. Mike turned away to pour another cup, while Bruno fought down a sudden urge to smash his handsome, dark-haired head with his coffee cup. He opened his mouth to speak but couldn't, and glanced around at his silent family, all inspecting him with annoyance.

Kathy stood up to clear away the remaining dishes. "Now boys," she said in her best maternal voice. "Remember, you promised you wouldn't argue this time. It's Easter, all right? Play nice — we don't have to solve all the problems of the Church today." She smiled thinly, handing the plates to her daughter who shot him a dirty glare as she entered the kitchen.

"That's for damn sure," Bruno finally said in a dangerously low voice, "but you don't understand."

Though he spoke softly, even the birds stopped singing as if frightened of the ragged edge underlying its tone. At that instant, his resentment came crashing down. The protective fortress of icy rage collapsed into dejected rubble. They didn't know, of course. How could he tell them, any of them? But how could he not?

Staring at the ground, he mumbled, "You don't get it, Mike. Don't you see? It was more than just being choked, or slapped around. They — they got me, man."

His face was burning red. The air was still. Mike leaned forward. "What do you mean, Eddie? Who got you?"

Before he could answer, Kathy suddenly spoke up. "Marie, dear," she called out, "why don't you go take the dogs for a walk? I think we grown-ups need to talk."

Bruno slowly looked up into Mike's worried blue eyes. "Somebody in a damned collar m-m-molested me."

"Are you sure?" Mike paled, but had to ask.

His older brother laughed bitterly. "Am I sure? You think I made this up? I may be crazy, but I'm not that crazy!"

He laughed again, wildly, crossing his arms and rocking back and forth. "Do you remember," he continued harshly, "the names we had for the priests at Soledad? You know, like Father 'Malarkey,' 'Deadeye' DeLaval, who could bean a kid with an eraser across a classroom, or fat old Monsignor 'Cold-cut?' Let's see, there was also Father 'Lush' who always emptied the wine cruet, and oh yes, good old 'Feeler' Wilson.

"I think I now know why we called him that." Bruno suddenly seemed very old.

Mike reached towards him. "Oh God, Bruno, no." Bruno abruptly stood. Biting his lower lip, the man trembled, close to tears, but he held himself rigidly as he backed away.

Mike's hand fell. All his pastoral training and experience suddenly failed him. He had no wise words to soothe a hurt this close and this deep.

Bruno raised his hands. "No please, not now. I need some time." He glanced at the priest with such utter, hopeless despair and freezing rage that his brother was taken aback. "For all I know, all you damn priests are in it together!"

He whirled and strode out the gate. Only silence followed him.

†

CHAPTER SIX

Wednesday, April 14

MIKE pulled into the deserted Catholic Complex in the relieved quiet of this Easter week morning. Spring break had left the parking lot almost empty, though the urgent bustle at the construction site next door more than made up for it. The builders had promised to do what they could to have their rising basilica ready for a papal benediction and the racket sounded like they meant it.

Bishop Chavez, the chancellor, and Monsignor Malachy were waiting by the door to DeLaval's office. The other two men nodded politely in greeting; the head of the diocese was talking to the custodian, Manny, about getting in.

"Yes, I know Consuela would have the key. I've called her," Chavez reasoned with forced patience. "But we need to get in now. Ahora. Surely you must have a master key, una llave maestra?"

The old paisano was nodding apologetically and picking through a clutch of keys as big as his fist. "Sí, Your Excellency, por supuesto. Somewhere here, I'm sure…

"¡Ah, está aquí! Muy bueno." The brown old man grinned through the gaps in his teeth, holding up a brass sliver indistinguishable from all the others. He shuffled over to the door, unlocking it easily. The bishop put his hand on it.

"That's fine, Manny," he said. "We'll take it from here."

The caretaker glanced around at the blank circle of faces. He shrugged and worked the key out of the door. Doffing his battered straw hat in respect, he bowed. "Okay, padres, there you go. I'll be outside if you need me."

"Gracias, tío," Chavez said with a quick smile. The old man ambled off, muttering.

Chavez peered over his men, suddenly all grim business again, dark circles under his eyes as if he hadn't slept. "All right," he said. "Let's get this over with."

"Excuse me, but just what's going on?" Mike burst out. "I'm still not sure why we're here."

"DeLaval's disappeared, son," Malachy said softly. "He never showed up at Ghost Springs."

Mike looked at Bob Cruz who nodded his head which was wrapped in bandages, and winced. He looked pale and thoroughly dejected. Before he could voice his concern, Bob cut him off with a gesture. "Later."

At a sign from their superior, the chancellor swung open the door — into chaos. In the gloom, it seemed like an earthquake had struck. Papers were strewn everywhere, every bookcase had been rifled and dumped on the floor. Even the prized collection of santos and icons were in disarray as if in shock.

"Good Lord," Malachy exclaimed. "What the devil happened here?"

The men waded into the room, trying not to step on anything. Mike flipped on the lights. "What an incredible mess," he observed.

Robert Cruz gingerly crossed the room to raise the Venetian blinds. "Ah here's how they must've gotten in," he said. The furled slats revealed an open window.

The men began picking through the piles. "Whoever did it was sure looking for something," Malachy said, straightening a precariously tilted Madonna. "This wasn't vandalism. Nothing seems deliberately trashed. No graffiti. Anything missing?"

"Hard to tell in this clutter," Mike replied. "Ah, what about this?" he exclaimed, pointing to the empty silver plaque above the monsignor's desk. "That big cross of his is gone."

He began to feel anxious. No one had even mentioned why he should be included in what was quickly becoming a search. "Uh, say," Mike hesitantly put forth, "shouldn't we call the police? We might be destroying evidence; I mean, you say he's disappeared. His office has been ransacked and he may be dead by now, for all we know."

"Ah, that would be too lucky," Malachy muttered darkly.

The men all looked at Chavez, who was bent over, poking intently around the desk. He straightened up. "Good point, Mike. This does indeed appear serious: after all, he left his pipe, which he almost never does," Chavez said softly, brandishing a well-used briar.

"But in any case," he said firmly, tossing the pipe back on the desk and wiping his hands together, "I think, that before we go jumping to conclusions involving the secular authorities, we should be sure what's happened. If the police come, the press will be on their heels, after all. For the sake of the Church, let's not get carried away until we have to."

The frowning prelate seemed completely determined. "Of course, Your Excellency," the chancellor said soothingly.

Mike stooped and picked up an old nameplate inscribed "*Thomas A. DeLaval, O.S.P.M.*" "Funny, I always thought Tom was a diocesan priest. I knew he got around, but I never realized he belonged to an order."

He waved at the wall over the desk where there was an array of certificates and photos of the monsignor with various notables, including several cardinals, Pope Paul IV, generals, politicians and various others — mullahs, archimandrites, rabbis, and lamas. There was even one of him in a jungle clearing with a voodoo priest holding a black chicken.

"I believe 'O.S.P.M.' meant 'The Order of St. Peter Martyr,'" Chavez remarked. "An honorary fraternity for specially dedicated priests, or something like that, which he belonged to a long time ago. Supposedly something of a charitable society and support group for clergymen."

"Named after Peter of Verona?" Malachy snorted. "Funny choice. A rabid inquisitor; crazy even for a Dominican, which is saying something. His crucifix scolded him, you know."

"Maybe for Peter the Fisherman then," Mike suggested. "The first Pope, see, with the keys to heaven."

"Whatever," sighed Malachy. "I've been involved in Catholic organizations from the Legion of Decency to the Equestrian Order of the Knights of the Holy Sepulcher, and that one always sounded bogus. I think it's been inactive for decades; why anyone would want its old emblem is beyond me."

They continued to poke around, Cruz soon despairing of piling up papers. Mike stepped gingerly over to where Malachy was peering darkly over the top of his glasses at the spine of a black-bound book. Next to him a lawyer's bookcase was nearly empty; the glass doors swung open wide, contents strewn across the carpet. "'*The Legemeton or Lesser Key of Solomon*,'" the old divine read distastefully from one cover, and picked up another. "'*The Grimorium Verum*' — 'True Grimoire,' I guess that means." He crouched and began picking through the pile, continuing to read titles aloud. "'*Goetia*,' '*The Grimoire of Pope Honorius*,' '*De Nigromancia*' — oh, and this certainly looks special: '*The Book of Black Magic and of Pacts*.'"

He dropped the heretical volume back onto the pile of forbidden lore and stood, dusting his hands against each other as disgustedly as Chavez had done. "Interesting references for the director of liturgy, don't you think?"

"Well, he is the diocesan exorcist," the chancellor explained uneasily. "Unofficially, of course."

"Yes," the bishop confirmed with a sigh. "We didn't want to alarm anyone by making any kind of official appointment, but Monsignor DeLaval was the one we'd call if there was ever any need. His interests and wide reading made him ideal for the task — since you turned it down, anyway, Sean. But we've never needed one, officially, so it doesn't really matter, does it?"

"How about unofficially?" Malachy demanded. The bishop and his chancellor exchanged glances. "I don't really know, Sean," Chavez admitted. "I never paid much attention to those sort of requests. I just passed anything to do with —"

"With 'that medieval nonsense?'" the old priest finished for him, close to detonation.

"Anyway," Chavez concluded lamely. "With his degrees in psychology and theology, Tom seemed really interested in all that spooky stuff."

"I turned it down only for health reasons," Malachy grumbled, his red face slowly lightening. "If I'd ever imagined it would be him…" He shook his head. Silence fell again.

Mike moved over to the closet door that stood ajar, if only to get away from the disquieting books. "He's a collector, that's all," he said dismissively, hand on the doorknob. "Look at all this stuff. He's like a kid, you know: if it interests him, he has to have it."

He pulled the door open and suddenly yelled, throwing up his good arm. A box precariously perched on the top shelf split apart, vomiting forth garishly colored magazines, books, and videocassettes.

A sudden deluge of pornography overwhelmed him.

He cringed in the midst of the avalanche of smut. He didn't have to read the titles — many weren't in English anyway — to realize what they had to be. The smiling, naked children, mostly boys, provocatively posed on the covers often with fat, hairy men only partly shown, revealed the unsavory truth.

"Oh my God," Mike moaned, suddenly wanting to hurl. He sat down heavily on the couch, unmindful of the mess. "I can't believe it. This is impossible."

Malachy moved over to him. "Are you all right, lad?" he asked. "Put your head down between your knees." He did so, fighting off the waves of nausea.

Cruz glanced in the closet. "There's several other boxes in there. This one's filled with videos, too." He dragged it out and pawed quickly through its contents.

"Well, it could be worse," the chancellor sighed with some relief afterward. "They're certainly obscene and probably illegal, but none are hand-labeled. If he shot any himself, they're not here." He began piling the porn up.

Mike sat, holding his sore arm limp in his lap, not knowing what to think. First his brother, and now this.

Malachy sat down beside him. "You know," he wondered, staring narrowly at his shocked superior, "I can't imagine any good reason why he or anyone would have this trash in his office. Can you?" Chavez said nothing.

"Oh my Lord," someone else exclaimed, startling everyone. Unnoticed, the Complex's chief secretary had entered the room. "Sorry to bother you, fathers," she began and stopped again, taken aback by the mess.

Chavez whirled, stepping in front of the mound of smut. "Why, what is it, Consuela?" he asked with a forced smile.

"You asked me to come down," she started, trying to see around her boss.

"Ah, yes, sorry," Chavez said, grabbing her plump arm and backing her up. "As you see, Manny let us —"

"No, that's not it, Father. There's a reporter outside from the paper and a TV crew just pulled up. The phone's ringing off the hook, and they all want to talk to you."

Bishop Chavez held up his hand imploringly and rallied his wits. "All right, Consuela, I understand. I'll be there in a moment." He led her back to the door. Closing it firmly behind her, he turned and hissed, "I want that disgusting filth out of here. Now. Discreetly. Very."

Mike was leaning back, hand on his forehead. "What should we do with it? We can't just go chuck it in a dumpster."

The bishop stood impatiently by the door. "I don't know, I don't want to know, I don't care. Just do it. Please," he pleaded. His shoulders dropped and for a moment he seemed all of his near-sixty years. "Guess this is it," he said, sighing loudly. "Bob, I'll need that statement you were working on. Sean, Mike, take care of this, will you?"

Cruz nodded, patting Mike sympathetically on the shoulder as he passed. "Be right there."

Chavez turned. "Oh, and if you come across a book in a black leather case with a latch like a old breviary, I want it," he demanded and left. Cruz shot a concerned expression at the others and followed his superior out in silence.

Malachy snorted. "Breviary? Not bloody likely. He did have a book, a vade mecum. I always assumed it was merely an appointment book; though now I dread to think what sort of engagements they might have been."

"So what that was all about?" Mike asked mournfully. "For that matter, what am I doing here?"

"Your guess is as good as mine, lad," Malachy sighed. "But I do know that our dear bishop is more than a little grateful for what you did the other night."

"Funny way of showing it," Mike mumbled.

The old priest clapped him on the knee and stood up. "Feeling better?" he asked. Mike nodded, and tried to smile.

"So what are we going to do about this?" he asked.

Malachy thought. "There's an incinerator down at the cathedral school. I doubt its been used in years, but it might still work."

"Excellent idea, Father. I think there's some empty paper boxes up by the copier; I'll go get them."

Mike went up to the front of the office, past the busy secretary and her blinking phone. He noticed Cruz and Chavez standing outside the front door of the chancery. Reporters surrounded them. Old Manny, leaning on his rake, had stopped even pretending to work on the lawn. Mike counted three TV cameras — all the stations in town were represented along with the newspapers.

"Something's definitely up," he announced to Malachy. The old priest began scooping up the piles of kiddie porn. Uncomfortable, Mike looked away. "There's a mob of reporters out there."

"It's likely some more questions about the accident," Malachy replied as he filled the box, "though I didn't think the building inspectors could've finished so quickly. You better be careful, or they'll probably want to talk to you again too."

"Ah, they'll forget me soon enough," Mike demurred.

"Be thankful if that happens before they can turn on you." Malachy said bitterly, folding several flaps shut.

"You sound like you speak from personal experience."

Malachy peered at him askance. "Oh, indeed, I do. Many years ago, when you were young, when that devil Wilson was murdered."

Mike stooped to help load. "I just can't believe this," the young priest said. "I've known DeLaval, and you also, for that matter, since I was an altar boy. He couldn't be a, a... Dear God, maybe Bruno was right."

Malachy gazed silently at Mike for a long moment, his face unreadable. "About what, Mike?" he asked softly.

There was another knock. "Yes?" Malachy said, voice raised. Consuela opened the door, even more distraught than before. "Father Malachy, por favor," she implored, "the bishop wants to see you. Right away. He said it's urgent."

"What's going on?" Malachy asked.

She shook her head, dark hair flying. "I don't know. But the reporters are asking all kinds of questions." She repeated even more forcefully. "Anyway, he wants to see you."

Malachy said, "All right, I'm coming." He turned to Mike, nodding at the stack of boxes. "Finish up here?" Mike suddenly wanted to shout "No!" but something prevented him. He nodded in acquiescence.

Malachy smiled gratefully and left. Alone, Mike looked around at the office, feeling as confused as it looked. Wondering, he picked up a magazine and thumbed through it. "*Let's Play House*," the rag said invitingly on the cover, showing a smiling little girl wearing only an apron. It was much, much worse inside, yet there was something nauseatingly compelling in the faces of the smiling, shy, and scared children, unaware of their innocence even as it was stolen from them.

Uncomfortably he stuffed the smut into the box with the rest. He felt suddenly scared, and incredibly filthy.

Before moving the boxes, he quietly brought his van around to the back door, well out of sight of the media circus. Returning to DeLaval's office, he experimentally hefted the first box. It wasn't very heavy but it made his arm hurt. Luckily he found a dolly from the front office. Mike loaded them up, checking carefully to make sure no obscene materials had been overlooked and finally locked the door behind him.

He hustled the boxes out to his van as swiftly as he could. Nobody was around. Ignoring his arm, he quickly manhandled them into the back.

Then he slowly drove out past the impromptu press conference, completely unnoticed. As he sped down the hill towards Plaza Vieja, a temptation whispered to him. Perhaps he should not be so hasty. No one need ever know.

Mike squared his shoulders. Mother of God, what was he thinking? No, that way surely lay sin and madness. Better he should burn the boxes than burn in hell. The sooner he did that, the sooner he could take a long, long run, have a hot bath, and forget all about it.

†

CHAPTER SEVEN

Thursday, April 15

BRUNO'S NERVE evaporated at the last second, stalling him in front of his ex-wife's door. He'd finally worked himself up to call and to apologize that morning. It was easier than he thought, even if he choked up once or twice. He'd quickly discovered that the only way he could talk about it was to distance himself, be as nonchalant as possible.

But Kathy had insisted on seeing him. So here he was, standing yet again in front of the Taos-blue portal of his former residence as the sun departed amid a swirl of spring winds, painting the mountains and puffy clouds pink and purple.

At least as nervous as he'd been on their first date over a decade and a half previously, like then he came armed only with a peace offering of a bouquet of roses. But he need not have worried; before he could agonize long, the door swung open.

She stood within; wearing a loose shirt and shorts, hand on hip. "Hi," she said. "I was afraid you wouldn't show."

Bruno spread his arms as if ready to be searched, turning around so she could see he carried no weapons. "I come in peace," he declared and thrust the flowers towards her.

"You're not getting off that easy," she smiled, "but I'll take those from you anyway." She opened the screen door for him. He squeezed in past her, careful not to let any beasts out.

Kathy went to find a vase while Bruno stayed and greeted the dogs. "You know, every time I visit, you seem to have more mutts," he said finally when she returned. She waited until he calmed the menagerie before placing the vase on the coffee table. "I can't keep up with them."

"Well, that's our daughter, you know," Kathy commented, returning. "Always the rescuer of creatures in distress. She's unable to stand seeing a lost, lonely or hurt anything."

"Must have gotten it from you," he replied, looking at her, "you took me in, remember?" True, Kathy had been expecting Marie when his fine Catholic guilt kicked in and he'd decided to do the right thing, trading in his Norton for an old Volkswagen. Ultimately, however, her wholehearted efforts at domestication had come to naught against alcohol, fueling resentment, feelings of imprisonment, and finally, betrayal.

Yet, she was still beautiful and openhearted, despite relaxing into a comfortably plump middle-age spread much as he had. Her round, almost Oriental face was downcast.

"Well, you were already almost house-trained," she tried to joke. "It was more our divorce than anything else that brought the Mother Teresa out in her, though Marie's always been very empathic." She paused, sipping a glass of pink wine, and said a little uneasily, "Where's my manners? Would you like something to drink?"

Bruno nodded. This was off to a great start. "Yeah, soda, coffee, cold water — anything. By the way, where is she?"

Kathy got up and brought back a diet cola but she seemed much more at ease. No guns or booze. She was obviously reassured that he hadn't fallen completely apart again. "Mike's tutoring her again tonight. It's just us," she said as another dog licked her free hand.

The small talk died. He sat hunkered over the cola can on the far end of the couch. She waited.

"With Mike, huh? Good, I guess." Bruno took a sip. "This, it's really hard," he began and stopped. He fiddled with the can. "It's hard enough facing you; I sure couldn't face her yet.

"Hell, I don't even know where to start, except to apologize again for being such an asshole.

"I sure didn't mean to blurt it all out like that," he explained, stealing a glance. "I really thought I could get through everything — Mass, the family scene. I just wanted to be there for Marie." He halted suddenly, unsure how to continue.

"Is that why did you brought the gun?" she asked softly.

Bruno shrugged awkwardly. "Yeah," he mumbled. "I guess I thought it might make me feel... safer.

"Anyway, the problem now is, what do I tell her? How do I explain it to our daughter?" He looked at Kathy and she stroked his hand gently.

Kathy shook her head. "Tell the truth," she replied. "Someday. Maybe not now, but you should talk to her about it soon. She's still a kid, but they learn awfully early these days, and she's curious. You wouldn't imagine the questions she's asked me. In any case, we chatted after you left. She understands you were hurt, as best a person could at her age, though not the details. She's just worried about you, as are we all."

Bruno hesitated and nearly said, "You should be." But instead he asked, "Has she, well, you know... had her first period yet?"

Kathy smiled. "Not yet, but it won't be long, I'm sure."

"Mother of God," he exclaimed. "My little girl growing up. Hope she follows your example and not mine. I don't know how either of us will survive if she acts like I did."

The woman gazed remorsefully at her former mate. "Maybe, if we keep her safe, she won't have any reason to."

Tears sprang to Bruno's eyes. Sympathy was hardest to bear, for it beckoned most to his newly-reopened wounds.

He waited for the next inevitable question but Kathy took another sip. In the silence, he became aware of the TV babbling. It was the local news. She noticed it too and reached for the remote, saying, "We can't talk with this thing on."

"No," Bruno choked out, "No. Turn it up. Please."

The screen flashed an old black and white picture of a skinny, almost cadaverous man; a long-faced priest wearing a stole and a gauzy surplice, with heavy, black-framed glasses and thinning dark hair. "Oh my God," Bruno whispered, "it's him!"

"— Father Philip Wilson, whose murder almost thirty years ago still remains unsolved. The alleged victims, over a dozen so far, mainly come from the Boston area where he began his career, but several, still unidentified, hail locally."

A man in a gray double-breasted suit with carefully styled-back silver hair and goatee was shown standing behind microphones. A caption read: "*NICK WEREGILD, attorney.*"

"We have filed suit today," he said in a sharp New York accent, "against the estate of Father Wilson, the Diocese of Alvarado, and the Ministers of Consolation, on the grounds that Father Wilson not only sexually abused my clients while a patient there, but that the Diocese conspired with the Ministers to conceal that fact, moving him from parish to parish.

"Only two people here have come forward so far," he said in response to a deleted question. "But as our investigation is just starting, we expect to hear from others." The picture then switched to Bishop Chavez outside the chancery.

Suddenly Bruno crashed to the floor with a heavy thud, kicking the coffee table aside, spilling everything, startling Kathy and the mutts. "Buddy," she said, reaching out, calling him by his old nickname, "are you okay?" She hit the mute switch on the remote. The TV flickered on unnoticed.

Bruno rolled up into a fetal position, arms tight across his belly, breathing hard through clenched teeth. His eyelids were screwed shut too, and he rocked slightly back and forth.

Awful visions swarmed through his mind as if the gates of hell had been torn open. He saw the tall priest's pale, moist face staring down hungrily; felt the grip on his shoulders and hot spittle on his back; heard the harsh threats and muttered curses. But there was more. Confused peeks of other encounters, even the glimpse of a slim, shiny blade. But most of all, an unbearable agony that seized his body and held it rigid.

Distantly, he could feel his ex-wife's gentle touch upon his forehead. He panted almost like a prayer, "Oh, shit. Cannot move... must be still. Must be still, be still, still... Mustn't move. Mustn't."

She held him silently. He stayed curled up tightly rocking back and forth on the floor. "Come on," she said, pulling his head into her lap. He complied without opening his eyes. As she stroked his hair, he began to cry, very, very quietly. "It's okay," she whispered, "it's okay."

Slowly, like the beginning of a long-awaited summer thunderstorm, his weeping grew louder and louder, finally turning into huge, racking sobs. The floodgates opened in his soul, and the hurt that he had denied for decades came pouring out. "That monster," he sobbed into her lap, "that miserable stinking bastard!" But slowly, like a passing thunderstorm, the sobbing slowed. "You want to know why I'm such a rotten father?" he panted. She continued to stroke his hair. "Because he used me like, like a girl!"

And then he was off again, his thick body shuddering. Occasionally he would stiffen and scream wordlessly between gasping as if in some awful, nightmarish climax. It took a long while but he slowly calmed down, the sobs draining away. At last, he gave a long, shaky sigh, and rolled slightly, looking up at her with despairing, bloodshot eyes through tear-smeared glasses. "Sorry," he mumbled. "I made a mess. Your lap's sopping wet now."

He rolled himself upright in a sitting position. She reached for a box of tissues, took some, and handed it to him. Bruno sat there staring at nothing, wiping and blowing his nose. He knew he looked like hell but didn't care.

"Well," he sighed deeply at last, slowly cleaning his glasses. "Does that answer any of your questions?"

"Yeah, a few," she replied tenderly. "When did you, ah, figure it out?"

"Friday," he sadly answered, and sighed. "Went back to the old church to get ready for Easter, and it hit me like a falling anvil. I've no idea what to do now." He shook his head.

"Poor dear, poor dear," she whispered, gazing sympathetically into his puffy blue eyes, softly brushing his disheveled hair. "You need to talk to somebody, Buddy. Somebody who knows how to deal with these things. Your therapist for sure, and maybe that lawyer, too."

Bruno nodded, and blew his nose.

Kathy hesitated, "Would you like to stay here tonight? I mean, just so you're not alone."

He smiled crookedly at her. "No," he said wearily, "better not. I'd like to, but don't want to raise anybody's hopes that Daddy's back, especially mine. Thanks, though, I mean it." They held each other for a long moment.

"I'd better go before the padre brings her home," he muttered into her shoulder. They pulled apart and struggled to their feet.

Arms around each other, they walked slowly to the door. He smiled wistfully down at her. "Sorry," he sighed. "I can't seem to get over saying that, like I'm drowning in an ocean of regrets — not least of which are about what's become of us, for which I am still to blame. But thank you," he said, "for letting me cry."

She hugged him. "We're family," she said, her voice husky. "Whatever has happened, whatever will happen, you are the father of my child. I still care."

Bruno noticed she did not mention love, not that he would ever expect to hear that particular word from her mouth again. This may have brought some understanding, maybe even some peace between them, but there was no going back.

He smiled mournfully into her eyes, letting her know he understood and accepted it.

"Buddy," she asked anxiously, "you take care of yourself, okay? I really think you should give Mike or somebody your gun for a while. And call me if you need anything."

"Sure," he fibbed. "I'll be in touch real soon." She stood on tiptoes and solemnly kissed him on the forehead. He forced a brave smile at her and then without saying another word, slipped around the screen door and out into the soft spring night.

☦

CHAPTER EIGHT

1962: Friday, March 23

AFTER THE ACCIDENT had been cleaned up, the rest of the Mass went very quickly. Always a fast one, Father Wilson blazed through the remainder like he had a big golf match waiting. Then the lanky priest skipped down the steps, genuflected crisply with the altar boys, and marched them double-time back into the sacristy. Before he even started disrobing himself, he barked, "Eddie, I want to see you before you leave."

Nobody said a word as the servers unrobed in the sacristy, not even Eddie's best friend, Ralph. The other boys were gone in minutes, the heavy oak door of the vestry sadly wheezing shut behind his pal, last to go. Instantly, Father Wilson strode in clutching a huge ring of keys and briskly locked the door.

Eddie politely stood up. The man leaned over to glare at the pudgy nine-year-old eye to eye, his pale, pinched face inches away. He pointed to the crucifix on the wall. "Do you see that? Our Lord suffered and died for you, and you let His Precious Body fall on the floor like so much garbage!" Eddie flinched from the sour stench of wine on the priest's breath.

"Come on, Eddie," he commanded and rose. Eddie started towards the priests' side of the sacristy, but Father roughly turned him aside past the closets into the middle section. It was a short hall with restrooms on either side. Beyond them were stairs that led up to the attic. "This way," Wilson said, producing another key and quickly unlocking the gate. Hunched over, he ushered Eddie up the stairs, stopping only to lock the gate closed behind him.

Eddie hardly noticed. He'd never been in the musty attic with its piles of pews, towers of stacked chairs, and colorful silk banners wrapped in dusty plastic bags. Wilson came up behind him breathing hard. "Stand on this kneeler," he directed Eddie. "Now, take down your pants. Underwear too."

Resigned to a severe paddling, the boy stripped. A glance behind showed the pale priest unbuckling his belt, nostrils flared, a strange, wild light in his eyes behind his large black frames. He said, "Would you like to know why girls, even nuns, can never be priests? It's because of this."

He unzipped his pants and brought out something that appeared as big as a snake, growing even larger as he stroked it. Eddie started to get scared.

Suddenly Father Wilson grabbed Eddie's shoulder hard with his free hand. He spun Eddie around; shoving down him so the boy grabbed the kneeler's armrest. Eddie stood there trembling, waiting for the belt to strike — but it never came.

Leaning over Eddie, Father Wilson began to pray. "In nomine Luciferi Lilithaesque. Hanc igitur oblationem servitutis nostrae," he muttered rapidly, placing his hands on the top of Eddie's head. "Amen," he said sharply and stepped closer, placing his feet in between Eddie's legs. He pushed forward and Eddie crashed against the kneeler. The boy felt the priest's moist hand groping around his private parts and then suddenly a burning pain in his rear. Eddie cried out. Wilson panted, "Shut up! It hurts less if you relax." He grabbed the kid by the back of his neck, growling, "You mustn't move. This is your punishment for dropping the Lord. Let go or it will hurt more."

Eddie could barely hear him. All he could feel was the hot agony in his butt, the weight of the priest bearing irresistibly against him, the man's foul breath wheezing, his hands gripping the back of Eddie's neck.

He let go, stopped fighting. The pain was indeed less but it didn't matter so much now. He floated up near the ceiling, unconcerned about the sharp thrusts that turned his vision into vibrating red patterns. Then, suddenly, after what seemed to be hours, the pulsating stopped and he was back in his aching flesh again. Wilson grunted and stepped back, making urgent sounds as he withdrew and shuddered violently.

He wiped himself with a pure white cloth — and Eddie's bleeding behind — carefully, even tenderly, then folded and reverently placed it in his shirt pocket. Grabbing Eddie's neck once again, he leaned close and recited in a low, threatening whisper, "Speak to no one of what we have done. Neither teacher nor preacher, friar nor nun. Damned be your soul if you tell anyone!"

He rose, brushing back his thin dark hair, and playfully slapped Eddie on the rear.

"There, it's over, boy. You've done your penance, but remember, if you ever speak of this to anybody, even your brother, your sin won't be forgiven and you'll burn in hell forever. Whoever you tell will burn forever too. Confession won't save them — or you. Now, get dressed." He stood up, refastened his pants, and straightened his shirt and collar.

Eddie, dazed, slowly rose, his buttocks throbbing, then bent down and picked up his trousers and underpants. He whimpered slightly, and Father Wilson, suddenly back to his old self, put his hand on the boy's shoulder. "I'm sorry I had to do that, Eddie, but it was for your own good. If we want to be saved, we must suffer like Jesus and never complain."

He crouched and searched the child's dazed blue eyes with his own cold, dark brown ones. "You'll be all right, Eddie if you don't tell anyone about this. Understand?"

Eddie nodded. Satisfied, Father Wilson stood up and rubbed the kid's bristly head. "Good boy, Eddie. There's still a while before school. Why don't you go get yourself some doughnuts from the bakery around the corner?" He pulled a dollar out of his pocket and gave it to the boy, then turned and followed the lad back down the stairs, humming.

†

CHAPTER NINE

1993: Friday, April 16

MIKE kept glancing around the study in the bishop's mansion at the exquisite collection of Southwestern art as he waited for the news to come back on. Priceless Navajo rugs graced a white adobe wall alongside a painting of a Native American Madonna. Small santos, black and white Indian pots, and even a few kachinas in niches adorned the opposite wall. In between, the room was full of massive Spanish colonial furniture, beautifully carved and upholstered.

He swirled his gin and tonic, ice tinkling, as the anchorpersons flashed back on in all their plastic perfection on the wide-screen TV. Malachy, sitting in the corner chair, grunted and reached for the remote. The sound boomed before the old priest got it right, drawing Chavez and Cruz back to their seats. The chancellor had just been informing his superior of the lack of results from his clandestine inspection of DeLaval's home.

"Another lawsuit has been filed against a local Catholic priest, this time against one of the most prominent clergymen in the diocese. Monsignor Thomas DeLaval," it continued as a clip of him standing beside Chavez flashed by, "seen here with Bishop Chavez last Christmas, has been accused of sexually abusing a woman, now an artist, who worked as a teen in his office in the 1980s, and her younger brother, the man who fell to his death from the roof of the cathedral, as well."

The TV now showed the lawyer next to a petite sable-haired beauty. She was dressed in a suit as black as her bangs, appearing resolute but very vulnerable. "Our lawsuit filed today," the attorney proclaimed, "for damages against Monsignor DeLaval and the Diocese, claims that he sexually abused this brave woman, Casandra Mondragon, as well as her late brother Carlos, for a number of years, that officials of the Diocese of Alvarado knew but did nothing to stop it."

Close up, her carmine lips turned down in determination. "I'm coming forward now," she was saying, "because only recently have I realized that I was molested repeatedly by Monsignor DeLaval while I was a teenager working one summer in his office. But I was not aware until the tragedy this last weekend that my brother was also involved with him."

The scene reverted to the Indian reporter standing once again in the late afternoon sun in front of the Catholic Complex, the blue Espiritu Santos mountains aloof in the northern distance. "Dan, Monsignor DeLaval has not been seen since shortly after the young man fell to his death. He was slated to be on retreat up at Ghost Springs this week; however, officials there say they haven't heard from him."

"Conway," the newscaster asked, "could the fatal fall be connected to Monsignor DeLaval's disappearance?"

"Well, the two men did know each other. The police would like to speak to him, but now that the building inspectors have concluded that the cross had been cracked at the base for decades, the death has been ruled as an accident. There's even been speculation that somehow the vibrations from the sprinklers combined with the weight of the man leaning on the cross caused the collapse. However, this lawsuit alleges that DeLaval somehow drove young Carlos Mondragon to do it."

"Thanks, Conway," said the Anglo anchor. A shot of DeLaval appeared. "One of the most popular priests in the diocese, Mons—" Malachy cut the TV off with a vicious click. "Don't need to hear that hokum again."

Silence filled the room. Finally, Mike got up and slid open the door to the patio, refreshingly cool in the evening shadows, birds singing high in the still-lit poplars. He sat back down heavily. Still no one said anything for a long time.

Bishop Chavez finally broke the quiet. "I talked to the chief inspector today. He assured me that we could continue holding regular services at the cathedral but under no circumstances are we to allow anyone up into the towers."

"We hadn't been," Malachy tiredly insisted. "That idiot kid kept climbing up the outside."

"He wasn't an idiot," Cruz said hotly. "He was troubled, all right, but if you knew his family, you'd understand."

He paused, rubbing his head, then said apologetically, "Sorry, Sean. They're my cousins, Carlos and his sister. We're all related around here, you know. I never approved of him having anything to do with Tom, but what could I do? He wouldn't talk to me. I felt something was strange but didn't know what to say. And to think I got Casandra that job as a favor..."

Cruz drained his margarita and went to the sideboard for a refill. Not looking at anyone, he said quietly, "I never liked that man. Both of them! It's unbelievable."

"We're all shaken up by all this," Malachy said, "even more so since we're being sued. God alone knows how many more there'll be."

"Something indeed must be done, and quickly," Chavez said somberly. "Before the story gets out of hand. We've got to show that we are dealing with it properly. But how?"

"Maybe we should start with what we should have been doing all along," Malachy said, "being good pastors. But we must do more — we can't wait this mess out, Excellency."

"That's assuming there really is a big problem," Cruz broke in. "I hope to God there can't be many more like Tom out there. Let's not leap to conclusions yet."

"Where there's smoke, there's fire," Mike said grimly. "Bob's family's not the only one affected by this. Easter morning, my own brother announced that he'd been molested, too."

"Ah, he did now, did he?" Malachy sighed. "Poor Eddie." He leaned back, shaking his head thoughtfully.

Mike nodded. "Makes a lot of sense, doesn't it? Anyway, we must not only be compassionate, we must be publicly compassionate. We are the Church, after all."

"But not rich, though people think we are," Cruz said. "We have to protect ourselves, even from our own."

"You have a point, Mike, and you, too, Bob. We must make sure that each charge is fully and fairly investigated, if we are to be just to both the alleged victim and the accused priest," Chavez pronounced. "The last thing we want is anything resembling a 'witch hunt.' We mustn't allow this to become a stick with which the vulgar media can beat us with, especially not with the Holy Father coming so soon."

"What we need," he asserted thoughtfully, "is a formal structure. A committee to dig into this to see if we do have a big problem and suggest solutions. A tribunal that could balance whatever claims come up with the needs of the Church."

"Of course," agreed Cruz. "Make it all aboveboard, with a wide representation. The members could examine any claim when it surfaces and recommend a course of action to you."

"Exactly my thinking," Chavez nodded. "They would have to swear to keep all their deliberations confidential, but that would allow them certain access to the files."

"Not all the files, Excellency?" inquired his chancellor.

"No, of course not," the bishop stated firmly. "What is most important is the person to head the committee. A cleric, of course, one with an unblemished reputation for frankness, even brutal honesty." He smiled knowingly at Malachy.

"If by that you mean me," the old priest said, "I'm flattered, but I think Robert would be better suited for the job, being chancellor. Or even Mike, since he relates to the kids better than any of us ancient relics can."

"Oh, no thanks," protested Mike, waving his hand. "Please, I'm not ready for such a position."

"I can't, because of my cousin's lawsuit." said Cruz. "Same reason applies to Mike, if his brother goes that way."

"I concur," Chavez said, smiling. "Don't worry, Michael. I've got a chore almost as difficult in mind for you."

The others exchanged glances, realizing they'd been set up. Their boss had planned this all along.

"As for you, Sean, I think you'd be perfect for the job," Chavez continued. "Bob, as chancellor, couldn't do it anyway because it could appear like a conflict of interest. But with your background in canon law, you are eminently qualified."

"You're right," Cruz agreed. "He's the best choice."

"Well and good," said Malachy, staring hard at Chavez, "but I don't want to be the figurehead of some board that's only for show. If you want me to do this, by St. Brigit, I'll do it, but give me real authority, a free hand, and access to the files."

"The personnel files will be wide open, of course," the bishop calmly promised. "But you realize there are others that should remain sealed."

"We'll see. How about investigators? Real private eyes."

"Too expensive," Bob objected, "unless we use our own people. I know a couple of ex-detectives who are available."

The bishop nodded approval without looking. "Excellent idea, Robert. I think it can be worked out. Okay?"

"Aye," Malachy said, sighing. The bishop said, "Bueno. Now then," turning to Mike, smiling again, "I'm sure you're wondering where you fit in with all this."

"Well, sure," Mike acknowledged.

"Simple. Since Tom's gone, and in these circumstances wouldn't be able to handle it anyway, I want you to be in charge of the Pope's visit. Completely. It's a big responsibility, but I think you are ready for such a challenge." He grinned.

Mike looked around, but the other two men were nodding their heads approvingly. Malachy slapped him on the knee. "Not to worry, my boy. You'll do fine."

"Well, uh, sure, thanks, I guess," he said hesitantly.

"Good. This will mean additional work for everyone, of course, as the life of the Church goes on the same as always."

"Now then," their boss continued, looking around his small circle. "I've worked out a plan that I think will make it a little easier all around. Sean, you and Mike will work at the Catholic Complex on these new assignments as much as possible. Bob's volunteered to help at the cathedral in return. And you, Mike, will be our new Director of Liturgy; you'll have to work very closely with all of us."

Malachy laughed. "Don't be so downhearted. At the very least, this guarantees that you'll get to meet the Holy Father personally when he comes to town!"

Mike swallowed hard. "Great. I'll do my best," he said, wishing that he sounded more confident.

†

CHAPTER TEN

Tuesday, April 20

THE RECEPTIONIST called out in that cheerfully neutral tone preferred in mental health clinics, "Dr. Blackstone will see you now." Bruno glanced up to see the pleasant, open face of his therapist, Sophia Blackstone, smiling at him from around the corner.

His crooked smile in return was only slightly forced. He was as happy to see her as he would be to see the dentist if he had a blinding toothache. Maybe talking to her would somehow relieve the mental fog, crying jags and the strange nightmares such as he'd had that very morning. Like the other walking wounded in the waiting room, it was becoming impossible to pretend that everything was all right anymore.

He stood up and strolled with her down the corridor. "Well, it's been a long time," she chatted easily. "Did you get into grad school?"

"Yes, thanks," he replied carefully as they passed other offices. "It's all because of you."

"Funny, somehow that doesn't sound like a compliment," she said, ushering him into her office. It was a cozy little room, not much changed since his last visit over two years before. It was comfy, crowded with a big, stuffed chair, a few potted plants, the expected clutter of professional books, a herd of stuffed animals gazing curiously out of one corner, and of course, strategically located boxes of facial tissues. Designed to put a patient at ease, it was well lit, soothing, and soundproof, without any telltale or distracting personal items.

He sank into the plush armchair and they made more small talk while she quickly handled the necessary paperwork. Bruno recalled the endless hours of therapy he'd spent there struggling with the bleak depression that had swallowed him like quicksand after his divorce, and the ever more severe bouts of drinking that ensued. The shrink had rescued him then, helping him clear away the debris and getting him into recovery, enabling him once again to pursue his interest in history.

Her curly blonde head nodded as she finished updating the forms and then leaned back in her chair, sparkling green eyes thoughtfully regarding him. "Well," she asked, "how are you? Is the depression bothering you again?"

He tugged his beard, unsure of how to respond. Now that he was here, all his carefully thought-out speeches seemed ridiculously trite. He was suddenly very self-conscious, aware that he must no doubt appear haggard and strained. "Uh, no, not exactly," he mumbled, twisting his hands together. "As far as that goes, everything's been fine, until recently."

She nodded attentively, allowing her listening to coax him to speak.

"You recall our very last session? I do. I remember vividly how you oh so casually asked me as you walked me out if I thought I had ever been abused." He stared shamefaced at the carpet, not daring to glance up as she nodded but rushed on, his body tautly quivering. "I laughed it off then, didn't even wonder why you asked.

"Well, guess what? You were right. I — I believe that when I was an altar boy, I was molested by a priest."

Quickly then, the story came tumbling out, with only a squall or two of tears and raging embarrassment. Soon, he had told her of the events that had happened in the last two weeks, though he didn't mention his gun. The time before Good Friday already seemed a distant era.

Finally he said, "I don't know what's worse: the memories — if that's really what they are — or these weird pains and weeping at odd times, even during sappy TV commercials. I am definitely dwelling in the land beyond fun."

Dr. Blackstone made another cryptic note on her legal pad. "You having any trouble staying sober?"

He sighed, hands twisting. "Only when I'm not feeling overtly suicidal. But no, I haven't been drinking, and no, I'm not going to meetings, either. It's been a while since I last spoke with my sponsor."

"Why?"

"Ah, hell, I don't know." He stewed for a moment. "Well, yeah, of course I do. Still not quite ready to go into a group and say, 'Hi, I'm Bruno, I'm an alcoholic, and you'd drink too if you got screwed up your butt by a priest.'"

"Why would you have to tell them?"

"God, how could I not?" Bruno whined, slumping down in the chair, staring bleakly at an abstract painting on the wall. "It's all I can think about, not that I want to. And it's having an effect. People are starting to worry that when they ask 'how are you?' I might just actually tell them. Much easier to hide from everyone, and feels safer too." He uttered a short, humorless laugh. "Hasn't helped my grades any, though."

"I'm concerned about those suicidal feelings you mentioned. Would you be willing to make a contract with yourself not to hurt yourself — or anyone else?"

He snorted again. "What good would that do? No stupid pledge is going to mean anything if I get that depressed. I know that already, so why make a promise I can't keep?"

"Well, could you promise to call someone before you do anything? Nobody can really stop you, you know."

"Yeah, I suppose I could go along with that." He punched the armrest. "Are you sure you don't want to put me in the nuthouse and give me the really good drugs? I'll go quietly."

"Only if you become a danger to yourself or others, but you keep insisting you aren't."

"Well, anything's better than believing this crap," Bruno complained loudly. "It just keeps getting weirder. For instance, when I saw DeLaval there at the cathedral, it really set me off, like some kind of alarm was triggered. I just had to get out of there right away."

Blackstone's face stayed professionally aloof but she was scribbling fast. "Interesting. What do you mean, 'triggered?'"

"Well, like a switch went on that I was in danger and sort of took over. I don't even remember how I got home." He paused, searching her face. "See? Sounds real nutty, doesn't it? As bad as the voices."

"Voices?" Her eyes got the tiniest bit wider.

He laughed and sank back in the chair, his hands behind his head. "Got you that time." He paused. "No, not voices outside that tell me to go save France, or the dog next door giving me orders, or anything like that, fortunately." Another pause and shrug. "It's just strange, random notions, I guess, that 'sound' — if that's the word — like my own thoughts, but they come out of nowhere at the oddest times. I'm afraid they'll slip out and I'll say something incredibly stupid right out loud. I talk aloud to myself enough as it is."

She glanced up. "Can you give me an example?"

"Oh yeah." He didn't even need to think. "When I left the party, the last thing I said to Mike was 'You're all in it together!' I was absolutely terrified that he'd come after me."

"Did anything happen after you got home?"

"Well, I was shaking so bad, a beer would have been real nice, but all I could do was lock everything up and go to bed. This was early afternoon. I slept until sunset when I woke up with a horrible headache, like my skull was splitting."

"What other things are these 'weird thoughts' about?"

Bruno hesitated. He folded his arms across his lap and finally continued, "Well, there's those memory flashes, or whatever they are. I keep getting glimpses of... really strange shit. Being abused, sure, but spooky stuff too like crosses and knives and weird prayers. I think that blackpriest was using the Catholic mind trip on me in a big way." He fell silent again, and did not glance up when he spoke.

"There are other thoughts, though, that are even more disturbing." Once again, she waited.

"Like, how I feel around my daughter and her friends sometimes. I mean, Marie's a beautiful kid, you know — but every now and then I find myself, like, attracted, sexually, that is, and it really bugs me," he babbled lamely, feeling his face burn. "For Christ's sake, she's barely twelve!"

"Have you ever thought of acting on this attraction?"

"Oh hell no," he asserted emphatically, sitting bolt upright. "I would never — could never — especially now. My God, I just look at her picture and I cry." No reason to mention the one truly serious compact he had made with himself long ago to blow his brains out before he would ever touch Marie or any child. Now at least he knew why he'd made such a promise.

"I think you're just being hypervigilant. It sounds to me like a natural sign of PTSD, Post-Traumatic Stress Disorder. Your daughter's growing up and it's perfectly natural for you to notice. I'd be more worried, frankly," she said, carefully watching him, "if you weren't concerned about it. If you haven't acted out by now you probably won't, especially if you continue to work hard on your recovery. You're a good man, Bruno, whatever you may think about yourself." She smiled kindly.

"Stay appropriate, but take it easy. You don't need another excuse to beat yourself up or isolate even more."

She scribbled out a prescription. "I think we ought to get you started on antidepressants right away, okay? Maybe some anti-anxiety drugs as well. And Bruno," she said, handing him the slip, "there are several other things I want you to try."

"I don't think I should be doing any drugs at all," he mumbled. "I have enough trouble believing all the stuff in the first place. Doping me up isn't going to help — hell, probably just put another monkey on my back."

"True," she cheerfully agreed. "Don't worry, I'm not about to prescribe anything even remotely enjoyable, and I'm glad you realize that numbing the pain won't work. Healing entails working through the long-suppressed hurt and those messy emotions it caused. Being all doped up doesn't help.

"These meds will just take the edge off the fear and depression so you can go on. The aches you mention sound like what we call 'body memories.' Your body has tightly held in all the pain, physical and emotional, all these years, and is now starting to release the accumulated toxins. Exercise and massage might help, although you might find being touched at all is rather too 'triggering' for awhile."

"Oh boy, what fun," he grumbled. "Well then, as long as we're talking ground rules, how's this: no hypnosis, truth serum, or any of that crap. I want to be sure that nobody can come along later and say that you put ideas into my head."

"No problem," she said. "I wouldn't recommend hypnosis now anyway. What's coming up seems more than sufficient for you to work on now, if not too much. No need to push it."

"What then?" he warily asked, expecting another lecture on the importance of sobriety.

"Two things. First, I was wondering how you felt about meeting others. Other people who share these issues, I mean."

Bruno shrugged. "Actually I was going to ask you about that. Should I? Would it help?"

"Quite possibly, yes."

"So what's the other thing?"

"I want you to buy yourself a teddy bear."

He gazed at her like she was the crazy one but she was dead serious behind her agreeable smile. "A teddy bear?"

"You don't have one already, do you?" He shook his head. "Well then, you definitely need one."

Dr. Blackstone held up her hand before he could object. "Go to a toy store, pick out whatever stuffed animal that makes you feel good, take it home and sleep with it. Not only that, I want you to talk to it."

Bruno looked at her a little perplexed.

"Yes," she insisted. "Talk to it, hold it like you did when you were a small child. You'll be amazed how much better it'll make you feel." She grinned. "I tell most clients that. Now, do you need a written prescription for this, too?"

†

CHAPTER ELEVEN

Wednesday, May 5

THE LEATHER-COVERED CHAIR beneath him hadn't finished wheezing from his weight when the lawyer charged into the office. Bruno was up on his feet again instantly, parochial school reflexes automatically rising to the occasion.

The attorney dropped his notepad on the mahogany desk and extended his hand. "Nick," he barked in his trademark Eastern accent, "Nick Weregild. And you must be —"

"Name's Bruno. Last name's Nolan." He almost stuttered, sounding like a bonehead even to himself, but carefully matched the attorney's quick, hard grip.

"Uh-huh." Weregild inspected at Bruno with a sharp, measuring gaze, sizing him up. Bruno could easily guess why the city's best-known litigator was called 'the Werewolf.' Impeccably groomed in a fine pin-striped suit with vest, he was gray from slicked back hair and small goatee to suede-shod toe, the only color being an improbably garish red necktie. He waved at Bruno's chair, which was now breathing back in. Both men sat simultaneously in the luxurious, talkative furniture, causing the seats to complain in unison.

"One moment, Mr. Nolan." He pressed the intercom.

"Marge, hold all calls — even the Pope's." He winked at Bruno, a slightly lupine smile behind his goatee. "And my rabbi's, for that matter."

"Your rabbi?" Bruno could hear the secretary's muffled laughter. "Yes, sir!"

"Well, that should buy us a few moment's peace." Weregild leaned back in his chair, put his elegant footwear up on the desk, and picked up the notepad. "You wouldn't believe the calls we've been getting." He was already scribbling. "And I don't mean reporters." He glanced up at Bruno. "So. I don't mean to be brusque, but I need some basic information about you and what happened before we can begin to decide how to proceed."

Bruno nodded, and swallowed hard. He noticed he was nervously twisting his hands together and deliberately unclenched them.

"Now then, Mr. Nolan — may I call you Bruno? So, Bruno, I guess the first thing I need to ask is, how long have you known about this? Do you remember when you first realized something bad had happened to you?"

Bruno laughed harshly. "Oh yeah, no problem. It was the Friday before the story broke on the news."

"Before, you say?" The lawyer stroked his neatly-trimmed beard, eyebrows raised.

"Yes, sir. I went to church that day — Good Friday — and it all suddenly came back to me." Bruno couldn't believe how suddenly lame this all sounded.

"I see. Tell me, are you in therapy at this time?"

"Yeah. I did call my shrink — I mean, a psychiatrist I'd seen previously."

"So you've been in therapy before." He made a note. "Are you currently on medication?"

"Yeah, I am. Listen, what's this about? You afraid that I'm crazy? I think I got a good reason to be."

The lawyer put down his pen. "If by 'crazy' you mean 'emotionally and psychologically impaired,' well, that's what these cases are all about." He smiled reassuringly.

"But I have to make sure right from the start that we are within the statute of limitations. The law says a person who discovers abuse as an adult has a window of opportunity of three years in which to sue. We can't afford any problems there. If you told anybody about it back then, it could be trouble."

Putting his feet down, he leaned forward, clasping his hands. "I must confess I'm not real experienced in these matters of sexual abuse and its aftermath. From what I understand, however, if this is what has happened to you, you're going to need treatment. Good, long-term psychiatric care, which is not cheap. One important thing I first want to establish right off is that you're safe. Not too happy or healthy — if we go to trial, we'll have to prove damages, after all. But safe. Frankly, I've had clients commit suicide on me before and I don't like it."

Bruno sank back in his chair, which sighed again. The gravity in the attorney's voice alarmed him. He repressed a sudden urge to flee, that the voices which said it was too dangerous to tell were right. But instead he said, "I don't think you have to worry about that: I have a daughter to live for. But if we have to show that this has harmed us, just look at our life. It sucks." He stopped abruptly, trembling slightly.

"From what you said on the phone, you were molested by Father Philip Wilson?"

Bruno cleared his throat. "Yeah, I think so, while I was an altar boy at Our Lady of Solitude in the early sixties. I was about nine at the time it started."

"What do you mean, you think so? Then you're not sure?"

"I'm sure something happened with Wilson, but I'm not absolutely certain he was the only one," Bruno confessed. "For some reason it's real hard to, to picture the guy." He sighed. "DeLaval or one of the others might have been involved, too."

"Well, what do you know?" the lawyer inquired softly.

Bruno felt his face redden. He hunkered down in the chair, his hands strangling each other again. "All I know for sure is that somebody got me at least a couple of times. The rest is still too fuzzy."

"By 'got me' do you mean —" The words hung in the air.

Bruno sat up and stared the lawyer directly eye to eye. "I mean he sodomized me on at least one occasion," he enunciated carefully. "And likely at other times, too."

"Okay. I know this is hard, but you must be able to talk about it just like that. If you wish to pursue this you're going to have to tell people — not just me, but the Church's lawyers, maybe even a judge and jury — exactly what occurred to you as a kid. Do you think you can do that?"

Bruno sighed, slumping and scratching his head. "Well, I know it sounds stupid, but I have this horrible feeling that if I tell anybody, something awful will happen." He opened his eyes and saw the expression in the other man's.

"But yes," he stated firmly, sitting upright and swallowing a sudden lump of rage, feeling it catch fire in his chest. "I think I can speak out if I have to. I mean, hell, it feels like I've told everybody in the whole world already."

"So your family knows? How did they react? Have they said anything to indicate that they might have known something about this in the past, maybe?"

"Oh God, no, nothing like that. My parents have been dead for years but even my ex-wife's been real supportive. I'm not so sure about my brother Mike."

An expression of astonishment illuminated the attorney's face. "Ah, I knew there was something about that last name. Your brother's Father Mike Nolan, isn't he; the one who saved Bishop Chavez?"

"Yep, that's my baby brother, all right," said Bruno resignedly. The shyster's attempt to hide his excitement was entirely unsuccessful. Bruno ignored it and took a couple of antacid tablets from a roll in his shirt pocket.

"You realize, Bruno, that if you go public with this, the media will go after you — and your brother — like a pack of crazed hyenas?" Weregild asked quietly. "It could rend your family apart."

"Not all that much left to tear," Bruno remarked, trying not to sound bitter. "As for the rest of it, what the hell. The damn nuns shouldn't have talked about the glories of martyrdom so much. If that's what it takes, so be it."

"'If that's what it takes' to do what, Bruno?" inquired the attorney suspiciously. "What do you want out of this? Sure, you can become a media martyr but it may not be necessary. You could sue as a 'John Doe,' if you want to." He paused. "However, the media attention could really help your case. We might be able to get you a lot more in the way of punitive damages. Because, you know, the one thing we can't get you is justice. Whatever happened thirty years ago can't be undone. The most we can do is get you some money. If that."

It was a good question, Bruno thought. What did he really want? He hadn't intended getting so materialistic about this; suing just seemed the American thing to do. It might not make the pain go away but he could imagine nothing else that might be able to relieve the fear and rage that now haunted him. "I want it to stop," he replied at last. "I want those sons of bitches to never harm a child again. And I want — I want some kind of validation. I want them to acknowledge what happened and that it was wrong."

"Well, frankly, we can't do that for you — directly." Nick sat up and waved at his richly wood-paneled office with its rows of law books in their glass cases.

"The most we can do in this kind of civil case is teach them a lesson in their pocketbooks. It's been my experience that money talks to institutions, even one this big, with amazing clarity. If they're slapped with enough big lawsuits and lose, they'll start paying attention. Hit 'em where it hurts — in the collection plate. Otherwise," he shrugged, "like any big corporation, they can keep stepping on whomever they like."

"God knows I could use some cash. I'm in grad school and have a lot of debts," Bruno admitted. "I've been paying my shrink on the installment plan and hoped the Church would pay for counseling like they've been promising. I hadn't really thought about therapy and those kinds of expenses."

"Well, maybe you should." Weregild checked his platinum watch. "Listen, I don't want to pressure you into this. We've plenty of time here — years, even. My first impression is that you're a pretty credible witness, and from what I've heard about Wilson, every kid he ever laid eyes on was in immediate danger."

The attorney peered critically at Bruno. "But you have to be absolutely sure just who was involved, first of all, and then you need to be strong enough to handle the pressure. I try hard to settle these cases out of court to make it a little easier on my clients, but it could come to trial. I advise you to talk it over with your therapist and your family before deciding anything."

He stood up and handed Bruno his card. "If you decide to sue and agree to the terms we discussed earlier on the phone, call my secretary. She'll draw up the paperwork and make an appointment for you to meet with my investigator to get started. Okay?"

Bruno stood, the chair sighing in relief. "Okay," he agreed. "Thanks. There's just one more thing..." For some reason, this was enormously difficult to ask.

"Do you know... anybody else I could talk to? Victims, I mean. Other victims of Wilson's. I think it would really help if I could get together with somebody else who's been through this." He felt horribly awkward and the attorney's metropolitan style of time management didn't help.

The lawyer shook his head. "Sorry," he said gently, stroking his thin mustache. "Both the other Wilson cases I'm handling right now insist on strict anonymity. One's in a psychiatric hospital, and the other comes from an old Hispanic family and is scared to death they'll find out.

"However, there's a support group for clergy victims starting up," he said. Weregild took the card back, and quickly jotted a number on the back. "Here, this is for Casandra Mondragon. She's one of the main organizers; she said she wouldn't mind talking to other victims. Who knows? You may find others yourself."

"Thanks," Bruno said with some relief. He shook the man's hand vigorously but nearly stumbled over the coffee table on the way out. He automatically smiled at the receptionist, though he was squirming with shame once more. He stuck the business card in his shirt pocket and tried not to think about it.

✝

CHAPTER TWELVE

Sunday, May 9

THE POPULAR STUDENT HANGOUT across from Alvarado State College was often full on weekend evenings. But it seemed especially busy tonight — no doubt due to the imminent onset of final exams, Bruno thought guiltily as he wound his way through the swarm toward the back room.

As he wove his way through the clots of students, bums, and other bohemian types, avoiding trays brimming with pungent chile, greasy burgers, or huge sweet rolls, his uneasiness grew. He wasn't sure he could even find the right group in this confusion or that he would be disappointed if it were so.

He needn't have worried. The back rooms of La Frontera Restaurant were considerably less tumultuous, given over to intense students piled about with books, couples quietly chatting in booths, and serious smokers. The walls were hung with Western and Indian art and artifacts ranging from cowboy paintings and old rifles to Navajo rugs. On the far wall, an enormous acrylic of John Wayne caught in the flaming glare of sunset squinted in unspoken disapproval of the motley collection of liberals, leftists, pseudo-intellectuals, and aging hippies.

There were four people hanging out at the table beneath the canvas. He took a deep breath and walked over. "Hi," he greeted a small, very attractive woman with fine porcelain features. She was a few years younger than him — mid-thirties, he guessed — clad in a tight black tank top and jeans. A small cross hung from a choker around her neck. She was coolly leaning back in her chair against the wall, idly twirling a shiny lock of raven-black hair. "I recognize the Duke, and I think I recognize you from TV, so this must be the right place," he said to her. "I'm Bruno." He smiled timorously.

Her crimson lips smiled warmly as she leaned forward and shook his hand, chair legs squeaking above the racket. "Yeah, hi. I'm Cas. Glad you could come, Bruno. Always glad — and sad — to meet another one of us. Welcome to the club."

He peered around the table as the occupants studied him, and introductions were made. Next to Cas sat Jesús Jaramillo, a Chicano in his early twenties with short black hair covered tightly by a bandana, a closely trimmed beard framing his lips. His skin was as dark as hers was pale. He appeared muy macho — solidly muscled, dressed in bicycling pants, and an armless shirt; his grip, however, was surprisingly soft.

"Call me 'Chewie,'" he offered with a slight smirk and an exaggerated cholo accent. "I hate to be called 'Jee-sus.'"

"Well, you do resemble him a lot."

Across from Chewie sat an equally young, pink-faced, strawberry blonde-haired Anglo, a nervous, pudgy guy in a white short-sleeved shirt. He appeared to be even more gringo than Bruno. "Hi, I'm Dick, Dick Ryan. I don't like to be called 'Jesus' either."

"Well, not to worry, guys," Bruno reassured them with a grin. "Don't think that'll be a problem."

The last person sat opposite Cas. She was also Hispanic but Bruno's age, or possibly older. A few veins of gray snaked through her dark wavy hair. She had a round face with a few worry lines and a patient, maternal air. "I'm Dolores, I guess you could say I'm one of the ringleaders, too."

Bruno sat down at the end of the table and glanced at her quizzically. "Yeah," Cas snickered. "Some ringleader. She's the one that talked me into seeing Weregild in the first place and then into going public. But you don't see her out there."

"What do you expect from a mastermind?" Dolores retorted with a smile. "Sorry, chica, I got a family to protect."

They all chuckled politely. An awkward silence fell briefly on the table while the din continued unabated around them. "You hungry?" Dick asked Bruno. A plate with a swirl on the bottom of melted butter and cinnamon sat in front of him.

"Nah, not really," Bruno answered. "Actually, I'm way too nervous even for coffee. I was really scared to come here tonight. My stomach's been acting up enough as it is."

"I can dig that," Dick said. "I was nervous as heck the first time I met these guys too."

They all laughed. "Hey, it's a great club to be in even if the initiation's a real bitch," declared Cas.

"Initiation?" Bruno asked nervously, and then realized it was just a joke. "Oh right. I get it." His chuckle was slightly forced. "Well, if that's the case, I've been paying my dues through the ass every day since this damn stuff came up."

The other four nodded knowingly. "So I take it you're just starting to get your memories back?" Cas inquired.

It was Bruno's turn to nod. "Yeah. Unbelievably, the first I knew of it was on Good Friday. I went to church and bam! There goes my life straight down the toilet. Whoosh." He made a flushing gesture. "Then I see you on TV. Talk about strange timing. By the way, I'm real sorry," he finished awkwardly.

"Thanks, I guess," she said with a sigh. She shook her head. "I hope it's all worth it. I'm not at all sure myself. Price seems way too high already."

"Yeah, I understand. I was there when he fell — it was awful." He didn't know what more to say.

"Man, if I could go back and forget everything, I would, gladly," Dick broke in. "It's almost been as bad for my parents, especially on my mom. Worse, I guess, since she was once a cloistered nun."

"Oh you poor bastard," Bruno laughed, then sobered. "Sorry, man, I didn't mean..." but by then everybody was laughing, Dick most of all.

"Orale, vato, mi familia won't even speak to me any more," Chewie said once the giggling stopped. "Coming out in a Chicano family was hard enough, but this... My mama said, 'How dare you, the way you live, speak against a holy father like that?' My old man didn't say anything, just looked at me like something he scraped off his boots."

"Oh, I know exactly what you mean, sweetie," Dolores agreed. "I grew up in a small town up north where everybody's related. Once they know something, or think they do, it's over for good and all."

She paused, as if startled by her own frankness. "I was only thirteen when our parish priest seduced me," she said simply. "And they blamed me. My own family, too." Embarrassed, she stared at her plate.

"Well, they might feel better if you get a big settlement," Cas suggested. "That's one big worry I have. If I get some cash out of this deal, I might hear from my mom again. I was actually relieved she didn't come to Carlos' funeral."

Another silence. "I guess I'm lucky," Bruno put in, emboldened. "My folks are gone, and the rest haven't a clue about what I'm going through, not that I understand it myself." He hesitated, feeling himself strangely blushing. "Especially my brother Mike, who's a priest..."

Dick's eyes lit up. "Father Mike? The one that pushed the bishop out the way?"

"The very same," Bruno rushed on, red-faced. "It's weird, but I almost feel like I've got to apologize to you guys about being related to him. I've always been proud of my little brother, but now, it feels like admitting to Holocaust survivors that my uncle's named Adolph."

"Well, we don't hold it against you personally. So don't apologize that he saved Arturo. Not yet, anyway," Dolores said with forced lightness.

"I know how you feel," Cas said sympathetically. "Being in a big family, I've got a couple of cousins who're priests, too. One happens to be the chancellor now, small help though that's been so far. He's very concerned with my soul, but just doesn't want to deal with this."

"I was a good friend of Carlos, too, you know," Chewie said, softly patting her hand. "He and I — let's just say we both knew DeLaval real well. Somehow that pendejo is as responsible for his death as if he pushed him." There was another uncomfortable pause.

"Kind of an admission of guilt to run away like that, ain't it?" Bruno commented.

"Yeah, where the hell is he?" Chewie asked. "They must be hiding him somewhere."

"Shipped him out," said Dick. "Wouldn't be the first time. I was, uh, done by Monsignor McCarthy. Once I convinced my mom, she complained to Father Busch, the chancellor then, who promised us with a great display of sensitivity that McCarthy would be taken care of and never be anywhere around kids again. Well, they took real good care of him, all right — they transferred him somewhere out of town for awhile and then back to another parish here where he once again ran the altar boy program."

"They sent him to that Ministers of Consolation place up north in the Espiritu Santos," Cas interjected. "Weregild told me he was let out on weekends as a supply priest just like Wilson, to help out in the parishes. I'd bet that's where DeLaval is right now."

"So how about you?" Bruno asked Cas abruptly. "It must have been very hard to stand up there on TV like that. Well, that and losing your brother." He felt idiotic but couldn't stop his mouth in time.

"Carlos and I really weren't that close even after my mom split," she said sadly. "He was so much younger than I and completely out of control. I feared it would be drugs or street crime or falling off a mountain that would kill him — if not AIDS."

"Weregild — and Dolores — talked me into going on TV. He said that I made such a good impression that I could be the poster child for victims and he should demand a lot more money from the Church. Frightening thing is that I'm not sure he was joking."

"Yeah, that hombre seemed awfully slick to me," Chewie snorted. "But I don't think he's so thrilled with my case." He laughed with bitter pride. "I've been such a bad boy, you know. DeLaval picked me up off the street after I got out of jail." He glanced around and dropped his voice. "I got busted for prostitution — a big mix-up. All I was doing was waiting for my buddies down on Main."

There was yet another pause.

Filling the void, Cas said, "I had no idea Carlos was mixed up with that pig. I moved back here last fall and when I heard that DeLaval was still around, I couldn't believe it.

"But it wasn't until I had a good talk with girlfriend, here," she said, grasping Dolores hand and smiling, "that I even realized I'd been abused. It wasn't that I didn't remember so much as that I just couldn't bear to think about it."

"What really infuriates me," Dolores said angrily, "is that Arturo keeps repeating the same old line that there were just a few bad apples; they didn't know that child molesters were uncurable, and that everything's just ginger-peachy.

"I think we've got to do something, something public. This special commission they're setting up is going to be more of the same garbage unless we pressure them."

"There should be a victim on board and a parent or maybe a spouse, at least," Bruno suggested. "It needs some public accountability to keep them honest."

"You're absolutely right," agreed Cas. "You know, I didn't file suit until I talked to Chavez and my extremely unctuous cousin Robert after the funeral. They kept saying very soothing things but didn't seem very interested in actually doing anything, the conceited asses.

"They keep telling Weregild, 'Oh, the commission will address this issue and that issue;' but they're taking their own sweet time in setting it up. And now, of course, they won't talk to me at all."

She shook her inky-black hair and sighed. "So what about you, Bruno?" she asked, after a long pull from her cigarette. "You mentioned Wilson."

"And maybe DeLaval. I've no memories about him, but he scares the hell out me," he admitted slowly. "I swear, if he came into this room right now, I'd have to kill him before he could open his mouth."

"I can relate," Cas sympathized. "With me, it's the tone of voice. I was powerless against it. DeLaval could paralyze me just by talking to me. I have nightmares about him coming back."

Bruno shook his head. "However, all I remember so far is 'normal' abuse from DeLaval — you know, slaps to the back of the head, ear-twisting. But they all did that."

They laughed. "With the little of my childhood that I recall, who knows? Like, I thought Kennedy was shot when I was in second grade, yet it happened when I was in sixth. Must not have wanted to think about those intervening years."

He sighed. "I guess my bottom line is that I just don't want whatever happened to me to happen to my daughter."

"Exactly," Dolores agreed, eyes flashing. "That's why we need a group, if only for the sake of the children. This has got to stop."

"Yeah, but how?" Dick asked. "What can we do? Hey, first time I tried telling my parents, I got whacked. What makes you think anyone would listen now?"

"We're not kids anymore, man," said Bruno. "We can fight 'em like grown ups now: sue the bums, raise an almighty stink, make their lives as miserable as they did ours."

"Something to consider, for sure," Dolores said. She glanced at her watch, "But for me it'll have to wait. I told my babysitter I'd be home a half-hour ago."

"Yeah," Bruno reluctantly agreed. "I should get going too. All these industrious students make me feel guilty."

That was the signal for everyone to gather their things. "Wait," Bruno implored. "I'd really like to do this again. At least let me get your phone numbers." Dolores sat down, pulled a notepad out of her bulging purse, and scribbled her name and number on sheets that she then passed out to the rest.

"Great," Bruno said. "You're the first people I've been able to talk to about this stuff without having to pay by the hour first."

"Let's do more than just talk," suggested Cas as everyone swapped numbers. "We need something more dramatic, involving everybody. Maybe I could get a list of callers from Weregild — I'll tell him we're contemplating a class action lawsuit."

"That'll light up his beady little eyes," Bruno laughed. "Why don't we protest? Let's picket a church!"

The others exchanged looks. "We're already there," said Dick. "We were just talking about that before you came in."

Dolores whipped a church bulletin out from her purse. "Over Memorial Day weekend Chavez will hold a special retreat for lay catechism teachers there at the Complex. How about then?"

"Okay with me," said Bruno. "My old high school I can handle; I just don't want to go anywhere near that damned old church again."

"Me neither," Cas sighed. "Both are bad for me, but the Complex isn't quite as creepy." Bruno nodded understandingly.

There was a decided difference now in the atmosphere at the table. Was it revolution in the air? At least the pall of helplessness had dissipated. "We need a name, people," Bruno pointed out. "Something to put on a press release, anyway."

Dick asked, "How about something simple and obvious?" "You know, something like 'Catholic Victims of Clergy Abuse?'"

"Much more dramatic," rebutted Dolores, "How about 'Alliance for Clergy Accountability?'"

"Why not 'L.A.M.B.S.' — 'Little Angels Molested by Sodomites?'" Bruno suggested sarcastically. It quickly got downright silly: "Veterans of Foreign Objects," "Catholic Catamite Club," "Clergy Kleenex," and even worse.

When the hilarity finally subsided, it was agreed that something serious was needed. "Not 'victims,'" Cas insisted. "If we don't want be victims, let's not call ourselves that. 'Survivors' are what we are, no matter how we might feel at times."

Finally they agreed on a more humdrum name — they would call themselves "C.A.S.A.," the "Clergy Abuse Survivors of Alvarado." The hat was passed and a whopping twenty-three dollars collected for signs and fliers. "Not bad for our first collection," Dick said. "Maybe we ought to start a church."

Bruno nodded reflectively. It was interesting being in on the beginning of something like this, he thought, and not just as a student of human events. Self-empowerment: fright replaced by anger. Maybe, he thought, if not a revolution, this is how the real healing begins.

"Good," said Cas. "Let's meet here again next week."

"Excellent!" Bruno exclaimed and stood up. He felt better, his arctic isolation thawed a little. "God, it was good meeting you all. Thanks."

They smiled uncertainly at each other as they stood around the table. "Would anybody mind?" Dolores asked finally, spreading her arms. "I could really use some hugs."

They circled around so everyone could get a squeeze. When it was Cas' turn, Bruno gazed down and saw her deep hazel eyes questioning him.

"This is going to sound stupid, but I have the weirdest feeling I've met you before," he said, suddenly embarrassed.

"Me too." Cas nodded thoughtfully. "But I can't remember where." She smiled. "Maybe at some big social function, a wedding or something?"

"Doubtful. I didn't have many friends as a kid and hardly ever went out. Were you at Soledad?"

"Our Lady of Solitude? No, I was incarcerated over at Queen of Peace. My guess would be the College, maybe."

"Could be," acknowledged Bruno. "But somehow I don't think so. That just leaves biker bars and strip clubs, I'm afraid."

"Sorry, afraid not," she giggled, shaking her head.

"Come on, you guys, knock it off," Dick interrupted playfully. "Are you practicing pick up lines, or what?"

Bruno suddenly became aware that he was still holding Cas lightly by her arms and she didn't seem to mind. He dropped his hands and stepped away. "Bitch, bitch, bitch," he sneered at Dick. "Who made you class monitor?"

"Well, I can see we're going to have a lot of work to do with you, young man, and your public school insolence!" Dick berated him in a high falsetto nun imitation, frantically wagging his finger at Bruno. "You've been talking to those Protestants again, haven't you?" They chuckled as they meandered through the rabble towards the front door.

When they got there, Bruno held it open for Cas. "Okay if I call you before then?"

"Sure," she replied casually. "If you want. I can use all the help I can get organizing this."

"Count on me," Bruno grinned. The hell with finals. This had turned out much better than he had imagined it could. "Talk to you soon."

†

CHAPTER THIRTEEN

Feast of Pentecost, Sunday, May 30

THE DUSK was already settling, relieving the day's heat as Bruno rattled up to the empty lot across from the Catholic Complex. The last rays of the sun painted the saw-toothed crests of the Sanbenitos across the valley a deep salmon while the Espiritu Santos to the north were already purple. Overhead swept a subtle gradation from the violet above the glowing peaks across the clear vault of heaven to the rich peach on the creamy clouds decorating the western horizon.

On the other side of the wide boulevard stretched their target, the Catholic Complex, a spacious compound of white-bricked, red-tiled buildings shining brightly in the sunset, surrounded by deep green fields lined with tall poplars. In the middle, the scaffolding and cranes enclosing the new cathedral, Nuestra Señora de Victoria, shone like some monumental abstract sculpture of birds building a nest.

Below the Complex, the valley already lay in shadows; the glittering city beyond mounted the eastern bluffs, spreading up to the very foothills of the mountains.

Another breathtaking sunset but Bruno didn't care. The small band of people milling around moved to greet him.

"Good Lord, is this all?" he said, shaking hands.

Dick laughed hollowly. "There've been a few desertions in the ranks, general."

Bruno was genuinely shocked. The last gathering had completely filled the back room of La Frontera. In all his years coming to the joint, he'd never seen such a large crowd.

Yet less than a dozen stood waiting here. Apart from the four he had first met, there was Irene, a steel-haired butch ex-nun; Rudy, a dark, wiry Mexican farmhand from down south;

Chuck, who was entirely round, and three or four more nondescript types whose names he couldn't remember.

"Is this really it?" he repeated in dismay. Dick nodded and handed him a stack of fliers.

"Afraid so. Becky, our sole parent, was asked by her son not to, so she's out. Several called but everybody else just ditched. So much for our great display of solidarity." He pointed behind Bruno. "At least some TV guys showed up."

Bruno turned around. On a rise in the tumbleweed filled vacant lot behind him, several television camera crews set up their gear. A young blonde woman, even shorter than Cas but wearing a business suit with shoulder-pads as thick as a quarterback's, interviewed her against the picturesque backdrop.

Dolores rushed over. "Thank God you're here." They hugged quickly. "If you're thanking God already," Bruno guessed, "things must be even worse than I thought."

They strolled over to the truck where Chewie was leaning, studiously bored. "Hey, dude, what's up?" Bruno asked. Chewie shrugged. "Just waiting for the show. Pick a sign, vato."

He gestured with his thumb at a pile of placards in the bed of Cas' pickup. Bruno chose one he'd made that read, "*WHERE'S DELAVAL?*" in bright red. Dick, rummaging around, exclaimed, "All right! Cas did it!" He lifted a bright yellow poster, beautifully block-lettered in black: "*BLESS YOU FATHER, FOR YOU HAVE SINNED.*"

"Should we go over?" Bruno asked. Across the street was the main entrance with a statue of the Virgin on top of a white brick wall. A banner hung on either side proclaiming "*CATECHISM TEACHERS RETREAT.*" Cars were already turning in for the Mass, the high point of the event. Bruno noticed several men with arms folded watching them from near the entrance.

Chewie said, "Weregild told Cas it would be legal as long as we stayed on the sidewalk. But I don't think we ought to get too near those hombres."

"Believe me, I'm not keen either. Haven't even been on the grounds since I got booted out of high school. But hell, I've fought worse looking guys than that." Bruno snorted. He stared across the river of traffic at the men. One, an old man, might have been a groundskeeper, but the others, dressed in windbreakers despite the warmth, one short, white-haired and fat, the other, tall, dark and skinny, might be coaches from the Catholic high school. "We ought to go over there and demonstrate anyway. They aren't going to attack us in front of these cameras."

"I recognize them," announced Irene gruffly, coming up from behind. The stocky woman stared intently. "I think they're the ones that have been following me. How dare they!"

"Maybe we ought to stay here where it's safe." Dick said nervously. "Let's forget about the fliers."

At that moment, Cas came up, hair tied back behind her black baseball cap. She took off her sunglasses and smiled at Bruno. On her black halter-top was a pin with bold letters that said, *"ALVARADO — THE LAND WHERE PRIESTS PREY."*

"Hi," Bruno said, pleased when she gave him a warm hug. "Hey, I dig that button. Got any more?"

She grinned briefly and handed him one out of her big black purse. "We got a problem," she said, suddenly all business. "The newshounds are getting mighty hungry."

Bruno glanced at her blankly as he fumbled with it. Dolores explained, "She means the reporters. The only way we could get them to come was to promise somebody would come forward tonight."

Cas took the pin, attached it to his shirt for him, and gazed up at him inquiringly.

Dick patted him on the back. "That means you, big guy."

"What?" Bruno exclaimed, his bravado instantly evaporated. He lowered his voice, trying not to let his apprehension show. "Why me?" They huddled more closely around him but the gathering had alerted the reporters. One was already zeroed in on them.

"Because you're the only one here who can," Cas stated softly but firmly. "We already have," nodding at Dick and Chewie. "But we have to give them something. The Diocese is already crying foul about 'nameless accusers.' If we want any of these media people to help us, we have to keep feeding them information. Besides, most of the others aren't ready — except for Irene. It was all I could do to get them to even show up."

"Well, yeah, maybe Irene's a little too gung ho, but why not you, then?" Bruno demanded, staring at Dolores. She ignored his glare as she watched the approaching journalist, and nodded to Cas, who slipped away to head him off.

Dolores turned and gripped Bruno's arm tightly. "I mustn't go public yet," she whispered. She searched his face. "I'm sorry. I promise I'll tell you everything as soon as I can. Honestly, I'm taking a big risk even to be here with you guys."

Cold resignation washed over Bruno, like he was a soldier about to hit the beach.

Cas returned to the group. "Well?" she asked quietly. "This is your big chance. Think what a difference it will make," she urged, "for the brother of a priest to come forward."

"I guess it's inevitable," he admitted, "and now's as good a time as any, I suppose." He sighed. "I just don't think I'm ready for this."

"Nobody ever is," Cas said gently. "But we're with you."

"Well, that makes it better." He sighed again even louder. "Okay, then," he said fatalistically, "let's do it."

She flashed him a quick, grateful smile and then stood on tiptoes to kiss him. "For luck," she said, blushed, and wiped the lipstick off, touching his hairy cheek before stepping back. She turned and fished out a sign from the truck. Hers was two-sided with "*CLERGY ABUSE SURVIVORS OF ALVARADO*" on one side and "*CLERGY SEX ABUSE IS A SIN*" on the other.

"It's not so bad," Dick consoled him cheerily. "Embarrassing your family to death might even be fun."

"Been there, done that," he muttered and shrugged. Why the hell not, he thought. Crazily, his hand itched for a gun.

But he realized that, paradoxically, if indeed he had been carrying a piece, he could never contemplate a confrontation. After all, things could get out of hand, like the anti-war riots at the College he'd ditched high school to join. With his record, he dare not afford the added penalty for carrying concealed, not to mention any temptation to actually use it.

Suddenly, an icy sense of outrage filled him. "Damn it, I'm not going to let those smug jerks bully me this time," he proclaimed. He turned to the small band.

"Well, folks, as somebody once said, the whole world is watching. I'm just pissed that they got some goons over there to intimidate us, so I say we cross the street and get right in their ugly faces. Screw 'em if they can't take a joke." Everyone looked around uneasily but nobody said anything.

Bruno shouldered his sign like a rifle. "Well, I'm going, anyway." He marched over to the corner and punched the button for the light. He heard them milling around but deliberately did not look behind him. When the light changed, he strode across the street, ignoring the honking, sign held high and planted himself before the Virgin.

Only then did he glance around. The others who followed him reluctantly across the asphalt Rubicon now stood uncertainly around him like a herd of skittish cattle. On the other side of the street, the TV crew was still shooting in the twilight, their lights brightening the cars that roared in between. A motorcycle cop had stopped to observe the scene.

"All right!" Bruno exclaimed. "This is more like it. Now spread out everybody. We need a song, or something."

Dick asked, "How about a chant?" He paused and then his face lit up. "Abused once but never again!" he shouted. "Yeah," someone called. The group raggedly picked it up.

Shouting their new slogan, Bruno led them towards the entrance. He stood there facing the three men across the driveway, ignoring the cars that drove past. The trio shuffled about defensively. The fat man focused a camera on him so Bruno shifted his sign to block the video cameras and flipped him off. The skinny Chicano had to hold his pal back, but the old geezer just laughed.

That felt great. The assholes just glared back at him, so Bruno turned to face traffic. He grinned with Cas and the others, waving at the curious, indifferent, amused, or irritated drivers cruising the warm weekend evening.

He rocked back and forth on his toes, feeling truly and marvelously alive. Energized, he accepted what he now knew he had to do — call Weregild and add his name to the lawsuit.

By now it was fully dark; the first stars shining above the Sanbenitos. The reporters crossed the street. TV lights flared on again as they began shooting the demonstrators from a new vantage.

Holding up their signs, led by Dick as before, they started chanting, "Bless me, Father, for you have sinned!"

Bruno decided it was time. He gestured to his companions. They silently grouped together behind him. Feeling a little like a deer in the headlights of hunters, he stepped forward into the blinding glare of the TV lights. He could see nothing but brightness, felt the heat of the lamps on his face like the furious electric concentration of all the eyes behind them.

His throat was parched. He swallowed hard and declared, "My name is Edward Bruno Nolan, and I was sexually abused by Father Philip Wilson."

Bruno could barely distinguish the flashes from the still cameras in the blaze of the TV lights. He struggled not to squint or blink but stared resolutely into the glare.

It quickly became an impromptu inquisition as the reporters grilled him from the shadows.

"Have you filed a lawsuit?"

"Not yet, but I intend to file individually or maybe join the suit already filed by Mr. Weregild."

"For how much?"

"I don't know; we haven't really discussed that."

"Aren't you the brother of Father Michael Nolan? Does he know? What does he think of this?"

This threw him but he should've expected them to make the connection to Mike immediately. Everybody in town did, it seemed. "Yeah, he's my younger brother. We've talked about it very little; you'll have to ask him what he thinks about it."

The interrogators intensified their assault. Questions came fast and hard: When did it happen? How often? Did you tell anyone? What do you think of the proposed Review Board?

He fended them off the best he could. The only answer he was at all satisfied with was the last. "The Review Board sounds good, but why let them investigate themselves? I'd much prefer a grand jury." Short and sweet.

For the final shot, the victims dropped their signs and stood behind him, hands joined, feebly singing "We Shall Overcome." Bruno was amazed and gratified to see that Dolores joined in next to Cas on the far end of the line.

Soon, though, the press was sated, however temporarily. One of the journalists from a newspaper in traditional livery of rumpled coat, dirty shirt, and badly-knotted tie wandered up to confirm his misspellings. The cameras turned again to the Catholic Complex, where his more photogenic colleagues stood by the Virgin's statue to offer their instant insights.

Bruno was exhausted, feeling like he'd been through a fistfight. The others crowded around congratulating him. "Good work, champ," Cas said warmly. Chewie added, "Way to go, amigo!" and Dick suggested, "Hey, let's get some ice cream to celebrate!"

By the time Bruno got home he only wanted to crawl under his bed, with his gun, cat, and stuffed toy turtle. His answering machine tape was full, but he didn't care. The heady rush of speaking up burned out fast, leaving behind a nameless foreboding in his churning guts. Exposed in the uncaring light of the public eye was not at all a comfortable feeling.

†

CHAPTER FOURTEEN

Saturday, June 5

BRUNO waited nervously by the statue of Pius XII in the very heart of the Catholic Complex. It was a hot summer evening, the bedraggled clouds loitering over the green heights of the Sanbenitos doing nothing to relieve the parched desert air.

He was sweating and not happy to be back on the grounds of his old high school, though he had been looking forward to this event where the Diocese would reveal its plans for dealing with the crisis. Tonight was a chance to get some answers at last or know why not.

The parking lot filled rapidly. To the left stood the classroom buildings of Pius XII High, to the right the cathedral's construction site, with the diocesan offices in between. A growing crowd milled uncertainly in the central courtyard.

"What's going on?" he asked the first person that didn't seem lost. The older man replied, slowing briefly. "They're moving us to the lecture hall. Too many people."

"Bruno!" He turned to see Cas, garbed in a loose top with thin spaghetti straps, black as always, hurrying towards him with a smile. She gave him a big hug, pulling back at his lack of response. "What's wrong?"

He frowned down at her. "I've been thinking. You and Dolores set me up. You must have told those reporters in advance I was going public before I even agreed."

"Bruno, we didn't want to," Cas confessed, stepping back. "I'm sorry. But they started bugging us the moment we arrived and by then we had to do something."

"Yeah, but how could they instantly know about my damned brother unless you told them?" Bruno felt his voice rise as his irritation surfaced.

Cas nodded miserably. "You're right, I did. But I had to, you see — they were starting to pester Dolores."

Bruno snorted. "So? What's she hiding anyway?"

"She didn't tell you?" Cas asked in surprise.

"She said she would, but she hasn't returned my calls." He stared suspiciously at Cas.

"Well, if she hasn't, then I can't," Cas stated firmly. "It's her secret and I'm not going to blow it for her. Sorry."

She touched his arm gently. "Believe me, Bruno, she'd speak out if she felt she could. I hope soon she will. It'll knock this town on its ear. Please don't press her."

Bruno was interrupted before he could retort. "Hey kids! How's it going?" Dolores called, waving at them. Cas flashed Bruno a desperate glance, and he rolled his eyes and nodded.

Soon, drifting with the crowd's flow, they entered a fair-sized auditorium. Bruno led them to his preferred spot — inconspicuous, at the rear, close to the exit. He gazed around curiously, not having been there since his last detention over twenty years before. The walls had mutated from revolting green to repulsive tan, but the squeaky chairs, dusty green board, and crucifix were the same.

"Jeez," he whispered to Cas, pointing out the carved initials on his desk. "Sure hasn't changed much." He shot a quick glance at her. She, too, seemed nervous as she dug in her purse for a cassette recorder. "You okay?" he asked.

She nodded quickly. "Yeah," she replied in a low voice. "Relieved, actually. I'm just glad we're not in any of the conference rooms. I had too many 'conferences' with DeLaval over there. But I've never been in here before. I take it you have."

"Oh yeah, plenty of times," Bruno laughed. "But yeah, I'm okay. Nothing happened to me here — at least, nothing worse than hanging out with the pachucos for always asking the wrong questions in religion class."

"Ah, so this is where you got your higher education," Dolores laughed.

On the platform below, people were moving in a long table next to the podium and setting up chairs. A genial-looking man in a fuzzy sports jacket and big bow tie wrote "*AD HOC COMMITTEE PUBLIC MEETING*" in large letters on the board. He waited patiently for people to sit.

"Oh hell," Cas whispered. "Should have known he'd come." At Bruno's inquiring glance, she explained, embarrassed. "My glorious cousin Robert, the chancellor." He nodded, "Well, I'm in luck, anyway; no sign of Father Fantastic."

The drab guy at the board was one of the more dismal lecturers from college, but Bruno recognized few others in the crowd — just Irene and one or two of the more outspoken mothers who had been on TV.

The multitude was quite diverse. A few men and women, probably lawyers or media, were dressed in business suits with had legal pads resting before them. Most everyone else was dressed casually, all adults of various ages and shapes, mostly parents and concerned citizens. He noticed a few people his age or younger who had the spooked air of victims.

Cas looked inquiringly when he started and followed his dour gaze. "Our friends are here, too." In the back of the hall by the upper exit stood the two men he'd faced off at the protest.

"Just ignore them," Dolores whispered. "Remember, we're undercover here tonight."

The professorial type on the stage prevented further discussion with a few feedback squeals as Father Cruz adjusted the microphone on the podium for him.

"Good evening," he said experimentally. "Uh, as I'm sure you're all aware this is the first public meeting of the Ad Hoc Committee on Clergy Abuse in the Diocese of Alvarado. We are here tonight to present the preliminary proposals for the Permanent Review Board, and to listen to your comments and questions on the, um, matters at hand."

Bruno noticed that Cruz and Malachy, sitting next to each other at the long table, had been having an earnest discussion. Cruz got up and whispered in the speaker's ear and then walked to the door where a camera crew was waiting.

"Ah, before we go any further," the speaker said, "due to certain concerns that have been expressed about privacy, no pictures will be allowed here during the meeting. The um, TV cameras will be set up outside away from the building. And, ah, no-one among the audience who wishes to make remarks will be asked to identify themselves. You may if you wish, of course, but it is in no way required."

He glanced at the panelists, who nodded in agreement while the crowd made approving noises and relaxed slightly as the camera crew packed up.

The man peered at the crowd over his glasses and continued. "My name is Dr. Nathan Dodge. I am Tenured Professor of Contemporary Religion at Alvarado State College. I was asked by Bishop Chavez as an interested outsider to help the diocese to, uh, look into the apparent problems here. In the past month, we've held many private meetings with the hierarchy and clergy, law enforcement officials and several, um, alleged victims and their families.

"In addition, we have consulted other dioceses and the National Circle of Bishops as to what guidelines and ah, policies may exist. Unfortunately, there aren't any. So we've devised a plan that we think is reasonable and fair to all concerned. But before we formally make our proposals to Bishop Chavez, he has asked us to consider the uh, input of the faithful. This is very generous, and I ah, think it shows that he intends to take this problem as seriously as you do. We've already had over a thousand phone calls and hundreds of letters, some sent anonymously.

"First, I think we, the members of the Committee, should identify ourselves." He detached the microphone, passing it to Cas' cousin.

"Father Robert Cruz," the olive-skinned priest said sweetly, smiling under his thick mustache. His slicked-down hair gleamed inky blue. "I am the Chancellor of the Diocese. Though I have been asked by His Excellency to help set up the Review Board, and will, of course, be working closely with it, I won't be on the Board itself." At a prompting from Malachy, he continued gently, "This is to prevent any appearance of a conflict of interest. Since I am also Vicar of Priests, I will be ministering to any clergy who may be accused of misconduct."

He passed the mike on. Malachy seized it and leaned forward on his elbows like a bulldog standing his ground. "My name is Monsignor Sean Malachy. For many years I have been rector of Our Lady of Solitude but Bishop Chavez asked me to head up this Review Board due to my training in Canon Law. I've also served on the Marriage Tribunal here for quite a number of years."

He paused and then said briskly, "I just want to make something clear at the outset. I didn't want this job, but I took it because I love the Church. She is as dear to me as my own sainted mother, and I will protect her like I would my mother. I don't like fakers and whiners but I utterly despise child molesters, so if you come to me, be ready to tell me God's honest truth, and I will do what I can."

"Classic Father Malarkey, all right," Bruno whispered approvingly. "Diplomatic as a junkyard dog."

Malachy deferred to a thin, auburn-haired woman in a red suit. "I'm Carolyn Kramer, a partner at Kramer, Sprenger and Associates, the Diocese's law firm. I'll represent the Diocese in any legal proceedings, but though on this committee, I will not be on the Board. I'm just here to discuss the legal aspects."

Next was a dark, heavyset man with a thick salt-and-pepper beard, but shiningly bald on top, dressed in an old rumpled suit. "My name is Jorge Gonzales," he said huskily. "I asked to be on the Board, because my boy, he —" He choked, cleared his throat, and went on, "my boy, Ernesto, was molested by Father Wilson. He took his own life last year."

He bowed his head and passed to the penultimate member of the committee, a thin elderly man in an elegant Western-cut suit complete with a turquoise-encrusted bolo tie, who automatically pushed a box of tissues towards Gonzales. "I am Doctor Vernon Van Kampf. I am a psychiatrist; my practice involves setting up treatment plans for both sexual victims and offenders. I am not to be part of the Board, but may be called upon to provide psychiatric evaluations if needed."

The final speaker was a small, smiling leprechaun of a priest with flaming red hair. He had a Celtic, almost elfin appearance to him, immediately confirmed by his lilting brogue accent. "Kevin Lynch, ladies and gentlemen, is my name, and I have the great honor to be Minister General of the Ministers of Consolation. Our Order has several retreat houses here in the Diocese, and a modern treatment center up at our headquarters, there in the lovely village of Ghost Springs."

The audience stirred. "This'll be great! What a line up," whispered Bruno. "Shouldn't we ask them something?"

"Only if we think of a really good question. Let's not blow this chance to nail them publicly," Cas whispered back.

The mike was passed back to Dodge at the lectern. Clearing his throat, he read, "Thank you all for coming. The ongoing onslaught of, ah, allegations of sexual abuse by members of the clergy of the Roman Catholic Diocese of Alvarado are naturally of grave concern. I'd like to ask Monsignor Malachy if he'd be kind enough to describe the proposals."

"Be happy to," Malachy said dryly as he took his turn at the pulpit and adjusted the mike stand. "I have an outline of these proposals in detail," he said, holding a sheaf of papers up. "Unfortunately, there aren't enough to go around. Please share them with those next to you." He waited for the noise to die down as the copies were distributed.

"The Review Board," Malachy finally began, "will have seven members: the Case Manager, which will be me; three other clergy, a layperson, a victim, and a victim's parent. Bishop Chavez has already appointed some members; others are still to be decided upon. All will be required to swear confidentiality."

Malachy began to outline the system, droning on about allegations, screening, and so on, but Bruno's mind soon drifted. How bizarre it was, he thought, that he should be revisiting the scenes of his past like this. To have such issues overshadow his life, and never even suspect. Had he always been lost in a trance?

He became aware that Malachy had finished. "That's all I have. I guess we can take questions now." Dodge stood up and took the microphone. "Thank you, Monsignor Malachy, for your succinct summation. I ask that those who wish to speak line up, one by one, in a nice, orderly manner before the microphone set up in the center aisle."

The crowd stirred, and slowly, like having received the call from the altar at an uninspiring revival, individuals rose here and there and hesitantly made their way over to the mike.

First up was a young, longhaired, nervous-looking man who kept his arms crossed. Another victim, Bruno guessed.

"Fa- Father Malachy, is the Church is going to pay for therapy for victims and their families? And if so, will there be any limits placed on it?"

Malachy stepped back up. "As Bishop Chavez has said, the Church has made a commitment to heal those who were injured, so the answer is yes. We will continue to pay for therapy." There was scattered applause. "However," he qualified, "we will have to be assured that the money is indeed going to healing. Our wealth is not great; but as for any practical limits, right now, I don't know of any."

"Unless you sue, of course," a burly African-American said, loud enough to be heard around him. Cas grabbed Bruno's leg as he laughed aloud and Dolores groaned. Even Malachy glanced up. The young man at the mike just seemed relieved. "Thank you, Monsignor," he said and quickly sat back down.

Cas whispered, "Actually, they'll pay only as long as we go to their shrinks who'll report back to them."

The hope it would stay non-confrontational was then shattered as the big black guy stood up and grabbed the center mike. "What I'd like to know," he boomed in a deep voice, "is why the Church sent a lawyer here." A murmur of agreement spurred him on. "We've gotten nothing but lawyers from the start. I don't want to talk to no more lawyers. If he cares so much, why isn't the Bishop himself here?"

This inspired a brief interchange between the Chancellor and the woman in red. Cruz finally spoke up. "Miss Kramer is here tonight because I asked her," he said. "She graciously came not to discuss cases but the overall legal situation. However, she has agreed to leave if that is what you all want."

A smattering of applause decided the issue. Cruz shrugged angrily, and the woman, face now as crimson as her suit, picked up her briefcase and purse, marching offstage as stiffly as a soldier.

His mustache drooping, the chancellor addressed the crowd again. "As for his Excellency, Bishop Chavez couldn't be here. He's on a speaking trip back East, raising funds for the new cathedral." He added defensively over the rising murmur, "This trip had been planned a long time, and with the Holy Father coming, we are naturally anxious to have as much done as possible, which takes money."

"How do we know these donations aren't going for lawyers and secret settlements?" the man demanded.

"Surely you must have some faith in us," Malachy began.

Bruno was startled to hear a muffled sob next to him. Dolores had started to weep, Cas already handing her some tissues, and firing a warning glare at Bruno.

By the time he glanced up again, a small, plump, blue-haired, grandmotherly old woman had replaced the large, dark man at the mike. "I just wanted to thank you for letting us chat together like this," she said pleasantly. "And to ask Father Lynch if he could tell us about the therapy program he runs up there in the mountains. My goodness, from the stories they show on the news, one would think it was some kind of resort for perverts."

CHAPTER FIFTEEN

THE AUDITORIUM gasped. Bruno and Cas laughed aloud and they were not alone. The color drained from Lynch's face.

Lynch jumped up and grabbed the mike from Cruz. He was too short for the podium so he stood beside it, feet braced apart, bouncing like a boxer. "Well, you can't believe everything you read in the papers," he said with a charming smile. "Rest assured, dear lady, that our Retreat House is not a resort of any kind. It is a lovely and restful place, to be sure, up there in the beautiful mountains, but it is a place of spiritual discipline and prayer; not luxury, much less depravity.

"The work of God can overwhelm even the strongest men," he declared, warming to his homily. "So it is to reinvigorate all priests and religious — and not just the troubled and sick ones — that we operate our facilities."

"But what about those troubled priests, Father?"

"It's true that they are our especial concern as an order. We have strict therapy programs, both psychological and spiritual, for priests who need help. Most who come to us suffer from emotional or alcoholic problems such as depression, and most ask to be sent. Those referred to us for sexual difficulties are really quite few," he said matter-of-factly. "And they have their own special programs, involving a great deal of personal reflection, as well as other treatment they may be required to attend." He paused for a sip of water.

From his seat, the large black man interrupted again. "But aren't these perverts dumped right back into our parishes afterwards — or even while they're there? What about Wilson? Didn't he molest kids while he was supposedly in your care?"

Lynch held up his hands. "Please," he pleaded. "If we can't be civil here, there's no point in trying to talk. As for the question, there were limited placement arrangements with several shorthanded dioceses, including this one, made for some who were doing well in therapy. As for Father Wilson, those cases are in litigation, so I can't discuss them.

"This was all quite a while back, you know," he earnestly declared. "Nobody knew how difficult these erotic paraphilias — perversions as you call them — would be to successfully diagnose and treat. Am I right, Dr. Van Kampf?"

The psychiatrist reluctantly stood. "Regrettably, that's true, Father Lynch," he said. "Recidivism or relapse among sexual offenders, especially pedophiles, is remarkably high even after treatment, and still not understood.

"Yet let me say that priests are no more likely to molest children than other men. Far more sexual abuse of children in this country is perpetrated by physical fathers and stepfathers than by spiritual 'fathers.' In my view, with all the sexual molestation going on in our society, those who are blaming the Church are just hoping to win the 'Catholic lottery.'"

Cas and Bruno stared at each other in amazement. "Did you hear that?" he asked, dumbfounded.

"Yeah. Remind me never to consult him professionally."

"Remind me to run him over if I ever get a chance."

An old, frail Hispanic woman, dressed in black, limped up to the microphone supported by an equally ancient leather-skinned cowboy. Clasping the stand for support, she earnestly said, "I belong to a prayer group at Santa Marta parish, in the valley, you know? This is a spiritual problem. We believe the Devil is attacking Mother Church. We must pray. The Blessed Virgin Mary has warned us."

The crowd muttered in a mixture of sympathy, disbelief, and amusement. Even Cas chuckled, but Bruno for once didn't.

Though he shared her cynicism, what the little old woman said was poignant. Of all these supposedly religious people here she was the only one to make a connection with spirituality.

Cruz answered in his smoothest style, not bothering with the mike. "¡Por supuesto, abuelita! We must first and always pray that the Lord will ever guide us and bless our work." This seemed to disarm her and the couple sat down contentedly.

Next up was another elderly pair, both heavyset and white-haired. "My question is for the professor," the man said in an unrecognizable Eastern European accent. Dodge looked up in alarm, but did not stand as the shrink eagerly passed the microphone to him.

"You said all letters sent to you would be handled confidentially," the man said slowly. "Why did we get a reply from the chancellor when we wrote to you?"

"I, ah, have no idea, sir," answered the startled academic. "Er, when did this occur?"

"Just last week." The man held up a typed letter. Even from this distance, a spot of color in the corner appeared to Bruno like it might be the Diocese's coat of arms.

Dodge nervously glanced at Cruz, who continued to sit impassively, and Malachy, who suddenly exhibited a keener interest. The old man continued angrily, "We asked you not to tell the Church about our son, that he was deeply ashamed. But the chancellor — whom we never talked to and did not want to — wrote us asking all kinds of questions."

The professor reddened. "I'm sure it must have been some sort of an oversight," he spluttered. "I, uh, just can't imagine how it could have happened otherwise. Perhaps it got mixed up when the mail was sorted."

"Perhaps you can't be trusted," the old man said. He glared for a moment and then turned away.

Cruz hesitantly rose to defend himself. But Irene strode up to the microphone, grabbing the stand as if it were a throat. "Father Cruz," she called out.

Cruz did not appear relieved to face her instead. "Yes, sis- er, madam?"

"Ah, so you do remember me. As you know, formerly I was a nun. My confessor tried to seduce me and when I told my mother superior about it, I was transferred to another convent and disciplined. So, finally I left. The priest is still serving in a parish here in town. But that's not the issue now."

She paused. "I wanted to ask you and Father Malachy if your investigations call for wiretapping, harassment, and stalking people."

"Wiretapping?" Malachy exclaimed.

"Yes, sir. My phone's been messed up ever since I first went public." She raised her voice over the rising hubbub, and pointed at the back of the hall, "And I've been followed around town by those two stooges of yours." The men stepped hurriedly out the door in guilty haste.

Malachy had turned tomato-red, redder even than Dodge or Kramer had been. He glared sharply at Cruz, who paled an similar amount instead.

"I never authorized that," Malachy spat. "Never."

That was it for the meeting. Pandemonium broke loose around Irene. Bruno had to laugh. This was just too rich. Too bad there were no cameras there to catch Malachy's reaction.

The meeting dissolved into many small heated groups despite Dodge's feeble calls for order. Malachy and Cruz were arguing and gesturing at Irene, who was defiantly pleased by the chaos. Several people were circling around waiting for their turns at them. The professor and the psychiatrist quickly and quietly grabbed up their papers to escape.

Bruno glanced at his companions. Dolores had finished weeping, but was a mess. She grabbed his arm and whispered harshly. "We have to talk, Bruno, now, but not here."

The trio made their way outside where the anarchy continued. The charismatics had been inspired to hold a prayer meeting in the middle of the courtyard, speaking in tongues, the whole bit. The TV crew was loving it.

There was a Sunday crush to get out of the parking lot. It took a while to get to La Frontera. Bruno drove alone, meeting Cas and Dolores there. This time they did indulge in some of the notorious oversize pastries dripping in butter and sugar.

By the time he returned with the tray, Dolores had started crying quietly again. "Thanks sweetie," she said in a low voice, accepting another tissue from Cas. "Thanks for being so patient."

Bruno passed the food and coffee around as she blew her nose. Finally, she began softly, not glancing up. "As you guys know, Father Kirk, the pastor of our parish, seduced me but I got blamed. After he died in a plane crash, I was so hurt and confused that, like a dope, I went to another priest for help.

"Well, you can guess what happened. Again, I stupidly fell in love. I thought he was in love with me, too — until, of course, I got pregnant. He insisted I go to Mexico for an abortion. I refused but I got some herbs from my grandmother who's a curandera — a healer, you know? However, I was too far along. I nearly died; they took me to St. Luke's and, being Catholic, they saved the baby so he could at least be baptized.

"I think now he was hoping they wouldn't save me too, but they did. Then he wanted them to take my child away and almost had me talked into it; but after all that, there was no way I was going to let anyone near mi angelito."

Her voice lowered. "He begged me not to make trouble. After all that, I still loved him, and yes, still thought of him as a man of God. I have stayed away from him all these years and he has helped my child. For although he survived, my poor sweet Esteban's brains were damaged by the herbs, and he needs a great deal of love and medical attention."

She wiped her eyes and looked up gravely at them. "I suppose you can guess who the father is." Bruno's eyes widened. "Not Chavez? Merciful jumping Jesus!" he exclaimed. "No wonder you couldn't speak out."

She nodded. "Anyway, for my baby's sake," she ruefully continued, "I went along with it even though I realized it was all wrong. But for my dear friend Cassie here, I wouldn't have had the courage to come this far." Dolores smiled through the tears and squeezed Cas' hand hard, and then released it. "But now something's happened. I — I don't know what to do."

She stared at her hands as they picked up a white paper napkin, twisting and shredding it. "I can't get through to him anymore. I mean, literally. I'm not supposed to call him; that was part of the arrangement. But my poor baby has not been doing well. He desperately needs another operation.

"So I've tried and tried and got nowhere. The secretaries hang up on me. I leave messages on his private line, no reply. I've even considered waiting for him at the bishop's house.

"He's cut me off for good, I think. But I have to do something. If I sue the Church over Kirk, this is sure to come out. So what can I do? Sell the story to the tabloids? I could probably get a whole morning to myself on a talk show." She chuckled humorlessly. "I know there were other women. I was pretty stupid at the time, though, thinking I was the only one. That he really loved me but had to put God first, and it was important to have someone leading the Church who was part of our traditions, nuestra raza.

"At least, that's what I kept telling myself." She disengaged and blew her nose again. "Then I got this the other day. She reached into her voluminous leather purse and pulled out a white envelope. "A large check, much bigger than usual. A little late — but it wasn't mine."

She opened the envelope. Inside was a check for seven thousand dollars from the "Sociedad de Nuestra Señora" typed out to "Kathleen Sullivan," and signed with an unreadable scrawl. Bruno craned his head to make out the note stuck on the side. "*Will call when I get to Seattle. Hug the little one for me.*"

He almost laughed at its banal tone, but Dolores trembled as if she held her own death warrant.

"It's, it's not just that there's somebody else." Her voice wavered. "Always before, he sent a personal check — or rather, I guess he had his secretary do it. I didn't want to know how badly he was betraying the Church as well as me."

She sighed, placing it carefully back into her purse. "I've been thinking hard about this. Maybe if I just threaten to sue over Kirk, it might scare Arturo into settling.

"I only know I've got to do something. For Esteban if nobody else. He's the only true innocent in all this. If I can get help for him, sure, I'll keep my mouth shut. But if there is no other way, I'll go public too. Before that I have to know what's going on, and only you can help me, Bruno."

Cas started to object but Dolores shook her head. "No, sweetie, you're already in too deep with the Chancellor — he'd never listen to you now."

"So what do you want me to do?" Bruno asked. "The situation's pretty bad between me and my brother, too."

Dolores hesitated. "I was wondering, what do you really think about Monsignor Malachy?"

Bruno shrugged. "Tough old bird; a hard-nosed, hard-line, old-fashioned priest." He pondered for a moment. "I don't think he's a perp. Never had 'Feeler' Wilson's slimy vibes, or those creepy moods of DeLaval's. Hell of a temper, but if he was abusive it was in the normal Catholic way." He paused again. "If I trusted any of them other than Mike, it would be him. If, that is. I'm not sure I trust Mike, either."

"I want you to talk to Malachy for me," she said pleadingly, placing her hand over his. "I just can't believe that Arturo would abandon his own son after all this. Especially when he knows I could ruin him. Somebody must be interfering somewhere.

"So," she asked, drawing back to study him. "Would you speak with him? Maybe he knows what's going on or could talk to the bishop. I have no other way of getting a message through other than hiding in the bushes when Arturo comes home."

"Please, leave that to Irene." Bruno held up his hands. "Okay, I'll do what I can."

"Good," Cas interjected. "But it's got to be soon." She spoke in a low voice. "Reporters are already sniffing around. They know something's up. I'm already walking a tightrope."

"Well consider this — if I take this to Malachy and he gets as pissed as is likely, what then? I mean, he's supposed to be checking into this stuff. He has to listen, but this would put him in one hell of a spot.

"And what if I'm wrong? What if he is one of the bad guys, too? This is real close to blackmail, after all. What's to keep those two bozos from knocking us off before you actually blow the whistle?"

"I have information hidden away. There would be no way they could cover it up," Dolores said quietly.

"Well, that's a relief." Bruno said sarcastically. "I'll be sure to tell them that before they shoot me."

"Blackmail?" Cas said bitterly. "Isn't that what all these confidential out-of-court settlements with gag orders are? It's all the same thing, only with lawyers rather than gangsters."

She sighed. "I still think you should just go public, chica. It's got to be safer that way."

Dolores shook her head. She appeared so miserable that Bruno could not refuse. He sighed heavily. "Like I said, I'll go talk to the man — but I want to borrow your recorder, Cas."

✝

CHAPTER SIXTEEN

Tuesday, June 8

BRUNO kept fiddling with the small cassette recorder as he waited. He'd much prefer the reassuring heaviness of his beloved Colt Commander but this would have to suffice.

He felt enough like a spy in the heart of enemy territory anyway but he was not about to let any opportunity slip to let Malachy put his foot in his own mouth. Meanwhile, he sat eyeing the large wooden statue of La Victoria that faced him off across the lobby from her shrine, candles reverently lit at her feet. A crude version of the elegant Spanish doll in the cathedral, the bulto was eloquent of the stubborn endurance of the conquistadors' descendants in these most distant outlands.

The statue though, was less threatening than the secretaries who kept eyeing him suspiciously as they quietly went about their work. He had little doubt they knew who he was even before he introduced himself, soon confirmed by the security guard discreetly watching him from the door.

Malachy recognized him instantly, too. The stocky old priest came striding briskly into the lobby, arms full of manila folders, and came to an abrupt stop, face undecided between surprise and dismay. "Mr. Nolan," he said flatly, "Surely, I wasn't expecting to see you here."

Bruno forced a smile and stood. "You said your door was always open. I decided it was time to take you up on that."

"Hmm," the priest grunted warily. "Well, now is not the best time. If you'd care to make an appointment..."

"Hey," Bruno said, expecting such a stall, "this isn't about me or the Review Board or any of that. I'm here for somebody else, somebody who really needs your help. I promise this won't take long."

Malachy studied Bruno critically, blue eyes squinting at him warily through the same heavy black frames he'd always worn, long enough for Bruno to remember many other such glares Eddie had endured. Now the old clerk had to look up at him instead of down, but it still had much the same discomfiting effect.

"Okay," the monsignor sighed at last. "You have five minutes." He turned to the secretary who handed him a sheaf of messages. "Consuela, would you hold my calls? Oh, and please let Robert know I'll be a few minutes late for the meeting with the insurers? Thanks."

Malachy pivoted around the corner and strode down the hall to the office that now had his name hand-lettered on a card taped over the brass nameplate. While he balanced the folders, unlocking the door, Bruno switched on the recorder.

Once inside, he glanced around curiously. There was a haphazard appearance to the various stacks of papers, like Malachy had created an uneven, chaotic layer of more recent stuff like new geological strata over those of the previous resident.

Whatever books DeLaval might have had were gone; the shelves now held more or less neat piles of folders. But there was a large glass case in the corner crammed full of gaudy religious trinkets and folk art, with more piled up next to it. It didn't take much to figure out the strange collection of icons and idols belonged to the missing monsignor.

But Bruno didn't have a chance to examine anything more closely. Malachy stalked over to the desk, dropped the files, and began scanning his messages. Without looking up he said, "The clock is running, Mr. Nolan. Sit down, please."

Bruno lowered himself nervously on the edge of the proffered chair and twisted his hands together. Malachy also sat but stretched out his legs, rubbing his neck. He remarked, "Can't tell you how hot this bloody collar gets on a day like today. It's pure mortification of the flesh. So what's this all about?"

Bruno had to smile at one of the old man's favorite phrases. He took a deep breath. "What have your investigators told you about Dolores Rael?"

"I have no idea who you're talking about," Malachy said icily, rubbing his neck.

"Don't pretend you haven't been snooping," Bruno said angrily. "We're a bit beyond that now."

"I haven't been snooping, Mr. Nolan. I was not lying when I said that I hadn't authorized anything. I didn't. The chancellor brought in those two nincompoops, not me. Nobody's told me anything about this person. Who is she?"

Bruno chewed his hairy lip. The hell with diplomacy, he thought. He could be blunt too. Offhandedly he said, "Oh, merely the mother of Chavez' love child."

"What!" Malachy sat bolt upright, the ruddy color draining out of his face. "Dear God, tell me you're joking."

"All I know is what I've heard." Bruno shook his head. "But I guess you hadn't heard either."

Malachy sat stunned for a long moment then his eyes narrowed. "Why are you telling me this? What is it you want?"

"Well, I wish it was because you're the head of the Review Board and this is a case of clergy sexual abuse," Bruno stated, shaking his head. "But not this time. I'm just trying to pass on a message, even though, I doubt it'll do a damn bit of good." He smiled. It felt wickedly delightful to swear in front of his former pastor. He held up hands disarmingly. "As for me, after I deliver this message, I'm out of it. I don't want a God damned stinking thing.

"Dolores, however, needs to talk to the bishop real bad, and she says he won't talk to her," Bruno went on. "So I'm here today to request that you ask him to call her. That's all."

"And what if he refuses?"

"She's in a very hard place. Her son — Chavez' son — is very sick, apparently. She's afraid the only way she may be able to come up with the necessary funds would be to sue the Church — but not about her baby. From what I understand, the bishop wasn't the first priest to get into her panties. That was a guy named Father Kirk."

Malachy reddened and Bruno almost smiled. He was quite enjoying this. "But if she has to sue, it could all come out. If he doesn't contact her, she feels she has no choice but to go public with part of her story, though she will avoid talking about 'His Excellency' as long as possible."

There, he'd said it. Bruno rocked nervously, closely watching Malachy's pale, lined face as the tired old man grappled with the situation, rubbing the stubble atop his head.

"Oh, and before I forget, she also wanted me to tell you that proof of this is in a secure place, and if anything happens to her — or me, for that matter — it goes to the media."

"Mr. Nolan, who do you think you're dealing with?" Malachy sputtered. "We're the Holy Catholic and Apostolic Church, not the Mafia!"

"And a great relief that is," Bruno replied caustically.

A buzz on the intercom made them both jump.

"Consuela, I told you —" Malachy began in aggravation.

"Sorry, Father, but the Chancellor asked me to buzz you. They're waiting in the conference room."

"St. Bertha's britches, I'm late," Malachy exclaimed, glancing at his watch. "Okay, tell him I'll be right there."

He stood, glowering. "Eddie — Mr. Nolan," he said. "Do not expect me to thank you for bringing me this information."

Bruno stood up also. "What are you going to do?" he asked uncomfortably, and not just because of the ill luck that tended to follow heralds. Hearing the old priest use his childhood name like that made him feel like a bad kid again.

"I must confront him," Malachy answered wearily. "What else can I do?" The old confessor suddenly seemed very worn.

Bruno felt guilty at the wave of relief that washed through him. The priest's slumping shoulders told him that he'd successfully dumped the burden on someone else, somebody who could — and should — take care of it somehow.

"Sorry — Father." The word still stuck in his throat.

Malachy coldly glared up at him but Bruno suddenly felt very small. "I hope you realize what this could do to the Church, Mr. Nolan. I understand you were hurt horribly; believe it or not, I've no doubts whatsoever about your case. But if this is true, a lot of innocent people will suffer. Ask yourself, is it worth it?"

"Don't blame me — I'm just the messenger," Bruno retorted hotly. "And don't fault Dolores either. She was lied to and screwed by two of these so-called 'men of God.' If anybody's responsible other than them, it's the rest of you — all of you. It's the fault of every single one of you supposedly 'good' priests who've witnessed this crap go on and on for years and years and haven't lifted a finger to stop it." He halted abruptly, shaking with barely-contained rage.

Malachy looked as if he had been slapped.

"I'm sorry, Eddie," he said. "I will do what I can. What I now see that I must." His bleak face had become as gray as his crew cut.

Bruno wheeled and strode to the door, stomach twisting with confused emotions. Hand on the knob he paused. "I sincerely hope so, Fath-, er, sir. Somebody's got to do something."

As he pulled the door shut behind him, he thought he heard the old sky pilot mutter, "Though surely there will be hell to pay." Bruno switched off the recorder in the hall, wondering if it caught that last remark.

✝

CHAPTER SEVENTEEN

Father's Day, Sunday, June 20

CAS announced, "Quiet now, it's starting!" Bruno leaned forward on the couch next to her, reaching for the popcorn. At her feet, Dolores sat on the floor, nervously clutching a pillow. Chewie and Dick flanked them on either side, sunk into matching plush chairs.

Cas hit the remote's recording button as the familiar electronic beeping that announced the opening of the show began. A dark-skinned man appeared on the screen, sitting comfortably in a director's chair. With his round head and heavy jaw covered with short grizzled gray hair, he gave the impression of being a particularly wise and urbane shaman.

"Good evening," he said genially, as a digital display in the corner of the screen began counting up from 0:00:00, beeping softly. "I'm Ben Morgan, and welcome to *Hour: Zero-Zero*."

The camera backed out and the background changed. A recent picture of Our Lady of Solitude with the broken stump of the cross on the roof between the unfinished twin towers loomed with the words "Sins of the Father" in garish red medieval lettering above it. "All right!" Bruno breathed.

"Today is Father's Day," Morgan continued. "And on this special edition of *Zero-Zero*, our main story tonight is about a spiritual father, a popular leader who has himself become embroiled in the sexual scandals that have rocked his church. Now it appears he himself has led a double life, a life that some say betrayed the very principles he has stood for."

The background switched to Bishop Chavez beaming in complete episcopal kit of miter and cope, crosier in one hand, blessing away with the other. "All that and more tonight on *Hour: Zero-Zero*."

The show cut to the first set of commercials, and Cas paused the VCR and muted the sound. "This is it at last," Dick said excitedly. "Whoo-hoo! Payback time!"

Bruno gazed down at Dolores. "How you doing, kid?"

"Okay," she said, plucking at the fringe on the pillow she cradled. "Scared. Nervous. I'm glad my grandma could take care of the kid tonight so I could be with you guys. I just hope she'll let me have him back after this. But I'm glad it's happening. I don't think I could take much more of this suspense but I'm surprised they put it together this fast."

"It's a big stink, for sure," Chewie said, "and will draw a swarm of reporters. Like flies to shit, you know?"

Cas patted her shoulder. "It'll be fine," she said. "You did the right thing."

"I hope so," Dolores said. "I gave Arturo almost a whole week after Bruno talked to Malachy, but I heard nothing." She laughed bitterly. "By the time I finally called the producer, they'd found two more of his women on their own and were going to do the story anyway. So I guess I shouldn't feel so bad about it but I still do."

"Any signs of the goon squad?" Bruno asked. Everybody shook their heads. "Good, I guess."

The general silence then stretched to the end of the ads for overpriced luxury cars and other geriatric aids. When Ben appeared again, he was in front of the cathedral dressed with a white straw hat against the afternoon sun, hands in pockets, speaking to the camera. He strolled across the ancient plaza amidst the tourists beneath the tall cottonwoods.

"The city of Alvarado is like many in the American Southwest, with a large Hispanic population that has deep roots and a sense of history as proud and old as the *Mayflower*. It is a strong, traditionally Catholic community, and when one of their own, a well-liked priest named Arturo Francisco Chavez became bishop here, there was a huge celebration, an outpouring of cultural pride, a feeling that at last they had come of age in America.

"But now all that may change. In recent months, as in many parts of the nation, the Catholic Church here has seen many of its priests accused of sexually abusing not only women, but children, boys and girls." He stopped strolling. "Unlike other dioceses wrestling with these problems, however," he continued, "it's the bishop himself who now stands accused of sexual misconduct."

The scene shifted to a conference room. "Hey, that's Werewolf's office," Bruno said. Chewie hushed him, saying, "Look, there's Dolores." She was the oldest of the three women sitting across the table from Morgan. They were similar in that they were all longhaired, professionally dressed and made up, and fairly pretty.

Morgan's voice-over continued. "Meet Guadalupe, Kimberley, and Dolores, all raised as devout Catholics. These three women, who never met until recently, say that they were sexually involved with Bishop Chavez, sometimes for years. And their stories, it seems, are remarkably similar in some ways."

Quickly he interrogated the women. The youngest, Guadalupe, told of how Chavez had fondled her one night on a camping trip, a retreat for young adults in the Espiritu Santo mountains, and how she then became his lover. She only stumbled when recounting how he had taken her in the chapel of his house after a private Mass he said for the biggest donors to the new cathedral.

"Wasn't that inappropriate?" Morgan prodded.

"I should think so," she huffed. "I was shocked. It happened actually on, on the altar itself in the chapel, but I felt completely powerless to resist."

"No, I mean, wasn't there something he said then, that made you wonder about the whole relationship?" he gently prompted.

"Oh yes." She flushed red. "He kissed me, and said, 'If only your father knew what he was missing.'"

"And that meant...?"

She appeared pained and twisted her hands. "It meant, he knew, you see, he knew he was like a father to me and yet he did it anyway."

The affair had died shortly after that because she became pregnant, although she did have the abortion he requested.

The next woman, Kimberly, was an Anglo, taller, slightly older, and with lighter skin and big puffy blonde hair, decked out Western-style with lots of turquoise and silver. She held her hands clasped on the table before her, sitting confidently.

In a soft Texan accent, she told how she had met Chavez while he was lecturing at the college before he became bishop. He dumped her as soon as he was promoted.

"It doesn't seem like it bothered you very much," Morgan commented.

She shrugged. "I'd grown up a lot in that time, and frankly, I was tired of him, all the sneaking around and the hypocrisy. I swear, honey, he would preach a sermon in bed.

"So I got my degree, moved to Dallas, and ain't been inside a church since. But I'm telling y'all: I knew there'd be others. A snake can shed its skin but it can't change its spots."

Then Dolores' face suddenly filled the screen. Everybody at Cas' house yelled but quieted down quickly. She blushed as her screen self told the story, illustrated with photos of the late Father Kirk, standing with her beside a small airplane and her in her Sunday best beside a young, fully vested Father Chavez.

The scene abruptly shifted back to Morgan standing in the middle of the downtown plaza next to the bandstand. "But Dolores' tale doesn't end there," he said. "Apparently, Bishop Chavez has been helping her pay for her son's medical expenses, running to tens of thousands of dollars, for years. If this is so, it isn't just Christian charity on the part of Chavez: bishops don't get paid that much.

"And Dolores may not be the only one to have benefited. Another woman who allegedly bore the bishop a baby has been identified in Seattle. However, she refused to talk to us."

A woman in a raincoat was quickly shown maneuvering a toddler out of a car and up a wet sidewalk while blocking the camera, then the scene cut back to Morgan on the sunlit plaza.

"So we sought to ask Bishop Chavez about these serious allegations. We were unable to get an interview but we caught up with him just this last weekend."

And there was Chavez himself hiking down a dirt road in the mountains, his familiar designer glasses darkened against the sun. He appeared tanned, fit, and as relaxed as ever, in the center of a group singing hymns in Spanish.

"Isn't that up by Ghost Springs?" Bruno asked.

"Could be. Looks like back up behind the Retreat House," Chewie whispered. "They have camp-outs every summer. I went on one with DeLaval last year."

The correspondent entered the frame from the left holding a microphone. "Bishop Chavez, Ben Morgan of *Hour: Zero-Zero*. How do you respond to the —" Suddenly a familiar white-haired hulk interposed itself between the men. "Hey, it's Laurel and Hardy!" Bruno exclaimed. "So that's where they've been."

The massive Anglo pushed Morgan back, while the skinny Hispanic guarded the bishop's other flank as Chavez nonchalantly continued marching along. Morgan came back again and there was a bit more shoving.

The scene cut. The group had now stopped, milling angrily behind the bishop, some with arms crossed defiantly. Yet Chavez looked as calm and benignly patient as ever. "Sorry," he explained to the proper time or place for these questions. Please contact our administrative offices, and I'm sure we can set up an appointment, okay?"

"We've tried that and gotten no answer," Morgan objected but the bishop was already moving away fast. The goons firmly planted themselves in the way. The bishop waved, smiling. "Call my office," he yelled encouragingly.

"Before we left, however, we did get a taste of what some of his followers thought." The camera showed a fat Chicana, feet widely planted in the road, waving her finger dramatically at the camera as the group escaped behind her. "Go away!" she screamed. "Leave the holy man of God alone. Don't believe those women who seduce priests! They're whores and worse than whores!"

The camera cut back to Morgan in the plaza. "We never did get a reply from Bishop Chavez, so we did the next best thing. We talked to the man asked by the bishop to investigate clergy sexual abuse here — Monsignor Sean Malachy."

†

CHAPTER EIGHTEEN

THE SCENE on the screen switched now to Malachy's office at the Catholic Complex. A small combination TV and VCR was set up on his desk. He stared intently at it; hand on fist, brow furrowed.

Among the gang watching at Cas', there was amusement at the inquisitor being put to the question.

"Well, Father Malachy, now that you've seen what these women had to say, what is your reaction?"

Malachy began to turn darken ominously. "I don't know what to say. I'm astonished and saddened that anyone could make such horrible accusations about Bishop Chavez."

"Do you believe them?" Morgan asked.

Malachy squirmed uncomfortably. Several times he opened his mouth to speak. Finally he said, "What I believe is not the point at the moment. Their allegations are serious, so I will examine their claims, and we'll go from there."

"Do you think you can do an honest job, seeing that you'll be investigating charges against your own boss?"

"Mr. Morgan, I promise you — and everyone else — before God and your audience," Malachy flatly declared, waving his hand in the direction of the camera as it closed in on his furrowed face, "that I will seek the truth out no matter where the trail leads."

The scene cut to Morgan at the plaza again. "We asked another's opinion — Nick Weregild, lawyer for several of these women and numerous other plaintiffs suing the Diocese."

Back in the lawyer's conference room, Weregild seemed as much at ease as Malachy hadn't. "There are many problems in this diocese," he said soberly. "It goes back long before Bishop Chavez came on the scene. But what he's done and failed to do is close to criminal in my view. If he has diverted

Church money, it certainly is indeed illegal and the District Attorney should look into it. My client, Dolores Rael, however, is innocent of any wrongdoing, since she was never made aware of the source of the funds.

"He has abused his position of trust at least, and his bad example to his clergy clearly enabled this problem to fester. He's been far too involved with his own sexual indiscretions to deal with them effectively, in my opinion.

"Indeed, Alvarado has become a dumping ground for child molesters disguised as Catholic priests. What Bishop Chavez' full role in all this is still unclear, but it is definitely something we will be investigating. It's my personal belief that we haven't seen anything yet."

Suddenly, the face of Father Mike, sitting alertly in the office of the rectory of Our Lady of Solitude beneath a mobile of whirling angels, appeared on the screen. Morgan's voice said, "The bishop is not without his defenders among the clergy. One of them is Father Michael J. Nolan. He saved the bishop's life recently, when a young man plummeted to his death from atop the cathedral in what has been ruled a freak accident."

A quick rehash ensued, ending with Bruno caught in the glare of public disclosure.

"Yet Father Nolan's own brother has recently gone public with his own story of abuse at the hands of the now-notorious Father Philip Wilson." Bruno blushed in his turn while his friends jostled him. "Quiet," he hissed. "I gotta hear this."

"Father Nolan, how do you feel about the situation, now that your own brother claims he was molested? Has this changed your opinions about how the Church is handling these allegations?"

Mike, fidgeting slightly, seemed nervous but sincere. He leaned forward as the camera zoomed in. "Not at all, Ben. While I feel sorry about what might have happened to my brother, I'm confident that the Church is doing all it can to clear up this mess, as quickly as possible. The Review Board Monsignor Malachy will head up shows our solid commitment to healing and prevention."

Bruno rolled his eyes.

"Do you have any regrets about saving the bishop's life, now that you've heard these allegations against him?"

Mike appeared startled. "No, of course not." He hesitated and continued gamely, "Whatever may or may not have occurred to my brother and most of the other alleged victims, was a long, long time ago. Before Bishop Chavez was even ordained as a priest. He had nothing to do with any of it."

"What about the accusations against him?"

"If indeed they are true, he needs help and forgiveness, like all us sinners. But I also see the great things that he's done for the Diocese, and I think that these unfortunate allegations will only increase his resolve to get to the bottom of all this."

"Sanctimonious simpleton," Bruno growled as the picture cut to Morgan walking down a country road. The reporter stopped in front of a modern-looking, whitewashed church. "Somewhere near the bottom of all this are the Ministers of Consolation, a Catholic order specializing in helping other priests. Here at Ghost Springs in the Espiritu Santo mountains, they have had a major operation since they were founded shortly after the Second World War.

"They've won high praise from various bishops and even cardinals in the Church for their treatment programs for alcoholic and drug-addicted priests. So during the nineteen-sixties, they expanded to treat clergy with sexual problems, including pedophilia. We spoke with the head of the order, Minister General Kevin Lynch."

The Irishman's head abruptly loomed large on the screen. He was seated in an office with a pine forest behind the picture window, hummingbirds diving around a feeder just outside. He was looking a bit cagey.

"There's a lot of unfortunate misunderstandings about our role here," he said soothingly. "Back then, it was a different world altogether. We didn't know about the extent of the problem of priests acting out sexually with minors, in terms of numbers or in how difficult such conditions are to treat effectively."

Morgan regarded him thoughtfully. "One report I read indicates that your founder, Father Fitzkennedy, actually bought an isolated tropical island to exile clerical sexual perpetrators for life. That he wanted nothing to do with them and thought them incurable monsters. Is this true?"

Lynch shifted uncomfortably. "Yes, I'm afraid so. A saintly man, and caring, but he could be very harsh in his judgments sometimes. The plan was scotched by the hierarchy before it could be put into effect, and for good reason."

"My God!" Bruno exclaimed, grabbing Dick. "*Gilligan's Island* for perps! How about that, little buddy?" Dick shook his arm off. "Hey man, chill out!"

"What reason might that be?" Morgan was asking.

Lynch was definitely squirming now. "Some thought that in such a restricted environment, unfortunate conditions like those that prevail in many penitentiaries might occur, where larger, stronger men take certain advantages of weaker ones."

"But you're talking about men of God here."

"I know," Lynch said unhappily. "Fallen, perhaps, but still ordained priests. It's a hard thing, to be sure. It was decided that to work to treat these men and give them hope was the most compassionate and Christian plan."

"For them, perhaps, but not for their victims?"

"In a few isolated instances, that has proven regrettably true. I know it may seem cruel to look at the figures, but the number of decent, hard-working priests we have saved is many, many times that of those who were not sufficiently helped."

The group at Cas' house booed loudly. Dick threw a pillow at the set.

"Was Father Philip Wilson ever sent here?"

"I'd have to check the records," Lynch stated disarmingly, "if any are available."

"It's stated in the lawsuit that he was."

"Since the matter is under litigation, I can't discuss it."

"What did you mean, 'if they're available.' Why wouldn't they be, Father?"

Lynch was sweating visibly now but still attempted to smile. He licked his lips and said, "There was a lot of concern about the privacy of our clients in the early seventies, and we were also quite short of room. So it was decided that the older records were not needed. Most were destroyed."

Morgan peered at him unbelievingly. "Destroyed?"

Lynch nodded. "On the advice of the bishops' lawyers, yes, I'm afraid so."

The scene cut back to the opening with a somber Morgan lounging in front of the "Sins of the Father" graphic. "One last note: the Ministers of Consolation face numerous lawsuits also and not just from alleged victims in the Southwest. Some of the priests they helped went on to allegedly abuse children in places as far from here as Minnesota and Ireland.

"Finally, we tried again to get a comment from Bishop Chavez before this program was aired. We were told he was unavailable, because he was on retreat again at the Ministers of Consolation center in Ghost Springs.

"*Hour: Zero-Zero* will follow this story, and keep you posted. Stay tuned for a —" Cas hit the remote and shouted, "Yes!" There was a great deal of whooping all around.

Bruno leaned forward and patted Dolores' shoulder. "Way to go, mama! That took some real huevos. You did great."

Dick jumped around the room. "Oh man, the expression on that old priest's face!" he exclaimed.

Chewie sat with arms folded. "Enjoy it now, amigo," he said. "I doubt we'll be dancing in the streets any time soon."

That slowed them down. "He's right, there could be a hell of a backlash," Bruno speculated. "We better lay low for awhile. No demonstrations."

"Fine!" Dick exclaimed happily, "We don't need to, now! It's in the hands of the experts, who will hunt it down, wring its neck and extract every cent of legal fees possible!"

"What do you think, Cas?" Bruno asked, but Cas was crouched over Dolores who sobbed quietly into the pillow she clutched. He sat on the floor beside her, and patted her gently too. "What's wrong, kiddo?" he asked quietly.

Dolores lifted her tear-stained face, contorted with misery. "I loved him," she wept. "I loved him so much. Now it's all over and I'm ruined. You heard what that bitch said. They're already calling me a whore." She started sobbing once again into the pillow, rocking back and forth.

Bruno gazed sympathetically at her, and then around at Cas, Dick and Chewie, all clustered around the weeping woman. No one could think of much to say that had any comfort in it. He grimly realized that, like it or not, they had to be committed to the struggle now more than ever.

He glanced out the front window. The report had taken a short time to air but the world had been changed like an atomic bomb had gone off over at the base. Not obviously — Cas' neighbor across the street still contentedly mowed his lawn in the sweet evening air — but Bruno knew that ripples were moving out all around them, invisible shockwaves of disbelief and denial. Nothing here would ever be the same.

†

CHAPTER NINETEEN

Monday, June 21

THE MORNING after the broadcast, the Catholic Complex was as bleak and tense as could be expected, like a hospital waiting room where relatives gathered after a disaster. As he sat in the lobby, Mike found the comparison all too apt. Watching Consuela doggedly fend off inquiries from all quarters, he wondered if he should have come, but he could think of no other place to be.

After what seemed an eternity, a buzz interrupted the ceaseless flow of incoming calls. The secretary nodded to Mike. "He can see you briefly. I'm glad you're here — he could use a shoulder to cry on." She glanced back at the blinking console in front of her. "We all could." Mike patted her softly on the arm as he walked by. "Hang in there," he said.

She shrugged and lit another cigarette before turning back to the demanding lights. Mike had noticed the makeshift ashtray on her desk overflowing with butts in the heart of this supposedly smoke-free office, but he wasn't about to say anything. Christ, if that was all it took to get through a day like this, then he had no complaints.

He tapped lightly and Cruz called tiredly, "Come on in." An explosion of newspapers strewn across the floor had violated the fastidious orderliness of the chancellor's office. An even more pointed symptom of his current state was that his collar was off — and he only wore bands that completely encircled the neck. Unheard of.

Cruz waved, hunched over the desk. "Join the party, Mike. Or the auto-da-fé, rather." He rubbed his face. "There's a lot of people right now — and not just reporters — who are ready to burn me alive." He paused. "By the way, good job. Thanks."

Mike nodded and studied his friend's face. Bob was sallow this morning, seeming years older, heavy bags under his eyes, black stubble darkening his chin.

"Man, you do look awful. You get any sleep?"

Cruz shook his head. "You look pretty bad yourself."

Mike searched for a place to sit that wasn't covered with huge headlines. There wasn't any, so he flopped down anyway. "Actually," Cruz continued, "I've been pushing most of the journalists off on Malachy so I can deal with the hierarchy myself. Their questions are much ruder. The nuncio's hysterical; several cardinals are taking turns bullying me; and nobody in Rome will give a straight answer to me, the lowly flunky just trying to carry the ball. You got any aspirin? I'm out."

"Actually, I do," Mike said, "antacids, too."

He tossed both bottles to Cruz, who gratefully downed several pills from each with the dregs of his coffee.

"So," Mike asked. "Have you talked with him yet?"

"Oh yeah," Cruz answered bleakly. "He's touching up his official resignation even as we speak. The Vatican's been breathing fire down his back and there's no other way out."

"How's he holding up anyway?"

"Not good. Acutely depressed — sounded fairly suicidal. I've asked Lynch to keep him under close observation, as drugged as needs be. A dead bishop is the last thing we need, though it certainly might simplify things, God forgive me."

"So he's at Ghost Springs?"

Cruz nodded. "Only place for him. Very private; supportive atmosphere; and the best psychiatrists we can buy."

There came a soft rapping on the door. It opened and Malachy stuck his head around the corner. "I heard there was a wake going on in here," he said.

He entered; all rumpled, collar undone too, carrying a bottle in one hand and a coffee cup in the other. "I found where that swine DeLaval hid his good stuff. Twenty-year-old single malt scotch with a name even I can't pronounce. I thought you might care for it?"

"I shouldn't — but I surely will." Cruz pushed his cup across the desk. A smile flickered beneath his thick mustache.

"Oh hell, why not?" Mike said. It violated all his rules to drink this early — except on the job, of course — but it seemed that the regulations had been pretty much ripped up anyway. Cruz handed him a mug.

Malachy unscrewed the top, poured a large slug into each of their cups, and set the bottle down on the desk still open. "Should we have a toast?" he asked.

"How about to self-control?" proposed Mike with a small, crooked grin.

"Self-control," Malachy said. "Amen," said Cruz, and they clinked their cups together. The whiskey's purity scorched Mike's unaccustomed throat and left him gasping. Malachy poured them both another round without asking and sat down heavily in the other paper-strewn chair.

"You know, what I don't understand is how Chavez could blow it like this," Mike said. "I'm certainly not defending his actions, but it's odd that he could blithely diddle around for years and then, just when the overall situation starts to heat up, suddenly screw up so bad."

"I've wondered about that too," Cruz said. "A cry for help, perhaps?"

"Then he certainly couldn't have shouted much louder," Malachy said. "It's not like he hadn't been warned — and even by me, of all people. I confronted him weeks ago about some rumors I heard. From your brother, no less, Mike — apparently Bruno's close to that bloody Rael woman.

"And you know what His Excellency did? Swore there was nothing to it, reminded me of my oath of obedience, and told me to let it be. I knew then something was up for sure."

"Smells like some kind of setup to me," Cruz snorted. "Interesting that the only thing that's really changed recently is that DeLaval, his right-hand man, is suddenly gone missing."

"Reminds me of Wilson's disappearance," Malachy mused. "Do you suppose Tom could have been blackmailing Art all along, and that once he was out of the way, Chavez thought he was finally free?"

"Well, I wouldn't imagine he was that stupid," Mike countered. "I mean, the women could have destroyed him at any time, with or without Monsignor DeLaval. Unless you're suggesting that DeLaval was somehow using them to get some sort of power over him."

Mike stared down into the amber depths of his glass. "I find that hard to believe." He glanced at the others, a pensive smile on his face. "You guys are almost as cynical as my crazy brother. Conspiracies. Sinister forces. Me, though I don't pretend to understand it, I blame it all on simple human weakness. The bishop's just a sinner, fallen like the rest of us. He was probably thinking only with his other head; you know, the one in his pants."

Malachy poured them another shot. "You realize, Robert, as chancellor, Canon Law puts you in charge now," he said. "It'll be up to you to keep the Diocese going until the Pope appoints a new bishop." Cruz nodded, his face hardening.

Mike sipped his whiskey. "That reminds me," he gasped. "What about the Holy Father's visit?"

"Oh, I bet we can forget all about that," Malachy sighed. "He's not going to want to come anywhere near this snake-pit."

"Tar-baby's more like it," Cruz agreed, leaning back. "If the Pope stops here, he could be seen as not being hard enough, if not actually condoning what's happened."

"Well, that's just plain wrong," Mike objected. "Don't we need his presence here more than ever? This is like punishing all of us, abandoning us in our greatest time of need."

"That may be so, Mike," the chancellor slowly admitted. "But John Paul was coming to celebrate the finishing of our new cathedral. It certainly won't be ready in time."

He gestured at an unruly stack of spreadsheets on his desk. "I'm not big into numbers but even I can tell we have a major financial problem here. Even without all these lawsuits. Unfortunately, it appears that His Excellency was using the building fund to pay for his mistakes."

"Lord Christ, no," swore Malachy.

There was a funereal moment of silence. "Where did it all go wrong?" Cruz whispered. "I keep thinking of what that blasted reporter said, about how proud we Chicanos were when Cruz was appointed bishop, almost twenty years ago now."

He leaned forward, cradling his cup. "You guys remember? We were deacons then, weren't we, Mike? The ceremony was held at the baseball stadium in the middle of the week and it was still packed. Bells rang all over the city. It was absolutely magnifico. I was so proud...

"If it hadn't been for him that day, I would not be a priest now," he continued sadly. "I decided then and there to return to Rome and finish my studies. Was it God's will I was following or just my pride?"

"Even Jesus had those same doubts," Malachy said. "All we can do is the best we can. That and pray that God will protect us from our own stupidity."

"That ought to keep Him plenty busy," Mike said darkly. He put down the empty glass. "I hate to break up a fine theological dialog, but it seems to me that our first concern must be for our people. What'll we tell them? And how?"

"You're right of course." Cruz sighed heavily. "The flock must be protected. However, I have to see what the lawyers say about what liabilities this opens us up to before I can make any public statement. I'm afraid today's pastoral reality is that we must first think of the Roman Catholic Diocese of Alvarado, Incorporated, before the People of God."

Mike scowled. "I know that offends you, Mike," Cruz said gently. "I don't like it either. But if we don't protect the institution, we can't serve the people."

He gazed somberly at the others. "Will you help me? This is going to be a very difficult time for the Church and we must all stand together."

"Of course," Mike answered. "Whatever I can do."

Malachy nodded in agreement.

"Okay, then, here's the plan." Cruz sat up straight, like a general back to running the battle again. "I'm going to have to pass the word around. I'll need you, Sean, to start working on a press release for the media, if you would."

"How about scheduling a press conference? Surely there will only be more questions."

Cruz groaned. "Yeah, but not right away. I just can't face them yet. In the meantime, Mike, would you start on a pastoral letter to be read at all Masses this Sunday? Something dignified but soothing, saying all the right things."

There was a light tapping on the door. "Yes?" Cruz said sharply as the chief secretary opened the door. "Sorry, Father, it's come." The fat woman could barely stop from crying as she stumbled across the room to deposit several curled sheets of thin paper on the desk.

She turned and fled, weeping openly. The ecclesiasts sat there for a long moment staring at the scrolls. Finally, Cruz sighed and unrolled the faxes.

The first was Chavez' resignation. Cruz checked it over silently scowling, and then turned to the next page. It was from the nuncio, the Vatican's ambassador. He read aloud: "'*With a heart full of grief and tender prayer, the Holy Father regretfully accepts the resignation of Bishop Arturo Francisco Chavez as Ordinary of the See of Alvarado...*'" He quickly scanned down. "Ah, here it is," he said. "'*Given the uncertainty of the situation there, and the heavy scheduling demands of World Youth Day, the Supreme Pontiff has decided to forego his announced visitation of the diocese. He has informed me he will instead address the people of Alvarado personally by radio as his flight traverses the region on the way to Denver.*'"

Malachy said simply, "For once, Rome moved quickly."

"Oh great," Mike said sarcastically, "The Pope's going to chastise us from above because Chavez was naughty. This isn't fair. We deserve better than that. He sighed. "Good thing we hadn't spent much on the planning."

"Hmm," Cruz grunted, not looking up. "Oh, this gets even better.

"Listen to this: '*The Holy Father desires that you, as Diocesan Administrator, along with your senior clergy attend on him at World Youth Day. I personally would like to take this opportunity to meet you, understand your situation, and offer whatever support I may. Perhaps, if time permits, an audience with His Holiness could be arranged.*'"

"Even worse, you mean," Mike said. "Now you're ordered to go up there, grovel, and beg, and maybe they'll let you kiss his ring?"

"Easy, lad; he is one of the last absolute monarchs, not to mention Vicar of Christ," Malachy calmly objected. "Sounds like you've been listening to your brother again."

"Not as much as you have," Mike grumbled.

Malachy said mildly, "Well, we can either feel sorry for ourselves or make the best of it."

"How about a penitential pilgrimage? Crawl there on our knees, whipping ourselves?" Mike asked sardonically.

"In that case," Cruz said, smiling grimly. "I should ask the Penitentes to lead us. Bet they'd love it.

"Seriously, though," the chancellor continued, "a big showing in Denver might be a good idea, despite the expense. Doing something — anything — could only improve morale. The more people of the diocese we could get to go, the more impressive it would be, especially under these circumstances. And you, old buddy, are the one to lead it."

"Me?" Mike said, taken aback.

"Sure," Cruz said. "You were in charge of the visit in the first place. And listen to yourself. If you're this bitter, then what about everybody else?"

"This diocese needs a spiritual renewal," Malachy agreed. "Bob's too busy being a bureaucrat and I've got my hands full being the grand inquisitor — that infernal hotline has been ringing constantly, even before this folderol."

He leaned towards Mike. "Besides, this is an event dedicated to the young. As I've said before, none of us old fogies can keep up with them like you can."

"And you still might get to meet the Pope," Cruz added.

"Okay, okay," Mike said resignedly. "I'll do it, if there's no actual flagellation involved. Is that all, boss?" he said, standing up. "I'll be back at the rectory, then, if you need me."

"And you know where you can find me," Malachy said as he rose. "Up to my ears in bloody reporters."

"Good, that's what I wanted to hear." Cruz stood up too. "Thank you, gentlemen. With your dedication and a major miracle or two, this diocese could just survive."

☦

CHAPTER TWENTY

Wednesday, June 30

B EFORE KNOCKING, Bruno paused briefly to look over the collage of cartoons surrounding the engraved plate that said, "*PROF. I. MITHERS Medieval History.*" An old engraving of the Holy Office plying its trade had recently been added. A new caption scrawled above the masked torturer gleefully breaking an unfortunate wretch on the wheel read, "*Now this is a curve I can grade on!*"

This made Bruno feel even uneasier about the upcoming interview but he had to smile. He just hoped Iggy would understand. If the rumors that pegged him as an ex-Jesuit were true, he might, but Bruno feared that it probably would just make things worse.

Sighing, he knocked. "Can't you read?" came an irritated voice from within. "Grades will not be posted until Friday!"

"It's me, Professor Mithers, Bruno Nolan. I got your message that you wanted to see me."

Bruno heard a chair scrape back and his mentor muttering as he made his way to the door. It cracked open and a dark brown eye squinted suspiciously through a thin tortoise-shell framed lens. Seeing Bruno, he opened the door wider and shoved his head out, glancing both ways down the empty halls.

"Come on in, Mr. Nolan; quick, before someone spots you." Bruno stepped past him into the room, shaking his head. Iggy was a very popular teacher, too popular, some said — particularly administrators annoyed by an outspoken but tenured gadfly. Iggy spent the minimum time required in his office, which often made it packed with students when he was there.

Bruno sat down carefully in a creaky chair opposite the desk. The small study was like Don Quixote's — dusty books and papers in uneven towers, strewn with toy knights in armor, heraldic devices, gargoyles, photos of castles and cathedrals, several swords and a piece of armor or two.

But on the only space void of shelves hung a framed, bloodstained, upside-down American flag, an honored relic of his role in the campus Vietnam anti-war protests. A sign of his ongoing radicalism faced outward in the window, demanding "*NO CIA ON CAMPUS.*"

Despite his bookwormish glasses, Iggy indeed seemed more of a old hippie than an academic. Everything about him was long — body, limbs, and hair. A serious runner, he was slim with an even tan, dressed casually in an old worn tee-shirt that said "*Not Medieval, Just Middle-Aged*," khaki shorts and sandals.

He flopped down behind the desk and leaned back, propping his legs upon a lump of ungraded essays. Smiling at Bruno he complained, "These kids can't spell without a computer anymore, not that they were any good before. You should be glad you're not my reader yet, though I could sure use you. I find myself wondering, though, after your performance last semester, if maybe you need to take some time off."

"Yeah," Bruno said. "My marks have slipped again, but..."

Iggy interrupted. "That would be enough, all by itself. But you seemed, shall we say, a wee bit distracted."

He gazed thoughtfully but not unkindly at his student. "You don't have explain, Bruno. I follow the news. Speaking out like that was pretty damn gutsy, and I certainly can imagine what hell all that has made of your life."

Bruno shrugged heavily. How was it that everybody who hadn't gone through this torment could imagine it so well when he still could barely face it? "I appreciate that," he replied cautiously. "It snuck up on me from behind, all right, and knocked me into a major loop."

Iggy nodded. "Take some time off to get your life back together, then."

Bruno shook his head. "Don't think so. Right now, I'll go nuts if I don't keep busy. I was actually hoping to start work towards my thesis." He didn't mention that if he didn't keep his nose stuck in books it soon might well be in a glass of beer.

"Well, what would you like to tackle?"

"I'm not sure, but something definitely more fascinating than problems of feudal landholding. I'm already starting to think the Peasant's Revolt wasn't such a bad idea."

Iggy chuckled. "You're not the first." He picked up his pipe and waved it airily. "Get crazy then, while it's still easy to change your topic."

"I've unquestionably become a bit obsessed with this church crap lately, but what could I do with it?"

"What can you do with an expertise in feudalism?" Iggy demanded. "Face it, kid, you're probably going to wind up baby-sitting in some dreary high school anyway.

"As the man said, 'Follow your bliss,'" he continued with a smile, "if not your great white whale. But you're not going to make it through the program unless your subject absolutely consumes you. Or you'll be so heartily sickened afterwards that you'll wish you were a truck driver instead."

Bruno shrugged. "Well, there should be enough to study. Kids being screwed by priests can't be anything new, even if the Pope blames it on our decadent days. Seems to me, though, that the real blame belongs to the guy where the buck stops, whose foot everybody kisses. If the underlings are running around wild, it's must be the leadership at fault."

Iggy smiled gravely. "The papacy's the world's oldest bureaucracy. It's meddled with everything — but you may be surprised to find out how little control the popes have ever really had over the whole Roman Church, much less all of Christendom.

"Besides that, there's been a great swing back and forth between corruption and reform throughout the centuries. Compared to some periods, the Church today is actually quite virtuous, almost saintly, believe it or not.

"Still," he concluded, "there are said to be over thirty miles of shelves in the Vatican Secret Archives alone — not to mention the Vatican Library. That's a whole lot of scandal to be covered up."

"So where do I begin?"

"Start with the papacy itself. The decrees of various Church councils and pontiffs should be quite helpful. They didn't fulminate without reason, though not always the ones they claimed. Compilations of canon law could be useful too: doubtless there's a historical precedent for every single rule."

"Hmm," Bruno said. "Why not make a virtue of necessity? Can't sleep anyhow. Okay, prof, if you're game, I am too."

† † †

BRUNO concluded, "At that point, I woke up with an incredibly stiff back. Still hurts." He twisted uncomfortably, waiting for Blackstone to catch up. "This was the most vivid of these kind of dreams I've had." The image of the vulture poised over the defenseless turtle was still very vivid.

"You've had it before?"

Bruno shook his head, as if to clear his vision. "Maybe two or three times. It's all your fault, though."

"How's that?" the shrink asked, pen halted in surprise.

"It's that damned stuffed animal you had me buy," he complained. "Just like you said, I went to the toy store and got the first one I liked — a fuzzy green tortoise with a sailor's hat. So naturally I called him 'Bert the Turtle.'"

"Why?"

"Remember the old black and white Civil Defense movies about how to 'duck and cover' from the A-bomb?" Bruno smiled crookedly. "He starred in them. Seemed appropriate somehow."

"Interesting," she said, nodding. "Often significant dreams will happen just before a session. What do you think it means?"

"Easy. I'm like the turtle. I feel totally powerless against the vulture, that blackpriest. I guess it cawing 'Recite' was from some religion class."

"What do you mean by that phrase, 'blackpriest'?"

"Did I say that? Well, it fits. I just wonder why it's DeLaval that haunts me, rather than Wilson?"

He paused, staring at nothing present. "And now my head is itching like crazy again. Damn, what's happening to me, doc? Am I completely losing it at last?"

"I don't think so," his analyst said patiently. "The fact that you are having these dreams means you're working very hard. They wouldn't be happening if you weren't strong enough to handle them."

"But I feel crazier now than ever before."

She considered him candidly. "How so? Suicidal?"

"No, homicidal. There's a lot of grief still, but more often indiscriminate rage. It scares me because I get some kind of kick out of it. Being pissed off all the time makes me feel much more powerful."

"That you should watch. Anger can be addictive too, you know." She glanced at her notes. "How's your sobriety?"

"I'm still hanging in there, even if I'm white-knuckling it," he said grimly.

She nodded but happily did not seem inclined to pursue it. "What else is happening?" she asked.

"Well, more new bad memories, vague and fragmented as always. But they're pretty weird."

She waited patiently as he picked at the armchair. "The stuff must have happened a bunch of times, because the scene keeps changing. The church attic, the rectory, the school basement — all over the place. And there were others."

"Others?" she echoed gently.

"Yeah. Definitely Wilson and DeLaval. But I think there, uh, were group things, with other priests." He shook his head. "I really don't want to go there.

"Could I be making all this up?" he whined. "Maybe all this New Age therapy stuff encourages it. Am I so scared of facing responsibility for my own messed-up life that I'm ready to blame anything else for it?" Fearing he was starting to rant, he halted suddenly, taking a deep breath and rubbing his face. "I'm sorry. This whole business has become something of a possession with me," he sighed.

He noticed she was peering oddly at him. "What?"

"Did you hear what you just said?" she asked, jotting fast.

"Was I too loud?"

"Not at all. Get as loud as you want," she said, but hesitated briefly. "You said that the whole thing had become 'something of a possession' with you."

"I did?"

She nodded.

He shrugged. "Well, I guess I meant 'something of an obsession.' Slip of the tongue, that's all. In any case, what I really wanted to talk about today was my relationships with women."

"Okay," she said slowly. While Bruno collected his thoughts, she continued to fill the legal pad with her notes.

"The strangest thing," he said, "there's this one gal, Cas. You might have seen her, she was on TV when the first DeLaval suit was filed — whom I swear I know from somewhere. Can't figure it out."

He corrected himself. "Two strangest things, actually, because I found myself instantly, enormously attracted to her. Well, maybe three, because she seems interested in me, too."

Bruno smiled at himself. "How's that for luck? After years of being alone thinking I'm doing fine, as soon as I tumble to how totally screwed up I am, I get hot for someone who's likely equally as loony. But there's some kind of strange karma resonating there, if not codependent craziness." He sighed dejectedly. "Maybe I'm so mad only a mad woman could love me."

"Maybe," Blackstone agreed with a smile. "Birds of a feather and all."

"Anyway," he said, shrugging, "I do appreciate that I'm in no shape to handle a relationship right now. But I just can't give up the delusion that there's still hope."

"Nothing wrong with hope," Blackstone commented. "But you're right; this is probably not the time for you to get involved romantically. Besides, you've just met her."

"True." Bruno admitted. "But I can't relate to 'normal' people anymore, not even alkies or druggies."

"Is she the person you said you'll call if you start feeling suicidal again?"

"Yep, that's her. It's a mutual thing, sort of a buddy system. Seems she's going through some heavy memories too."

Once again his therapist studied him long and carefully before speaking. "You know, Bruno, if you're determined to pursue this, it is possible to make a relationship between adult sexual abuse survivors actually work. After all, who knows what's going on better than someone who's been there, too?

"But sexual relationships between abuse victims are very difficult, Bruno, no matter what," she continued intently, "much, much harder than those between 'normals' because it's so easy for one partner to trigger another. Most victims have serious problems with boundaries, too, especially with lovers."

Smiling wistfully, she said, "In any case, it would be an interesting ride. If you want to face your issues head-on and fast, you're on the right track. But I caution you to go very slow, because it could easily end up like a train wreck."

"Sometimes I have this weird feeling that I've already decided," he said. "Somewhere a long, long time ago."

†

CHAPTER TWENTY-ONE

1962: Thursday, October 11

LOOMING IN THE DOORWAY of the rectory, Father Wilson said, "Ah, Eddie, you're early for your Confirmation lesson. Good. Come on in." He held the screen door open, smiling coldly.

The boy's shoulders slumped and he reluctantly waved to his dad. Harry waved back and the truck slowly pulled away, coughing like an old man.

Father Wilson was alone tonight. The office was closed and dark as were all of the bedrooms but one. In the front room, the television flickered with a gray image of Pope John XXIII passing by on a throne borne on the shoulders of a squad of costumed men. Wilson paused briefly and picked up his drink. "It's the start of the Ecumenical Council," he explained. "It may change everything. Soon, the altar might be turned around, and Mass no longer said in Latin anymore, I hear. How'd you like that, eh?"

Eddie was dubious but approved of the latter idea. Wilson turned off the set and they continued down the hall.

The priest's room was simply furnished with a small, hard looking bed, a tall oaken wardrobe, a couple of chairs and a roll-top desk, and, of course, a crucifix on the wall. The priest sat down at the desk and had Eddie remove his jacket and sit in the other chair.

He smiled. "Eddie, I'll be honest. You don't need special tutoring for Confirmation. You're doing fine. I wanted you here tonight because you are a very special boy," the priest confessed. "I think God has given you a rare gift and an extraordinary vocation. One that's much more important than being an altar boy, higher than becoming a priest or bishop — maybe even better than being the Pope. Are you interested?"

Eddie gazed at him doubtfully. "Sure, Father," he said.

Wilson grinned, rolled his desk open, where a small pottery bowl with strange writing sat on black velvet beside a small notebook. He filled the bowl with water from a small bottle next to a towel, and lit a black candle.

Closing and locking the bedroom door, he turned off the overhead so all was dark save for the flame's wavering glow. Finally he pulled out a large prayer book bound in black leather. This he reverently unlatched and carefully opened.

Many of the unreadable words were in red like a regular prayer book, but Eddie could tell it was very old and handwritten. Wilson followed his gaze and covered the text with his hands. "Some people would kill to see this, so I only ever show it to a few. You must prove to be very special indeed to be worthy to read this, one day."

He got up and dragged Eddie's chair to face the candle. "Now, Eddie, I want you to sit here and look at the flame.

"Just gaze at it and listen to me," Wilson said slowly and softly. "Pay no attention to anything else. Just look at the light..." He kept talking softly but firmly. Within several minutes, Eddie was in a deep trance, face relaxed and peaceful.

Wilson checked his book and proceeded to the next step.

"Hold out your left hand." The priest fished in his pocket and pulled out a quarter. He placed the coin in Eddie's open hand, and folded the kid's fingers over it. "Now Eddie, I have just put a consecrated Host in your hand. Can you feel it?"

The boy nodded. "Think about when you dropped it, Eddie, and what happened afterwards. Have you ever told anyone about it?"

Eddie shook his head. "Now remember your worst sin ever. While you're thinking about it, the Host in your hand will start getting warm. It will get hotter and hotter the worse that sin was. The more it hurts Jesus, the more it hurts you. The hotter it gets, the harder you must squeeze. But you can't let go until I tell you to."

He watched Eddie closely. The boy breathed in suddenly, sharply. His hand trembled as his pudgy fist clenched ever tighter. Sweat gleamed on his pale, freckled forehead. In moments, the child was whimpering in pain.

"Okay, Eddie," Wilson said. "The pain is gone. Jesus takes it away. Your hand feels cool and unhurt. You can open your fingers now and give me back the Host."

Eddie's face relaxed. Wilson took the quarter, warm from the boy's grip, and examined his palm carefully. The indentation was deep. Around the edges and on the tips of his fingers were small blisters. Wilson smiled approvingly.

"Why did your sin hurt you so much?" he demanded. The boy faltered. "Confess, Eddie; tell me everything and your hand will heal quickly," he said.

"I hate... I hate you, Father Wilson. You hurt me."

"What else, Eddie? What else do you hate?"

It was even harder for the boy to answer. "I lied to my mom about what happened just like you said."

"That's good, Eddie, real good. But there's more, isn't there? You must tell me everything."

"I hate her too," Eddie whispered desperately. "She drinks all the time. I wish my mom would just die."

Wilson wrote rapidly on the notepad. Hiding his delight, he pronounced as sternly as possible, "You hate your mother? That is a wicked sin against the Fourth Commandment. No good boy hates his mother. Only a demon could, a devil named," he hesitated as he checked the text, "Murmius. Only a devil would hate a holy man of God who punished you for your sins. I deny you forgiveness for this and whatever other sins I choose. You must carry this sin in your heart and suffer for it until I and I alone absolve you.

"Now get up. You'll seem to be awake, but you will do only what I say. Whatever happens, you will not truly wake up until I command you to. Do you understand? Stand up and gaze into the bowl!"

Shamefaced, the boy rose. He timidly leaned forward, gazing into the bowl of water. His reflection floated on the surface and the candle dimly lit the inside, where a spiral of unreadable black bug-like letters wound down to a crude female figure in the center.

"Gaze deep into the water, Eddie, so deep that it's dark as midnight, as black as space. It is outer space, and you can see stars all around. Out of the darkness, a woman is coming towards you. Her hair is like smoke and she is very beautiful. Her wings are like an angel but fiery. She's richly dressed in purple and crowned with gold. See her? She's opening her arms to embrace you."

The boy nodded, his fascinated face hovering scant inches above the surface of the water. Wilson silently stole up behind Eddie and positioned his hand delicately on the back of the child's neck.

"And now she takes you!" He quickly dipped Eddie's forehead into the bowl. Wilson gripped his neck tightly and growled viciously, "Immolo te diabolo! In nomine Luciferi Lilithaesque, appello te 'Murmius.' Fiat, Satanas!"

The kid gasped but did not break the spell. The priest smiled — he had chosen well indeed. Wilson set him on the bed and wiped his face gently with the towel. "Relax, Eddie.

Everything's okay. You just had another baptism. Go back to sleep, that's it. A deep sleep, Eddie, but you must keep listening to every word I say."

Wilson spoke tenderly. "Now your hand will stop hurting and heal. You will not remember any of this, and you will now drift off into a peaceful sleep until I call you again."

The boy's head fell forward limply. Wilson took a few minutes to consult his text and make more notes, and then roused the kid again. "Now Eddie, I want you to open your eyes like you are waking up, feeling very good. From now on, whenever I tell you to recite the Act of Contrition, you'll fall asleep again until I order you to return, at which time you'll wake up fully, feeling refreshed and remembering nothing."

Wilson pulled the tab out of his collar and began unbuttoning his shirt. "Hear me. I have given you a new name, a special name. It is 'Murmius.' Repeat it for me."

The boy mumbled. "No, louder. Repeat your new name."

"My name is Murmius."

"Good. Hide it deep in your heart with your anger. Murmius is the one who holds the pain, who loves to hate. Repeat after me: 'My name is Murmius. Murmius is a devil.'"

He made the boy repeat this several times. "Now when you are punished, it is Murmius who is punished. When you hurt, Murmius hurts. When you get angry, Murmius is angry. All the bad things belong to Murmius.

"And you, Murmius, must only call me Xaphon, Master Xaphon. Now, Murmius, get up on the bed and take off your clothes."

"Yes, Master Xaphon." The boy crawled out of the chair onto the bedspread. He had just started to strip off his underpants when Father Wilson suddenly halted him. A low throbbing of a big car engine cut off abruptly, followed shortly by a door squeaking open and slamming shut.

"Damn! Who the hell could that be?" Wilson muttered to himself. He quickly blew out the candle and closed the desk. The sound came of the rectory's heavy front door opening.

Wilson turned and hissed over his shoulder, "Eddie, return! Get dressed, quickly! Wait here and be quiet." Then he slipped out of the bedroom and silently locked it behind him.

In a daze, Eddie found himself nearly naked in a strange room. He scrambled back into his clothes as quickly as he could, fumbling in fear. As soon as he pulled his jeans up, he crept over to the door.

"Where is everybody?" came a deep male voice. Lights flashed beneath the door while Eddie struggled into his shirt.

"Tom? What on earth are you doing here?" he heard the startled voice of Father Wilson.

"Oh, hi, Phil. For a moment there, I didn't think anybody was home." He heard the sound of a suitcase dropping. "Sorry, if this is a bad time. Hope I'm not interrupting anything."

"No, not really — just not expecting anyone, that's all. I knew you were coming back for All Hallows, of course, but I don't think we have your room ready yet."

"You didn't seriously imagine that I'd ever miss the revelry on the Thirteenth, did you? Anyway, I'll sleep on the couch, if I have to. Even that's better than those racks they call beds up there in that pious little prison in the woods. What I could really use, though, is a drink. A stiff one."

"Of course. Scotch is still in the study."

"Actually, I think they sent me back to keep an eye on you." His laughter receded as they went into another room.

Eddie had just finished laboriously tying the laces of his hi-top sneakers and was worming into his jacket when the door flew open again and Father Wilson loomed uneasily in the hall light. "Are you ready? Good, come on," he whispered, striding to the window. Opening the window to the crisp autumn night, he pulled a lever beneath the sill that opened the security bars. He held out his hand, beckoning impatiently.

Lifting Eddie up, a cold laugh stopped him dead.

"I thought you had something going on, Phil. Who is it, one of the Nolan boys?"

Wilson put the boy down and spun around. Eddie peeked past him at the other priest. Father DeLaval stood in the hall, drink in hand, collar undone, smiling evilly at them.

Seeing him stare, DeLaval's leer grew even more unpleasant. "Ah, the older one. Afraid I'd want you to share?"

Eddie shrank behind Father Wilson. "He's my novice, now, Tom, mine. I just initiated him. Take his brother if you want, but stay away from this kid," he scornfully ordered. "Mess with Eddie, and you'll never get anywhere near the *Codex*. Not while I live, anyway. Clear?"

There was a brief, tense silence. Then DeLaval chuckled. "No problem, Phil. Plenty of other lambs in the fold."

Wilson protectively herded Eddie past the other priest out into the front room. Turning on the TV, he smiled reassuringly at the confused boy and said, "Don't worry, Eddie. It's all right. We'll just watch the Council until your father comes." Eddie wasn't clear about what just happened, but he was pretty sure it was not all right.

CHAPTER TWENTY-TWO

1993: Saturday, July 3

MIKE sighed, "I can barely recall the last time I went to the mountains, it was so long ago." Cruz' white jeep toiled up the long grade, trapped behind a dilapidated camper hauling a boat. But Bob didn't seem to mind; casually dressed in a light shirt, shorts and silver shades, he was clearly on vacation. He grinned hugely behind his mustache, glancing smugly over at his friend.

"Well then, this was way overdue," he said confidently. "I haven't been up in ages either, but after the last couple of weeks, we both really needed it."

"I'm already glad you kept nagging me," Mike agreed. For a while both were silent as Cruz managed to get his shot at the passing lane. An indefinite line of traffic snaked both fore and aft fleeing the city on this hot holiday weekend. Behind them lay Alvarado shimmering in the desert crucible, molten in the hot, dry air of late morning.

The road gradually climbed, winding north among scattered piñons and tufts of wilted prairie grass, chamisa, and sage along the tops of the mesas. Ahead the Espiritu Santos beckoned, promising pine woods and meadows strewn with wildflowers. A small halo of cloud struggled to form over the tallest peak, a hopeful portent of the summer rains to come.

"Maybe this'll help restore my perspective. It's all been so confusing lately," Mike said. "I feel sorry for Chavez, and his women and their kids, and also all those little old blue-haired ladies that can't believe this has happened." He hesitated. "Must be even worse for you, knowing how much you admired him." Cruz only shrugged.

"But DeLaval," Mike continued, "that really bugs me."
Cruz shot him a glance. "How so?"

"Oh, just that I've known him since I was a kid and never had a clue about what was going on. If half of what I've read in the papers is true, he's a monumental, ecumenical pervert. He apparently molested his assistant, that Mondragon woman, right there in his office as well as her brother." He shook his head sadly. "Unbelievable."

The conversation lapsed as the traffic snaked along the narrow road paralleling the Rio Espiritu. The line of cars slowed as they approached the speed trap at the sleepy Hispanic farming village of San Martín where Cruz turned off towards the blue-green dome of San Pedro Peak.

Once past the village's ramshackle adobe church and the last cop lurking in the shade of a half-dead tree, they sped up again. But soon they caught up with an old pickup loaded with furniture, dogs, and giggling brown children.

The truck turned off at the Pueblo of San Tomás, past an Indian cop blocking the entrance. The pueblo was a compact village not much different from San Martín save that the mud-built houses huddled together as if for protection. There was a lot of traffic down around the central plaza. Parked cars lined the highway, where Indian ladies sat in rickety booths selling home-baked bread, watermelon, and early sweet corn.

"Today's their feast-day, too, of course," Cruz said, smiling. "Saint Thomas the Apostle. But nowadays you must be invited by a member of the tribe to attend their sacred dances. Too many drunk tourists, I fear. In any case, they rarely invite white priests. Did you know that they even have a 'Priest-Killer' kachina? The pueblos may be nominally Catholic, but there's still a lot of bad memories and they absolutely refuse to give up the old ways.

"Up the road, Ghost Springs, all-American town that it is, takes the Fourth of July quite seriously and the feast-day of the original mission's patron saint merely adds to the celebration."

Passing the last cornfields beyond the pueblo, huge mesas rose up on either side. Erosion had sculpted the mountain's outskirts into vast undulating walls. Crowned with pickets of ponderosa pines, the forbidding ramparts of pink and ochre stone stood like God's own battlements.

"So what about the Ministers of Consolation?" Mike asked. "All I know is what my mom said once when we passed old guys along the road up here when I was a kid: that they took care of the poor priests who'd worn themselves out in service to God. How'd they get into this work?"

"Long story, I'm afraid. Short version is that since this is the only order dedicated to helping clergy that who'd lost their way, there simply was no place else." Ahead the line of taillights suddenly glowed, a clear sign they were nearing the congestion of Ghost Springs. Cruz carefully slowed down to a crawl as the first buildings and tourists began to appear by the side of the road. The faint sounds of a band began to be heard.

"They came here because it was remote and they got a good deal on the old spa, not because of the shrine. The sex stuff happened by accident. Their main focus is on alcoholism and depression but they found they also had to contend with thorny sexual issues which kept getting raised in treatment."

The white car crawled past the town's church, where a procession seemed to be forming out of a crowd milling in the parking lot. On the other side by the original bathhouse lay a spacious open park with a bandstand where a small group was valiantly attempting music. Rows of booths offering food, drink, and arts and crafts were set up on the lawn. Families were picnicking everywhere. Every possible parking space on either side of the highway was already filled. A banner stretched across the road between the sole coffeehouse and bar in town announcing the holiday art festival.

"The important thing," Cruz continued, "is that the Ministers are totally independent from this or any other diocese, answerable only to Rome. If we don't like how they run their program, not much we can do about it."

"Was DeLaval ever here?" Mike asked nonchalantly.

"Since he fled, you mean?" Cruz replied, startling him. It hadn't occurred to Mike that the monsignor might be lurking so near. "Malachy says Lynch assures him that Tom has never shown up. I've heard that the investigators for the other side think he went to the West Coast or even to the Philippines. He was, of course, often up here on retreats, but if you mean as a patient," he shrugged. "I don't know. Such information is generally not kept in the ordinary files. Ask Lynch. Maybe he'll tell you — but I wouldn't hold my breath waiting."

On the right side around the next corner there suddenly appeared the massive dry-stone ruins of the original mission church of San Tomás, now a state monument. White-stuccoed buildings with bright red metal roofs surrounded by a tall fence loomed across the road opposite.

"May not mean anything if he was. Even Sean's taken a turn through one of their programs, you know." Mike tried not to show his surprise.

Before he could frame another question, Cruz skillfully turned without slowing through a hole in the oncoming line of cars. He whipped the vehicle around into a parking lot and into a shady spot under the portico of the red-roofed building with practiced ease. Outside the gate, a sign read:

MINISTERS OF CONSOLATION
Motherhouse and Retreat Center
Closed to the Public

Below a piece of cardboard was taped that read "*OPEN HOUSE TODAY.*" They had arrived.

Mike opened the door. A soft breeze touched with the scent of pine sighed through the cottonwoods bringing hints of the cool, quiet heights above.

The men climbed out and stretched. The lot was nearly full and other visitors were strolling about the grounds. A neat flower garden with statuary had rock-lined paths which led to a white clean-lined church several stories high. A slender bell-tower overlooked the entrance.

"First we check in," Cruz said, leading the way. Inside the main building seemed much more like a hotel lobby than the austere monastery that Mike had expected, tastefully adorned with comfortable sofas and chairs and a few green plants. A radio played softly in a nearby room. Only the religious art on the walls gave it away. The quiet, purposeful, and above all, totally masculine atmosphere reminded Mike instantly of the seminary.

"Have you seen Father Kevin —" Cruz began to ask the balding, middle-aged receptionist. "Robert!" came a cheerful greeting behind them. Cruz and Mike turned to face a small, wiry man in short-sleeved shirt who had materialized from nowhere and was already opening his arms wide to greet Cruz.

"Father," the chancellor said, smiling. "It's good to see you. Peace be to this place and all who dwell in it."

The men clasped each other's elbows and stately bobbed their heads together on either side, once, twice. Mike smiled.

Clerks doing the formal kiss of peace always reminded him of birds performing a bizarre mating ritual.

"Peace be to you — and to your friend as well, here." Lynch grinned broadly. Breaking loose from Cruz, he thrust his hand forward into Mike's and gave it a firm squeeze. "You must be Mike Nolan," he said. "Heard great things about you. Be welcome. Mi casa es su casa."

"Thanks, Father. I'm glad to have this opportunity to be here and learn about your work."

Lynch rolled his eyes comically and held up his hands. "Ah, don't try to sweet talk an Irishman, especially one who's actually kissed the Blarney stone. I know you're here just for the weekend. Relax. Enjoy. We can talk later, if you must."

Mike put up his hand. "Actually, I have just one question, but I really would like to know. Was Monsignor DeLaval ever here? I mean, as a patient."

Lynch and Cruz shared glances. "Well, now, I'm not sure," Lynch said slowly, "but he often came up for weekend retreats. I think he also taught theology here occasionally. Why do you want to know, if I may ask?"

"I've known him since I was a boy," Mike said simply. "I have to know if there's some truth to all these accusations."

Lynch's face became suddenly sympathetic. He glanced around and answered softly. "I understand. I'm sorry, but in truth, it was long before my time as Minister General. And really, with all these lawsuits, even if I knew, I couldn't say." He glanced at his watch and smiled apologetically.

"And now, I must be off. Lots of guests, barbecue to attend to. Gordon, please give these gentlemen keys. We start serving at six!" With that, he was gone, quickly as he came.

They signed the guest register, collected the room keys, and got their bags from the back of the car. Strolling down the hill behind the main building, they came upon several clusters of small dormitories.

Cruz handed Mike a key and pointed to one on the right. "Let's see, you're in Yucca and I'm in Spruce. I think I'll visit the shrine before the procession gets there. How about you?"

"I'll probably watch the parade for a bit, check out the ruins, maybe take a hike up the hill." Mike nodded at the top of the piñon-covered slope beyond the dorms where a thin trail snaked down the cliffs.

"Sounds good," Cruz nodded and veered off.

The room Mike found was much more in keeping with his image of the place. Small, equipped with a few modest pieces of furniture including a squeaky iron bedstead with a thin mattress and thick blankets, and a small lavatory. For decoration, a crucifix and a window framing a vista of the creek and the far canyon wall sufficed.

He'd barely put his bag down when there was a light but insistent tapping on the door. Mike did not recognize the figure on the other side at first, dressed in a khaki hiking outfit, hat pulled low, wearing a small backpack. The face was familiar, but gaunt and lined; the slim torso that countless numbers of generous grannies had tried to fatten and failed was thin, frail and stooped. The brown eyes no longer sparkled behind the gold frames but held a haunted, despairing light.

"Bishop Chavez!" he exclaimed. Chavez' fingers flew to his lips as he stepped into the room. "Shh," he whispered. Without speaking he sidled up to the window and glanced carefully around outside then quickly glanced under the bed. As

Mike watched this exercise in astonishment, Chavez strode over to the sink and turned the water on.

Finally he turned to Mike and smiled wanly. "Sorry for the melodramatics," he whispered, "I saw it in a movie once." He seemed on the verge of tears. "Oh thank God you came, Mike. It's the answer to a prayer."

Mike hugged him. "Good Lord, Excellency. What happened? Please, sit down."

Chavez pulled back. "No time," he said. "They keep me on a pretty short leash. We've got to talk — alone. You know where the ruins are, don't you?"

"Sure, but what —"

The bishop bore on, unstoppable. "Go there and wait by the entrance. When the parade goes by, make your way up to the sanctuary. If it's safe, I'll signal you."

There was more tapping on the door. Chavez jerked as if shocked by a live wire. Looking desperately at Mike, he whispered imploringly, "Tell no one." Mike nodded, and went to the door while the disgraced prelate turned off the faucet.

"Sorry to bother you, Mike, but I was going to lock the car and —" Cruz began as Mike opened the door. "Your Excellency!" he exclaimed, catching sight of Chavez. They hugged, Chavez more stiffly than before. Turning to Mike, Cruz smiled and said, "Well, that was quick. I'm glad you found each other so soon. So, Mike, our little secret is out. Here's the real reason I insisted that you come."

Chavez nodded tiredly. "There's much we must discuss. I've been cooperating, you know, but some things 'they' don't need to hear. Nor do the lawyers lined up to grill me like St. Lawrence, as Malachy might say."

"But why include me? Isn't that Malachy's job?"

Chavez glanced at Cruz. "Yes, but we must guard his — what's that phrase — 'plausible deniability?'"

"Some things might put him in a difficult position as head of the Review Board if he were to hear of them prematurely," Cruz explained smoothly. "He's got enough problems as it is. This is really just to protect him."

"If you say so," Mike said dubiously. "When do you want to have our little talk, then?"

"After dinner," Chavez suggested quickly. "Yes, between the fireworks and Evening Office would be perfect."

"Fine," Cruz said. "Let's discuss it then. In the meantime, shall we go down to the parade?"

"Not me," Chavez said. His smile was forlorn. "There might be reporters, and I'm still too well-known to appear in public. I think I'll watch from atop the hill."

Cruz nodded. Mike, not knowing what to do, held the door open for the men. Gazing after the skinny figure trudging up the trail, Mike said softly, "Good Lord, Bob. Two weeks? Looks it's been more like twenty years."

"I know," Cruz said, as Mike shut the door. He clapped his colleague on the shoulder as they started back towards the road. "I just hope we can help unburden him."

The men walked back to the parking lot. Cruz turned off to get his camera from the car, while Mike, thankful not to have to make some excuse, hurried down to the highway.

✝

CHAPTER TWENTY-THREE

FOLKS had already lined both sides of the only paved thoroughfare through Ghost Springs. Mike wandered over to the entrance of the monument where a thick, twisted cottonwood offered the only shade on that stretch. He stood making small talk with an elderly Italian in a loud Hawaiian shirt. Was the old guy a patient of the Ministers, Mike wondered, or does he think that perhaps I am?

Finally, the parade began, led by a cop cruising slowly down the median, lights flashing, in front of the color guard.

Mike made his excuses and slowly backed up. Peeking back around the corner of the visitor's center, he saw that even the park rangers were watching the spectacle from the porch. The last few kids ran down from the ruins.

Shrugging off his gloomy thoughts, Mike followed the trail through the piñons around the massive outer walls of what remained of the three-and-a-half centuries old Mission of St. Thomas. The four-yards-thick masonry showed that the Franciscans had meant to stay, but it hadn't saved them during the great Indian Revolt. Yet two centuries after the pillaging, the thick, solid octagonal watchtower and most of the walls of the Mission itself still stood when the nearby miraculous spring with its healing mud returned the place to Catholic maps.

He came into the empty nave. The ceiling was long gone, of course, and the rubble removed from the cavity. A few crumbling stone steps led up to the bare grassy spot where the high altar once stood. The place seemed deserted.

Suddenly, a small rock thumped on the lawn beside him. Glancing up, he saw a hand beckoning through the narrow opening in the tower twenty feet above. Wondering how he was supposed to get up there, he wandered around the other side through the maze-like ruins of the attached priests' quarters.

The church, he saw, had been built into a shoulder of the hill and at the rear the slope almost reached up to the tower's opening. He struggled up the steep trail, loose shards of rock making it tricky. Finally reaching the window from which he had seen the hand, he found nobody there.

A scrabbling sound, and Chavez crouched on the trail above him. "This way," he whispered, offering Mike his hand. Scrambling up the hill they finally stopped beneath a large juniper. The birds chirping around them made pleasant counterpoint to the noisy celebrations echoing up from below. A squirrel scolded them and retreated further up the mountain.

Mike waited for Chavez to speak. "You must think I'm crazy," the former bishop gasped at last. "I mean, all this paranoid stuff." He tried to smile. "I wish I was, I truly do.

"But what I really wish is that I was more suspicious, a lot earlier." He studied Mike, who was listening worriedly.

"Don't get me wrong. I've sinned. I'll admit I abused my position for sex. You know, Mike, some women like to tempt priests. Some do it to get back at men and all they care about is to toy with us. Others are a much bigger problem. Maybe they want to save themselves by saving a lonely man or some such romantic drivel. Most have some kind of daddy issues.

"In any event, more insane women seem available as you advance, rather than less. God knows that our poor Holy Father must have to beat them off morning, noon, and night."

Mike stared at him, bewildered. "Bishop Chavez, let me stop you for a moment. Are you wanting to make a confession?"

"Oh no," Chavez yelped.

In a lower voice, he said, "All kinds of people down below — priests, therapists, and lawyers — would love me to tell them all my faults. Some even want to strap a thing on me called a 'plethysmograph' — a peter-meter — and show me dirty pictures. 'For my own good,' they said.

"I do not want this under sacramental seal," he said sharply. "You may have to tell what you've heard someday."

He sighed. "I'm not trying to justify what I did. I realize I failed miserably. But you don't know how I was trapped."

Chavez paused, staring at the small cloud growing overhead. "When DeLaval was released from here the last time —"

"Hold on. He was here?"

"Yes, of course, how else do you think he came into our diocese? And just like his pal, Phil Wilson, he returned here often. Anyway, after the last time he was caught, they required somebody to monitor him in a residential setting for awhile and Bishop Lewis gave me the job.

"We lived in the same rectory for maybe six months. But we were never really friends, despite what the newspapers say. He was seldom around. One time that he was just happened to be the day that Dolores Rael first visited me. She'd had an affair with Dick Kirk, who had recently been killed in a plane wreck, and she badly needed counseling."

He hung his head. "Some help I gave her. God forgive me, but I instantly fell in love with her, little more than a child though she was, and even while I knew I could never leave the priesthood for her. And then she became pregnant."

Chavez stared intently into Mike's eyes. "Here's why I'm telling you this. DeLaval soon found out. The filthy *pendejo* began to collect evidence even as he encouraged me — letting me use his house, lying for me and so on. He found out about others; I swear to God, he sent several of them to me.

"After Lewis died and I was consecrated bishop, DeLaval quickly began to blackmail me. His demands for money steadily grew. I had to pay him off with cash donations I received for speaking engagements. When we decided to build the new cathedral it just provided greater opportunities for him to squeeze me. And then he wanted more."

A long pause ensued. Mike finally prodded, "Like what?"

"Like access. Access to certain churches at certain times. He also wanted to control many assignments in the Diocese, who went where. Not just at churches but at schools and hospitals, too. He even had me put him on the Retirement Board."

"Why on earth would he want such things?"

"I asked myself that, and started noticing he wasn't alone in those desires. Odd coincidences showed others were involved somehow; men would ask me for something DeLaval had 'recommended' a day or so previously.

"As you know, competition for the better parishes can be quite fierce. But he wasn't just stacking them with his old cronies, but new ones, many of whom had been put up here.

"As for the Retirement Board, that's pretty obvious: controlling pensions gave him a lot of influence over any priest that might oppose him, especially elderly ones." He hesitated.

"At first I thought it might just be a ring of homosexuals running some 'lavender rectories,' like Olly and his pals. That's one of the things I want to talk about with you and Bob tonight. But it's way beyond that. Some of these priests were associated with him in other ways — private pilots, chaplains, members of the 'Morning After Club.' Kirk, for example, was thick as thieves with DeLaval yet there was nothing at all queer about him.

"That bloody 'Order of St. Peter Martyr' he joined was behind it all somehow, I'm sure. He wasn't the first; an Austrian priest named Urwald introduced it here right after the war. I finally realized that they were the key, but I didn't know who all 'they' were." He paused; when he spoke again, his voice was low and heavy.

"There's a shadow on the Church, Mike, a deep, dark shadow. These 'blackpriests' are up to things, unspeakable things. Molesting kids isn't all of it, not by any means — I think they murdered Wilson. Why I don't know; but it was not long after Malachy was sent by Lewis to investigate the financial situation at the cathedral. But they surely used and destroyed me, and I fear they'll attempt to do it to you, too."

"Me?" Mike exclaimed, jaw dropping.

"Yes. Isn't it obvious? You're a rising star, Mike. DeLaval was in some ways your mentor and patron, after all." He paused, searching the younger man's face. "In fact, he wanted you posted to Our Lady of Solitude as much as Malachy did."

Mike was aghast. Chavez continued, "Again, I have no idea why — because I don't believe they got to you yet. Not only did you save my life, but your astonishment at his stash of filth seemed genuine enough. Though if you are his creature, well, then I'm dead already."

He gripped Mike's forearm urgently. "Beware, Mike — they will tempt, twist, and manipulate you any way they can, ways you can't even imagine. You must trust nobody. I mean no one: not even Sean or Bob. Either or even both may be in on this, though I hope to God not."

"Is that why you ignored Malachy's warning?"

"What warning?" Chavez demanded harshly. "He came to me, saying that he'd found out about Dolores. It sounded just like another shakedown to me, with him picking up where DeLaval left off. But I knew it meant I was doomed.

"I didn't have any time to waste," he continued hastily. "So I gathered everything, all the secret files, my evidence and suspicions." His smile was quick and crooked. "While they thought I was shredding everything, much I copied instead. This, then, is for you."

The bishop dug into one of the backpack's pockets. "Here. Nobody knows I had this made." He handed Mike a small silver key. "It's a duplicate to the secret archives in my office, where I hid it all. But you must hurry. The chancellor also has a key. If he's one of them, it may already be gone."

Mike moved to hand the key back. But Chavez grasped his hands together tightly. "Take it. It's all I can do to make up for my sins. You're my only hope, Mike. There's a sealed packet there that you must give to the Holy Father."

"The Pope!"

Chavez nodded. "Him and only him. I know you can do it, Mike. Like I said, you're being groomed for higher things; you may not have to strive to actually get to meet him. But push to be presented if you have to. Then you must hand the packet to him. Not to one of his aides, but to him, John Paul himself, directly and personally during the audience."

Mike didn't know what to say. "I'll do my best. But how?"

The bishop smiled shrewdly. "Like it was a personal gift." He pulled out an envelope out of the pack and passed it to him. "This goes with it. Tell him the packet contains proof from Bishop Chavez that the Devil's own disciples are at work here. This letter will explain it to him. I pray it's in time.

"Promise me you'll do it. This is more than a request from your old bishop whom you swore to obey. The whole Church may depend upon it — certainly the diocese does. Promise!"

He held Mike's hands fast. "Okay, Father, I will, if I get a chance." Chavez did not release his grasp but continued relentlessly. "One more thing, and this is for your own safety. Promise me that you will not look within the packet or at the files yourself. Do you understand? Not for any reason!"

Mike's gut twisted in a sudden fluster of fear. He nodded. "Say it!" Chavez insisted.

Mike's mouth was dry. He swallowed. "Okay, I won't look." He gulped again.

Chavez' face twitched with a tiny smile and relaxed but only briefly. Suddenly, he heard something coming up the hill below. "We'll talk more later," he whispered and disappeared into the bushes.

Mike was still numbly staring at the key and envelope when a cocker spaniel burst through the bushes below, bounding up to lick his face. The excited voices of children followed behind. The parade had passed and life returned to normal. He pocketed the items and composed himself, smiling to face the little girl who had followed her pet alone deep into the piney woods.

†

CHAPTER TWENTY-FOUR
Independence Day, Sunday, July 4

IN A TONE of great authority, Dick said, "The story I heard is that Chavez is hiding in a convent back East."

"No way," Chewie said. "I'll bet he's stashed up there at that Ministers of Consolation place."

"Maybe," allowed Cas, "Apparently, even Nick's not sure. Malachy won't say."

"That's no surprise. That old fart could out-stubborn the devil," Bruno said, "and probably will. I just hope Chavez is in one of the Church's prisons, like they had back in the Middle Ages — those rugged 'monasteries of the strict observance' I've read about where they slept on boards and consumed only bread and water."

"Ah," Dick said, "what we used to call 'summer camp.'"

Everybody laughed contentedly. With Dolores absent, they were could still relish the fall of the bishop, though the threat of the backlash had scared off the remaining activists.

Fortunately, their fears hadn't materialized. The media kept trying to goad them for some opinion to balance the dismay of the flock. But the faithful seemed to have suffered sufficient humiliation already. So, apparently, had Dolores, who was not returning anyone's calls, not even Casandra's.

However, nothing constrained the rest around each other. So they'd gathered this hot holiday afternoon on the veranda of the Heavenly Hippo to celebrate with ice cream and lemonade. Few people were about in the heat of the day, and the cicadas in the mimosa trees droned hypnotically.

"So what do we do now?" Bruno asked.

"Now?" asked Cas. "Now, now, or just now in general?"

"Well, in general, actually. I mean we can't stop yet."

"Why's that?" Dick asked, gesturing with his spoon. "Hey, we won, haven't we? The wicked bishop has been run off with his tail between his legs. It'll all come out now and our lawyers will make us rich. If that ain't winning, buddy, what is?"

"Hombre," Chewie said, "that stuff must be freezing your brains. It's a war, no? They're not going to lie down and give up now, but hit back even harder."

"Exactly what I was thinking," Bruno agreed. "Besides, what about the kids? They ain't that much safer yet."

"Sure," Dick said. "But the best way to teach them is to beat 'em economically. If they let it go on they'll have their asses sued off. So they'll stop — simple as that."

"Wow, check your meds, vato," Chewie laughed.

"Damned Marxist thinking for a Catholic," Bruno added.

"Hey," Dick said angrily. "I'm not like you. You've all lost your faith. Given it up completely. I can understand that, but I haven't — and I believe in the Church, too. Yeah, you heard me. I bet if the Pope knew he'd be as angry with this mess as we are. Maybe more so. So quit treating me like a cretin."

"Whoa. Sorry, dude," Chewie said, holding up his riding-gloved hands, startled by the outburst. "Just joking. Really."

Dick flashed even more crimson with embarrassment. "Yeah, okay," he mumbled. He tossed his half-empty dish into the trash in disgust. "It's all wrong — very exciting to see such a hypocrite exposed but I sure haven't felt real good since."

"Me too, but it had to be done, man. Remember how he screwed Dolores over."

Suddenly a thought occurred to Bruno. He squinted calculatingly at them. "So, Dick," he said abruptly. "You really meant what you said about the Pope, huh?"

"Dang right I did. Why?"

"Uh-oh, watch it," Cas said softly. "Bruno has an idea. He's got that funny grin on his face."

"It's okay," she said, her voice dropping conspiratorially as she leaned forward. "Actually, it's interesting seeing you switch like that." She lowered her sunglasses so he could see her hazel eye wink theatrically. "Don't worry, your secret's safe with us."

"Uh, thanks," said Bruno, unsure of the joke. "Well, if John Paul doesn't know," he continued, "maybe we should just go and tell him."

"Tell him," Dick repeated unbelievingly.

"Sure," Bruno insisted. "What better way to get our message across than to protest at World Youth Day in Denver?"

"You're even more loco than he is, chico," Chewie said. "Too scared to hold one here, and you want us to demonstrate in front of zillions of screaming fanatics? ¡Qué cojones!"

Bruno held up his hand. "This is still America. There will be all kinds of people protesting there, you can count on it. Women's ordination types, gays, pro-choice, who knows?"

"True," agreed Cas. "The authorities have to allow demonstrations but they certainly won't want a riot on their hands any more than the Church would."

"It's not the cops that I'm worried about," Chewie said. "It's everybody who's even higher on John Paul than our very own saint here."

"Well, I like the idea," Dick said, "but not because I want to see the Pope. I imagine that's not too likely. But if we went with the right attitude, maybe it would be okay. Like not saying it's his fault, just that we're trying to bring it to his attention. Faithful Catholics come in simple humility to petition our Holy Father to notice and redress these wrongs."

Bruno peered at Dick with amazement. "Damnation," he swore, "you say I'm the cynical politician? That's a beautiful idea. As crazy as the Children's Crusade, but it just might work. What about the rest of you guys? Interested?"

"I'm not so sure," Cas said. "If I could talk Dolores into coming, maybe. It would certainly help her to do something."

"There is one more thing I should mention," Bruno drawled in his most seductive tones.

"Yes?" she dubiously inquired, cocking an eyebrow.

"The Pope isn't coming alone, you know. He's bringing lots of pretties to show off — tapestries, gold and silver work, paintings, sculpture."

"Oow," she moaned. "Yeah, that might just do it."

"Thought so," he said smugly. "But if we're going to do this, we need to make museum reservations soon. Who wants in? The more the merrier, you know."

Dick eagerly agreed but Chewie said, "I'm game for the trip, but not to see a bunch of churchy shit."

"Fine," Bruno shrugged. Turning to Cas, he said, "Please work on Dolores. It'd really help if she would participate."

"Well, I'll try," she replied unenthusiastically. "Girl's in a bad way. Still on a guilt trip."

Bruno smiled and patted her on the arm. "Well then, use that Catholic guilt to get her to come. Call me afterwards?"

"With pleasure," she promised.

† † †

DROPPING the lumpy duffel bag at the door later that afternoon, Bruno said, "Thanks for having me over. I really appreciate you letting me do this while I'm here.

I don't have enough extra time to waste it in a laundromat, especially on a holiday."

It was breathlessly hot, with only a small thunderstorm building over the Espiritu Santos to the north soon to be painted pink by the exiting sun. The pink Sanbenitos in the east seemed like flat cardboard cutouts. Even the monotonous hum of the cicadas seemed sluggishly oppressed by the heat.

Kathy opened the door and shrugged. "No problem," she said graciously. "But it's odd that you're not the only Nolan who needed to use the washer recently."

Mike's maroon minivan was nowhere to be seen. "Ah, you mean the Reverend Father? The washer at the rectory gave out again, huh? If he's here, I should go. I don't want to cause any trouble."

"Well, he's not, so you'll just have to stay and enjoy yourself," she said, patting Bruno's arm.

"Yeah, okay," Bruno said, trying to hide his relief. "Oh, and here's my humble contribution to the festivities." He pulled a paper bag out of the bulging duffel and handed it to his ex-wife. "Don't worry, it's all sedately legal."

Kathy glanced doubtfully at the sack but accepted it. She held the door open while Bruno hefted his laundry into the house, past the eagerly sniffing dogs.

"How are you doing, anyway?" she asked.

Bruno shrugged uncomfortably. "Other than... all that stuff, not too bad. I do wish I could talk to Mike, though."

"So things are still tense?"

He snorted. "That's an understatement. This could become the new Cold War."

"You guys have argued before," Kathy said, "but always managed to work it out somehow. Just try to keep it out of the papers, okay?"

"Bit too late for that, I'm afraid."

From behind the house came girlish laughter and splashing sounds.

"You didn't?" Bruno asked in surprise.

Kathy beamed. "Oh yes I did."

They went within. Bruno dumped his bag by the washer in the laundry room and walked out onto the back porch, where the girls splashed about in the brand-new hot tub.

"Hey, hey, hold it down," Kathy called. "That's not a swimming pool, you know!"

"Yes, Aunt Kathy," Beth said with exaggerated patience, as she surreptitiously flicked water at her younger cousin. "Hey," Marie said, "that's not fair!" and began another explosion of aquatic combat that drenched the small wooden deck surrounding the pool with water.

Kathy shrugged and picked up her margarita. "I suppose I should be happy they're not diving," she said. "Anyway, they're watering the garden at least."

The pool was large, surrounded by a low deck with a railing on one side. The girls were sitting comfortably on ledges, foaming water swirling up to their brown shoulders.

"Hiya, pumpkin," Bruno said to his daughter. "Forgive me if I don't give you a hug."

Marie pouted prettily. "Brute," she said. "That's child neglect, you know." She aimed a splash at him with her open hand, which he almost managed to avoid.

"Hey," he said, startled. "That's cold!"

"Of course it is, Uncle Bud," Beth laughed. "Who'd have a hot tub in summer?"

Kathy brushed Marie's hair back. "That's right. Though I can hardly wait to sit in it this winter all wonderfully warm while the snow gently falls. I hear it just sort of evaporates above the water."

"Sounds excellent," Bruno admitted. He glanced around at the yard, partly to avoid staring at the kids in their swimsuits. Kathy had done a good job of placement. It did not take up much of her garden, nor did it come anywhere near encroaching on the old Marian shrine.

"It's big," he said. "Big enough," Kathy replied. "It's supposed to hold four adults easily, six, if they're friendly. Want to try it?"

"Ah, not now," Bruno hedged. "No trunks."

"Don't need any, Dad," Marie said. "Shorts are good enough."

"Yeah, but I really should do my laundry now," he said uncomfortably. "Besides with all the fat I've put on, I'd push all the water out."

The others smiled but said nothing. He had gained some more weight, true, but his well-known body shyness had gotten far worse since Easter.

He turned back to the house. "Dad?" Marie called.

Bruno glanced back. His daughter leaned on the edge of the pool. "It's all right if you don't want to get in. I understand. But I would really like to see your tattoos again someday."

He reached out and mussed her wet hair. "Aw, you don't fool me — you can't have one, kitten. Your mom and I had this discussion before you were even born," he said, oddly amused.

Glancing at her lightly freckled back, "You've put on sunscreen, I hope?"

She smiled. "That's my dear old Dad, always able to find something to worry about. I'm okay: Mom made me put some on already."

Bruno nodded and went back to the laundry room, where he quickly started the first load. He got some iced tea and wandered out to sit on the back porch.

"So what's with Mike, anyway?" he asked. "Not like him to miss a party — or to leave his clothes in the dryer."

"Oh, did he?" she replied with a laugh. "I shouldn't be surprised. He was all excited about going up to the mountains for the weekend. First time in years, he said. I'm sure he needed it, especially after this spring," she said and immediately looked like she wished she hadn't.

Bruno smiled. "Don't worry — I'm cool. Anyway," he continued, as if to prove he could separate past from present, "I imagine he's awfully busy with the Denver expedition."

"How on earth did you know about that?" Kathy demanded. "It was only announced today at Mass."

"Hey, I never miss my Sunday obligation." Bruno grinned. "I watch 'Perp of the Week' er, '*TV Mass for Shut-Ins*' every Sunday." His ex didn't laugh, so he hastened to ask, "Are you and Marie going?"

"No, just the girls, I'm afraid. Beth's mom's still working nights at the hospital and with the new jacuzzi, I can't afford it either," Kathy said regretfully. "I hope you don't expect your daughter to pass on such a fantastic experience just because of your problems, do you?"

Bruno shrugged. "Nope," he fibbed. "Of course not. I just would have liked to have been consulted, that's all." Before his daughter's legal custodian could rejoin, he quickly added, "I mean, maybe she'd like to go with me instead." Then he chuckled in recognition of the notion's preposterousness.

She shook her head, sipping her drink with a frown, so Bruno decided it was a good time to check his clothes. The wash room was stifling, barely affected by the swamp cooler's heroic efforts, so he opened the door to the porch and began to unload Mike's clothes from the dryer.

They were his, without a doubt — among the socks and towels were several clergy shirts and cassocks. He roughly dumped them into a laundry basket.

As he refilled the machine, he could hear splashing as the girls climbed out of the tub. He peered around the edge of the door. Beth and Marie stood there speaking softly, a dyad of naiads unaware of his presence; rubbing their lithe young bodies dry with towels.

Bruno breathed out quietly, at first unaware of what they were discussing. In the flaming orange of sunset the girls were stunningly beautiful — slick and gleamingly lissome in their wet swimsuits, as vibrantly glowing as fire.

Now a teen at last, Beth was rapidly blossoming into a woman, her curves more pronounced, a fine, even tan across her flawless skin, brunette hair henna-red in the golden light.

Marie, a year younger, was just entering the transformation, but her father could see that she had matured even since Easter. Her breasts had barely begun to swell on her willowy frame. Her cheeks and lips blushed with health and her red hair wetly glistened like dark flames in the sunset.

Uneasily feeling like a voyeur, Bruno glanced away as they bent over to stroke their legs. But he continued to listen as he quietly refilled the washer.

"I'm really glad your dad was kidding about wanting you to go with him," Beth said softly. "That would have been so utterly bogus."

"Ultimate," Marie agreed. "Can you imagine hanging out with him and his weird friends? He'd probably want us to carry signs too. I'd be so embarrassed. It'd be fatal, just fatal."

Bruno smiled to himself.

"I'm so glad we get to go with Uncle Mike," she continued. "It'll be so cool to see all that neat stuff with him. Camp out together before the Mass. All the other kids will be totally jealous — maybe he'll introduce us to the Pope!"

The girls giggled and began to curtsey, daydreaming about being presented to His Holiness. Bruno frowned. Marie's unthinking idolatry of the pontiff was even worse than her adulation of Mike. She thinks they're all supermen, he thought resentfully, right next to God Almighty. If only he could get near the damned Pope, he'd show them all otherwise.

Suddenly he froze. A new idea intruded, dangerous in its simplicity, awful in its potential. Maybe he could get close enough to John Paul after all, it whispered, if he had the right disguise. The sudden lure of completing Mehmet Ali Agca's work seized him — after all, the near-miss had shown that a few ounces of lead, properly placed, could gain more attention than all the protests in the world. Death and eternal shame would inevitably result but so what? He feared not the former, having already tasted too much of the latter. Chewie was right — it was a war, a guerilla war.

It was pretty damned unlikely he could pull it off, but would it not be worth the price? No matter how the Church cursed his name afterwards, it couldn't ignore the problem then. He'd win some sort of martyr's crown after all.

He frowned at the mound of Mike's clothes. They were mostly black clergy shirts — surely his little brother wouldn't miss just one.

He didn't have time to think it all through. If he changed his mind later, he'd claim the load in the dryer got mixed up by mistake. Since Mike had started running again anything new would be impossibly small, so Bruno quickly stuffed the oldest shirt into the bag. Heart pounding, he then continued with the laundry and put it resolutely out of his mind.

Afterwards, Bruno stepped out into the holiday evening. The sky was purpling, a huge full moon rising behind the silhouette of the Sanbenitos among the first exploding rockets of the night. Already the patriotic aromas of burnt flesh cooking on countless outdoor barbecues and burnt gunpowder from expended fireworks filled the air. It felt dangerous, a little like a battlefield. Bruno smiled, breathing deeply.

†

CHAPTER TWENTY-FIVE

Saturday, July 10

BRUNO exhaled loudly, his face as purple as an Advent candle. The pilfered clergy shirt strained at the buttons, but held. Clearly, though, either he was going to have to lose a lot of weight within the next month, or find another black shirt. No way he could button the collar.

There came a brisk rapping at the door.

"Who is it?" he called, frowning at the mirror.

"It's Cassie," came a cheerful response from outside. His heart skipped a little at the not-unexpected sound of her voice. She'd said she would come over and help him with his outfit, but this was a bit early.

"I was just thinking about you," he said as he undid the deadbolt. "I don't think this will —" He stopped abruptly.

Cas stood there smiling, radiant in the lavender afterglow of the setting sun behind her. Eyes sparkling green, she seemed strangely younger. Behind her bangs, her straight, raven-black hair was tied back in a ponytail by a pink ribbon and her face was brightly made up. But what really took him aback was her costume. She was dressed in her old school uniform; white blouse now generously filled out, a pleated plaid skirt; navy blazer complete with the Queen of Peace monogram. Short white socks with frilly tops and saddle shoes finished the girlish image.

"Well, good evening, Father," she giggled. "Would you like to hear my confession?"

"Uh, yeah, well, I guess. You look, well, fabulous, in a retro sort of way. What's the occasion, kiddo?"

"I heard you were going to play dress-up," she said, teasingly. "I've been such a bad girl, Father. I need to be punished. Aren't you going to let me in?"

"Yes, of course," he stammered. "Come on in, Cas, Casandra."

"It's Cassie tonight," she said, flouncing in. "Casandra is such a serious name, and Cas is too short."

Bruno shut the door behind her, perplexed. "Sit down," he said. "Can I get you something? A soda?"

"Do you have any beer? Wine?"

"No, you know I don't drink."

"Sure," she said lightly. "But it never hurts to ask. It's okay, though," she continued. "They say I shouldn't be drinking either. Brings the bad ones out."

Bruno went to the refrigerator and brought back two colas. He had no idea what the woman was talking about. She was clearly playing a major mindgame of some sort, one that would somehow end in his total humiliation.

He handed her the drink and sat down on the sofa next to her carefully, not wanting to pop any buttons. "So," he said. "What's new with you?" His cat, Clio, seized the opportunity to jump in between.

Cas laughed; a clear, delightful peal. "Silly old man," she said. "Trying to be so cool but I know how you really feel."

Bruno instinctively glanced down, afraid he was somehow exposed. He wasn't, but he was stirring at the sight of her. She sat on the chair, with legs curled underneath, shoes kicked off, smiling at him with teal-green eyes. They held laughter and something he couldn't identify for a moment, something he hadn't seen in a long, long time. Then it hit him — desire. She gazed at him as if she actually wanted him.

He cleared his throat. "Maybe you do. You sure are cute in that outfit. Why that one, though?"

"Thanks, I knew you'd like it." She sipped her soda and said, "What else could I wear?" She shrugged, "Cas has got such dull taste in clothes. All black or white. An artist should have a lot more variety, don't you think? Me, I like colors. Not that this has much but it's the only thing she'd let me try on, even if she's so fat that we can barely fit anymore.

"I wore it just for you." She stared up at Bruno with studied coyness. She set her can down carefully on the end table and ran her finger along his arm. "You know I've liked you all along," she said softly, "but the others, well, they tried to get in the way. But I won't let them anymore."

"Others?" he asked feebly. She said nothing but gazed at him expectantly.

He set his soft drink down. This was suddenly moving way too fast, but as it was the first motion in this direction he'd felt in years, he wasn't going to blow it simply because she was being strange. If she wanted to play this game, fine by him.

She leaned forward, her eyes luminous, lips parted slightly, utterly luscious. The cat meowed uncomfortably and jumped to the floor. Bruno felt Cas' breath electric on his cheek as they moved together. Their lips met and slid together, tongues reaching for each other. She clasped him hard and he wrapped his arms around her.

Their hearts wildly pounding, she squirmed forward into his lap, pushing him backwards. Her hands ripped open his shirt, buttons flying everywhere, groping downwards. He could feel her breasts, unencumbered by any bra, press against him as her tiny nipples stiffened.

He pulled her blazer off roughly. She nuzzled him on the neck as he eagerly strove to undo her blouse with fingers as urgent as they were clumsy. His right hand snaked up across the slickness of her slip, engulfing the softness of her breast.

"Oh, baby," he whispered hoarsely, grabbing her asscheek with his other hand. Her cotton panties were already soaking wet. "Oh baby, I've wanted you so much."

"Yes," she moaned. "Oh yes, daddy, yes, daddy, take me!"

That did it. Suddenly Bruno stopped. He released his clutch upon her privates, deliberately grabbed her arms, and forced her back away. At first, she laughed, thinking he was playing but he continued holding her wrists tightly. "Hold on a minute," he panted. "This is too weird. We've got to talk."

"What's the matter?" she hissed. Her eyes flashed green with sudden fury. "Don't you like girls? Better let me go, little boy, or you won't have a pee-pee to piddle with."

Then, just as suddenly, "Eddie, you're hurting me. Let go. Please, Eddie!"

"Will you stop fooling around?" he demanded.

That brought another frenzied outburst of squirming. She bit him on the left arm and he flung her back on the couch, cursing. She was upon him in a flash, pinning him. As she sat on top of him with a hungry, disdainful sneer, grinning at him now like a predator that had cornered her victim, she rocked slowly back and forth. He found his erection returning.

"I'm sorry," he grunted. "This is really entertaining, but I — don't — think — so." He lurched up, twisting his arms easily out of her grasp. She fell backward. He grabbed her wrists together and pushed them hard down into her lap.

"What the hell are you trying to do, woman?" he yelled. "I mean, fun's fun, but this is getting too strange, too fast." He took a deep breath. "And besides, that reminded me a bit too much of my parents," he muttered.

He looked at her. She was devastated, her lower lip quivering, eyes brimming with tears.

"I'm going to let you go now. I don't want you jumping me, or kicking me, or scratching my eyes out, okay?"

He let her go and sprang back. Instead of attacking him, she curled up into a fetal position, covering her eyes which immediately overflowed with tears. Black with mascara, they flowed down her face and all over her hands as she howled.

Bruno stood there, wondering what the hell to do. As she continued sobbing loudly but wordlessly, he slowly sat down on the end of the couch. He reached out cautiously but she pulled away, so he sat back for a moment and thought. Then he rose, went to the bathroom, and returned with a spool of toilet paper.

This she accepted. He sat down next to her. He softly smoothed her hair as she wiped her face and hands with the soft paper and blew her nose on it.

"I'm sorry, dear. I just got scared that's all," he tried to explain. "I didn't mean to hurt you." She did not reply.

Finally she whispered in a tiny, hollow voice, "I know what I'm going to do, Eddie. I know how to kill her. I'll just roll up into a ball on the floor, just like this, see, and when she comes over, I'll bring her down and have her by the throat before she can make a sound."

Hair rose on the back of his neck. "Kill who?" he asked, slightly choked.

"My therapist, of course," she said in the same strange voice which slowly grew softer and somehow dreamier. "I have to stop her, you know. It doesn't work any more and I've failed Master Raume yet again.

"We can't go on," she continued softly. "She knows too much. Cas too. It's them or us. Master won't be able to stop us from killing the body then."

"No," Bruno replied. He tried to sound confident and unconcerned. "Nobody needs to die just yet. Just calm down and everything will be all right."

She suddenly grabbed his legs, levering her head up to stare in his eyes. "Please, Bruno," she whispered in an altogether clearer voice. "Please, just let me spend the night. Just hold me. We don't have to have sex. Just hold me."

He peered searchingly at her. Her hazel eyes were wide with fear, but otherwise rational. She seemed like herself again.

"Okay," he said at last, sighing. "If you want to stay, let's go to bed. I'm too old to cuddle all night on a couch."

Bruno gently led her to the bathroom and cleaned her face up. She was as compliant as a sleepy child.

Finally they climbed into his small, lumpy bed together. Cas fell asleep at once, clinging to him, but Bruno didn't sleep well at all. He had far too many questions he needed to ask when morning came, but perhaps not the courage to utter them.

†

CHAPTER TWENTY-SIX

Monday, July 12

THE CHANCELLOR glanced up as Mike flopped down wearily in a chair before his desk. "Here are the estimates for the school buses to Denver you wanted."

"Ah good." Cruz capped his fountain pen and reached for the folder. "It's not going to be cheap," Mike said, "so maybe we should also encourage as much car-pooling as possible.

"There's still lots of enthusiasm, so there should be sufficient adult supervision. But we've only got a month. We really need to get on it right away. Perhaps I should do the TV Mass again soon to whip up support."

"Good thinking, Mike." Cruz finished examining the documents and dropped the folder back on the desk, and nodded. "You seem to have a knack for this stuff."

Mike smiled glumly. "Not to brag, but I was twice president of the St. Dominic Savio club in grade school, you know."

"Impressive," Cruz chortled. "I should make a note of that for your permanent record."

There was a brief moment of silence, then Mike asked, "So why did you really ask me here today, anyway, Bob?"

Cruz smiled grimly. "You know me too well." He sighed, "We never did discuss what to tell Malachy."

"I don't know what you should say," Mike replied truthfully, recalling his private conversation with Chavez.

"Yes, it's thorny," Cruz concurred. He leaned back and toyed with his pen. "If he doesn't need to know as Case Manager, why bother? His plate is overflowing as it is."

"I feel overwhelmed, too. I can't tell you how depressing this is," Mike said. "I can't speak for you, of course, but I find myself wondering if I'm the only celibate left in the diocese."

The chancellor laughed humorlessly. "No, thank God, you're not, but I can see how you might feel that way. The latest statistics indicate only twenty percent of us always stick to our vows. No wonder the priesthood's in such bad shape." He shrugged. "But what can we do?"

"Are you saying, then, that if these guys aren't taking advantage of women and kids or causing scandal, maybe we shouldn't bother?"

"A lot of bishops would — privately, of course — advocating the theological principle of 'compromise,' that a lesser evil is better to be tolerated than an even greater one endured."

"Is it pure pragmatism," Mike asked, "or perhaps laziness? Sure, half the parishes that still have priests would be empty if you take a real hard line. But you can't abandon all discipline. That one guy Chavez mentioned — Garcia, the one going into the gay bars with his collar on; well, that shouldn't be allowed any more than patronizing strip joints would be. Just not seemly."

"True; I don't think we need to bother Malachy with these minor sorts of problems. If he hears about them from other sources, however, I don't think I dare interfere."

"Absolutely. You must be discreet. Not only keep your hands off the Review Board, you must be seen keeping your hands off," Mike concurred. "Especially in regard to the situations that seem like they're about to blow up. Like the business with Olly Griego at St. Albert's."

Cruz nodded. "Yeah, pretty amazing. I can't imagine why Chavez let it go on so long, considering how much he knew about it." Mike shrugged; he'd heard rumors about Olly's parties for years but he'd never been invited. Just as well. Mike knew a few gay priests, all fine pastors and good men, but there was something indefinitely slimy about this guy. "Well, he is a friend of Tom's..."

Cruz peered at him oddly, so Mike hastily moved on. "What about those other situations Chavez spoke of? The long-term relationships?"

"Well, we can't sell the women and their bastards off into slavery like they did in the Middle Ages, no matter what Malachy might want," Cruz replied. "We dare not alienate some of the best we've got left, yet the lawyers tell me that if we continue turning a blind eye then we are exposed to all kinds of nasty liabilities.

"Yet some situations do seem to work out. Torres, for example, has been living quietly with his housekeeper for twenty years; everybody at Visitation knows it, I'm sure, but nobody's complained. At least not to me."

"But we're already completely at the mercy of these guys' partners, aren't we? Maybe if we don't bother them, they'll keep quiet," Mike said. He rubbed his temples. "Perhaps you, as Vicar of Priests, should visit the ones whose names came up and suggest they clean up their acts before Malachy or the media does it for them."

"Yeah, I suppose I should," Cruz sighed, "and as soon as possible. Meanwhile, let's bring our Torquemada in here." He dropped his pen on the desk and pressed his intercom button. "Consuela, come in for a moment, please."

The large secretary entered silently. Cruz handed her the papers he had just signed. "Here, these are ready to go out. And please call Father Malachy in." She nodded and left.

"I remember you saying that the financial situation was bad," Mike said. "How is all this going to affect our little pilgrimage?"

"Funny you should mention that —" Cruz began, when Malachy's brisk rap upon the door interrupted him.

"Come in, Sean. How's it going?"

Malachy came in almost as fed up as Mike felt. He sat down heavily and waved his hand. "Between this infernal heat and the bloody phone, I'm toasted," he explained wearily. "I've just been informed by Miss Kramer that five new lawsuits are being filed today. Against Schmidt, this time — and the diocese and Chavez, of course. She didn't have any details."

He glanced over at Mike as if noticing him for the first time. "Hi, Mike. You seem tired. Mountains too much for you?"

"Loved it, but got a little sunburnt. Too long since I last took a hike that high." He paused. "How'd it go on Sunday?"

The older man laughed. "Fine, just fine. I'll say this for your nieces, they're good servers all right, especially the young one. No mistakes, kept right on top of the ball."

Mike smiled. "They're good kids, the best. I'm not surprised, though. After all the horrible stories Bruno and I have told them about you, they were likely terrified."

Malachy chuckled. "Your brother I'd expect, but you? Telling tales out of school about me to those innocent girls?"

"Only enough to keep them on their toes," Mike smiled.

Malachy snorted and turned to Cruz who had been quietly watching the exchange. "Well, is it as bad as we thought?"

"Worse," Cruz said. He explained, "The auditors are still digging but the first estimates are in." He picked up a paper off his desk. "It appears that His Excellency was even more generous with the diocese's money than he's admitted so far. There's half a million dollars unaccounted for from the building fund for the new cathedral."

"Half a million?" Mike repeated in astonishment.

"At least. With this and all the lawsuits, we're going to have to sell the land the old cathedral's on for sure. Sorry, to crush your dream, Mike. No way we can rebuild."

They quietly absorbed the news. Mike's depression deepened. Our Lady of Solitude had always been the living heart of the lovely old section of town. A church belonged there.

"The land in Plaza Vieja is worth millions; that might just be enough to save us. Because if it isn't, we may have to do what no diocese has ever done before: declare bankruptcy," he stated grimly. Malachy and Mike glanced at each other in dismay and the old priest began to glow with anger.

"Well, by St. Michael and all the archangels, we shouldn't go down without a fight," he fumed. "Just as we mustn't allow these perverts to destroy this diocese, neither must we allow these leeching lawyers to get rich off of us."

"What can we do about it?" Mike asked.

"Well," Cruz suggested, "we've got lawyers and private eyes of our own: let's use them more aggressively. Offer quick settlements to those who don't sue. Those 'victims' who want to play legal hardball, fine. We'll see them in court. Dig up some dirt on them in the meantime. And let's stop paying for therapy for those who condemn us publicly — even your brother and my cousin, if necessary, Mike."

"Tell the world how broke we are," Malachy proposed. "Take up a special collection to get the people involved. Ask for money from the dioceses which sent these blackguards here in the first place. Request help from the Ministers — the bishops give them enough — and threaten to sue them too if they don't fork some over. Demand that the insurance companies pay up or face the same fate."

Mike was horrified by this display of righteous sacerdotal dudgeon. He was sure they meant every word; faced with danger to Holy Mother Church, both priests had reacted as instinctively as guard dogs. Against real human suffering, however, Mike doubted either his friend or the old Irishman could be so heartless.

Or would they, if they belonged to "them?"

Mike shook his head. Already he was infected by the new climate of paranoia. He ought to toss the key on the table and tell them everything, right now. But glancing from Malachy's ruddy visage to Cruz' hard one, he decided that this was not the time. Neither appeared particularly infused with Christian charity at the moment.

"Thank God you're on our side, fellas," he said sincerely.

"All I want is that you just let me do my job." Malachy waited a moment to see if Cruz would take the bait, but the Chancellor remained silent, so he continued. "I was charged with thoroughly investigating this mess and I'm still not being allowed access to the records I need to see."

"We've been through this before. Most of the problems those records dealt with have long been settled."

"Maybe canonically, but not necessarily spiritually or even according to civil law. Some of these lawsuits, as you know, refer to events thirty years ago. If we'd dealt with the situations properly then, they wouldn't be attacking us now."

"We're talking about the archives," Cruz explained to Mike. "The secret ones. Have you ever heard of them?"

"Something," Mike cautiously admitted.

"Most people other than canon lawyers haven't. Suffice it to say that anytime a priest is caught in a big no-no, a record is kept of how it all turned out. But those documents are kept under conditions of strict confidentiality for the sake of the privacy of all those involved."

"And I need to see them," Malachy interrupted.

"I'm certainly not going to hand you the key and let you rummage around," Cruz stated emphatically. "I can't allow any fishing expeditions. That's not your job."

"Oh, and what is that, then, if not to track down the beasts in our midst?" Malachy said with all the sarcasm he could muster.

"As I recall, the duty of Case Manager is to investigate the cases brought to him. Individual, specific cases. Give me names and show me the allegations."

"Now I've got him. Watch this," Malachy stage-whispered to Mike. He leaned forward. "I have given you one name over and over: the Very Reverend Thomas Antoine DeLaval. As for the allegations, how many do you want? There's a new one almost every week against that obscene fiend!"

Cruz shook his head. "Quit grandstanding. As a distinguished canon lawyer you know perfectly well that no matter how notorious he is, I couldn't give you his dossier — if there is one — because no documents may be removed."

"Yet, as diocesan administrator, you can look at them?"

"Yes, in cases of genuine necessity."

"Well, what could be more necessary than this?"

"More necessary than this?" Cruz repeated angrily. "The future of the Church!" He exhaled loudly and took a deep breath, calming himself. "I'll admit it," he said, lowering his voice, "the secret archives are a time bomb. Everything's in there, all right: the results of every inquiry ever done, the names of the priests involved, and the outcome. It's all spelled out there in black and white.

"If any of this material got out, the media would crucify us. It doesn't matter how old the cases are, nor what the results were. The mere fact of its existence is so sensational that it would scandalize the faithful. We dare not risk it."

"Well, now we're getting somewhere," Malachy said with some satisfaction. "Aren't you glad you dropped by, Mike? You're learning something."

Mike was acutely uncomfortable. "Why are you so interested in this, Monsignor Malachy? If, like Father Cruz says, it's mainly old stuff?"

Malachy glanced from one man to the other for a moment. Then he said in a calm and thoughtful voice, "Because I'm thinking that these damned pedophiles have been around here for quite a while. They're organized, and I believe that if I had free access to all the files I could prove it."

"Oh my God," Mike said, letting himself be shocked.

Cruz made a derisive noise. "Organized? You're starting to sound like Mike's brother, Sean. Most of the guys accused so far can barely even run a bingo game!"

That broke the tension a bit. Malachy checked his watch and rose. "Well, I lost this round, but I'll keep trying.

"Anyway, I must put that press release for the evening news together, so I'd better get on it. Good seeing you, Mike." Glaring hard at Cruz, he said, "We'll talk more later."

Cruz did not smile. "I can hardly wait."

Malachy shut the door firmly behind him.

"I better go too." Cruz, not looking up, waved his hand in dismissal. Mike closed the door softly behind him. He turned and jumped. Malachy stood there, gazing at him somberly.

Before he could speak, Malachy put a finger to his lips and grabbing his arm, herded him away from the door.

"Just thought you should know, there's more to it than that," he whispered. "Did he mention what the private investigators discovered?"

"No, not a word. Why?"

Malachy's tone dropped even lower and he glanced around before speaking. "I am not supposed to know, but unofficially, I've found out that they have developed a list of about two hundred victims that haven't come forward. Most of the cases are fairly recent, too. Your pal Robert won't let me see it, won't even admit it exists."

Mike looked at him questioningly.

"Why?" the old man shrugged. "Money, no doubt. If a victim doesn't come forward threatening to make a big stink, we don't have to do anything. Not a bloody thing. 'Let sleeping dogs lie,' that's his philosophy, I'm afraid."

"Why tell me, Monsignor Malachy?"

"Because, Mike, deep down we both know your brother's right," he said bleakly. "There's been a lot of wickedness in this diocese going on for a long, long time. If we're going to confront it, we can't afford to have any blinders on."

†

CHAPTER TWENTY-SEVEN

Wednesday, July 14

BRUNO cleared his throat. "So then we went to bed," he said, twisting his hands, "but that was it. She went out like a light."

Chagrined, he stole a glance at Dr. Blackstone, listening to his tale in frank amazement, all the validation he needed. "I know she did, because I sure didn't sleep a wink."

"What happened then?"

He sighed. "In the morning, she seemed okay. Quiet, like she was embarrassed. When we finally talked over breakfast, it was as if it all involved somebody else and she'd just heard about it. She tried to laugh it off, but I wouldn't let it go."

"Did she explain anything?"

"Yeah, and that's what really freaked me," Bruno said dejectedly, "why I had to see you today." He'd called at the first opportunity; fortunately, a cancellation had provided an opening. No playing with toys or visualization exercises today; he needed some serious couch time.

"She said was that she was 'MPD.' I asked what that meant, and she stared at me like I was the one that was nuts. 'I'm multiple,' she said, 'I thought you knew; after all, you're one too.'" He threw up his hands. "I didn't know what to say."

Pushing back in the recliner, Bruno examined the holes in the ceiling panels yet again. "She said that one of her 'kids,' as she calls these other personalities, spooks, beings, or whatever the hell they are, came out. A real wild child with a crush on me, I suppose.

"I asked her if this happened often, and she said no. She said the reason her 'system' had allowed it then was in order to, ah, test me."

"To test you?"

"Yep, she said that some of her 'alters' — that was the other word she used — wanted to make sure that I was safe. Not some kind of a perp, that is. So they let the kid, 'Cassie' out to tempt me. I got the feeling, though, that if I really had tried to have sex with her, the pain today would be somewhat worse than just blue balls." He smiled crookedly.

"Anyway, though she didn't recall the part about killing her shrink, she believed me. I think it scared her. It sure as hell did me. She promised to talk to her therapist, but maybe you should let her know too, just to be sure."

Blackstone jotted a separate note.

"Since I didn't freak out," Bruno concluded, "she seemed rather relieved, but anxious because I obviously had never heard any of this stuff before.

"The real irony, doc, is that she's the first woman interested in me in years, and I couldn't make love to her because it'd be like... like doing a child. The fact that I really wanted to is bad enough. But the idea that I might be just as crazy as she is terrifying. Utterly terrifying."

"First of all, give yourself some credit," Blackstone said soothingly. "Your refusal to take advantage of her shows great moral courage, in my opinion. Secondly, she trusts you. Before this, I mean, or it wouldn't have happened. Some part of her was pretty confident you'd pass before she even attempted it.

"But you really need to understand what having multiple personalities — or, as its now called, 'Dissociative Identity Disorder' — is all about. It's not like it's shown in the movies."

"Multiplicity's not schizophrenia, though that's not mutually exclusive, either. Schizophrenia involves chemical imbalances in the brain which lead to hallucinations, paranoia, psychotic thinking, and the rest.

"It's not being 'crazy,' it's an adaptive survival response to a crazy situation.

"Every child," she continued, putting down her pen, "comes into the world totally helpless, absolutely dependent on its parents. If the parents do not love the baby and tend for it constantly, it will inevitably die.

"So what happens if the caretakers don't really love it, and traumatize it with serious abuse or neglect? The child cannot face this intolerable situation because to win the adult's love is absolutely necessary for survival."

"Sound like a situation like with the evil stepparent in those fairy-tales," Bruno commented.

Blackstone nodded. "Quite. Since a young child can't deal with this reality, sometimes it doesn't. The kid trances out, pretends nothing bad happened. This is dissociation and it often saves the child. If the trauma is severe and prolonged enough, the consciousness of such a person can actually become divided, with some parts of the mind holding the abuse and others knowing nothing of it.

"Worst of all, sometimes trauma is deliberately inflicted to make sure the abuse is kept secret," she continued sadly. "Victims so stressed that they dissociate completely often keep it hidden because they don't or can't let themselves know."

She sighed. "However just about everyone dissociates to some extent. It can be very handy. It's one way to get through difficult situations even in such mundane matters as, say, going to the dentist or sitting in a jet for hours.

"What you must realize is that it's not a black and white thing — like you're dissociative or you're not — it's a rainbow," she continued earnestly. "At one extreme are fully-blown multiples with distinct and often rival personalities that can switch in and out of the driver's seat like a Chinese fire drill, while at the other end are poets and daydreamers. Cas seems closer to the far end; you to the nearer. Does that help?"

Bruno shook his head. "There's a big difference between doing the Walter Mitty thing and having somebody else whom I don't even know living in my brain."

Dr. Blackstone nodded. "Bruno, I've diagnosed you as having PTSD and Dissociative Identity Disorder, but that does not mean you are fully multiple. You have not exhibited or demonstrated any such symptoms to me. So, in all honesty, to some degree you are — but not extremely so, I think."

She paused. "Clients often have problems with this prospect. Most are afraid it means they're out of control. Does that sound right?"

"Oh baby, does it ever."

"Well, you haven't experienced missing time in quite a while, is that correct?"

"Yes. Not since blacking out back when I was drinking."

She smiled and shrugged. "Good — yet another reason to stay sober. So then, it doesn't sound like you're switching from one autonomous ego-state to another like your friend was."

Bruno smiled ruefully. "I hoped all it meant was that I hadn't been abducted by space aliens."

"That too, I suppose," she laughed. "Okay. So then, you haven't woken up someplace strange, or had people come up and greet you by another name, or found clothes in your closet or other items you don't like and can't remember buying?"

"Nope. But there are certain people, like Cas, who I feel I should know but can't remember. Does that count?"

"Possibly. Might just be getting old, too." She tapped her pen on the pad. "Do you frequently misplace or lose things?"

"Constantly." Bruno said and she scribbled. "The only missing time I'm sure about is the number of watches I've lost. As a kid, Mike used to say it was my poltergeist, or that I was possessed. God, could that be it, doc?"

She raised one eyebrow as she finished writing, and gazed at him soberly. "I don't know, Bruno," she said. "I doubt it. I'm not an expert on spiritual entities. But psychologically speaking, I can assure you that alters are not in and of themselves demonic. And as fragments of the psyche, they can't be exorcized. The attempt usually just shatters them further."

"What were we talking about?" Bruno asked abruptly. Dr. Blackstone looked surprised. "You were telling me what you feared about being dissociative," she said slowly.

"Oh yeah." He frowned. "Having other people living inside my head? That still doesn't seem possible. I wish there was some way I could tell."

"Maybe there is," his therapist tentatively suggested. "If you do have some semi-independent sub-personalities, perhaps you could communicate with them. What about the 'voices' you mentioned?"

"If I pay much attention to them, they shut up."

"Well, we could try automatic writing or perhaps a pendulum..."

"Hey that gives me an idea." He flopped his left arm loosely on the armrest of the chair. "Tell me; if I had these other selves, couldn't they raise my arm if they wanted to?"

"Maybe," Blackstone admitted. "It depends on a lot of different things. They may not be accessible, especially if they were progr-." She bit off the word sharply, but Bruno did not seem to notice.

He relaxed his left arm as much as possible and closed his eyes. "Okay, guys, if anybody's there, any time will do." Not a single muscle in his arm twitched.

Bruno smiled. "See, ain't nobody —" he began. Suddenly there was a ferocious itching on the left side of his head. His scalp tingled painfully as if bitten by an army of ants.

"Ouch," he exclaimed. Instinctively, he raised his left arm to his head to scratch. The torment ceased immediately.

"Oh shit," Bruno groaned, staring at his uplifted limb. "I think we're in trouble."

"No, Bruno, this is good, very good," Blackstone said enthusiastically. "It's a sign they're ready to talk with you."

Just then, the grandfather clock in the corner softly chimed the third quarter hour, startling them both. Bruno's eyes flew open even wider. "My God, like the bells! The church bells! I remember now: the sacristy. But it wasn't just Xaphon," he said in horror, turning to Blackstone, face suddenly ghostly. "It was Master Baalberith — he was behind everything! He wanted Xaphon's book. He forced me to tell him!"

He leapt to his feet, babbling. "This is way too much, doc. I really gotta go," he babbled. "Time's up, I think. Yeah, gotta go. Right now. Sorry."

She rose but before she could say anything he was gone.

†

CHAPTER TWENTY-EIGHT
1963: Saturday, April 20

EDDIE knelt at the altar railing as Father DeLaval had ordered. The bad taste in his mouth and knot in his guts left no doubt that he was really in for it this time. He tried to pray as he waited for the fat old priest to finish locking the doors of the church. The sincerity was there but he was too scared. All he could think about was the day before, flinching as the sound of each latch clanking solidly shut echoed through the vacant cathedral. Meanwhile, the bells unhappily tolled the hour.

Eddie stared desperately up at the harsh, reproachful face of Our Lady of Solitude above him. "Holy Mother, I'm sorry. Please, please don't let him hurt me," he whispered. "It wasn't so bad, really, was it? I'm sorry, and I'll never do it again."

The words were almost exactly what he had said to Father yesterday at the time of the incident, and again a few minutes ago in Confession. And about as effective.

It had all started innocently enough. Big Brenda, largest girl in the whole school, and Mean Monica, unafraid of pounding on any kid unwise enough to notice the hair on her upper lip, had caught Eddie on the girls' side of the playground, chasing an escaped dodge-ball from the boys' half of the yard.

They'd trapped him red-faced and gasping up against the cathedral's sandstone wall. Desperate to get away, he'd yanked the side door open, and fled inside the church, claiming sanctuary. Smelling victory, the two girls had started to follow but stopped on their heels, turned and ran.

Hearing the unseemly disturbance, Father DeLaval had erupted from the sacristy in righteous rage. He'd yelled at Eddie for allowing girls to desecrate the church. Grabbing him hard by the ear and forcing him to his knees, he'd ordered him to come to Confession on Saturday.

Yet when Eddie presented himself at last in the confessional today, Father DeLaval gruffly told him to wait outside. The concluding penitents filed through and muttered their token prayers. Finally DeLaval emerged and began silently locking up the place.

Securing the last door, the same one by the sacristy Eddie had blundered through, he summoned the youth with an imperious crook of his finger. Eddie followed into the priests' section of the sacristy. DeLaval turned and suddenly grinned, gray eyes sparkling, anger melting away. He gestured for the boy to sit down on the bench. "Eddie, aren't you supposed to be serving tonight?" he asked casually, leaning against the cabinet.

"Yeah," the kid answered. "Mom doesn't like me out late but Father Wilson insisted."

"Good. You know, Eddie, my lad, it's a very important occasion and quite an honor for you. I've been thinking. You're a big boy now. Maybe I was too harsh on you about those girls. Who can blame a handsome lad like you for being chased, eh?"

He unlocked a cabinet and pulled out a bottle. "So how can I make it up to you? How about a special treat? Have you ever tasted sacramental wine? No? Well, if you're thinking about becoming a priest, then you should." He got two paper cups from above the sink in the bathroom.

Then they drank up. In no time at all, Eddie's face became slack. After a short while, he began to nod.

"Oh no, no, this is not nap-time," the priest said, rousing Eddie with sharp pats to his face, hoping he had rightly calculated the dosage. "Stay with me, kid. You've got some questions to answer.

"Eddie, recite," he said carefully. Obediently, the boy began the Act of Contrition as he had been trained, "Oh my God, I am heartily sorry..." DeLaval let him finish, and then said sharply, "Eddie, be gone!"

There was no response. "Who is there?"

Eddie, head hanging limply, spoke, "You are not my master. My lord is Magister Xaphon. I answer only to him."

DeLaval smiled. It had worked. And his old friend was now claiming the Magistracy, was he? "Wilson, er, Master Xaphon sent me to test you, that you may be ready for tonight.

"What is your name?" he demanded again.

The boy mumbled something. DeLaval slapped him. "What?" he roared. "Speak up when Master Baalberith questions you! Who are you?"

"Murmius," Eddie growled. DeLaval repeated it silently to himself several times. Now to see how far that scoundrel had gotten with the boy's training.

"Who are the Blackpriests?" he barked.

"The Blackpriests of the Order of St. Peter Martyr, are the instruments of God's love hidden in His anger, through the ministry of the great archangel Lucifer, Our Dread Lord, also called Satan, whom men fear as the Devil, and his consort, Lilith, Our Dread Lady."

"What is the ministry of the Devil?"

"Satan's ministry is to scourge unrepentant sinners and test the righteous, as Jesus' was to forgive those who feared him. The Blackpriests, who are Satan's Chosen Ones, are the sublime agency the Dread Lord uses to accomplish this."

Kid had it down pat. DeLaval skipped to later points of the Order's diabolical catechism.

"How is one Chosen by Satan?"

"Satan elects one to be His special minister after the Candidate successfully passes the Ordeal, through proving his openness to the Devil's Will by his lusts, by conformity to the Discipline of the Secret, and by the full and voluntary offering of a victim's Blood."

"What do the Blackpriests gain from serving Satan?"

"The Blackpriests acquire mighty powers of sorcery, and all that is forbidden the other followers of Christ is granted them to enjoy in this world and in the next."

DeLaval smiled with dour admiration. Most of the nuns would be as astounded at such marvels of memorization as horrified by its content. Wilson, damn him, had done his job well, but then again, he had the *Codex*. Possessing it would certainly make what he was about to attempt much more likely to succeed, but also totally unnecessary.

He glanced at the wall clock and smiled. Time enough for a little fun before getting ready for the big event that evening. It should at least cover his tracks; ultimately it just might provide the groundwork whereby he pry the information he needed out of the boy.

"So, Eddie," he said thoughtfully as he undid his collar, "you're going to have a new Master, and a new name. It'll be our little secret. I think I will call you 'Kazideel.' And someday, you're going to tell me all about that special book of his."

†

CHAPTER TWENTY-NINE

1993: Sunday, July 18

AS HE slowly drifted into wakefulness, Bruno sighed contentedly. Without opening his eyes, the smooth, warm body breathing softly next to his, the perfume of her hair tickling his nose told him exactly where he was. It was no dream; he was in Cas' bed with her, spooned together, as shamelessly naked as Adam and Eve.

He raised his head, which caused her to stir. "Cuddle me," she mumbled and snuggled up against him, which he gladly did. She sighed blissfully, dozing off once more. No wonder. They had expended a great deal of energy on lovemaking after a long conversation that had lingered long past midnight.

They had been very mature, open, and honest, but it didn't matter. From the very moment she opened the door, Bruno knew that he would end the night in her arms. She did too; neither spoke of it, but it gave a magic glow of delicious expectation to the entire evening's extended preliminaries.

Bruno recalled the evening as they lay breathing together. When at last they had entwined, it truly was love that they made, not sex that they had — or almost, anyway. But even with a tenderness he had never known before, the pleasure had been tainted with poison.

How could it be otherwise when he saw Wilson's ghostly face straining with desperation every time he closed his eyes, or DeLaval's, gleaming with unholy delight? How could he hope for the sweet tenderness he craved, when her gentlest caress could feel like their brutal mauling?

And why, when she cried out in passion, should he gaze into her green eyes and see them as much younger than her years, screaming at him in silent terror?

So here it was the morning after, and all he wanted was a drink. Well, that at least seemed normal enough.

He sighed softly and slowly disengaged himself, despite a sleepy complaint. He slipped quietly into the bathroom, took some much-needed relief and a hot shower.

Returning to the bedroom, he heard Cas in the kitchen, which gave him a chance to gather his scattered clothes and quickly dress. Brushing his damp hair back with his hands, he joined her. "'Morning," he said, entering as nonchalantly as he could. Cas turned around with a nervous smile, putting out her cigarette, and pulling her bathrobe a little tighter.

"Hi," she said. "You okay?"

Grinning, he chivalrously declared, "Oh, way more than fine. Great." He opened his arms and she nestled against him.

"How about you?"

"I'm good. Real good."

"Just good?" Bruno chuckled, and after a moment, so did she. "Look at us," he said, pulling back to examine her. "We're as nervous as a couple of virgins."

She laughed, putting a loose strand of his graying hair back in place. "Ex-virgins, you mean. Last night was really something, wasn't it? See, it can have its advantages, baby. We can be anyone we want to be, anyone at all."

He smiled because he dared not speak, and they kissed lightly before she pulled away again. "No, I reek," she said. "I really need to bathe." Bruno, all too conscious of her sour, smoky breath, could only nod, so with another peck and a pat on the rear, she skipped off into the bathroom.

As her shower started, Bruno went into the front room and found the air conditioner switch. He sat down and realized that his joy had already evolved into jitters. Now that they'd become lovers, now what?

Not wanting to dispel the residual afterglow by facing that question just yet, he reached for the TV's remote control.

"Ah, 'Perp of the Week's' already on," he mumbled as he heard the familiar tinny piano banging away for the *TV Mass for Shut-Ins* from the Catholic Complex. He stretched out on the sofa and put his feet up.

The picture swam into focus. A woman prattled a reading in Spanish while type crawled along the bottom of the screen begging for dinero. Then the camera panned right to the rustic wooden sanctuary of a Southwestern-style chapel and the priest standing there ready in a green chasuble. "Holy cow, it's Mike! What the hell's he doing on?"

Bruno sat up, watching intently. His brother, tall, handsome, dark brown hair slicked back and blue eyes twinkling with joy, smiled easily into the camera, every inch a confident, professional apostle.

"A reading from the Holy Gospel," the priest began. Bruno replied, "Please, little brother, I'll pass," and hit the mute button.

He watched as Mike read the scriptures. His brother had style, no doubt about it; the optimism of his faith shone around him like a nimbus. Bruno felt a spasm of envy. How serene it must be to be celibate, not consumed with the crap that haunted Bruno's every waking hour and all too many of those asleep. "Yeah, but I'm allowed to get laid, even if it only happens once every seven years or so," he muttered.

Bruno turned up the sound for the homily. "Today's Gospel, the story of the weeds sown amid the grain, is somewhat apt, I feel, for us at this time.

"There has been an enemy among us, who scattered seeds of evil in our fields," Mike said firmly. He raised his hand. "I'm not talking just about the horrible stories in the newspapers about priests betraying their trust, and I certainly don't refer to those who say they have been hurt by them —"

"Damn well better not be!" Bruno growled.

"— but all the weeds of doubt and confusion, of selfishness and despair that these things have nourished.

"In the story, the disciples ask the Lord if He wants them to pull the weeds up. Jesus tells them no, because they might accidentally pull out the good grain as well. Better wait until harvest, he says.

"My friends, is that not what is happening now?" Bruno snorted and hit the mute button. Mike continued blathering silently, smiling as enthusiastically as any used-car pitchman. Finally, Bruno flicked the sound on again.

"But time is running out. Permission and reservations for the buses to Denver must be in by the end of the month." Spreading his slim hands wide, he concluded, "Please don't let this once-in-a-lifetime chance slip by. Call the number on the bottom of your screen for more information." The phone number for the Catholic Complex appeared.

Folding his hands again, he closed his eyes and intoned, "And so we offer up our prayers to you, O Lord, first for the children of Alvarado that —"

Bruno cut the sound again and leaned back. He heard the bathroom door open and Cas came into the front room, turbaning her hair in a towel. "I heard you yelling at the TV. What's up? Hey, isn't that your brother?"

"Yep, the Pied Piper himself is putting on the magic show today," Bruno replied. "Gotta sell that snake-oil." He lightly stroked the inside of her leg below the bathrobe and she did not pull away. Suddenly leaning forward, he exclaimed, "Hey, he even brought the girls."

In tandem, Beth and Marie helped Mike with washing his hands and bringing the bread and wine to the altar, demurely innocent in the loose white albs.

"Which one's your daughter?" Cas asked.

"The short one," Bruno said proudly. "The other's my niece. Damn, Marie's good at this. Thank God the Pope won't allow women priests!"

Cas laughed. "Hey, be nice. You know I've already sacrificed one relative to the Church," he complained.

"If she takes after you at all," Cas said, bending down to kiss him, "the Pope will surely have his hands full."

As she leaned, the robe fell open to expose her left breast like a fresh, dewy peach, tiny nipple erect from the cooling air, a small tattoo of the Sacred Heart nearby. Happily leering, he reached up but she playfully slapped his hand away.

"Don't even think about it, buster," she said, shaking her finger, scolding him with a smile. "Not in front of God and your family and everything. What would the nuns say?"

"Oh, probably something like, 'See what good things the Lady has given you,'" Bruno laughed. Cas grabbed his arm suddenly in alarm. "What? What did you say?"

Taken aback, Bruno floundered. "Just a joke. I was just kidding. I, I — don't know where I heard that."

Cas' hazel eyes glittered wide and unreadable as she searched his. "You don't know what you're saying," she hissed. "Don't ever, ever say that to me again."

"Sure sweetie, just ease up a little, will you?" Bruno said, touching her arm. Her grip relaxed. "Are you okay, dear?"

Shakily, Cas released him and reached for a cigarette. "I'm sorry," Bruno began, but she interrupted, and her smile was very shallow. "That — it was something my mom used to say, before she abandoned us."

"I see," Bruno lied, not really understanding, but sympathetic. "You want to talk about it?"

"No," she said shortly, shaking her head, then glanced up at him with a more genuine smile. "Thanks, though. I'll be okay. But I'd like to be alone for a little while. Please?"

"No problem, dear," Bruno said gallantly. He stood, uncertain he should reach out to her. He raised his hand as if to touch, and then dropped it.

He opened the front door, glancing back. Cas was staring dejectedly at the floor, surrounded by smoke, nervously twirling a sable lock of hair with a finger. Bruno felt a stab of sympathy and foreboding and sighed loudly, thinking about Blackstone's sour predictions. "I'll call later," he said, but there was no reply.

Bruno gingerly closed the door.

†

CHAPTER THIRTY

AFTER THE FINAL BLESSING and dismissal, Mike waited, smiling blindly into the impassive eye of the television camera until the red light blinked off. "And we're clear," said one of the technicians loudly and suddenly the hot lights faded out.

Mike blinked until his vision returned to normal. "Ah, that went well, didn't it, girls?" He ambled over to the closet that served as a vestry.

Beth and Marie quickly put up the Mass dishes. As Beth poured the leftover wine from the cruet carefully back into the bottle, she said, "Yeah, I guess it was okay, Uncle Mike."

"You sure don't seem excited by your big TV debut."

The brunette shrugged. "No big deal, just that creepy camera staring at you."

"Yeah," added the redhead, "I didn't like it much either. I thought there would be more people here or at least a monitor to watch or something."

Mike smiled, doffing the chasuble. "First time on TV, and already you want star treatment. Sorry. Place is too small to hold all your fans, anyway."

The girls giggled as they stripped off their robes and hung them up in the closet. "Can we go now, Uncle Mike?" Marie asked, straightening her halter-top.

"Yeah, sure, go on out, have fun. I'll be with you shortly."

Forgetting they were still in church, they skipped to the door, Beth grabbing the bag with their skating gear. It was part of his bribe to get his nieces to serve for him on such a gorgeous summer's day.

The TV crew packed up their equipment as efficiently as the girls had. Mike said good-bye to the readers and the cantor and slowly got his stuff together. Finally he was alone in the chapel. Taking his briefcase, he slowly, almost reluctantly, went to the door and turned off the lights.

Manny waited in the lobby, watching the girls twirl and squeal outside. Hearing Mike approach, he rose, removing his greasy straw hat.

"Thanks, Manny, you can lock up now."

"Sí, Padre," the old man said, pulling his key ring out. He nodded at the window. "Your nieces are full of life, Father."

"Yes they are. So much so, I'm glad I'm just their uncle." He hesitated. The carefully planned moment had arrived but he was curiously hesitant to proceed.

"Manny, before you go, could you let me into the bishop's office? I'm seeking some information for the Denver trip, and I need to get it before Monday." He smiled, hoping he hadn't betrayed his edginess, but the old man just shrugged and examined his key ring again.

He shuffled across the lobby, and with a clatter, opened the thick oak door to Chavez' deserted sanctum. Mike turned on the light. The room was a little dusty, but otherwise as neat as if the bishop had just stepped away from his desk for a moment, which made it seem even more desolate.

"How empty it is. I haven't been in here since Bishop Chavez resigned," Mike said. "Hard to believe it was just a month ago."

"Yes, Padre, it was very terrible," the paisano said patiently. "Do you need anything else, Señor?"

"Oh, no, nothing, Manny. I'll close it up when I'm done. Sorry to keep you — and gracias!"

The old man touched his battered headgear, muttered, "De nada," and left.

Mike glanced around the office uneasily, unsure of where to seek the secret archives. He had no clue where they would be stored — in a simple file cabinet, bank vault, or concealed behind a bookcase.

He began searching randomly, afraid to disturb the dust or leave fingerprints. The file cabinets did not seem to hold anything unusual nor did the key fit the desk's locks.

He finally located it, appropriately enough, in the closet. The repository was a sturdy-looking, three-drawer file cabinet of heavy battleship-gray steel, with a lock plate and handle that meant business, sitting unobtrusively in the far corner. Tucked in beneath Chavez' still hanging jackets, it was not otherwise hidden, nor, for that matter, even labeled.

The cabinet opened effortlessly with Mike's illicit key. He held his breath as he pulled out the middle drawer and began to riffle through the folders from front to back. There must have been dozens of them in alphabetical order, each with the name of a blameworthy priest or religious.

Unhappily, he recognized most of the names. As he half-expected, there was a fat folder with the name "*GRIEGO, ORLANDO PABLO*" on it. But it was the thin one labeled "*MALACHY, SEAN PATRICK*" that grabbed his attention. "Oh God, not you, too, Father," he whispered, feeling sick. He closed his eyes, shut the drawer, and opened the one above. There were almost as many files in the top drawer — more than fifty, Mike guessed.

The thickest was nearly an inch wide, and it was marked "*DELAVAL, THOMAS ANTOINE.*" Mike held it for a long moment, debating what he should do, torn between his promise to his bishop and a terrible curiosity that welled up within him. The answers to all his questions were probably in there.

The temptation to take the file with him was nearly overpowering. But would anyone know it was there to be missed?

In the very front of the top drawer was an ancient brown ledger book. As the canons prescribed, it contained a list of all the cases left in the archives since the foundation of the diocese of Alvarado, handwritten by all the bishops from Laretz to Chavez. DeLaval's name appeared frequently near the end.

Theft would undoubtedly be detected. Somewhat guiltily relieved, he slid the top drawer closed. "Sorry, Buddy," he muttered, "can't do it. Not even for you."

The bottom drawer held an older set of files. Most of these names Mike didn't even recognize and contained very little, usually just several sheets of thin paper. He felt less guilty about peeking at these as he picked his way through them.

Most seemed to be summaries of cases and judgments, letters to or from the Apostolic Penitentiary in Rome. This didn't faze him; he knew it wasn't a prison for erring evangelists but an ancient clerical tribunal. His Latin wasn't good enough to catch all the ecclesiastical legalisms, but he recognized some phrases such as "in res turpi" and "stuprum pueri" which indicated the corruption of altar boys and perhaps worse.

Behind one last rather thick folder branded "*URWALD, HEINRICH*" he came to the very last, even fatter, labeled "*WILSON, PHILIP PETER.*" It burned his hands even more than the others had, so he shoved it back down quickly.

But that was it. Nothing more. A wave of anguish washed over Mike. Was Chavez right? Desperately he groped beyond the metal divider at the end of the drawer. His hand came upon a bulging portfolio crammed down behind, hard to pry loose. Plain, reddish-brown, the flap was taped shut and secured by a wax seal. He hesitated briefly, feeling the weighty bundle of papers several inches thick inside. But then he saw what his erstwhile superior had scrawled above the red seal, "*For the eyes of the Holy Father alone. ☦AFC 6/16/93.*"

He set the packet down like it might explode. Nervously, he checked the old ledger again but found no mention of any special item for the Pope. Of course, Chavez would never have listed it. He closed the book gently and returned it to where it belonged.

Placing the portfolio gingerly in his briefcase, Mike carefully straightened the folders and locked the cabinet. With a final glance around or three to make sure his tracks were covered, he turned the lights off.

As he softly shut the office door, there came a banging from the front of the building. Mike nearly dropped the briefcase. Heart pounding, he turned around, desperately thinking of an excuse in case he was busted.

The pounding continued as he rounded the corner of the lobby. But it was just Marie, hot and tired. Her cousin sat next to the door pulling off her skates. As he hurried to the entrance grinning with relief, Mike checked his watch. Almost an hour had passed since Mass. Definitely time to leave.

As he opened the door he asked, "Shall we go for pizza?"

☦

CHAPTER THIRTY-ONE
Denver: Friday, August 13

STRETCHING HIS BACK for all it was worth, Bruno said, "Now everybody remember where we parked. And what we parked."

The others stumbled out of Dolores' station wagon bitching at the sweltering Colorado afternoon. It had been a long trip; they'd left Alvarado well before dawn to get here in time. Nobody had slept much the night before — making signs had gotten everyone too pumped up for the adventure ahead.

The call to demonstrate had produced little save for a sudden flurry of media attention — most victims thought them completely insane. It came back down to the core "Gang of Five" once again, but despite his efforts to enlist them, Bruno was ambivalent about associating them with this potentially stupid stunt. He sure didn't mention the .45 semiautomatic carefully tucked in the bottom of his bag "just in case."

Exiting the freeway, it had been just a brief cruise around Capitol Hill before he found a parking space behind one of the big apartment buildings he knew from his biker days. Within easy walking distance to the Civic Center and the Museum, the spot was a blessing on such a hot and cloudless day.

Cas made sure the signs were well hidden in the car, and they made their way towards the Museum disguised as turistas. Soon they ran into a trickle of people, then streams, rivers and ultimately a surging flood that sloshed around the Colorado History Museum. But this was just the high tide of the sea of humanity that filled the center of the city. Beyond the Museum, an ocean of people extended up the hill to the golden-domed state capitol building and across the wide green lawns to overflow the esplanade and porticos of the Civic Center opposite, renamed "Celebration Plaza" for the weekend.

THE HARROWING

The youth of the planet had apparently taken the Pope's invitation seriously. The vast pilgrim horde consisted mainly of spirited teenagers, in all shapes, sizes, and colors imaginable, dressed for the heat with hats, sunglasses, colorful tee-shirts, shorts and sandals, and packs with extra water bottles.

All were squeaky-clean Catholic kids on tight budgets whose faces glowed with youthful fervor. Few tattoos, colorfully-tinted hairdos, or anything pierced other than girls' earlobes were to be seen among them.

A scattering of adults shepherded them — nuns, priests baking in black, and parents basking in their offspring's zeal. Little groups, often dressed in identifying garb, greeted other clutches in a Babel of languages, excitedly hugging and swapping pictures. The concessionaires did a lively business selling fast food and cold drinks, but despite the festival atmosphere, there seemed to be few other merchants about.

"Good grief, it's a Catholic Woodstock," Cas muttered as they waded downhill past the Museum.

"More like a Nuremberg Rally," Bruno replied. So many, and so young, all radiant with health, happiness — and something else that it took him a moment to identify. A look of easy, confident self-satisfaction with the world as if they knew God had made it just for them. Beyond the invincible exuberance of adolescence, it could only be the assurance of untouched faith, Bruno realized. These kids were sharing their naïve trust in God and the Church like his generation had shared pot.

"Stay away from the yellow holy water," he said, covering his mouth with his hands to imitate a loudspeaker. "The yellow holy water is a bummer. The clear holy water is okay. Repeat: do not use the yellow holy water."

His friends laughed but Bruno still felt inexpressibly melancholy. The beautiful innocence of the young, smiling unsuspectingly at him as he passed among them, was poignant. The whole scene had an air like something out of the mythic era of the hippies, except much less odoriferous. But he felt as strange, as old beyond his years, as a scarred war veteran amidst dewy flower children.

He masked his alienation behind a big friendly smile as they strolled through the crowds, lest his curse, like the Ancient Mariner's, blight their joy.

"I'm going to search for souvenirs," Chewie announced, stopping to snap a photo of the crowd. "There's got to be a soap-pope-on-a-rope for sale around here somewhere."

"Yeah, me too," Dolores agreed. "It's nearly time for our admission," Bruno said, glancing at his watch. "Meet you up there by the entrance afterwards, around five?"

The group split up. Chewie and Dolores disappeared into the mob, while the trio slowly made their way back uphill to the Museum. Easy to spot, it was hung about with huge banners announcing "*Treasures of the Vatican*" with scowling medallions of Peter and Paul. Groups of kids lounged on the steps outside in the shadow of the building.

After confirming their tickets, Bruno bought sodas for the others. "Wonder if Mike and the girls are here yet," he said. "If they don't make the showing, there's sure not much chance of running into them in this crowd. Heard somebody say there were two hundred thousand already here and more expected."

"Jeez, where are they all staying?" Cas asked.

"Every hotel room is booked, of course," Bruno said. "I heard there are kids sleeping in parking structures, even in an empty department store downtown. The clergy are staying at the Catholic college. Every rectory, convent, and monastery within fifty miles doubtless has prelates stacked like plates."

"But aren't the kids supposed to camp out at the Mass site down at Cherry Creek Reservoir?" asked Dick.

"Tomorrow night, I think," Bruno said. "No doubt my brother will be there, too."

"Any ideas on where we're going to crash, by the way?" Dick inquired cautiously.

"Nope," Bruno said. "Interesting question. All I know is that it sure won't be at Cherry Creek." He was prickly, since all their delays had rendered hopeless his original plan to camp out in the mountains above the city.

"Relax," Cas said, squeezing Bruno's hand. "You got us here on time. Try to enjoy it. Worst case, we can always crash out on somebody's lawn like Deadheads before a concert."

Bruno's rejoinder was cut off by the announcement of the three o'clock admittance. They leapt to their feet. Still playing the paternal role, Bruno doled out the tickets. "Remember, Dick, you still owe me."

"Hey, I'm good. Just as soon as I win the suit, really, you'll be the first to know."

"Like hell," Bruno laughed loudly, and instantly clammed up again when he caught distressed glances from several young girls standing nearby. This was enough to make the trio giggle like kids themselves. They'd barely calmed down by the time they were finally let into the exhibit.

Inside, it was hard not to feel reverential. The display was large, serious, and magnificent, beginning with several gorgeous tapestries at the entrance. The air was deliciously dark and chill; all it lacked was incense. Men's voices chanted Latin softly in the background. The rooms were dimly lit but spotlights brilliantly illuminated the exhibits. People strolled slowly and quietly, murmuring comments to one another or listening intently to the walking tour on their headphones. Occasionally, kids would joke and flirt with each other.

The exhibit began with the history of St. Peter's and commemoratives of various big-name pontiffs. Beyond that, the ascendancy of the papacy in prestige and power was illustrated with examples of exquisitely wrought reliquaries, monstrances, processional crosses, and brocaded copes embroidered in gold.

At the heart of it all sat the papal regalia — several enormous bejeweled tiaras, shaped like silver and gold beehives with tiny crosses on top, and white silk ribbons hanging down behind like miniature stoles. A golden baroque throne upholstered with a tapestry of Christ giving Peter the keys to the kingdom stood nearby.

Drawn together in front of the opulent crowns, Dick whispered, "It's so lavish, it's almost idolatrous."

"Oh baby," Cas breathed. "Gimme just one of those hats and we'll call it all even."

"Sorry, but they're needed for the pope's job. Only he can wear the triple tiara, you see," Bruno pontificated. "It started with stacking crowns on a dunce's cap. A king got one coronet, an emperor two, but the pope outranks them all and so rates three. And of course, the cross on top gives him infallibly clear reception from You-Know-Who."

"How could anybody wear that?" Dick asked. "You'd have to have neck muscles like an ox."

"Must be where the stiff neck comes from," Bruno laughed. "Job must be quite the literal pain. Maybe that's why they used to carry them around in chairs back before the modern invention of the popemobile."

"You know," Cas said after a moment, "I've never been too keen on cherubs. But all those naked little boys floating around in these paintings here are starting to creep me out."

"Yeah, me too," Dick said. "Maybe we should move on."

Just then, Bruno caught a familiar voice behind him. "And this is the tiara of Pope Paul VI," Mike was saying. "The three coronets symbolize the pope's power over the Church on earth, in purgatory and in heaven. But Paul didn't wear it much and neither have his successors. After Vatican II, the pope has wanted to be seen as a pastor rather than a king."

"Or the superior of kings?" Bruno asked, stepping forward into the light where Mike was holding court with a dozen or so kids, some in Our Lady of Solitude tee-shirts. The opportunity to show up his kid brother before a captive audience was an irresistible temptation. "Howdy, bro, girls. Good to see you." he said pleasantly. He nodded at Marie and Beth, who greeted him tentatively, whispering with their friends.

Mike was obviously not thrilled to see him. "Hello, Bruno," he said cautiously, shaking his brother's hand. "Last place on Earth I thought I'd run into you."

"Well, I was in town for the weekend and decided to check out the exhibit. You know history's my thing."

"I see," said Mike, deciding not to ask for details of his activities. "What do you mean 'superior to kings?'"

"That's what it says here," Bruno said, pointing to the description on the base of the exhibit. "It says the band's inscribed '*Regum Atque Populorum Patri*:' 'To the Father of Nations and Kings.' From the coronation rite, I do believe. The line above calls him 'Supreme Governor of the World,' I think."

"And the line above that calls him the 'infallible Vicar of Jesus' which he also is," Mike said, not to be outdone.

"Very good. Wasn't aware you did Latin anymore."

"Still taught it when I was in the seminary," said Mike, recalling long nights sweating over strange grammatical terms and endless lists of word endings. "Not much need of it these days, but like the tiara, it's still there just in case."

"The papacy's never thrown any claim away, has it? Is Boniface VIII's famous declaration that 'it is necessary for the salvation of every living human person to be subject to the Roman Pontiff,' still valid?"

"If you're talking about salvation outside the Church, Vatican II declared it's entirely possible," Mike countered impatiently. "Once again, brother, you're confusing past with present. Of course, the pope had to appear, talk, and act like a king in the Middle Ages because that's all they knew."

"But why shouldn't the Holy Father be in charge?" a boy ion a tee-shirt with an image of a giant John Paul blessing the Mile High City broke in anxiously. "Jesus said he should be. He gave him the keys to heaven. Sorry, Father Mike," he concluded, apologizing for the interruption.

"That's okay, Marty," Mike said, smiling. "It's a good point. Our Lord did indeed give St. Peter the power to permit and to forbid on earth and in heaven, and that power has passed down through the centuries through good popes and yes, bad popes too. It's what makes the Holy Father infallible."

Bruno was momentarily speechless at Mike's catechismal oversimplification, but rallied quickly. "Okay, then, if the Pope has this God-given ability to choose what's good and what's bad, why doesn't he use it? I mean, really and truly use it?

"Why hasn't he excommunicated any of these perverted priests?" he demanded. "Not just boot 'em the hell out of the priesthood, but out of the Church entirely?"

Mike looked to heaven for guidance. He stepped forward, and grabbed Bruno's forearm. "Please, brother, not here," he begged quietly. "Can't you just let it rest for a little while?"

Bruno scowled. "These kids should be told that you priests aren't God," he said bitterly. "Nobody ever told me."

"I understand," Mike said patiently. "But why disparage this for them?" Bruno opened his mouth to retort, but Cas grabbed him by the other arm. "Are you nuts, Bruno?" she hissed. "Look around; do you want to get us arrested?"

The impromptu debate had already drawn a sizeable crowd through which a pair of security guards was already worming towards them. Bruno's sophistry had not won any points with the rest of the audience, either. Even Dick had forsaken him like the apostles at Gethsemane.

Sheepishly, he took a deep breath, and held up his hands. "Okay, sorry, man. Sorry I got angry. I'm cool."

"It's okay, Buddy." Bruno suddenly seemed so lost and vulnerable that Mike drew him aside. "I know you feel betrayed," he said in a low voice, glancing around. "But we priests are not all evil, no matter what you think. I shouldn't tell you this, but something will be done about this, I promise.

"The Holy Father is going to find out, this weekend. I, I've got some information to give to him that should straighten it all out."

"What information?" Bruno demanded.

"I can't tell you that." Seeing his older brother's face harden, he continued, "I don't know what it is; I promised the one who gave it to me I wouldn't look."

"Let me do it, then."

"Oh no," Mike said, realizing he'd blundered by mentioning it. "You can't imagine what kind of trouble I'd get in."

"Well, I wouldn't want to tarnish your career," Bruno said sarcastically. "Guess I was right, after all. You want to keep the secrets hidden too. What makes you think the Pope will be any different?"

Mike shook his head, trying not to recall how he'd burnt DeLaval's incriminating collection of obscenity. "No, you're wrong. Something will be done, Eddie; you'll see."

The crowd began to drift away, bored. Though the guards lingered distrustfully, it seemed they were glad to let the priest handle it peacefully.

"Okay, then," Bruno shrugged, searching for something positive to say. "Well, I'm glad you're here with Marie." he clapped Mike on the shoulder. "Enjoy the show, and that goes for you too, kids. And, and if for some reason, I don't see you later, don't think too ill of me."

"You okay, Buddy? You're not going to do anything stupid, are you?"

Bruno smiled dourly. "You know how unlikely that is."

"That you will, or won't?" Mike asked sadly. Bruno nearly replied, but changed his mind, shrugged again, and waved good-bye to Marie, who waved timidly back. He tried not to notice that she appeared as stricken with shame as the Sorrowful Mother herself as he turned and walked slowly away. He dared not glance back, nor think of what they might feel if somehow he got lucky.

"Hear that?" he whispered to Cas. "He says he's got information to give the Pope. As if that'll accomplish anything. God, I wish I could lay my hands on it."

Outside, Chewie and Dolores were waiting with Dick, the latter trying on a huge foam-rubber bishop's miter. "Can you believe it?" Chewie complained. "This is the only thing we could find anywhere. There's all kinds of official souvenirs," he continued. "But it's all the same junk. We even went down the side streets, but no luck. Man, if anyone was selling silly stuff, the cops or nuns or somebody must have run them off."

"They just don't want anybody to spoil their fun," Bruno said darkly. "Well, that's what we're here for, isn't it? Tomorrow could be one hell of a day."

"Oh yeah, can't wait to see who you're going to pick the next fight with," Dick mumbled.

†

CHAPTER THIRTY-TWO

Saturday, August 14

STEPPING BACK to examine Bruno in his fake black clergy shirt, Cas declared, "Now that's scary." From a short distance away, it did indeed appear authentic. Only a close examination of its cowboy cut and black pearl buttons betrayed its origins.

Bruno fidgeted with his homemade plastic collar biting his neck. "How do they stand these damned things?" he grumbled, removing it to attack it again with Cas' nail file. That helped; though stifling, it didn't cut into his throat as much.

"Not done yet; needs the crowning touch." He groped around in his bag, bypassing his holstered gun. Turning back around, he placed a pair of plastic devil's horns atop his head.

"You know, impersonating a priest really is excommunicable, I think," Dick said. "You better hope they're not checking IDs — Oh my God!" The others, lounging around the car in the shade, laughed too.

Striking a heroic pose, Bruno proudly held up his sign. hand-lettered by Cas with thick black medieval-looking strokes. On both sides it read *"KIDS — Beware of Pervert Priests!"*

Chewie dropped to his knees before Bruno. "Bless me, Father," he prayed, signing himself, "for I face great trials this day." He easily dodged the swat Bruno aimed at him.

They all needed a good laugh. Quickly tiring of the crowd, they'd gone to eat and spent the rest of the evening searching for a hotel out along East Colfax Avenue, but the few vacancies left charged by the hour. Exhausted, Bruno and Cas had taken turns making phone calls but eventually gave up, camping out with supplies from a convenience store at the end of a nameless, freshly-cut dirt road that would one day be in the heart of another suburb far out on the plains.

Bruno was the only one in costume for this event. After some discussion, they had decided to dress discreetly — no printed tee-shirts or buttons. Only signs would carry their message, as easy to discard as his collar and horns if necessary.

This morning they were still game, though already a bit gamy. After a decent breakfast and wash-up at a pancake house, they sat around the parking lot, waiting to go. Only Dolores seemed to be unhappy, having said or laughed little. When Cas asked, she just said she missed her little boy.

"Okay, troops, we'd better saddle up," Bruno said. "The paper says to get there plenty early because of security."

Slowly they bestirred themselves from the pleasant, grassy shade, so different from the bare, lumpy prairie they'd slept upon. They loaded themselves back into the car. Bruno once again took the wheel.

"Think you ought to drive wearing those things?" Cas asked. "Whoops, sorry, they felt so natural," he grimaced, doffing the diabolical headgear. As they headed downtown, she reminded them, "Now, remember, the idea is to avoid confrontation. Don't stop to talk to people, don't get in their way, and if they want to argue, don't respond but be respectful. Okay?"

"Gee, mom, you never let us have any fun," Dick whined.

"Don't forget to put on your sunscreen, either, kids," Bruno ordered paternally. "It's going to be hot."

The day had already warmed considerably from the early morning chill. They soon arrived at McNichols Arena, where the pope was to speak that afternoon. An army of cops directed traffic. Bruno could not believe his unbelievable luck in being ushered into one of the very first lots off the street.

"Hey, this shirt actually works," he said. "Maybe I could sneak in — wouldn't that show up Mike."

"I don't think you'd get very far," Cas said. "Even without the horns. I mean, check out all this security," she said, pointing out armed men on the roof.

Bruno parked at the far end of the lot. Opening the tailgate, they dragged out their signs as the place began to fill up with cars. Pilgrims streamed towards the arena's entrances. "Funny, I almost feel like we should say a prayer before we go," he mused.

"Not your fault, it's that collar," Chewie shrugged, matter-of-factly. "It does that to people, no?"

"How's this?" Bruno intoned piously, "Please don't let any of your precious fanatics rip us limb from limb as we miserable sinners truly deserve." "Amen!" everyone chorused. And give me a clean shot at the Pope, he thought.

"Damn, you're right, Chewie," Bruno exclaimed, picking up his sign. "It does take over." Donning his horns again, he said, "Okay, let's do it." He shouldered his sign and began marching towards the street, the others walking alongside. Cas' placard read, "*BAPTIZED, CONFIRMED, MOLESTED*"; Dick's, "*HOLY FATHER, PROTECT YOUR CHILDREN*"; Chewie's said simply "*STOP CLERGY SEXUAL ABUSE;*" while Dolores' proclaimed "*CLERGY SEXUAL ABUSE IS A SIN.*"

Cas approached the traffic cop idling at the lot's gate. "Officer, we're here to demonstrate. Where should we go?"

"Well," the mustached policeman drawled, unimpressed by the strange group. He gestured across the street. "You can march over there across from the entrance. Don't block traffic."

"Thanks, officer," Cas said. "You heard him. Let's go."

Crossing to the other side of the street across from the main entrance, they began their vigil. Under Cas' direction they spread out, signs facing the street, walking slowly back and forth along the sidewalk. Few seemed pleased to see them, though most ignored them completely. Soon the sidewalks were bustling with Catholics headed towards the dark entrance to the arena, gaping like the gates of hell, where cops in black armor scanned them with devilish metal detectors.

To keep their spirits up, Dick led the gang in a round of chanting, "Abused once, but never again!" which only increased the numbers of glares they received. They took it up again whenever a news crew came by. Dolores and Cas stepped out of line to do a brief interview with a reporter from Alvarado while the others resolutely marched back and forth behind them. Dick held his sign defiantly above his red sunburnt face for the entire world to see while Chewie discreetly hid behind his.

Naturally, most attention fell on Bruno. A tiny white-haired nun of some unidentifiable order approached him and asked politely, "Are you really a priest?" Bruno hesitated, but she said with great relief, "Oh, you're not! Thank goodness!"

"I was molested by one, ma'am," he confessed, "when I was a nine-year-old altar boy."

She handed him a white rosary made of plastic beads on a string and squeezed his hand. "I'm so sorry. Pray to Mary," she said sincerely. "Our Blessed Mother will not forget her children. And I will pray for you too."

All his snide comments evaporated in Bruno's mouth. "Thank you, Sister," he mumbled, oddly touched. He stuffed the chaplet into his back pocket.

Just then a flotilla of women religious cruised by, obviously from south of the border, one translating the signs into rapid-fire Spanish as they passed. "See that?" Dolores exclaimed when she next crossed Bruno. "They didn't even bat an eye. Don't tell me this is only a North American problem."

"Where are all the other demonstrators that were supposed to be here?" Bruno asked on the next pass. "There are only a couple of gays down at the other end."

They continued the circuit as the temperature soared. Only once did anyone try to start an argument. A bulging-eyed man far fatter than Bruno planted himself in front of Dick and demanded, "Hey, this is our event. Why are you here trying to spoil it for all these good people? How dare you criticize the Holy Father!"

"I, too, am Catholic —" Dick began hotly. Cas, right behind him, interrupted, "Sir, we're just here to march, not to debate. We mean no disrespect to anyone." She put her hand on Dick's back and propelled him past the scowling bulk. "Go join the Protestants!" he said loudly as the line behind him impelled him forward again.

Then two black-suited feds came strolling across the street. A tall, darkly handsome man accompanied by a short, redheaded woman, both suited up in black, broad-shouldered, full-length coats despite the sun.

"Good morning," the man said. "How's it going?"

"Well, it's pretty warm, especially in black, as I'm sure you know." Bruno smiled in his best nice-and-easy dealing-with-cops fashion. There was response to his attempted small talk. "Real good, sir," he continued quickly, "just peaceably assembling."

"Uh-huh." The agent's eyes were unreadable behind his shades. The woman asked, "Are you getting enough water? Sunscreen?"

"Yes, ma'am, we're taking care of ourselves," Cas said, holding up her half-empty bottle.

The man touched his earphone, and then spoke briefly into a lapel mike. "Keep moving, and stay on this side of the street," he ordered them. "Let's go, Dana."

"Yes sir!" Bruno said, glancing wide-eyed at Cas as the pair strode off. They resumed pacing. The crowds started to thin as the long processions wound their way through the carefully watched mouths into the belly of the arena. Finally the dark maw swallowed the laggard tail of the snaking line.

Chewie wearily dropped his sign. "Hey, can we stop now? Everybody's gone!" By this time, only a few latecomers were left hurrying in from the most distant parking lots.

"You bet," said Dick, "Let's go."

With aching feet, they plodded back past the cops hanging out at the entrance to the parking lot. The car seemed miles more distant than when they had arrived.

"Oh man, are my dogs sore," Dick whined, leaning against its side. "I'm tired, hot, hungry, and thirsty too," added Chewie. "I sure wish we had a hotel with a swimming pool to go back to. Let's at least go find a nice, dark bar."

Bruno opened the back of the station wagon and threw his sign in disgustedly. Roasting in his black outfit, he jerked the makeshift tab out and unbuttoned his collar. The relief was so profound that he continued with his shirt.

"Sounds great, but we should at least wait until the Pope gets here," he said, checking his watch. It was a quarter to four. "Any minute now." He pulled a clean tee-shirt out of his bag.

"What do you want to do, moon him?" Dick asked.

Bruno laughed. "Who's to stop us?"

"Oh, just the police, Secret Service, FBI, and Swiss Guards," Cas said tiredly, plopping down on the tailgate, "to start with."

Bruno glanced around. There was a cop at the far entrance to the lot, several more gathered in the nearby street intersections, and one visible on the arena's roof. "All they could do is shoot us," he muttered, shrugging. "Big deal.

"Now," he declared, climbing into the car. "I'm changing into my shorts. Don't anyone peek."

"You wouldn't say that if you didn't really want us to," Dick said. "But I'm not about to fall for it." He giggled. "Hey, you weren't kidding about those angel wing tattoos!"

Bruno quickly put on the shirt. As he stripped off the black pants, he noticed that suddenly the traffic noises had become muted like birds quieting down before the onset of a storm. He glanced around. Indeed all movement had stopped — police cars blocked every intersection. In the distance the heavy, rhythmic sound of big helicopters coming towards them could be heard.

"Hey, look, here he comes," Chewie said, pointing west.

Bruno slid out, pulling up his shorts. Only fifty feet above the ground, two huge green and white helicopters flew directly towards them like monsters of the Apocalypse. I'll be damned, Bruno thought, it's a chance. A real chance at last.

Everyone watched the choppers grow larger. "Wouldn't you love to have a bazooka right now?" Dolores asked petulantly. Bruno silently put his hand in his bag. He touched the rough grip of his .45, waiting in its holster. This is it, he thought, undoing the snap, heart thudding louder than the whirling blades. Take out the pilot or a rotor at this low altitude and the crippled copter would crash. No one could stop him.

Time seemed to slow down as he stood in an agony of indecision. He could feel the cold, demanding steel of the Colt Commander as his finger slowly curled around the trigger, thumb on the safety, ready to erupt, blazing death.

The dust began to fly around them in slow motion as he peered at his friends, all laughing and staring. Cas, standing beside him, was watching him with a puzzled expression. Her hand reached out infinitely slowly and softly touched his arm as it trembled with indecision.

That ended it. He let go and slammed the gate shut. Time unexpectedly sped up again.

"Hey, Dick, great idea!" Bruno shouted above the whooshing of the great whirling blades. The helicopters were almost directly above, tiny faces peering out of the windows.

There was a crazy grin across his face as he turned his back on the choppers, already slowing for their landing beyond the stadium. In one quick gesture, he dropped both short pants and underwear and stuck his bare, pink buttocks high in the air. "Kiss my ass, Daddy-o!" he howled.

Waving signs, the others jumped about shouting but he couldn't hear them.

A hot blast of wind smelling of oil and exhaust beat down on them as the first aircraft overshadowed them, then from the second which bowled Cas and Dick over. The machines disappeared behind the arena. Dust swirled around as they picked themselves up and gathered the scattered signs, laughing hysterically.

"Come on, let's get the hell out of here!" Bruno shouted as he hiked up his britches. They piled noisily into the car. Since nobody had shot them after all, he wanted to peel out and get as far away as possible. It required all of Cas' urging to quiet them down before he dared start the car.

As sedately as he could manage, he slowly drove past the totally bored and indifferent cops. Instead of taking Colfax back east, however, he got on the interstate. He felt a need to speed, and as soon as they were safely on the freeway, they began whooping like madmen.

They'd done it, protested in front of thousands. Even better; if not actually offing the old geezer, he had publicly mooned the Pope. And somehow gotten away with it scot-free.

†

CHAPTER THIRTY-THREE

*World Youth Day, Feast of the Assumption of Mary,
Sunday, August 15*

BOB CRUZ exclaimed, "Ah, so there you are." Mike squinted up into the golden sunlight, surprised to see the chancellor, especially this early in the morning. His heart jumped in hope; maybe this was the good news he'd been praying for.

"Looked everywhere for you," Cruz continued. He sat down on the other side of the picnic table, and sipped from a large, steaming plastic cup. Mike patiently folded up the morning's paper, and shoved it aside, picking up his own coffee.

Cruz studied his friend. Usually sunny in the early hours, Mike appeared exhausted, his normally well-groomed hair pointing in random directions. "Boy, it's almost chilly this morning, isn't it?" Cruz said cheerfully. "Did you sleep well?"

"No, of course not." Mike rubbed his face. "It was the world's biggest slumber party, just like the night before. The kids gabbed almost until dawn. The air mattress leaked; I'll sure be glad to see my own bed again in my peaceful rectory."

Cruz laughed. "Well, my evening was a little bit similar. Lots and lots of talking but I dare say I got to sleep earlier though the cot I had wasn't much softer than concrete either. So how'd it go otherwise?"

Mike grimaced. "The hike to Cherry Creek here was long, hot and tiring, but the kids kept their spirits up pretty well. Thank God our people were prepared — I didn't hear of any cases of heatstroke or dehydration. One boy from Queen of Peace sprained his ankle but the last time I saw him, he was being nursed by some girls, having a pretty good time."

He paused. "Mike, I —" Cruz began, but halted suddenly as Marie, Beth and several other kids approached the picnic table with their breakfast trays from the yellow-arched franchise. Seeing the other priest there, they hesitated.

"Good morning," he said, smiling. "Good morning, Father Cruz," they chorused back respectfully. He held up his hands. "Sorry, kids, I need to talk to Father Mike alone now."

Dejectedly they hunted a table nearby. Marie glanced back over her shoulder with concern.

Cruz waited until they'd seated themselves, blowing softly on his coffee. "Well, bad news, Michael," he said in a low voice at last. "You don't get to meet John Paul. Not at this time, anyway."

Mike nodded passively. "I knew that the moment you chased the girls away." He shrugged. "Just as well — I'm totally unpresentable. I couldn't even find my favorite shirt when I was packing. I can wait until the audiences after Mass." He sighed and gazed at Cruz, who sat there frowning and stroking his mustache. "What else?" he demanded. "That scowl tells me there's more."

"Oh, it does?" Cruz shook his head. "I guess you know me too well. You see, I mean, really not at this time." He sighed and set his cup down.

"I heard a story yesterday from an assistant to one of the bishops who flew in with the Holy Father to McNichols," he began slowly. "Seems that just before landing, they were mooned by a protestor in the parking lot. Thank God that the media didn't catch it, or there'd be a real hullabaloo."

"Protestor?" Mike asked weakly, certain he knew who.

"Yes, I'm afraid so," Cruz replied. "It was indeed your brother. He, my cousin, and several others were there demonstrating — I saw them on the news last night." He hesitated. "Might as well hear it all from a friend, Mike, but Bruno was wearing both a Roman collar and devil's horns. He carried a sign that said something about 'perverted priests.'"

"Christ Almighty!" Mike said harshly, loudly enough that the kids at the tables around them noticed. Clenching his fists, he glared at the heavens but the Lord was nowhere to be seen.

"Apparently," Cruz went on softly, "some senior members of the papal entourage were not amused."

"He saw? The Pope saw my brother's naked butt?"

Despite himself, Cruz smiled. "Supposedly close enough to personally bless, or as my source put it, asperge."

Mike flopped forward in shame, burying his face in his arms. "So that's it," he moaned, voice muffled. "You mean I don't get to meet him, ever."

"No, just not now," Cruz said softly, placing a hand on Mike's arm. "I'm sorry, Mike, I truly am. But Bruno created quite an uproar among the hierarchy. Many of the bishops I've run into here have asked me about him — they've heard or seen the news stories and they're curious.

"Nobody blames you. I've got a relative that I'm ashamed of, too, you know — even Jesus was embarrassed by his own family. But I thought that it would be in your best interests, and the Diocese's, if you weren't presented to His Holiness just yet. Why associate your name with such unpleasantness?"

"You blackballed me?" Mike asked indignantly, straightening up in disbelief.

"I wouldn't put it that way," Cruz hedged uncomfortably, "but the Camerlengo himself asked me, so what could I say?"

"Yet you met the Holy Father."

"Well, yes, I was presented to him briefly after my meetings with the nuncio and the others. But it wasn't much — just a handshake. I didn't even get a picture out of it."

"Oh well, in that case," Mike said resentfully, staring off towards the reservoir dam. "Isn't there anything you can do? Slip me in somehow? Please? It means a lot."

The chancellor's silence was answer enough.

"I can't tell you how much I was really looking forward to actually meeting him. I even brought a present —" Mike stopped suddenly, his pursed lips biting off his words.

"A present? Well, arrangements could be made to pass it to one of his aides," Cruz said. No response. "Even if you handed it to him directly in person he'd just give it to someone else to deal with." He paused again. "What was it, anyway?"

Mike dismissed it with a grimace. "Never mind. Doesn't matter now."

"I'm sorry, Mike. I'll try to make this up to you somehow. With the situation as strained as it already is, I really felt I had to make the call."

Mike sighed heavily. "It's okay, Bob. I do understand. I don't blame you," he said. "Bruno, on the other hand...

"All my life he's interfered, trying to prove he's better than me. Even at the Vatican exhibit he tried to start an argument! He's constantly trying to save me from myself — like I'm the one getting into trouble and not him."

Cruz shook his head sympathetically, letting Mike rant, but he was already running out of steam. "Sorry, Bob," Mike sighed at last. "It's just so frustrating. He's like a millstone around my neck. I try to be patient, I'm always praying for him, but he just gets worse. He only gets worse."

"It's the cross you must bear, old friend."

Behind Cruz came the sound of someone loudly clearing her throat. They glanced up to see Marie standing behind the chancellor, nervously twisting her fingers together.

"I'm sorry to interrupt, Father Cruz," she said, stepping forward next to Mike, "but I couldn't help overhearing. Uncle Mike, did Dad — did my father get you in trouble?"

Mike sighed, and patted the bench. The redhead sat down timidly, and Mike put his hand lightly on hers. "Yeah, a little bit, I guess. Don't worry, kitten, it'll all work out."

Marie shook her head. "I could see it upset you when he started talking crazy in the museum like that. I try to pretend like it doesn't matter, but he's really embarrassing. Sometimes I get scared that he's going to hurt someone."

"Well, me too, actually, princess. I don't think his new bunch of friends are any help."

"Yeah, they're pretty weird, too, especially that goth chick." She paused. "Has he — Dad — always been like that?"

Mike nodded glumly. "Since we were kids. He was always pretty wild but good-hearted. He mainly beat up on bullies."

They chuckled. "But since he got these so-called 'memories' back, he's really changed," Mike said seriously. "He's so sullen and bitter now. There's no way I can reach him."

Marie searched his face earnestly. "There's only so much you can do, Uncle Mike," she blurted. "He should be proud of you. I know I am. Sometimes, I, I really wish you were my father instead."

She suddenly flushed as scarlet as her hair and she hugged him tightly for a moment.

"Well," Mike said, flustered. "thanks, I guess."

She stood up hurriedly but her uncle reached out to prevent her fleeing. "You're a good kid, Marie. If I had a daughter, I'd want her to be just like you." He smiled reassurance. "Why don't you start getting the rest of them ready? We should be all packed so we can leave right after the Mass."

"Sure, Uncle Mike, of course," she said in almost a whisper, backing up quickly, still self-conscious.

"You're a very lucky man to have such a caring niece," Cruz said. "Count your blessings, Mike."

"She does make up for her dad a bit," Mike agreed. He shook his head and rose. "Well, what now, boss?" he asked with only a trace of sarcasm as he stretched his back.

"Me, I've got to get back to the school and make sure our colleagues make it over here in time. Then yet even more discussions afterwards, no doubt. You have no idea how much ecclesiastical ass I've had to kiss this weekend. I envy you — I'd love to duck out and go home too."

"Ah, the price of greatness," Mike said sardonically. "Don't look here for sympathy."

"I guess I deserved that." Cruz stood up. "Listen, take care of yourself," he said. "I'll see you when we get back into town." They went off to locate their charges.

† † †

MEANWHILE, the shadows shortened as the sun crawled above the plains. The clouds building over the Front Range of the Rockies promised little relief from the heat as Thomas DeLaval plopped down in another concession area near the Cherry Creek Reservoir with a groan. He doffed his straw hat and mopped his brow, yearning for a tall, iced drink. Even a nonalcoholic one.

Around him the swirling throng of teens drifted off towards the Mass site but the monsignor showed no interest. He had much more important things to concentrate on.

THE HARROWING

At first DeLaval had enjoyed being able to walk about openly in his Roman collar once again after months traveling incognito, basking in the respectful greetings of all the lovely boys and girls he encountered. There was something wonderfully tonic about the normalcy of it; he could almost imagine that he was not a hunted animal. Yet even as he enjoyed the parade of beautiful youth, his eyes constantly probed the recesses of the crowds, uneasily peering about for faces that might recognize his.

Ah, but all this opportune young flesh! Many young people who had come together for the love of Christ this weekend were ecstatic to find so many congenial companions. With the ease that divine and human love commingled at such tender ages, the chaperones would surely be hard put these sultry summer nights if baptisms of many little John Pauls and Marys next summer were to be avoided.

DeLaval smiled benignly as another happy couple, gawkily holding hands, strolled by. He wiped his round face once again, still not used to his coarse beard. He was sweating like a parched pig but felt safest brazening it out openly in his black monkey suit. Who on earth would expect him to dare? Now if only he could be sure he was at the right place.

His anxieties were immediately answered. "Mind if I join you?" came a thin, well-known, Italian-accented voice from behind him.

He sprang to his feet. "Luminence! You startled me!"

The Grand Master cackled evilly. The old man was decked out in a bright Hawaiian shirt, big straw hat, and thick wraparound sunglasses, leaning on an ebony cane.

"Sit down, no titles, please — Order or otherwise. No names, either. One can never be too careful in a public place."

DeLaval glanced about warily, but nobody seemed to be paying them attention. He sat down again as the skinny old man perched vulture-like on the bench opposite him, and removed his shades. His rheumy blue eyes glistened maliciously. His smile was equally cold and cruel.

"Good to see you again, sir, so soon," DeLaval began.

The supreme head of the Black Order irritably dismissed the formalities. "Forget the flattery. This heat is worse than Rome's. Do you want to talk seriously or not?"

DeLaval swallowed and nodded. "Of course, Em — sir."

"So, what have you been up to?"

"As you suggested, I've been visiting those groups you were interested in, as well as old allies. I must say your word opened many doors." His master's glare did not soften.

"Good. You may have to stay underground," the Grand Master said. "While your place has been severely compromised by your indiscretions, your ties to your old rival's demise —"

"Are unprovable, I assure you —"

"Don't interrupt."

DeLaval bit his lower lip.

"As I was going to say, matter naught to us. You're clever; not the best teacher, but you could be useful in some agreeable haven elsewhere, even if you may not return to Alvarado. If, that is, you have not endangered the Book or the Cross."

This did not surprise DeLaval. "Fear not, lord. They are safe but currently unavailable, even to me. But I trust I should remain their custodian. Not only should I have inherited the *Codex*, I took it only to keep it from being revealed."

"Oh, so you've a right to it, do you?" the old man asked mockingly. "What else do you have a right to? Magistracy of the Alvarado chapter, perhaps?"

DeLaval was sweating profusely. He swallowed hard. This could go very wrong.

"Never, lord," he lied most sincerely. "I've worked hard to keep everything safely hidden — even now, with all the scandal and publicity, the Order is unknown. Our secret devotions to the Dread Lord and Lady remain concealed."

DeLaval shut his mouth, suddenly fearful.

The Grand Master said harshly, "Yet you would dare set yourself up without our blessing. For that you had to be punished. But mindful of your great devotion, we were merciful, which is why we allowed you to be forewarned."

DeLaval's stomach dropped. So the old man himself was involved? The Great Council's tentacles stretched further and deeper than even he'd thought possible. "Sire, I was only preparing for the day when the chapter could be restored, but allow me to demonstrate my loyalty yet again. Last night at the hotel, I learned that certain information is to be delivered personally to the Pope today, which could reveal all our operations in Alvarado. I intend to intercept it." And enhance my power, he thought. "Fittingly," he couldn't resist boasting, "this will be accomplished by means of the very minion who figured in Xaphon — er, my enemy's overthrow."

"Interesting." The old man tapped his cane.

"This information should allow me to return to Alvarado in safety. With it as leverage, I can then rebuild the Order there even stronger than before. Our grip will be unassailable."

DeLaval knew he had him then. "If so," the old man scowled, "you may come out quite well, but I warn you that I judge by the old rules. You wish to fight for the province: so be it. Compromise our secrets, or lose to your challenger, though, and you'll find I'm still as pitiless as Our Dread Lord."

"When shall the trial be?" DeLaval asked uneasily. "At the Chapel in Alvarado on All Hallows as is traditional?"

The Grand Master snickered evilly, bouncing his cane. "If so, we'll be meeting in a vacant lot," he sneered. "You're not quite as well-informed as I thought. Did you not know that the cathedral is to be demolished by then? After due consideration, I have chosen the Feast of the Thirteenth as the best time to settle this dispute."

Taken aback, DeLaval swallowed again, despite his desert-dry mouth. "As you will, lord. I'll be ready by then."

"You had better be," the old man said as he stood. "I'll expect full details of your efforts to secure that leak. Now, however, I've several more meetings to attend. This event has been an excellent occasion for many diverse parties to come together."

He smiled with malign irony. "I must remember to personally thank the Holy Father when we get back to Rome."

✝

CHAPTER THIRTY-FOUR

BRUNO couldn't keep from bragging as they hiked. "Compared to yesterday, this is bound to be an anticlimax," he said. "Mooning the Pope! You guys should've joined in. If only a TV camera had been there."

"Then you'd be in jail right now," Cas countered disgustedly. "And we'd have been thrown in with you."

"Hell, they couldn't do nothing to us," Chewie boasted with a cholo swagger. "This is America. We got freedom of speech, ain't that right, dude?"

"Don't count on it," Dick said. "Maybe there's no law against exposing one's buns to the view of foreign heads of state, but if the crowd had seen you, it would've been our asses for sure. You're nuts, man."

"I still wish we had a bazooka," Dolores said wistfully. "I'd love to blow those pompous hypocrites out of the air."

"Careful what you ask for," muttered Bruno under his breath. A bit more loudly, he said, "Ah, we're getting somewhere at last."

It had taken them hours at an amusement park to settle down after the papal exposition. But they'd wound up once again without a pillow for their heads. Ultimately they located another vacant lot a few miles from Cherry Creek State Park and passed the night even more uncomfortably than before.

It turned out they weren't allowed to park much closer than that anyway. Already they'd hiked towards the entrance of the park in the early morning air for at least a half-hour.

The crowd thickened, pooling in front of the park gates. Once inside, a deputy mounted on horseback unexpectedly barred their way. "Where d'ya think you're going with them signs?" he demanded with the arrogance natural to a man commanding a quarter-ton of muscular flesh between his legs.

Cas went into her routine. "We're here to peacefully demonstrate, sir. Just tell us where we can go."

The cowboy cop stared down at them as if they were completely insane. "What do you intend to do with those?"

"Just hold them up. Quietly."

"Uh-huh." He thought for a long moment. "Well, I can't let you go down there. They could tear you apart."

"See?" Dick hissed. "Just wait," Bruno replied.

"Sir, perhaps there's some designated area we could go to?" Cas asked politely.

"Well, hold on, little lady, I'll check," he said, pulling out his radio. Several loud but unintelligible minutes of static-filled jargon later, he stuck it back in its holster.

"Here's the deal. There's a corral for demonstrators on the far side of the park, near the southern entrance. That's where you're gonna have to go."

He held up his hand to stifle any objection. "Now, I'll let you go across the park to that area rather than make you walk the long way around. But you're not to stop between here and there or carry your signs down into the Mass area. If you do, you will be removed from the site and arrested for disturbing the peace, pronto. Comprende?"

"Yes sir," Cas said, as everyone nodded vigorously. "Can we hold the signs up on the way?"

He thought a moment then said, "Okay — but keep it quiet. We'll be watching you."

"Thank you, sir. I'm relieved that you will be," Cas said as the man wheeled his steed out of their way.

It soon became apparent why the cop was so concerned. The density of the crowd closely approached a mall on Christmas Eve but with even less forbearance. Their muttered comments were much easier to overhear; some of the kids got quite vocal. One girl followed them loudly wondering why they didn't protest "bad dads and stepdads" instead of the holy fathers until her friends led her away.

By now they'd crested a small hill and away down below them, nestled in an immense grassy bowl next to the shrunken waters of the reservoir, stood the Mass site, already swarming with hundreds of thousands of humans.

Behind the hordes, the bare earthen dam rose like a backdrop to the vast stage. Bleachers for bishops and musicians flanked the altar, which was no larger than an aspirin at this distance. Beyond sat the dais with the papal throne. A swooping white pavilion that vaguely appeared like an enormous miter overshadowed everything.

On either side of the huge sunshade, hung giant swathes of fabric emblazoned with the official logo. Beside them stood enough racks of giant TV screens and speakers for a major rock concert. The far sides of the field were lined with rows of portable toilets while near them at the top of the hill were even more rows of potties and vendor booths.

Despite themselves, Bruno and the others gawked, amazed at the vista. Behind them the crowd continued to overflow the top, flowing down into a boiling caldron of over a half million human beings. They kept coming, young and old, people pushing wheelchairs or baby carriages or on crutches.

"Wow, Cas, you were right; it's a Catholic Woodstock," Bruno marveled.

"No, I was way too optimistic: it's more like Dante's Inferno," she countered.

Just then a cop behind them interrupted, "Hey, you, move along there!" So like Jesus on the way to Calvary, they picked up their burdens and continued to march in the direction indicated by the secular authority. This turned out to be along the ridge to the other entrance. Every time they slowed, there seemed to be some cop waiting to urge them on again.

The second time this happened, Bruno noticed someone was missing. "Hey, Dick, why do you have two signs? Where's Chewie?"

Sure enough, Dick was bravely carrying both his and the other's signs. Chewie himself was nowhere to be seen.

"He said he wanted to go take some pictures of the crowd," Dick replied helpfully.

"Damn it," Bruno cursed. "We've got to keep together. We'll never be able to find him."

"Relax," Dolores said unconcernedly. "He knows where we're supposed to go. He'll find us. He better — I gave him the keys."

"You what?" Bruno barked.

"Yeah, he told me he would go and wait in the car if we got separated. Maybe he was afraid we'd leave him," she said lightly. This in no way reassured Bruno, but there was nothing to do except swear uselessly.

Eventually they arrived at the holding pen. It was set twenty yards from another path into the park which was fairly deserted this close to show time. Hidden behind a low rise, the corral was completely invisible from the Mass site.

The protest area was a bare acre of land surrounded by a tall chain-link fence. Inside were four plastic potties, three atheists with free literature, two bearded men holding a banner calling the Pope the Antichrist, and a trash bin.

"This really sucks," complained Bruno. "What the hell are we supposed to do now?"

"Maybe we can get nearer once Mass starts," Dick optimistically suggested.

Suddenly there was the same rhythmic, deep-bass, whooshing noise they had heard the day before. The two giant green-and-white helicopters appeared overhead, circling the field beyond the hill counterclockwise, once, again, three times. Below the crowd screamed out its welcome, a howl more befitting the flashy arrival of a different King than the Vicar of Christ and Sovereign of the Holy See. A roar that made their hair rise.

"Good Lord," Dick swore. "Did he bring Elvis with him?"

Bruno glanced quickly around. Once again, a deserted spot — he caught Cas watching him. "What?" he demanded with a wicked grin. "I was just thinking. Don't worry — I know I've already stretched my luck this trip."

"No doubt," she agreed, smiling. "Let's shake the dust off our feet and go before something really bad happens."

"Fine with me, too," Dolores said disgustedly. "I've just about had all I can take of these people."

"Well, we've done what little we could," Bruno said. He crunched up his sign and threw it into the trashcan. "Might as well leave this crap here."

The others joined in. Bruno gratefully undid his collar and broke the band holding the horns, and chucked them too.

The ceremony had just commenced by the time they climbed back up the hill overlooking the Mass site. John Paul II's severe visage, strained from the heat and pace of the last several days, scowled down from the giant TV screens while the choirs sang vigorously.

"Hey, let's check out the vendors before we leave," Bruno suddenly suggested.

Cas gazed at him curiously. "I thought you didn't want any souvenirs, Bruno. You switching again?" He ignored her.

"Yeah, I'd like to look for souvenirs one last time too. Won't get another chance, you know," Dick said.

After availing themselves of the facilities, they wandered down the long line of booths selling World Youth Day junk, still at outrageous prices, even as Mass progressed. "I guess we'd have to wait until after the show to get any good deals," Bruno commented. His girlfriend made no reply but grabbed his arm tightly with a gasp.

"Ow, honey, what is it?"

Cas stared past him into the vast swarm of human bodies. She was white as a sheet, as if she'd seen a ghost.

"Oh hell, it's him! DeLaval!" she whispered.

"And what the hell's my brother doing there?" Bruno added. A mere dozen yards separated them from the priests.

† † †

THOMAS DELAVAL rumbled, "Ah, it's good to see you again, Michael." The younger priest spun around. He'd been standing at the end of the concession booths as the note asked, peering around, but the monsignor still managed to sneak up on him.

Being on the run had somehow been good for the old man. In the few months since he'd last seen him, DeLaval had grown a grizzled beard, tanned, and lost weight. But his gray eyes were still as cold and intent as ever.

"So this is your doing," Mike said, waving the slip of paper he had been handed by a boy shortly after arriving. "What do you want? Come to give me 'important information'?"

The older priest smiled darkly. "Oh no, my young friend. I've not come to impart information, but to take it."

Mike reflexively tightened his grip on his pack's shoulder strap and stepped backwards. He shook his head. "No way. This is for the Holy Father, not for a serpent like you."

DeLaval chuckled. "You wound me, Mike. Am I so bad you won't even hear my side of it?"

He stepped closer and his voice dropped. "I had high hopes for you, boy. Still do. I can help your career, you know, get you the best appointments, prestige. And more." He spread his arms wide at the surrounding sea of perfect young bodies. "You could have pleasures and power you cannot dream of."

Mike shook his head, continuing to back away. "Oh, no. I've seen your damnable pleasures and I want no part of them. And besides, without Chavez, you have no power. You're finished, old man."

"Not quite yet," DeLaval said, smiling. Mike followed his glance. Bruno in black was running full tilt towards them.

"Here comes my brother now. You better leave if you don't want to get hurt."

"Thanks for your concern." DeLaval laughed, a harsh, full-bodied, dangerous laugh deep as thunder. "I'm afraid you've earned a little demonstration of what I can do, Mike, for having spoiled my last surprise. Let this be a lesson to you and don't get in my way again."

He turned calmly to face Bruno who skidded to a halt, panting, face red and strained.

Mike said, "Buddy, am I glad to see you!"

By now a ring of spectators were gathering. The Mass proceeded with readings in various languages in the background, but around the three men there fell a strange stillness.

"Eddie, be silent!" DeLaval barked at Bruno. "Kazideel, come forth and obey! Baalberith commands!" Bruno recoiled as if whipped.

Mike stepped forward. "Leave him alone! What are —" His question suddenly ended as Bruno growled speechlessly, punching Mike once in the gut, hard. The priest doubled over in agony and fell to the ground. Through the ringing in his ears, he could hear DeLaval. "Very good, Kazideel. Now get me that package."

Hands roughly tore open his backpack, and removed the carefully wrapped bundle within.

Other voices grew loud and angry, appalled that a priest was apparently being beaten and robbed by another. Mike looked up as a Texas high school football squad finally intervened. The skinheads vigorously pounded the old hippie, who offered little resistance. DeLaval was nowhere to be seen.

"No," Mike croaked, stumbling to his feet. "Stop it!" With the help of several others, he managed to pull his brother, bloody and confused, out of the fray as Dolores and Dick came up with Cas in tow.

"Bruno, let's go to the first-aid station," Dick admonished, but Bruno shook his head, sending more streams of blood dribbling down his fingers. Dolores helped him stand, brushing the dirt off his back.

Cas was close behind them, trembling like a trapped animal. She grabbed his arm with a grip of iron. "We must get out of here," she insisted. "Right now." She glanced at Mike. Still bent over, he gasped, "Go, quick, before the cops arrive."

"Let's go," Dick said, taking Bruno's other arm.

Bruno didn't argue as they began the long march out. They paused only to grab some paper towels for his nose from a concession stand. Though broiling now even by desert dweller standards, Cas, pale but determined, set an unrelenting pace.

Their legs were already sore, slowing them down. It took at least a mile of trudging before they could no longer hear the massed choirs or the announcer prating behind.

Finally the bedraggled group exited the park and headed ever more slowly towards their distant parking spot.

"Hope to God we don't have to wait for Chewie," Bruno grumbled. "Traffic's going to be an absolute nightmare."

"Well, better start thanking Him, dude, because I think we've just been saved," Dick exclaimed. He clapped Bruno on the back and whistled loudly. Chewie was slowly driving Dolores' station wagon towards them, waving back wildly and honking.

"It's a miracle!" Cas said, hugging Chewie hard through the window as soon as he pulled up. "I was afraid he got you too. What happened?"

"The crowd freaked me out," Chewie admitted downheartedly, "so I thought I should get the car so we could leave pronto. Afraid who got me? Hey, what happened to you, vato?"

Bruno, still bleeding, silently climbed into the car.

"Get out of Denver, baby, go! Go!" Dick crooned.

"Go west, young man," suggested Dolores. "The interstate's undoubtedly already bumper-to-bumper."

"Sí, señora," Chewie said, and soon they were headed towards the cool, green slopes of the Rockies. Already dark clouds churned over them, threatening a thorough drenching later on. There was little traffic behind them — most of it was on the other side of the highway, people returning to the Mile High City from God's country.

Cas was silent, pale and more doleful even than Dolores, but the others wanted to hear more about the event they had just escaped. Dick fiddled with the radio until he found a live broadcast from the Mass, only now slowly winding to an end.

"Hospitals and first-aid tents are being overwhelmed by the numbers of people needing attention. We're told there are well over ten thousand already overcome by the heat.

"Paramedics and volunteers are using whatever they can to carry people out — stretchers, sleeping bags or just their own hands. The crowd has even blocked emergency vehicles. One reporter said he saw ambulance drivers pleading with a line of priests serving Communion to move aside.

"If Pope John Paul wanted to see the 'culture of death' he decries, he only need come down into this crowd of his faithful followers. As one boy told me, 'Everybody's fainting down front — they're passing out like flies.' There've been no reports of fatalities yet; let's hope it stays that way. Back to you, Dave."

Chewie cut it off right there. "¿Quién sabe, did we get out of there just in time or what, compañeros?"

"If nothing else," Dick said with some pride, "we have accomplished a great Catholic ambition today — we were the very first people out of the parking lot after church."

"Amen to that, brother," agreed Bruno, dabbing his nose.

"No thanks to you, pal," Dick said. "You could've gotten us all killed."

Dolores said nothing. Cas just stared at the mountains ahead with a haunted, unseeing gaze.

☦

CHAPTER THIRTY-FIVE

Alvarado: Tuesday, August 17

BRUNO sat stiffly in the psychiatric facility's waiting room, staring blankly at the pastel canvas hung on the opposite wall. It was an abstract, maybe, or a Southwestern landscape of mesas and gorges, or both. Not that it mattered — the piece performed its function admirably as a soothing, gentle distraction like the canned music in the background of this antechamber to purgatory.

This softly-carpeted, bright place had little in common with the dark, cramped hardwood halls of that sanitarium, he told himself. This was not like that other place, the gloomy asylum where they had tortured his mother with electricity.

Perhaps his unease was from a suspicion that he should be confined here as well.

He shook himself from such dark thoughts and resolved to increase his antidepressants immediately. His funk had steadily grown since the end of the Mass. He could not figure out what had happened there. Some kind of fight, obviously — he still ached all over — yet now none of his friends would talk to him. Except poor Cas.

And she was locked up here. Because it was safe, and at her own request, but still locked up. Once back in town, she'd calmly demanded that he bring her immediately as soon as they'd finally said good-bye to the others.

At first Bruno did not understand. She'd been so quiet during the whole drive home that he'd thought she'd been peacefully asleep.

"I need to go to the hospital," she'd said flatly. "Now."

"Why, dear?" he'd sputtered. "You seem fine."

She'd silently rolled up the sleeve on her left arm, scored with dozens of neat slices from her fingernails, the most recent still oozing blood. One glance into the glacially blue depths of her eyes and he drove her straight to the nuthouse.

It was little reassurance that the hospital staff knew her like she was a regular. They'd whisked her away, asked him a few questions, gave him a bandage and some aspirin, and told him to go home. There, despite his aches, he fell asleep quickly, but not restfully.

Now he was back, sitting alone. All the others in the waiting room had been finally let in to visit their own unhappy kin, and still he waited.

He was little surprised, then, when a young, thin blonde in starched lab coat came out and briskly introduced herself. "Mr. Nolan, I'm Dr. Oretsky, Casandra's therapist," she said, holding out her hand as he rose to his feet automatically. He noticed her glancing at his black eye, but she said nothing.

The handshake, like everything about her, was pure business. "I understand you're quite a good friend of hers."

"Well, yes, I hope so. How is she?"

"You can see for yourself." She smiled. "I just wanted to talk to you for a moment before you went in. Please, sit."

Bruno lowered himself back down onto the edge of the seat as she lightly sat in the chair opposite. "How can I help?"

"Can you tell me anything about what caused this latest episode? I've never seen her triggered quite this badly before. It's a good thing you brought her in when you did."

"Well, she was rather insistent," Bruno said with a shrug.

"Yes, but you did the right thing. As you did passing that information to me through Dr. Blackstone about that particular alter. It saved Cas and I a lot of trouble."

"Oh, yeah." He'd somehow managed to completely forget all about that.

"But I didn't come out just to thank you," she continued. "So you were with her when she saw Monsignor DeLaval?"

"Me and about half a million other people. I'm not sure what happened, actually. It was all over so fast."

"Did he see her? Did he say anything to her?"

"I really don't think he was that close. I'm a little fuzzy about it — apparently he attacked me. Afterwards she seemed frightened but said little. She seemed withdrawn on the way home but there wasn't any obvious switching. Why do you ask?"

"I hope I'm not betraying her confidence, but I know she doesn't talk to her family, and that you two have become, well, involved," Oretsky said. Bruno nodded, blushing slightly.

"Casandra's been quite a handful this time. We medicated her, of course, but she keeps switching to alters that resist sedation. Most seem bent on her own destruction.

"I'm afraid to give her anything more, in case she triggers a personality who is hypersensitive or allergic to the drugs, which could kill her either way. We dare not restrain her so she's had to spend a lot of time under watch in the safe room. I think we've managed to calm her at last. Hopefully, she'll get to sleep soon."

"My God," Bruno breathed in horror. "I had no idea."

The doctor nodded sadly. "Oh yes. Often multiples have personalities as different physiologically as psychologically, with different tolerances to pain, allergies, even visual acuity and eye color. I have one client whose host is stone deaf although his child alters hear perfectly well."

Bruno felt even glummer. "So what should I do?"

"Just what you're here for — see her, support her. You are, after all, the only one she will allow us to let in." She stood and Bruno instinctively followed.

"Well," she concluded, "I'm glad I met you, Mr. Nolan." measuring him with her eyes, not unlike a nun sizing up a student, Bruno suddenly thought. He stood a little straighter. "Yeah, me too, Doctor." He smiled and shook her hand. They strolled together towards the thick doors with the wire-reinforced glass that led to the bowels of the hospital.

"You'll be fine," the shrink reassured him. "Just remember that her system is very unstable right now. Be gentle."

"Of course, Doctor."

They'd reached the doors. The doctor turned and nodded at the receptionist in the booth who pushed a button. The door popped open with a loud buzz. "Don't forget your tag."

Bruno retrieved it while she held the door. "Careful, we won't let you out without one,' she cautioned with a smile.

"Right. I won't lose it," he said, perhaps too sincerely.

The doctor gestured down the hall. "I think Casandra's waiting for you in the cafeteria."

"Great, thanks."

Bruno quietly padded down the carpeted corridor, trying to calm down. If the shrink's purpose had been to rattle him, she'd succeeded grandly. But he need not have worried.

He rounded the corner into the cafeteria and there she was, waiting at a table with her head propped languidly on a bandaged arm. The room held a scattering of small knots of visitors and inmates and a couple of burly orderlies lounging like bouncers in the back.

Cas rose slowly when she saw him, her smile hesitant but real. She looked like shit. Her face was even more wan than usual, save for dark puffy circles under her eyes. She seemed even thinner and was having the mother of all bad-hair days.

Gently they embraced. She encircled him with her taped-up arms, clinging wordlessly for a long time, the fingers of one hand toying with the back of his hair with a will of their own. He kissed her delicately, and was relieved when she responded just as gingerly. She still hadn't bathed or brushed her teeth since they'd gone to Denver.

He pulled back a little and gazed into her morose hazel eyes. Doped up and very fragile, even childlike; it was his Cas that looked back at him and tried to smile.

"Hey, sweetie, good to see you again." he said softly. "Sorry they made me wait so long."

She said nothing but seemed shyly uncertain of whether to laugh or weep. He gently but firmly untangled her arms from around his neck, careful not to touch the bandages. They sat down at the table, and she held onto his hands as tightly as she could. "How are you doing?"

"I want a cigarette, but they won't let me."

"What's with this?" Bruno asked, nodding at her arms. "We were bad," she said sleepily. "They tried to lock us in, so Sneak dismantled the locks. Then they tried to make sure we wouldn't cut, but Slasher got the light bulb in the ceiling. They finally put us in a tiny little closet with nothing at all in it and watched us until we promised to be good." She yawned. "Now they want us to sleep."

"Why cut yourself?"

"For the blood, silly," she replied. "You remember, no salvation without blood. We like the way it flows, the taste, how it blackens as it dries. Besides," she continued sleepily, "the pain is so clean, so pure. When it hurts, I don't have to think —"

Her eyes snapped open and she was there with him again. "I'm sorry, Bruno. It's been real hard. I don't know if I'm coming or going or flying on standby."

"Jesus, sweetie, I'm the one who should apologize. I had no idea you were this bad off."

She gazed tiredly at him. "Neither did I. That trip; all those kids wandering around like sheep; trying not to strangle you or Dolores when you started yelling at each other — it really took it out of me.

"And then seeing him —" She turned away, her face clouded. "My God, a day doesn't go by when I don't flash on something, anything, a whiff of pipe smoke, maybe, or the way you clear your throat sometimes, that reminds me of DeLaval. I wish I could forget that monster, Bruno, I really do."

"Believe me, honey, I know. A lot is coming back now."

"He looked right at me, Bruno. And he knew me. He looked right at me and smiled." She broke down and started sobbing, burying her face in his shoulder. He moved closer and held her, rocking ever so slightly back and forth, stroking her hair as he had sometimes done for his daughter so long ago. His lover poured out a flash flood of hopeless grief and the unspoken terror that always lurked in the dark corners of her world.

Slowly the sobbing stopped. "I just wish I could have gotten that evil son of a bitch," he growled. "I don't know what happened, but I couldn't. He spoke to me and I was gone."

"Poor dear, always wanting to rescue me." She snuggled closer. Bruno's heart glowed with protective masculine feelings banked behind a somber melancholy as thick as ashes.

"It's the least I could do —" he began and then stopped. Cas raised her head from his shoulder, a haunted expression again in her eyes.

"You do remember, don't you, Eddie?" She clung even harder to him.

He shook his head but the pictures there would not depart. Standing naked with the other kids, holding a snake before a robed man with a dagger in some candlelit place, a glimpse of her face twisted in fear. "Honey, I'm not sure of anything anymore. I've been sorry so long that apologizing has become a habit." He gazed at her in utter sincerity. "But if ever I hurt you, I'll make up for it somehow."

Her eyes searched his. "You couldn't stop them, Eddie, we know that. But you must remember. You must."

She pushed away. "You must remember, Eddie. We were there at the altar, and so was he!" By now the other dysfunctional groups were all watching and the bouncers stirred. One talked into a radio and a nurse strolled into the room.

"It's okay," he said calmingly. "We just need a little time, that's all, baby. We'll work it out together."

"Okay," she said in a tiny, little girl's voice. "Hold me?"

Bruno tenderly embraced her. By the time the nurse came over to return her to her room, Cas was asleep in his arms.

☦

CHAPTER THIRTY-SIX

1963: The Feast of St. Peter Martyr, Saturday, April 20

THE SPRING AIR was still warm and fragrant with early blooms but it was already dark when Father Wilson brought Eddie back to the church. The boy could tell that something strange was going on. There were other cars in the parking lot, but Our Lady of Solitude was black within.

Father knocked in a funny pattern on the church door. A nun cloaked entirely in black opened it, and whispers were exchanged. She was not alone, as other figures were bustling silently around the sanctuary in the gloom.

Wilson hustled him into the sacristy, dimly lit by a few flickering candles. The priests' room was full of men taking off all their clothes with quiet indifference to everyone else and putting on loose, hooded vestments with odd crosses.

There were a few kids in the servers' section, including a dark-haired girl, which Eddie thought was very strange. Years younger than him, she was sitting on a bench, dressed in a Queen of Peace uniform, swinging her skinny legs. She smiled. Before Eddie could speak to her, Father DeLaval rounded the corner and roughly ordered him to leave her alone and get robed like the rest.

Several other boys, older and also unknown to him, were already silently doing so. Eddie went to the rack to get a cassock but DeLaval hissed at him, commanding him to strip instead. Eddie wanted to object, but when he turned around the girl was gone.

He slowly disrobed. Before he got very far, a dark, heavy-set woman sent the girl, now in a loose dressing gown like a hooded bathrobe, over to Eddie with a similar garment. She seemed embarrassed too but neither one dared speak.

Eddie had been too busy to see what Father Wilson was doing when he suddenly appeared again. He too was in a long, monkish robe with a hood and a cord about the waist. Around his neck hung an a strange cross. He presented a chalice to the woman with both hands.

"Time for our special Communion," he proclaimed. "All of you must take a sip. You first, Black Madonna?"

She bowed and eagerly took a draft. One by one, they all dutifully lined up. Eddie didn't want to, but everybody was watching him, so he took a sip too. It tasted funny like the wine he'd had earlier: a sweet, thick red liquid, much like cough syrup but with a bitter aftertaste.

Wilson finished it off with a big show of smacking his lips, which made the children laugh. Eddie felt pretty good all of a sudden, and no longer afraid, though the shadows danced spookily across the walls and dark wooden cabinets.

One by one the grown-ups individually took aside the kids they had brought, whispered to them, and returned them silently to the line. Wilson smiled proudly when Eddie instantly fell into trance. DeLaval, though, had trouble. His boy, an older blonde kid, seemed hardly under the spell at all.

At a given signal, the kids lined up. Flanked by the adults, they squeezed through the sacristy door.

The sanctuary was lit by several tall candelabras and a tripod filled with fire, though the red flicker of the presence light showed that God was still locked within the high tabernacle. Below it stood a brand new altar, the first of the promised changes to the Church. It was a thick, rectangular wooden table, standing on two huge legs on a carpeted platform built out from the steps to the old altar. Faint scents of sawdust, glue, and the sweet sacred chrism from its recent consecration lingered beneath the strange musky vapors that boiled out of the caldron.

Even more imposing was the figure standing before it, lit eerily from below, in flowing robes of red and black embroidered in gold with a large serpent wrapped around a cross. He held a snake-headed staff and wore a strange miter as well, turned sideways so that the two peaks were like horns.

Raising his staff, he thumped it on the marble floor, once, twice quickly, then with three slow strokes. A hooded figure on his right bowed, and read loudly from a sheaf of papers, "Grand Master Abbadon, we Brothers of the Hidden Order, the Black Priests of the Province of Alvarado, are most honored to greet you at our celebration here tonight of the solemn festival of Our Order. With your permission, we will begin our ritual."

The leader swept his staff in a circle. "Let all the entrances to our place of working be shut and warded," he solemnly declared in a thin voice with an Italian accent. Vague figures could be seen stationed at the doors.

Suddenly, the atmosphere seemed closer, warmer; shadows more intense. More incense was thrown on the fire, thick smoke curling upwards. The priests walked counterclockwise around the sanctuary, stopping at each side with much bowing and chanting.

Brought forward by their masters, the children were then brought out individually to undergo a simple test. A basket was brought forward and placed on the altar.

One by one, the kids stepped up to lift a snake out. It was a small green boa constrictor with a bulge midway showing it enjoyed a nice big rodent recently. But it was not happy about having its digestion repeatedly disturbed. It writhed about, tongue flicking angrily.

Eddie was next to last. With a hand at either end, he carefully lifted the heavy reptile like an offering, straightening it as best he could.

"Salve, Matrona tenebrae," he began shakily, "quid homini mortali abhorre." Somehow he made it through the whole thing without error. The tall, blonde boy after him was not so lucky. "Hail, Mother of Darkness, whom mortal men abhor," he began fearfully in English. Then the serpent twisted around and headed up his arm. He screamed, trying to shake the boa off, which only made it squeeze harder.

His master, DeLaval, standing behind him, needed assistance to free him. The snake was placed in its basket and removed. The boy was also hauled out of the room, crying loudly for his mother. Eddie never saw him again.

"Well done, Master Xaphon. We commend you, Frater, on the thoroughness of the training of your novice. You have well earned the privilege of being the new Magistrate here. Too bad we cannot say the same for Master Baalberith." The man's eyes gleamed evilly in the flickering light. The tall priest stood a little prouder, while DeLaval frowned and hung his head.

"Anoint the child as an accepted Neophyte." The woman knelt before Eddie and rubbed him all over with a warmly tingling oil. Then Wilson marked a huge cross upon his body with fetid, black goop.

"Take now the symbol of our Order and sign the Book with your life's Blood, that your Pact with Our Dread Lord may be sealed," the Grand Master continued.

Face fearlessly blank, Eddie silently held out his right hand. Carefully his master took a slim, crosshilted dagger and pricked the boy's thumb, then pressed it down in the Book next to the kid's entry to confirm his admission.

The Grand Master smiled. "Your soul belongs to the Order now. It is ours to wield, to make and to break." He raised his arms. "Let us now make our offerings to Our Dread Lord and Lady," he cried. "Let us stain this holy table of sacrifice in their name — but first take the catechumens away."

The nude children were swiftly ushered back into the sacristy. The dark woman laughed, bent down to Eddie, and said, "Now taste what good things the Dark Lady gives those who serve Her." She grabbed him by the neck and kissed him fully on the mouth; her breath tasting of cigarette smoke and wine, while she insistently fondled his privates.

Eddie squirmed uneasily but became excited. She pushed him then into the group of kids in the center of the room, a groping, giggling mob. The bodies closed in around him, not much older than his own, touching him, tickling. He reached out and felt child flesh, all smooth as silk with the oil. Wriggling around, he found himself face to face with the girl he had recognized earlier. They rubbed their slick skins against each other, laughing happily.

The adults waited long enough for the children to become playfully aroused. Then suddenly, without warning, the grown-ups switched on the glaring fluorescent overhead lights and waded into the mob.

"Shame on you, children," the woman screamed. "You filthy little beasts! Come on, clean up, right now!" She flailed about at the blinded kids who cowered in embarrassment.

Father DeLaval joined in, too, yelling at the children. "Wipe yourself off right now," he demanded, distributing towels. "For shame! What would your parents think?

"All children, return!"

Eddie came back to himself in a whirl of confusion as the little girl was jerked away by the woman. DeLaval threw him a towel. Like the others, he wiped himself off as thoroughly and quickly as possible.

Father DeLaval worked them like a drill sergeant. "Come on, clean yourselves up and get dressed," he demanded, "It's late. Time to go home, kids, to your loving parents. They'll be so ashamed of you if they ever find out what naughty things you have done tonight. Quickly, let's go!"

Once dressed, the children were rapidly inspected and herded to the door. With a final hiss to be quiet, the blackpriest turned off the lights, opened it and then the outside door too.

As he squeezed past DeLaval, Eddie glanced back into the sanctuary. In the darkness beneath the unseen frown of the Sorrowful Mother, he glimpsed flashes of candlelit skin as men and women threw off their robes around the new altar. Four dark figures held the black-haired girl spread upon it as the Grand Master slowly approached her, arms opened wide apart like a priest accepting a holy offering. Her small, nude body twisted like red flames as she hopelessly squirmed.

Terrified, she looked up, imploring eyes great with fear, right into Eddie's. Then he was outside, and quickly put into a crowded van that was already idling, ready to go.

Eddie and the other kids curled up in their seats as it drove off and desperately tried to forget everything that had just happened.

☦

CHAPTER THIRTY-SEVEN

1993: Monday, August 23

MIKE trotted into the lobby of the Catholic Complex just in time, announced by the rattle of the first wave of hailstones on the roof. The thunderhead rising like a mushroom cloud behind the Sanbenitos had finally let loose. Distant flashes of lightning played along the crests as dark waves of rain rolled down the fir-clad slopes and on across the city. A mixed blessing — the desperately needed water could bring the fire of heaven down with it upon the dry woods. Yahweh in his most ancient role as god of thunder was up to his old tricks again, he thought darkly.

The secretaries were off somewhere, so he marched up to Malachy's office and rapped sharply. He heard a muffled "Come in," followed by a flash and a crack of thunder that rattled the windows.

The old priest was standing, staring out the pane at the storm. Hailstones bounced off the pavement and cars like popcorn but Malachy had a wistful smile on his face, remembering distant climes from his moister youth, perhaps.

He turned briefly. "Mike, what a surprise! You know, I'd been wanting to call you to find out how it went."

Mike joined him watching the storm sweep across the valley. Cranking open a window, Malachy continued, "Nothing like the smell of the desert after a shower, the sage especially. Like dawn in Heaven."

Finally he turned and examined the younger man. "By Columba's coracle, boy, you look like you just returned from the Crusades!"

Mike smiled crookedly. "That bad?" he asked, plopping down into a chair, "I feel it. Children's Crusade, perhaps — I think I've earned enough indulgences for all my sins and then some. We were ready for the heat and the sun, but nobody was prepared for the big storm that hit Sunday afternoon after the Mass." The heavens chuckled as if in recollection.

"I'm still getting over a cold, and I'm not the only one."

"I hope it was worth it." Malachy sat down behind the desk and leaned forward. "You really must tell me: how was it? What was it like to actually meet the Holy Father?"

"I wouldn't know," Mike said woodenly, with a disgusted wave of his hand. "Ask Robert; he did, I didn't."

"Oh, I'm sorry," Malachy said, surprised. "It meant a lot to you, I know. But you're young, even if the Pope is old. You'll get a chance to meet the Holy Father, someday, maybe not just this one."

"No, I don't think so," Mike disgustedly replied. "I've got an albatross around my neck, Father. Or a curse. Or the mark of Cain — whatever metaphor you want. I am my brother's keeper after all, no matter what."

"Ah, Bruno was there. I saw him on TV."

Mike nodded affirmatively. "With his squad of lunatics."

"What do they call themselves? 'C.A.S.A.' or some such silly thing?"

"Whatever. A handful of them anyway. Father, you would not believe Bruno's arrogance. First off, he actually tried to debate me about the papacy at the Vatican Treasures exhibit! But that was just the beginning," he blurted. "That brazen nutcase had the insolence to moon the Pope!"

To Mike's consternation, Malachy laughed heartily, so hard that the red-faced priest took off his heavy glasses and wiped them. "Sorry, lad, I'm sure it must have been distressing, but that's such a ludicrous image." He chortled as he put the thick black frames back on. "Anyway, John Paul's outlasted both the Nazis and the Reds. I'm sure he's faced far more pointed displays of disrespect in his time. Don't worry; he even forgave the man who shot him."

Mike was still angry. "But my own brother? I swear; I'm just glad our mother's not alive to hear about this." He sighed heavily. "I just don't know what to do, Father Malachy. Haven't I've turned my cheek for Bruno plenty — even more than the 'seven times seventy' Our Lord tells us? He's still after me. Even if he was abused by Wilson, why can't he just get over it?"

Malachy peered compassionately at him. "I fear this is how he's trying to, though it's surely not very fair to you."

Mike's reply was drowned by a sharp flash and a blast of thunder. The lights in the office went out as a new barrage of hail bombarded the roof. As the rain intensified, there came a light tapping on the door, barely audible above the storm. Robert Cruz stuck his unsmiling head in.

"Ah, Mike, thought I saw your van being pelted outside." He entered the room and sat down. "Well, that one just crashed my computer. So much for the latest financial report."

"He was just telling me about his brother's antics in Denver, mooning the Pope and all. Too bad you didn't get a picture, lad; certain bishops would be willing to pay for a copy of something like that."

"Or at least some cardinals," Cruz added, chuckling.

"I was just hoping Sean could shed some light. I mean, I'm really at the end of my rope, Bob. Bruno's, well, he's become dangerous. Oh, and before I forget — I just heard from Kramer that his lawyer wants to schedule my deposition soon — yours too, Father Malachy."

"Yes, I'm quite aware of that," the old man said gruffly. "Not that it will do much good for anyone."

"Well, you've known Bruno and I for a long time. Weren't you at Solitude while Wilson was a curate there?"

"And DeLaval, too," Malachy pointed out.

"Yes, of course." Mike paused. "Does that matter?"

"More than I can say, to you or the lawyers," Malachy replied grimly. "And I mean that quite literally, lad, for it's covered under sacramental seal. Believe me, I wish to God it wasn't but there it is."

Mike sat in stunned silence as the rain continued steadily. Their old pastor invoking the secrecy of Confession in regard to his brother's claims was as good as a Mob boss calling on the Fifth Amendment — a sure sign there was something to them. The world outside flickered as lightning sparked between clouds, followed by a long, low chuckle of thunder.

"My God, that crazy moron was telling the truth all along! But why on Earth would he help him?"

"What do you mean, Mike?" Cruz asked sharply.

"Ah," Mike said, suddenly flustered. "There was one more thing I hadn't mentioned: I also encountered Bruno at the outdoor Mass. Monsignor DeLaval was there, too."

"What!" the chancellor exclaimed.

"Yeah, I guess Tom wanted to talk to me about his situation," Mike improvised. "Didn't get much of a chance. Bruno spotted us, came over, and nearly started a riot." He rubbed his abdomen lightly, but suddenly got a faraway gaze.

"I never really believed it." Mike spoke like he was talking to himself. "I'd forgotten: he told me, when we were kids, that Wilson and DeLaval were both very bad men, but that you, Father Malachy, were okay. It was like a warning or something. I didn't understand, then, but I think it was shortly before Wilson disappeared and DeLaval first went away."

"But doesn't your brother claim he just recently remembered being abused by Father Wilson?" Cruz inquired.

Mike spread his hands. "And that he never said a word to me about it when we were young. He must have forgotten, too. I mean, I sure didn't recall him telling me until just now."

There was quiet in the room as the downfall slowed.

Cruz and Malachy exchanged sharp glances. "That's real interesting, Mike," the chancellor finally said. He stared at him, suddenly concerned. "So what happened at the Mass? Is everything okay?"

"Yeah, DeLaval took off as soon as he saw Bruno," Mike said, avoiding his gaze.

Suddenly, the sun came out, turning the fringes of the rain into a shimmering screen of crystal. The lights suddenly came back on, too, hardly noticeable in the sparkling brightness outside.

"Oh boy, power's back," Cruz said. "Lucky me; if the computer's not fried I get to compose that report again." He stood up. Mike did too.

"I should go too. Thanks for lending me a shoulder to cry on, Monsignor Malachy."

"Absolutely anytime, Mike. You know that."

Cruz and Mike stepped into the hall. "Oh, almost forgot," Cruz said as they strolled to his office. "It's official. The old cathedral will be shut down before Halloween. I managed to hold it off until after Our Lady's feast day, but just barely. I was wondering, Mike, since I really don't have a clue of what this might possibly entail ceremonially, if you'd see about it?"

"A 'decommissioning' ritual? Sure," Mike said.

"Great, thanks," Cruz smiled amiably. "Well, I have some calls to make."

"Oh, sure, good-bye then," Mike said, but the chancellor's door was already closing.

He sighed, turned, and went outside. The world was sparkling like it had been reborn, but he had a ominous feeling that lingered. Time for a nice long run, he thought, just the thing to calm him right now. It was good that the parochial school year was starting soon; he needed his routine back.

He could do no more for Bruno than he could affect the weather, anyway. As he left, Mike glanced back at the black cloud above the Catholic Complex, receding westward but still grumbling.

†

CHAPTER THIRTY-EIGHT

Tuesday, August 24

DR. BLACKSTONE said firmly, "Bruno, you should consider going to the hospital, too." Bruno was waxen, drained of all emotion, reclining with arms crossed. He barely shook his head in reply and cleared his throat. "Not safe."

"What's not safe?"

He sighed. "I don't want to be locked up; I'm afraid I'd go nuts, really nuts."

She tried another tack. "You were begging to be locked up a couple of months ago."

He stared at her flatly. "I was in denial then. No more of that, unfortunately. Used to be I couldn't remember. Since I returned from Denver, I can't stop."

"So now you're flooding. You need a safe place to process all this." She gestured at the wild stack of scribbled papers on the desk. "For goodness' sake, you've got more recollections there than most clients piece together in years. Your system's bound to be badly shaken up, and there may be some serious repercussions."

"But I'm still not getting it. There's more; it's important, I know it!" Bruno exclaimed, rubbing his head. "There was Wilson and DeLaval. There were group rituals, too, and other kids took part — Cas, for sure." He stared at the ceiling as if trying to augur through the pattern in the tiles.

Blackstone tried again. "That's precisely why you need a safe place to deal with all this." No response. "Well, I'd still like you to put away your gun for awhile."

He shook his head sharply. "I'm neither suicidal nor particularly homicidal. But paranoid, yes. My weapon lets me sleep much better than any damned stuffed animal, which is another reason I refuse to go to the loony bin. I'm keeping it."

She tapped her pad with her pen, and sighed. "Okay, Bruno, there's one more option I can suggest. I have a small group of people who meet here, cult survivors, mainly. They might be able to help you cope with these new memories."

Bruno laughed bitterly. "Why not? The last group I got involved in at your recommendation worked out so well."

Blackstone ignored the remark. "How is Cas anyway?"

Bruno shrugged. "She's still in the hospital, but now she won't talk to me either. I know something strange happened in Denver. It must have really pissed them all off somehow, but I can't remember it." He paused, appearing troubled.

"What's bothering you, Bruno?"

"I keep seeing Cas at that ritual I mentioned. It involved some weird test — we had to hold up a snake and recite some horrible prayer." His face burned with shame. "There were naked people, too. That's where I first encountered Cas, but I can't see it all clearly yet.

"I don't know what to tell her, and even worse, today I'm to give my deposition for the lawsuit against Wilson. Do I dare mention any of this? What if they ask me?"

"As I'm sure your attorney has advised you, don't volunteer anything. But don't lie either. However," she said positively, "they probably won't ask you anything even remotely about what we've been discussing." She glanced at the grandfather clock. "There's some time left; what can we do to get you ready?"

† † †

CAROLYN KRAMER shuffled her papers. "So, Mr. Nolan, I'd like to ask you again about when you first realized Father Wilson had sexually abused you," she said. "Now, this was on the ninth of April this year?"

"On Good Friday, yes," Bruno replied, nervously toying with his newly-trimmed beard once again. He glanced over at his own lawyer. But Nick Weregild, sprawled comfortably in his chair, making notes or maybe doodling, was apparently unconcerned that once again the Church's lawyer had circled like a vulture back yet again to pick on the memory question.

They'd been over it all, the whole sordid saga of Bruno's molestation at the hands of the infamous Philip Wilson thirty years ago before, with all the unsavory details. Many of the questions, oddly enough, concerned bodily positions. Kramer asked them in a dry, almost medical tone, and Bruno tried to respond in the same vein.

At first, he was embarrassed, partly because the court reporter was a young, pretty Hispanic woman. Her open face reminded him of his daughter's, so Bruno dared not glance at her, though she seemed so detached, he might as well be discussing the finer points of scholasticism rather than sodomy.

"And other than possibly trying to tell your mother about it at the time, you never told anyone else about what happened, is that correct?"

"No, as I said, at one time I complained to Father Busch in confession and he made me apologize to Father Wilson."

"Did you ever mention it to any of your friends, perhaps, or your brother?"

"I don't think so. The only other person I think knew at that time, Ralph Shore, was probably also abused. He helped me get away once. Died of an overdose in his twenties."

"Did you ever try to warn anyone, even if just to say that they should avoid Father Wilson?"

Bruno shrugged. "I didn't have to. The other kids knew he was creepy. We called him 'Feeler' Wilson behind his back."

At this point his lawyer stirred, noting the time. "I think my client has repeatedly answered these questions already. I would ask, due to the lateness of the hour, that you either move on to new ground, or continue this another day."

Bruno inwardly groaned. Another day! Though this hadn't been quite the inquisition he had dreaded, it had been torture. Talking about the molestation had been bad enough, but telling of the effects was even more painful. The isolation, self-hate, drunkenness, alienation, inability to form relationships; his completely pathetic, futile life, he'd laid out before them in textbook clarity with remarkably little whining. But it almost overwhelmed him. His lawyer had to ask for several breaks, and during one recess, Bruno hid in his old Volkswagen in the parking lot, despite the heat and his too-tight suit, sobbing and pounding the wheel.

Kramer replied frostily, "I'll ask what questions I need to ask, Mr. Weregild. You may object in court but not here. However, it is late, and I don't think any of us wants to do this again." She pushed her papers around a bit.

"Okay," she gazed steadily at Bruno. "Mr. Nolan, why are you doing this? Why are you suing the Church?"

Finally, the question he'd been waiting for, but all his indignation, regrets, and even fury, had been worn away by the unceasing trickle of questions.

"I have a twelve-year-old daughter who recently became an altar server," he said tiredly. "Some day she may even want to be a priest. In any case, I don't want her or any kid to experience what happened to me. Maybe if the Church has to pay up, it'll wise up and prevent this from happening again."

Kramer seemed unimpressed, but Weregild appeared satisfied. The girl finished typing calmly and waited.

"Okay," Kramer said, "that's it then. I don't have any more questions. Let's go off-record. Let's see, the deposition is ended at four twenty."

The reporter finished typing and dutifully turned off her recorder. Everyone relaxed. The attorneys cordially chatted as they gathered their papers; Kramer even thanked Bruno, and he and Weregild left.

Once outside in the noise and heat of rush hour downtown on a summer afternoon, the lawyer was positively elated.

"Great work, Bruno," he said, resolutely slapping him on the back. "You did very well. Answered accurately and consistently, and stood your ground, too.

"Yes, sir, I think I might up our demand to half a million. They'll settle — like Casandra, you're the last kind of witness they want on the stand."

Bruno smiled but his mind was reeling. The amount of money Weregild mentioned was far, far more than he'd ever let himself dream of. 'Winning the Catholic lottery' indeed. But in the back of his mind, he wouldn't let himself believe it. He'd heard too many grandiose promises from his alcoholic mother and her Church. Only when the check is in my hands, he thought, only then; but still, until then, it wasn't a bad fantasy.

"What about DeLaval?" Bruno asked. "I'm sure it was him we encountered in Denver."

Weregild waved his hand in exasperation. "I have no idea, Bruno. We're checking. I'm pretty sure he went first to California, but we've heard rumors that he's hiding in Canada, too.

He's still getting paid by the diocese, you know, so our one big hope is to follow the money trail." He looked quizzically at Bruno. "Sure you don't want to go after him also?"

Bruno shook his head. "Not now," he said. "I, I don't doubt he got me too, but it doesn't feel safe until he's caught."

"Well, it's your call. I don't think he's going to come after you if you sue. You'd be at the end of a long list.

"When you do speak to Casandra, tell her we're still searching and wish her well. But just between us, it's not likely we're ever going to find him. For one thing, it's obvious someone or some group is hiding him. For another, he hasn't been accused of any crime, so the police aren't even looking."

"What?"

The lawyer nodded glumly. "I took it to the district attorney, and he said none of the cases come within the criminal statute of limitations. Even Cas' brother was above the age of consent. If we had anything on him — such as kiddie porn, say — it would be different. I hope that the publicity of her case will draw other, more recent and underage victims out."

As he walked through the heat to his car, Bruno had a sour taste in his mouth. His elation evaporated. They were all in it together, all the lawyers too, needing ever more victims on the altars of litigation. He felt like he was as much a piece of meat to Weregild as he had been to Wilson, maybe even more.

Bruno sat in his Beetle wishing he were drunk. He really needed to go to a meeting, but he'd done far more than enough talking today. So much more pleasant it would be to have a couple of tall, cold ones in a shady, tranquil bar instead.

He shook his head and started the engine. No matter how desperate he felt, now was not the time to start boozing again, not when his financial troubles might soon be over.

CHAPTER THIRTY-NINE

Thursday, August 26

BRUNO shifted uncomfortably, his attempt to appear confident entirely unsuccessful. But if the others noticed, it did not seem to bother them as Dr. Blackstone began the introductions.

"Folks, meet Bruno. I've told you a little about him before. I think he's ready for this group."

"Ah, he's remembered killing babies, then," commented a nondescript, sandy-haired man, nestling in the corner with a menagerie of stuffed animals. His broad, innocent smile did not hide the sardonic twinkle in his blue eyes as he hugged a huge pink teddy bear to his purple tee-shirt.

"Frank, that's no way to greet a newbie," a stunningly beautiful, slim blonde woman perched in the stuffed chair opposite chided. Elegantly dressed, hair in a modest bun, she was quite a knockout. Her tan silk blouse and slacks exuded quiet sophistication by their simplicity as much as by their quality. They didn't call attention to her: they didn't need to.

"Hi, I'm Tamara," she said in a voice like a fine liqueur, smiling at Bruno. "That," she nodded, "is Frank, at least at the moment, I think."

The man nodded his head vigorously but said nothing.

"Come on, people, you'll scare him," piped in the last member of the therapy group. She was a slight young woman, curled up on the floor surrounded by papers on which she constantly scribbled with crayons in either fist even while she talked. Her mousey hair was wildly frizzy, and she wore 50s-style cats-eye glasses and baggy bib overalls over a bright, tie-dyed shirt. "You know how scary it was the first time," she said in a high, childish voice. She glanced up at Bruno with a brief, reassuring smile. "We're Debbie," she announced.

Dr. Blackstone gazed inquiringly at Bruno.

He cleared his throat. "Yeah, well, I'd say I was happy to be here except that I'm not. But Doctor Blackstone assures me that I needed to talk with other people that are dealing with, with all this crap." He cleared his throat.

"I was one of those altar boys you may have read about in the papers recently. Started getting my memories back just this spring, but lately they've become a lot weirder. I don't know what to believe, but I'd sure like it to stop." He shrugged. "If that's denial, fine by me."

"Denial's okay," Debbie said. "Enjoy it while it lasts."

"For me," Frank broke in, "it was like one of those cartoons where the creature falls through floor after floor until it winds up the basement. I first recalled dear old dad raping me and went through hell, but finally got to where I could say, 'Whew! Glad that's over. At least mom wasn't involved.' And wham! I'm flashing on mom and her wicked sisters taking turns, and from there it got really bad." He smiled sweetly. "That's why I mentioned killing babies. Best to get the worst over with."

Bruno snorted. "Considerate of you, but no thanks, I don't think there were any babies. The sex stuff was bad enough. I realized from the start that the abuse was funny, I mean, rather ritualistic, but I thought it was just because the guy who buggered me was a Catholic priest. He said creepy prayers both before and afterwards, too."

He paused. "I recall now that there were others involved, and some weird initiation they put me through."

"Maybe you were intended for a leadership position in the cult, then," Tamara said. "Mere victims and slaves rarely ever escape, and certainly are never initiated."

"What confuses me is the point of it all," he complained. "Separating the mind games out on is so difficult."

Tamara nodded sagely. "Usually is with satanists."

"Oh hell, now you've done it," Bruno groaned woefully. "The 'S-word.' I was really hoping to avoid that."

Frank chuckled. "Hey, you said these guys were priests. What else could they be?"

"I can't imagine."

"Well, what do your kids say?" asked Debbie.

Bruno shrugged in confusion. "Well, I've only got one daughter and I'm not going to tell —"

"I think she means your 'inner children,' Bruno," Blackstone interrupted. Debbie conceded with a shrug. "Sorry. I just wanted to make sure you're all speaking about the same thing."

"Inner children? Other personalities? I used to think that stuff was nuts." Bruno laughed harshly. "Better than possession, I suppose. What I really need to know is how the hell to deal with them."

Debbie glanced up somberly. "We just let everybody come out and talk when we feel safe. Like here. That's why we like to color so much. We like it here."

Blackstone nodded. "Yes, we do a lot of art therapy. Coloring, collages — or we can do visualizations or even sand trays. You can talk about anything here, too, because whatever is said in here is strictly confidential, just like in any regular therapy session." She glanced around and they nodded in agreement.

"So, what'll it be this evening?" she asked. "How about some art?" No one objected, and Debbie was already at it anyway, so Frank passed out big sheets of newsprint and crayons.

After a few minutes, Blackstone noticed Bruno struggling with his picture. "This isn't art class," she suggested gently.

"Let go; be as free and spontaneous as possible. You might even try using your other hand."

"I draw bad enough already," he griped. "Hate to think what my girlfriend would say."

"I'm sure Cas would tell you that technical excellence is really not the point here."

Bruno was dubious but shifted the crayon to his left hand. It was harder doing it as a southpaw. But when he gave up in frustration and let his hand scribble freely, the drawing progressed as if by magic.

Excited, he grabbed a handful of colors. As he did, the details filled in by themselves. The altar, the snake they made him hold, the strange implements, the robes the adults wore, all tumbled about chaotically in his head.

He drew a rough altar and a small black-haired figure held down upon it by a mass of dark, sinister shapes. In front stood one with a black book, another with a cross, and a third figure, a woman, was surrounded by smaller ones. Suddenly, from out of nowhere, it seemed, he remembered.

"Oh hell's bells," he swore, sitting bolt upright. "That's it." He jabbed at the drawing with his right hand. "She was there too. The little girl on the altar was my girlfriend, Casandra! I saw her through the back door as I left.

"I most clearly remember her eyes looking at me really scared. But it wasn't me she was afraid of," he exclaimed in relief. "I thought that — I didn't want to hurt her, and that's when I first decided I had to get away!" His face reddened.

"We understand, Bruno," Tamara sympathized. "Watching others get hurt is sometimes more difficult to bear than being hurt oneself. Don't take it too hard."

"She's right," the psychiatrist agreed. "So Frank," she said, continuing around, "what do you have?"

Sitting in the midst of a pile of stuffed animals on the floor, Frank glanced up. "Oh, me?" he asked, then held up his sheet, showing a crude bear-like figure covered with tiny stick figures, looming over a rainbow and other stickmen running in fear. "It's my Higher Power — an eight-hundred-foot tall teddy bear, and he's talking all my kids away from the bad men."

"Excellent. How about you, Tamara?"

"Something that came up recently," Tamara said, holding her paper up. She'd drawn a short, wide triangular blade with a simple, pencil-thin hilt. "Not for rituals," she said offhandedly, "but for wet work, bedroom jobs. Stab just under the skull in back of the neck to penetrate the spinal cord. Quick, clean, and unnoticeable, especially once the handle is snapped off."

"I drew a knife too. But ours were different," Debbie interrupted in her high, childish voice, presenting her own drawing. It showed a long blade with an elaborate guard made out of a ram's skull with jeweled eyes like a Georgia O'Keefe image gone horribly heavy metal. "The only bad stuff we had to do was in the magic circles with all the mean people and the animals."

"Jeez, that must've been one hell of a finishing school you ladies went to," Bruno awkwardly joked. "But you know, I saw a strange knife too," he continued quickly. He grabbed another sheet of paper and began to sketch rapidly with a stick of charcoal. A picture of a crosshilted dagger with a slender blade soon took form.

"This was a very special knife," he said, absently scratching his right thumb. "It was alive — or so he said, anyway. Any time it was drawn it had to taste blood. He cut me with it." He peered down at the scar on the digit in surprise. "Oh Jesus, that's where it came from!" His eyes moistened. "But why? Why all this? This is awful — even worse than perverts getting their rocks off."

Tamara silently passed him a box of tissues.

"They're psychopaths, Bruno," Blackstone gently explained, "so cut off from life, from God, if you will, that the only way they can stand their own pain and emptiness is to inflict it on the weak and the innocent.

"It's all tied into their insane beliefs," she continued. "Serious black magic requires exalting the powers of evil, which means profaning the good and the holy. Pagan good, Christian good, makes no difference to them. Logically, the more vile the desecration of the best, purest, and brightest, the greater glory it gives to the dark powers. The psychological energy generated by such inner tension must be incredible."

"So that's why the blackpriests buggered altar boys in church," Bruno said in horror. "Christ, this only gets worse."

"You're lucky, Bruno, about your girlfriend," Frank said, attempting to comfort him. "You must have gotten out before they could turn you against each other."

"Be glad you didn't have to do anything to her," Tamara agreed. "Soon or later, you'd have been forced to betray her somehow, maybe even kill her, just to survive. These people don't like nice relationships, you know. They need everybody kept alone and afraid."

†

CHAPTER FORTY

Friday, September 10

HOPING to see him alone early in the new semester, Bruno had made a point of procuring an appointment with his committee chairman. But no use. Once Mithers' door was open, they always came.

He was relieved to find that there were no adoring undergrads today, just a fellow grad student.

"Hi, stranger," Emily said with a smile as he entered.

"Hi, yourself. Good morning, Prof. Hope I'm not late."

Iggy Mithers was leaning back, his slim body stretched out, feet propped up on the desk. He toyed idly with his pipe. Waving at Bruno, he said, "Oh no, early in fact. I was just congratulating Emily on her defense of her thesis."

"So the dragon can be defeated, huh? Well, that's great." Her grip was firm when he shook her hand. A strong, large-size brunette, almost severely academic in manner, her face became remarkably more agreeable with a smile.

"It was classic trial by ordeal," she bragged, "but it nearly became trial by combat."

Iggy chortled. "At one point, I thought she was going to challenge Dodge to a duel over the Cathar influence on courtly love. Rather romantic, I thought."

"If he'd made one more snide comment about female knights I'd have decked him," she sniffed, rising. "Well, I don't want to cut in on anybody's time, so I'll be off. But I want to invite you both — and your dates, of course — to a big bash I'll be having a month from today, Columbus Day weekend, when it's all official. Then I'll really feel like celebrating."

She shouldered a bookbag the size of a small suitcase. "Hope you can come — especially you, Bruno. We never see you around here anymore. It'll be fun — a barbecue for all you carnivores and a keg of imported beer." She smiled promisingly.

"I'll see if I can make it," Bruno said, noncommittal.

"Uh-huh," she said dubiously and with a wave was gone.

Iggy uncoiled himself, rose, and closed the door. "Ordinarily I'd say let's go get some coffee, but undoubtedly we'd be interrupted by more of your fans."

Bruno snorted. "My fans? Yours, you mean."

Iggy sat down again and picked up his pipe. "Hey, I saw the way she smiled at you."

Bruno made a grim half-grin. "Yeah, well, if her girlfriend didn't kill me, mine would. Besides, I find her somewhat... intimidating."

"Self-assured is how I'd put it." He checked the draw on his pipe and lit it, sending up billows of white smoke. "So tell me, how's it going? You run into trouble already?"

Bruno tried not to cough, and suppressed a desire to flee. Everything reminded him all too much of DeLaval nowadays.

"I may be in a bit over my head," he admitted. "All I wanted to do was study the institutional mechanisms the Church developed in the Middle Ages to deal with errant priests and naughty nuns. You were right; there's no dearth of material. Lordy, but there's been some bad boys in the cloth.

"It goes way back, but the really disturbing thing is that the sex goes hand-in-hand with sorcery. Get this: the synod in the fourth century that first demanded clerical celibacy was also the first to forbid them from performing magic."

Iggy nodded thoughtfully. "So what's the problem?"

Bruno sighed. "It's gotten, well, personally weird."

The professor's arched eyebrows crawled even higher.

"I don't know if it's my studies interfering with my therapy, or vice versa, or what, but they're coming together more than I would like."

"How so? If you don't mind me asking."

Bruno sighed heavily. "Well, for instance, the other day I read an account written by John of Salisbury, about how the priest that taught him Latin tried to use him to see the future using the names of demons and a polished basin." He paused and said in a low voice, "That was in the middle of twelfth century. Just about the same damn thing happened to me eight hundred years later." He grimaced. "I don't like it. Validation sucks, but this bites and chews as well."

Iggy clucked. "Hmm. It's still not too late to choose yet another subject, you know."

"Yeah, but I don't want to do that again. I must deal with this, one way or another; if I can squeeze some academic juice out of it, so much the better." He sighed. "I just want somebody who's not a priest or a shrink or another nut to tell me what's going on. Could this stuff be real?"

"Are you really asking or is this just rhetorical?"

"If you really think you know, then I'm really asking."

Mithers knocked the dottle out of his pipe bowl and watched it flare and wink out before he answered. Then he steepled his fingers and peered directly at Bruno. "Religious and magical practices can indeed linger unknown for centuries. Even here. Did you know, there are Jewish families hereabouts who came over during the Spanish conquest to hide from the Inquisition, and are still in concealment even today? 'Crypto-Jews,' or 'marranos' I believe they're called."

"Who wouldn't hide from the Spanish Inquisition? But it's easier to conceal secrets in a close family setting," Bruno countered. "What I want to know is if there could be a secret organization of black magicians lurking within the Church."

"A cult, you mean, a secret one — in the modern, rather than the traditional sense?"

"Yeah, I guess."

"Well, let's examine the evidence," Mithers said in a lofty academic tone. "From the grimoires and other books on magic that have been preserved, we know that belief in the occult in general and demonic magic in particular was prevalent throughout the Middle Ages."

"Sure," Bruno agreed. "And the whole sacramental system of the Church could seem quite magical, especially to the uneducated. There are all those decrees against peasants stealing Hosts to cure their cows."

"Ah, but they're not the ones to worry about." Mithers waved his pipe like a wand.

"The peasants, after all, were peasants," he explained. "Folk magic plus a few half-forgotten remnants of paganism, tinged with popular Christian heresy — that's pretty much what 'witchcraft' actually was, I fear, despite all the wild claims circulated both then and now."

He smiled, "Though of course if you tell Emily that I said that, I'll deny everything.

"Anyway, who were those books on magic written for? Who could read or write spells, or anything else for that matter, during the Dark Ages? Who had the leisure time, ready access to the right equipment, and the interests to pursue a serious study of magic? Not your peasants, lords, or townsmen."

"Ambitious nobles at royal courts?" Bruno said hopefully.

"Yes, certainly, during the Renaissance, once education became fashionable again." Iggy banished it airily with a wave of his hand. "But you know who I mean — the professional clergy, who guaranteed their own monopoly on spiritual power by defining all spiritual practices they didn't approve of as heresy, including magic. Remember, too, that the ecclesiastical class was a far broader group then than now. Even university students were given tonsures and minor orders in the Church as a matter of course.

"So when things got tight — by the late thirteenth century, like today, there was a huge surplus of college graduates — a ready underworld existed of overeducated, underemployed clergymen clearly ripe for the temptation to improve their lot with a sly bit of trafficking with devils.

"Of course, the Inquisition ensured all that would stay underground, but the Church's own legal system usually took care of its own. All along they've quietly shipped offenders off to monasteries or the missions. Something which a determined, savvy group like a religious order could use to their own benefit. And often did, especially in the cloistered orders."

"But that was back before the Protestant Reformation — before the Black Death, even. It got cleaned up, didn't it?"

"Things haven't changed that much." Mithers shrugged. "Each and every year the plague still claims a few victims up in our mountains. I imagine there also could be some highly frustrated, highly ambitious priests out there with far too much time on their hands as well."

"That is precisely what I didn't want to hear," Bruno admitted. "It means that my memories might actually be true."

"More than that, my friend. It could still be happening right now, today."

† † †

BRUNO tried ignoring the phone but it wouldn't stop ringing. The damnable answering machine was acting weird again. Slowly he opened his eyes. The light slanting through the windows indicated it was late afternoon, and Clio sat heavily on his bladder scowling at him.

He got up, spilling the cat and his book onto the rug. While Clio headed optimistically to her food bowl, Bruno fumbled the phone up to his ear, and mumbled, "Hello?"

The sharp, quick voice of his lawyer echoed grimly in his ear. "Bruno? Nick Weregild here. We've got to talk."

"Yeah, all right, I'm here."

"Are you okay? You sound like you just woke up."

"Yeah, I fell asleep. All right now." He rubbed his face and blinked, trying to clear the last shards of strange dreams of books and knives and glowing eyes, glad to be awake.

"Listen, maybe I should call back later," Weregild said. From the tone, Bruno knew it could only be bad news.

"No, I'm okay, just hold on for a second, please?"

As the attorney waited, he stumbled into the bathroom, and performed the necessary ablutions. Returning to the phone, he felt much better though the kitty glared at him from beside her bowl.

"Yeah, I'm back. So what's up? You sound pissed."

"Well, yes, Bruno, I am, a little. I thought you were absolutely sure you never, ever told anybody about your abuse from the time it happened until you remembered it this year."

"Yes, that's right. So?"

"So your brother the priest testified in his deposition that you had warned him about both Wilson and DeLaval when you were kids."

"What? That's impossible!"

"Impossible or not, that's what he said, and held to it."

"Oh my God, wait a minute. This can't be happening."

Weregild let him rave. When Bruno finally paused for air, he said wryly, "Obviously, you have some problems with your brother you need to work out.

"But the bottom line is this: it's your word against his. Whether or not you actually told him after it had happened, if that's what he maintains, we're screwed. Plain and simple."

Bruno tried to object but the lawyer bore on relentlessly. "In that case, the Church's side will argue that you recognized the injury at the time and therefore bore the burden of reporting despite your tender years. Whatever Wilson did, your suit was then filed oh, say, nineteen years too late. Frankly I don't know why they haven't already asked for summary judgment against us. Oh, and since he mentioned DeLaval also, we're blocked there, too."

"Jesus Christ almighty! It's not fair! I didn't remember!"

"As I told you before," the lawyer said somewhat less acerbically, "I can't get you justice, only money and damn little of that, it seems. I think our only chance is to settle quickly."

"What if I insist on fighting it out?" Bruno asked hoarsely.

"Unless you can punch holes in your brother's story, you lose. I should point out that in that event, you'll undoubtedly have to pay court costs and my fees at least. You might even get counter-sued. Not to mention what it would do to your family."

"Crap."

"Exactly. But there's still hope. Monsignor Malachy admitted some suspicions about Wilson but refused to say much about DeLaval because of the confidentiality of Confession. Legally, we can't touch him on that, but since he's the one we'll finally have to deal with, maybe he'll be reasonable, as he obviously knows something. If you don't piss him off too much in the meantime, that is. So, what do you want to do?"

"I don't know. How long can I think about it?"

"Not very long. If we're going to settle, I think we should do it soon, lest they start relishing the feel of your balls in their grip."

"Yeah, yet again." Bruno sighed. "I know Mike. If he said it under oath, he surely believes it. Nothing I can do about it."

"I'm sorry, Bruno, truly I am. I'll try to cut the best deal I can, but if you can still pray, now's a good time."

"To who, the devil?" he snorted. "No, sorry. I know you worked hard and I thank you for it. I'm just real disappointed."

"Yeah, me too. Okay, tell you what. Think about it over the weekend. If there's any way you can refute your brother, we still have a chance. Otherwise, we go for whatever we can get."

After he put down the phone, Bruno stood there, trembling. "God damn it!" he shouted suddenly. Cursing like a drunken sailor, he pounded the pillow until it disintegrated into a cloud of feathers. His cat hid until he collapsed on the floor weeping, and then calmly resumed her station by her bowl.

"Sweet Merciful Jesus," he groaned, "I just want to get drunk."

†

CHAPTER FORTY-ONE

Saturday, September 25

THE RESTAURANT was busy late this weekend night with the after-theatre crowd, and Malachy was dressed in a long-sleeved turquoise jacket and slacks, but Bruno had no difficulty spotting him. It was reassuring that his priest-radar was still working. He straightened his leather jacket; the weight of the pistol holstered behind reassuring, and went in.

"Evening," he said gruffly, plopping down opposite the gray-stubbled old man in the booth. "Don't take this the wrong way, but you appear odd dressed like a civilian."

Malachy smiled warily, playing with the handle of his coffee cup. "Feel strange, too, like I'm working undercover."

That made Bruno even uneasier, but the arrival of the waitress distracted him. He glanced longingly at the beer and wine list but said, "Just coffee, please."

Malachy nodded approvingly and ordered more for himself. He casually asked, "On the wagon still, or is this for me?"

Bruno snorted. "No, I'm still dry. Why should you care?"

The priest shrugged, gazing at him thoughtfully. "I've been hoping for a chance to tell you that it's something we have in common. You see, I'm an alcoholic, too."

"Really?" Bruno was genuinely nonplussed. "You, a boozer? I've never seen you at any meeting. Besides, you're a priest. I mean, how can you say Mass?"

"The group I attend is only for professionals — doctors, police, and others who don't want to run into those they serve under such circumstances." He shrugged. "As for my Eucharistic duties, I'm duly authorized to use mustum — unfermented grape juice — rather than regular wine for Communion. I'm just forbidden to share it with anybody."

The waitress came by with a pot of java. After she left, Bruno asked, "Well, this is all very interesting, but why tell me? Why did you ask me here, anyway? If this is about my case, shouldn't you be talking to my lawyer instead of me, seeing that we're on different sides?"

"Actually, we ought to be on the same side," Malachy sighed. "We should work together, despite our differences. This goes beyond your settlement. I thought you should know, because my boozing has a lot to do with the amends I need to make to you." Bruno stopped, cup midway to mouth, surprised at hearing a priest use those words he knew all too well.

"Don't be so amazed. I owe you several, actually." The old man sighed heavily again. "Like you, Bruno, I'm cursed with a flaming Irish temper and the pride that goes with it. When that woman called the Ghost Springs Retreat House a 'pedophile resort,' for instance, I saw red.

"It may have become so; I don't know. Much has surely changed, but the stories in the papers are incredible.

"What I do know is that they saved my vocation, and probably my life as well. If it weren't for the Ministers' treatment, I hate to think what would have become of me.

"And I've been in a rage at you a long time too, son. I nearly lost it when you put me on the spot about Chavez. I was more furious at you than at him."

His old pastor appeared completely abashed. This was beyond mere novelty. Bruno completely forgot everything else and set his mug down.

Malachy took a sip and cleared his throat. "You see, I must confess that all along I suspected Wilson." He cradled his cup in his hands, like a candle in the wind, gray face gaunt.

"Oh Mother in Heaven, where do I start?" He paused. "Do you recall the day I first came to Our Lady of Solitude?"

"Sure — the day after President Kennedy was shot."

"I met your mother and brother first that day," Malachy continued. "They were praying before La Victoria, and well, I've never seen a kid appear more devout."

"The word everyone always used was 'angelic,' I believe," Bruno offered dourly.

"Exactly. Then I ran into you, kneeling on the porch before Wilson. You seemed defiant, even then. What, by the way, was really going on there? I knew something wasn't right."

"Oh, nothing much. What I've remembered is that Father Busch hauled me over there right out of the confessional to apologize because I had griped to him about Father Wilson."

"Out of the confessional?" Malachy was shocked. "And he told Wilson what you said?" Bruno nodded matter-of-factly.

"Villains! Bloody sacrilegious bastards!" Malachy exploded, clenching his fists. "And to think I've kept their black secrets all these years —" He bit the words off and sat there glowering.

Bruno waited as Malachy's color slowly cooled back down a shade of pink or two. "What happened was this," the cleric said at last. "I first arrived at the cathedral to check into some financial irregularities. I thought DeLaval was involved but I couldn't prove it, so when old Clausewitz had his stroke, Bishop Lewis put me in charge, much to the dislike of both DeLaval and Wilson. I remained as vicar until, well, all this."

"That's when Wilson was murdered, wasn't it?"

"That happened a little later, around May Day, 1964, but from the beginning, the situation wasn't right. They kept bringing kids over to the rectory all the time — including you and Mike. There were sleepovers, wrestling bouts, and other inappropriate activities. I've told the attorneys all I saw.

"It became even worse after Wilson's murder, believe it or not, so I one day I finally confronted DeLaval.

"Instead of denying anything, the fiend admitted everything. I was still fairly new as a priest, so when he broke down and wanted to confess, I took him at his word. Caught me completely off-guard." He paused, staring into his bitter cup.

"Even if I could, I wouldn't repeat the monstrous things he said. He boasted of — of what he had done. When I denied him absolution, he laughed hatefully and said it didn't matter because my lips were now sealed.

"And of course, he was right. Canon law absolutely forbad me to tell anyone — even my superiors — what he told me, for any reason, even without absolution. Breaking the seal of the sacrament of Penance is considered a far graver offense against the sanctity of the Church than mere crimes of violence and perversion, I fear.

"That's why I took to the solace of the bottle; to try to forget. But drunk or sober, it haunts me still, so Christ forgive me, I had to talk to you."

"For God's sake, man! Couldn't you have done something? You could at least have told the bishop or someone what just you told me!" Bruno had difficulty keeping his voice low.

Malachy said softly, "Wilson was found dead in his car at a highway rest stop, blood drained from his body. Tom's cronies backed his alibi. I knew I could easily wind up the same way.

"Despite his implied threats, I wrote a letter to Bishop Lewis stating all I had seen, strongly recommending that he be sent away for evaluation, and that's exactly what the bishop did. Wilson was conveniently blamed for the missing money.

"Things settled down, but the Ministers soon returned Tom to us with a clean bill of health. For whatever it's worth, Bruno, I've fought him all the way ever since. I've opposed him at every turn, but he's as clever as he is wicked, with many allies. Some, I think, even within the chancery itself."

He sighed sorrowfully. "I gladly took the job on the Review Board as my own penance. Just as I've watched over Mike all these years — because I wasn't able to save you."

"What do you mean?" Bruno croaked.

There was an expression of enormous sadness in the old man's colorless, deeply furrowed face, but he said nothing.

Bruno rubbed his forehead. "You mean, he confessed it."

The old priest peered at him. "Worse things than that."

Bruno chuckled bitterly. "So you knew all along about DeLaval buggering me, and were never going to tell?" His hand itched again for his gun.

Malachy leaned forward and gazed at him with great sincerity. "I couldn't. In good conscience, I couldn't. But you needn't worry about your settlement, Bruno; I swear before God it will be generous."

"Great," Bruno said with poisonous sarcasm, churning with fury. "What about the others? At least call off the countersuit against Dolores."

Malachy said, "Gladly, if you'll end this silly feud between you and Mike. He did not willingly torpedo your case. He mentioned what you said in front of Father Cruz and I. It was Cruz who told the lawyers, not I, and certainly not Mike."

He paused, regarding Bruno narrowly through his thick glasses. "It's not a one-way street. You've treated your brother quite poorly. I heard about your schoolboy stunts in Denver.

Did you know you cost him his big chance to personally meet the Holy Father?"

Bruno was torn between a flash of mean satisfaction and embarrassment. Then Malachy said, "Indeed, it almost sounded as if you and he got into a fistfight."

"Is that what he said? I wouldn't hit Mike, certainly not for — whatever reason." Suddenly Bruno's internal struggle was between indignation and panic.

The old priest shrugged. "I don't know what passed between you two at the Mass and I don't care. Mike didn't say, but remember, I taught both of you to box. I can tell when you boys've been at it."

Bruno leapt up, shaking his head. "No way, that can't be, Father. No, he's lying. He must be under DeLaval's spell!"

He stepped back, babbling in fear. "You nearly had me there, Father Malarkey. I know I failed Mike bad when we were kids, but this is nuts."

The old man sadly gazed up at him, anticipating another disappointment. Bruno drew a deep, shuddering breath, and determinedly sat back down again.

Aware of all eyes in his direction, he leaned forward, clasping his hands together. "Okay," he said shakily in a low voice. "Maybe you're right. Sorry."

He stared hard at the priest. "You want to try working together; okay, I'll give it a shot."

He sighed heavily. "I remember some pretty weird shit that you might not want to believe." He gestured at the waitress. "We'll need more coffee. This is going to take awhile."

☦

CHAPTER FORTY-TWO

1964: The Feast of St. Peter Martyr, Monday, April 20

ONLY PURE WILLPOWER kept Eddie in bed until Mike had finally left with Father Wilson, but he dare not move until after his mother came in to check on him again. He wanted to throw the hot, suffocating blankets off, but he needed a convincing temperature.

Eddie did indeed feel sick to his stomach, partly through blame. His guts twisted again in a knot when he heard the screen door slam behind the whiny little brat at last, and there was a sour taste in the back of his mouth.

He wasn't sure what he'd set his brother up for, but he had to do it. In the sacristy after Easter Mass three weeks before, Father Wilson had mentioned that "it's almost that time of year again," with an unlikely twinkle in his eyes. DeLaval had laughed too, giving him a funny look. He didn't know why but it had made him queasy, and that suggested it.

He heard the door swing open, and someone tiptoe through the scattered toys and comic books to his bed. Slowly rolling over, he sleepily peeked up at the concerned face of his mother as she bent down to gaze at him. Martha was wreathed, as always, in stale cigarette smoke.

She gently touched his forehead. "Still a little warm," she said. "Are you feeling better, honey? Would you like something else to drink, maybe some soup?" His glass of ice water was untouched. Eddie had actually thrown up earlier, and though relieved at proving his excuse, he didn't want to risk it again. Since serving Mass with Father DeLaval yesterday, though not feeling really sick, he couldn't keep anything down.

Now he just shook his head. "Naw, thanks, Mom. I think I just want to get some sleep right now." He tried a yawn to see if it would help.

His mother gazed down at her eldest son with an unreadable expression, and he felt even more uneasy.

Martha sighed. "Okay, honey. Sleep tight," she whispered, kissing him on his clammy forehead. There was a slight smell of sherry, which for once was odd. She drank a lot, but rarely when one of her boys was sick.

He stirred and peered at her guiltily but gratefully. "Mom, thanks for not making me go tonight."

She smiled sadly. "Don't thank me, thank Mike. And Father DeLaval." Turning off the overhead, she withdrew, leaving the room in gloom.

His gut twisted again. Since he hadn't shown up at school, Father Wilson had kept calling all day. But for once his mother had supported him. Not only keeping him home; she'd even refused Wilson's demands to talk to him on the phone, which is what saved him. Eddie knew he could never refuse that gruff voice.

And Father DeLaval had been a most unexpected ally, calling his mother up to suggest that Mike take his place.

Eddie had spent much time trying to talk Mike into it. The kid smelled a rat, though, and Eddie parted with his most prized Marvel comics in the end. Convincing Father Wilson through his mother was even more difficult. The priest insisted; Eddie, trying to eavesdrop, could not make out his words but sensed his worry. Finally, Wilson had given up and raced over after dinner to pick Mike up.

During the wait, Eddie had nearly blown it. "Listen, shrimp," he'd said, throwing off the covers, "we gotta talk." He'd sat down on the floor next to his little brother.

"Don't trust Feeler Wilson," he'd told him. "He's bad. Really bad. Don't be alone with DeLaval either."

Mike continued to read his new comic so Eddie punched him in the stomach. "Ow!" Mike whined. "Knock it off!"

"Listen, I'm not kidding! These guys can hurt you!"

"Well, then, I don't want to go!"

"You gotta go. You promised Mom, remember? But you can trust Malarkey. He's okay."

Mike had kept whining. Feeling guilty, Eddie then had given him his prized but already tattered first issue of *The Amazing Spider-Man* as well, and crawled back into bed.

Luckily, Father Wilson was so anxious about the time he had forgotten completely to check in on Eddie. So they had left quickly, and now Eddie tossed and turned, feeling alternately glad and awful by turns. He couldn't read; all he could do was wait alone in the dusk, for what, he did not know.

He silently cried himself to sleep.

† † †

THE ORANGE had faded to purple on the crests of the Sanbenitos in the gathering twilight when Wilson's big gray Chevy screeched into the rectory's driveway, momentarily overwhelming the Italian opera that flowed out the bedroom window. Malachy turned around in surprise from the flowerbed, glass of wine in hand, but kept the hose trained on the roses.

With a scowl, Phil Wilson leaped out of the vehicle, slamming the door. Ignoring Sean, he wagged his finger at the small shape inside, "Stay put! I'll be right back."

The lanky priest then dashed into the building with long strides. Malachy set his glass of wine down and calmly dropped the hose before wandering over to peer into the vehicle.

"Hello, Mike! What're you doing here?"

"Oh, hi, Father Malachy. I'm subbing for Eddie tonight."

"Really. What's going on?" the priest asked, leaning on the car door.

The kid shrugged. "I don't know. Eddie said it was a Mass of some kind. I think he said it was a black one."

Malachy went rigid. He could hear Wilson banging around in his own room, then cursing in DeLaval's next to it. "Come on," he said after a second, opening the door, "get out."

"But Father Malachy," Mike began. The porch door behind them slammed. "Hey, you!" Wilson shouted. "I said stay in the car."

The other priest did not let go of the car door. "What's going on, Phil? Where are you taking this boy?"

"None of your damned business," Wilson growled. He clasped and unclasped his hands and appeared like he wanted to strike Malachy. He lunged towards the vehicle.

Malachy blocked the taller man, hands suddenly turned into fists. They glared at each other through their mask-like eyeglasses. "Yes it is my business," he said. "Bishop Lewis put me in charge here, not you."

Wilson grunted in scorn. "You don't have to remind me," he growled. He fought for calm. He said in a placating tone, "The boy's to serve at the annual Mass tonight for the prayer sodality Tom and I belong to."

"You should have mentioned this before. You know we require posted schedules now. And for a server this young, on a school night, a note from his parents is also needed."

"I'm sorry, you're right," Wilson said with a forced smile and strained lightness. "I'll do better next time. But now, I'm quite late and I can't find my, my liturgy. You haven't seen a black book anywhere around here, have you?" There was a desperate edge beneath the attempted casual tone.

Malachy shook his head. "Maybe Tom's got it."

This did not seem to please Wilson. "In that case, everything's fine, just fine," he grated through teeth clenched like a grin of death. "Except that we're late. We really ought to go."

"Well, how about it, Mike? Wouldn't you rather stay here?" Malachy asked, never taking his eyes off Wilson.

The boy's face lit up then he looked warily between the priests. "Well, I did sort of promise —" Wilson moved forward but the shorter priest stayed in his way, swaying slightly.

"Michael, you don't have to go if you don't want to," Malachy said. A tenor warbled in the background.

"Cool," Mike said. He jumped out of the car.

Wilson's face went dark then pale. "Sean, I must at least bring a server," he implored. "It's important; really, it is."

Malachy's stance shifted, and his fists came up slightly. "Okay," Wilson said with a long, shuddering sigh. His shoulders dropped. "I suppose I can get along without one."

"Fine," Malachy said gruffly. Eyes on Wilson, he reached out and took Mike's hand. The boy huddled behind him.

Wilson drew himself upright and nodded fatalistically. Malachy shut the door hard. Without another word Wilson climbed into the station wagon and roared off into the night.

Malachy smiled and patted the boy on his head. "I've got to finish watering the garden, and then I can take you home," he said. Picking up his wineglass, he gazed up at the first stars twinkling above the mountains and took a deep breath of the perfumed evening air as the aria continued. "My, it's surely a beautiful evening, isn't it, lad?"

CHAPTER FORTY-THREE

1993: Feast of Our Lady of the Rosary, Sunday, October 10

CAS grumbled, "I'm not sure about this," as she tucked her hair beneath the wimple, frowning at the side mirror of her truck. "Why costumes, anyway? I thought this was supposed to be a graduation party."

"A Master's party," Bruno replied edgily, "with a Halloween theme. 'Come as your favorite historical or mythological character.' I thought you were looking forward to this; after the last few months, I know I could sure use some fun."

Cas finished adjusting her black and white nun's habit and began to touch up her crimson lips. "Yeah, I was." She sighed, peering around uneasily at the old houses surrounded by dead leaves from gnarled elms. Some places were already decorated with ghosts and witches. "I just detest this season." She turned to offer Bruno the lipstick.

"No thanks, I've got the real thing going. Ouch." His homemade crown of thorns was proving all too realistic as he gingerly adjusted it upon his head. He posed briefly, looking heavenward, holding up a plastic goblet like a chalice. "Well?"

Despite herself she had to laugh. His hair was almost shaggy enough, and with his scruffy beard, the thorns, and dirty white tunic, red-stained like his counterfeit hand wounds, he made a passable version of a suffering, albeit pudgy, Jesus. "Even more blasphemous than your last outfit. Thank God your family's not here to see it."

"We could favor Mike afterwards with a vision over at the rectory," Bruno grinned nastily, "but I'd rather have a more private communion of saints. Give your savior a kiss, little bride of Christ." He advanced, puckering, and she batted him away.

"No!" she said and meant it. "My make up," she explained, softening her tone. "It took forever to get this vamp look." Bruno backed off and said nothing about the lack of observable difference from her usual appearance.

"Oh, sorry." He held out his other hand. "Okay?"

Cas nodded but her frown lingered. Holding hands as they strolled along the cracked sidewalk through the crisp twilight, Bruno tried small talk to ease the tension. "Where'd you get that habit, anyway?"

"I made it to model for a painting of St. Rita, patroness of hopeless cases. Maybe I should've come as her."

Bruno said no more after that.

Emily's house was an old two-story Victorian in the student ghetto, a still ungentrified section of town near campus. It wasn't hard to find, with the loud mideastern music and a skinny Union officer talking to an immensely fat Cleopatra on the steps of the front porch.

Cas asked, "Remind me again why we're here?"

"Purely political, my dear," Bruno said out of the side of his mouth. "I need to kiss up to the head of my committee tonight."

"Smooch away, but please, let's not stay too long, okay?"

"Just give me the high sign, babe," he sighed, but he was already greeting fellow partygoers. It seemed like the entire graduate division was present. They climbed the stairs, passed through the crowd of Vikings, Romans, and a space alien or two gathered around the keg on the deck and on into the house.

The front room was filled with men appreciatively watching several belly dancers writhe to loud, rapid drumming from a couple of authentic-looking Arabs with dumbeks. Bruno and Cas proceeded past a closed bedroom reeking of skunky pot to the back room, a converted porch. Lounging in a plantation chair, Iggy was holding court there in a knot of rapt students.

Wearing his academic robes over black tights and shirt, he managed to appear vaguely sinister.

He broke off in mid-diatribe at the sight of Bruno and sprang to his feet. "Should I drop to my knees, or call for the centurion?" he exclaimed. "Merciful Lord!"

"Yes?" Bruno asked calmly and displayed the marks on his hands. "Easy now; it's been a rough weekend."

Iggy finally stopped laughing enough to notice his companion. "Ah, you must be Cas," he said, shaking her hand warmly. "I'm Iggy Mithers. Very pleased to meet you."

Cas smiled. Not to be outdone, she said sweetly, "Actually tonight, I'm Heloise, and this is Abelard." Out of her sleeve she drew a realistic rubber dildo. The clump of intellectuals caught the reference and cracked up again, Bruno included.

They were still chuckling when a voluptuous woman swept into the room. It was their hostess, decked out as a Minoan snake goddess in flounced skirt and tight-waisted corset. A real python encircled her shoulders, but fake rubber serpents wrapped her arms. A thin bodice covered her enormous breasts, dark nipples perky in the evening chill.

"Jesus, Bruno, you look heavenly!" Emily proffered her hand regally to be kissed. A bottle of red Grecian wine that she had obviously been enjoying was in the other.

"As do you, goddess," he said gallantly, but carefully shook her hand instead. "Emily, may I present my friend, Cas?"

"Charmed."

"Likewise."

But the women were already shooting daggers at each other from their eyes. Emily continued her progress, a thin, boyish blonde dressed in a Greek chiton taking her arm.

Cas hissed angrily, "Your 'friend?' Is that all I am?"

"No of course not, dear." Bruno went into the kitchen, fished a soda out of an ice chest and dumped it into his cup. She followed him. "I think we need to talk, Bruno. You act like you're ashamed to admit we're together to that big-titted bimbo. I thought you wanted me to come so we could meet your friends. What's wrong? Is there somebody else? Is it her?"

Exasperated, Bruno grabbed her by the elbow and dragged her over to a corner. "Keep your voice down, for God's sake. You're the one making a scene here. There's nothing going on — especially with Emily, if that's what you think. As for us, well, maybe we do need to talk, but not here."

"What do you mean?"

"I mean we're at a party, damn it! People are staring."

"Don't evade the question. What do you mean?"

"I don't know," he mumbled, eyes lowered. She put her hand under his chin and forced him to look at her. "I remembered more stuff," he said flatly. "Not much, but you, the chapel, us, and, and I don't know how to deal with it."

"I see," she said, turning even paler. She seemed to shrink, and abruptly tossed the sex toy into the garbage with a clatter. Almost absently she pulled her keys from her other sleeve. "Well, yes, I do understand. I think I'd better go now, if you don't mind." She bolted out the back door.

Bruno caught up by the backyard gate. "Cas! Wait! I'll go with you!" He grabbed her by the wrist. Her mascara was already streaming down her face like a heavy-metal rocker from her weeping. "No. I, I need to be alone. Stay here with your friends. Maybe you won't feel so strange with her!"

She twisted out of his grip and slammed the gate, which caught him on the knee. He stood there cursing himself while people pretended not to notice. Limping back inside, he kicked the trashcan hard, hurting his other foot as the dildo rattled mockingly. He found his goblet and drained it. Iggy ambled into the kitchen with an inquiring gaze.

"You okay? I couldn't help overhearing."

"Yeah, neither could the greater metro area. So much for staying cool and calm. Somehow I still create a scene."

"This sounds rather odd coming from a crucified man."

Bruno snorted. "I suppose it does at that." He peered longingly into his cup. "This is one of those days when I wish I could do that water into wine trick."

A jug materialized seemingly from nowhere above his fake chalice and red liquor miraculously splashed into it. He felt a warm presence suddenly close as a low female voice huskily murmured, "You don't even have to ask."

It was Emily, sans snake, swaying just inches away with a knowing smile. "With the Goddess, all things are possible."

"Ah, what the hell," Bruno said, mainly to himself. To Emily, he toasted, "Ave, Dea Bona, morituri te salutant!" Iggy choked a guffaw, spun on his heel and tactfully retreated. Bruno took a long draft, nearly gagging on the piney taste. Greek wine had never been a poison of choice, but didn't that make it better if he was going to drink? He swallowed hard.

He fought down the urge to retch and slammed back another gulp. Less trouble this time; his long-starved alcohol sensors, jolted into action at last, eagerly alerted the rest of his nervous system. The third swallow was easy, almost pleasant.

Bruno smiled back at his tipsy hostess. She threw her arms around him, sloshing cold booze down the back of his tunic onto the linoleum floor. He put his arms around her to steady her. She leaned against him and whispered, "Don't be sad, little Messiah. You don't need Mary Magdalen or whoever she was." She kissed him full on the lips, her mouth wet and hot on his, tongue probing like a viper's.

He pushed her away, gently. "Let me show you what a real woman can do," she breathed. She suddenly noticed her skinny, winsome friend standing nearby and kissed her hard too. "You don't have to be such an inhibited old redeemer," she teased Bruno, draping a rubber-snake wrapped arm around the slender woman's shoulders. "This is Andrea. You can have your cake and eat it too, you know."

She whispered into the young blonde's ear and they both giggled. The other smiled promisingly, slipped out from under her arm and disappeared down the hall.

Emily grabbed Bruno's crown of thorns and tossed it into the trash. She kissed him again with a sustained intensity that left him breathless. "But we don't have to do the entire suffering corn-god thing tonight, okay?"

Smiling, she took him by the hand and silently led him up the back stairway, past the upstairs bath and a bedroom already in service. At the end of the narrow hallway, her sanctuary was warm and softly lit with a dozen fat white candles. Festooned like an Arabian Nights fantasy, the boudoir had Persian carpets scattered about the floor, vases filled with peacock plumes and a large, well-lit glass box housing her pet snake. The walls were hung with tapestries and the bed was a pile of colorful cushions on a dais, surrounded by gauzy white veils.

Emily sat him down on a plush ottoman and refilled his cup. She began to massage his twisted neck muscles with strong, skilled fingers, humming to the insistent beat reverberating up through the floor. Bruno began to relax almost against his will.

Then Andrea sat on the edge of the cushions and slipped the chiton off her shoulder. Waif-like, her breasts were very small, with not even a sag to them, hips hardly larger than her waist. Emily stopped kneading Bruno's shoulders and reclined on the pillows. The women kissed deeply. They both smiled invitingly at Bruno as the blonde undid the tight lacing of Emily's corset.

Bruno's mind spun even as his body responded to one of his great erotic fantasies coming true. Emily smiled languorously as she leaned back. The blonde pulled down the bodice past Emily's jiggling brown nipples. Emily spread her legs, pulling up the many-layered dress, and toyed with her dark-haired crotch. Andrea, still silent, beckoned with a knowing grin.

Bruno rose, weaving slightly. He took another sip of courage. Emily opened her arms receptively for him, rubber reptiles still coiled about, and murmured enticingly, "Come and taste the good things the Goddess has to give you!"

Suddenly aghast, his face drained of color. He stumbled backwards, dropping the cup. "Mother of God! Now I remember!" he exclaimed.

Without another word, he groped for the door and fell through it, tripping over people in line for the toilet. He didn't hear their cursing but he knew where he must go.

†

CHAPTER FORTY-FOUR

BOB CRUZ lamented, "Ay, my friend, have you ever seen anything so sad?" His dolorous query echoed in the shadows of the Cathedral of Our Lady of Solitude. The scraping noises and whispers of the two men in the empty void as they strolled made it seem even more forlornly deserted now that La Victoria's last feast there was done.

"No, I must admit, nothing on God's Earth," Mike replied softly, patting his old seminary classmate on the back. The sounds softly bounced around them. They were taking their final tour of the first bishop of Alvarado's great dream, named from the loneliness he'd endured on the frontier, at the closing end of the very last day of services ever to be held there.

"Is there anything more we have to do? You sure there's no special deconsecrating ceremony?" the chancellor asked.

Mike shook his head. "None that I could find. Theoretically the decision to destroy it is sufficient. Sure doesn't seem right. The old place deserves much better than that."

"At least, I suppose some consolation is that so much of her will go to enrich her daughter churches," Cruz noted sadly.

The racks of votive candles, the holy water and baptismal fonts, the Stations of the Cross, the statuary, and everything else that had made this place a living church would soon be gone. Nuestra Señora would be moved secretly to a temporary home in the TV chapel. The altars, old and new, with the tabernacles and carved stone reredo from old Mexico in her chapel would be carefully disassembled and lovingly restored before being installed in the new basilica on the hill.

Everything of value that could be taken would be reused; from the pews, stained glass windows, and other architectural fixtures to the bells in the crumbling towers above and the dead bishops rotting in the crypt beneath. All, that is, save for the huge mosaic of the Sorrowful Mother on the rear wall. She cost too much to rescue and thus would perish beneath the wrecking ball. Only her memory would linger.

The two priests had been ordained together beneath her stern gaze, and Mike was posted there shortly thereafter. His whole life had been spent in Our Lady of Solitude's snug and pleasant shade. For him, it was as much a fortress of faith as any of the ancient missions, and he still dearly loved it.

He shook his head sadly. "Oh, I know it was a colossal financial drain and out of place, but still, we have such times gone by here, you and I."

Cruz nodded again as if unable to speak. Mike continued, "And as for the new one, well, I doubt if it'll ever have anything like her colorful history: shoddy construction, that horrible accident, the infamous kidnapping of La Victoria — not to mention the founder miraculously rising from his grave."

Cruz had to smile at the last. The floating of the coffin of Bishop Laretz from out of the crypt in the great flood of '72 was legendary, seen by many as an omen from God condemning the place. It was surely a sign that the poorly laid foundations were being undermined but the millions spent shoring the foundations afterwards had bought only a few decades more.

"Speaking of which, will the tenth bishop of Alvarado ever be buried in the new cathedral?"

Cruz dismissed the idea with a snort. "Not likely. Chavez will be lucky if he gets a plot in his hometown."

"But shouldn't he, who did so much to build it, someday have a memorial there?"

"He's left enough of one in all those bloody lawsuits sucking us dry. Malachy refuses to see how desperate our situation is. We could still be forced into bankruptcy, leaving the new cathedral unfinished, too. 'Laretz' folly' might still be outdone by Chavez," Cruz said vehemently.

Mike glanced with concern at his friend, who appeared as much betrayed as the Mater Dolorosa. It was as if the upcoming demolition was threatening to tear him apart too. The chancellor had been virtually living at the old cathedral lately, coming by daily to help clean out all the closets and the attic.

Mike said, "Well, at least we got to celebrate La Victoria's own feast day here one last time. For that, I'm grateful. Next year, in her own cathedral, you can have that grand procession like you've always dreamed of."

That cheered him a bit. By now they had reached the switchboard by the sacristy and Mike started to turn off the lights. Suddenly, they heard a racket at the side door.

"Come on, come on," a man shouted impatiently.

"All right, Bruno! Be careful." There was a clatter, the door flung open and Malachy and Mrs. O'Leary scurried in. Behind them, dressed in a stained white tunic, hair wild, painted like a medieval vision of the damned, followed Bruno, gun in hand.

"What in God's Holy Name?" Mike demanded.

"Ah little brother! Good, I wanted you to see this!"

He waved the pistol, herding them all forward. Malachy huddled with the weeping housekeeper, a little Navajo woman as round as a dumpling, trying to comfort her.

"Come on, into the chapel!" Bruno yelled. "Now!"

Reluctantly, Malachy unlocked it and turned on the lights. Bruno drove them all inside.

Nuestra Señora de Victoria stood in the gloom within her niche in the altarpiece, as ready as ever for a fight. Vases of red and white roses in honor of her feast overflowed her altar below.

Dimly lit by banks of votive candles, she smiled fearlessly down. Bruno stared back blankly as he stood, swaying slightly.

"Bruno, what are you going to do?" Mike implored as Bruno abruptly approached the altar.

"Don't you dare touch her," Cruz called out.

Bruno ignored them, feeling around the top with one hand while keeping the .45 more or less pointed in their direction. "You'll see, it's got to be here, under the white lady!"

He pushed back the linens, knocking over an urn, which shattered loudly on the marble floor. Everyone jumped save Bruno, who intently examined the exposed altarstone. A square block engraved with crosses was set firmly in the center of the slab. "What's in there?" he demanded.

"A few holy relics like in any altar," Mike said, "just scraps of saints' bones, bits of cloth. No gold or silver or anything of any monetary value, if that's what you're thinking."

Bruno didn't reply. Groping around the decorations on the marble front he finally pressed the right rosette and released the hidden spring. "Hah! I knew it!" he said as the front panel popped open. He pulled it wide. Amid the cobwebs within lay a thick book, bound in tooled black leather with a brass latch, and propped behind it, a cross of ebony and gold.

Bruno gestured to Mike. "You see? Bring the book out." Dumbfounded, the priest knelt and cautiously extracted the tome. Wiping the dust off revealed an embossed relief of the cross entwined with a gold-stamped serpent. "Heavenly Mother," Mike prayed, "what is this thing?"

Mike unlatched the cover carefully. On a handwritten title page, yellowed about the edges with time, in swooping letters, the schoolbook-perfect penmanship of an earlier age, was written, "*Codex de Arcanorum Diaboli.*"

"'*The Book of the Secrets of the Devil*,'" he translated.

"What in hell?" Cruz exploded, and strode up the steps. He bent over the book in amazement.

"See, I was right!" Bruno crowed, waving the gun about. "I knew it — Xaphon kept it here, just like I told Master Baalberith!" His face gleamed with a beatific leer that made him resemble Manson far more than Christ. He spread his arms wide. "Who's crazy now, eh?" he cackled, "Who's crazy now?"

And then he fell over in a dead faint.

†

CHAPTER FORTY-FIVE

Columbus Day, Monday, October 11

THE ROOM lazily swam back into focus. Bruno felt so relaxed that it was like drifting on a cloud, listening to chimes tinkling peacefully far off in the distance.

There was something shiny hovering above him in the early morning light. He blinked several times. The blur gradually resolved into the shape of a smiling angel, one of a flock of winged messengers soothingly orbiting overhead.

He shook himself at the bizarre vision, but everything stayed out of focus. Was he on the couch in his therapist's office? Dr. Blackstone was seated by a desk, seeming more frazzled than usual. A black book sat on top of some papers in front of her, an equally ebon cross next to it. Mike sat nearby, leaning on his knees, hands clasped, watching Bruno like a hawk.

"Oh man," Bruno yawned. "Sorry I dozed off like that. Don't know what got into me." He wanted to take off his glasses so he could rub his eyes, but the spectacles were gone and he couldn't move his arms. His wrists were bound to the armrests of the chair by a knotted stole.

He did a quick double-take. "What the hell is this? And what is he doing here?"

"The question is, what you are doing here, big brother," Mike replied. This wasn't his shrink's office after all, but one he once knew also too well: the pastor's study in the rectory of Our Lady of Solitude.

Bruno glanced over at the psychiatrist, confused. She appeared pale, tired, and nervous, as if she had just seen a ghost. "Well, ah, I thought I was in your office for a session."

"There was a session, sort of," she confirmed. "You remember anything?"

"Certainly not any strange bondage scene." Bruno peered towards the angels, thinking, and shook his head. "Actually, not much since early evening, except, maybe a costume party?"

He gaped at her in alarm. "What happened?"

She nodded at Mike and they both relaxed slightly. He rose and untied the cinctures around Bruno's arms. "First of all, how do you feel?" she asked.

Bruno rubbed his wrists. "A little weird, like there's something important I'm forgetting, but otherwise fine. Great, in fact, but stiff." He stretched and gratefully accepted his glasses from his doctor. "So what the hell's going on, anyway?"

"Sorry I had to tie you up, Buddy, but I didn't want to risk being hit again. You don't recall bursting in here and pulling a gun on Father Malachy and Mrs. O'Leary, do you?"

Bruno shook his head numbly.

"How about these then?"

"They resemble things I've been dreaming about recently," Bruno stammered, "along with a knife. I'm afraid to ask you what this means."

Mike shook his head resignedly. "We were hoping you could tell us." He rubbed the dark stubble on his chin. "Actually, Sean, Bob, and I stayed up most of the night trying to translate the damnable thing." He shook his head. "I'm just sorry that I ever thought you paranoid, brother."

"I did hit you, didn't I, there in Denver?" Bruno asked abruptly. "Funny, I didn't remember that before. DeLaval must have done something to me. I think he spoke to me first," he mused, shaking his head, and then looked at his brother. "Sorry, Michael, for whatever I've done. It's so confusing."

His brother patted Bruno's knee. "It's okay, Buddy. I understand a lot more now. It's amazing you survived any of it."

His voice choked. Mike stood unexpectedly, chair scraping loudly. "Anyway, coffee should be ready by now."

"What are you doing here?" Bruno asked his counselor.

"Monsignor Malachy called me in the middle of the night and persuaded me to come right over. Honestly, I didn't know a man of God could swear like that."

"Well, I heard he was in the Navy once," Bruno said dryly.

"Incredible," Blackstone remarked, perching her reading glasses on her nose for a better view. "And awful." She ran her fingers lightly over the embossed Cross of St. Peter Martyr on the battered leather skin of the book warily as if afraid the snake might bite. "I can't get over that this is real."

"You can't?" Bruno exclaimed. "Hey, you said you believed me. Or was that just shrink talk all along?"

The blonde woman tossed her curly head, flustered. "No, Bruno, I believed you, all right. But it's one thing to hear some wild story from somebody's childhood and quite another to hold the horrifying proof in one's own hands."

She opened the book, turning its pages cautiously. The *Codex* was upside down from Bruno's vantage but still very unsettling. The unpleasant diagrams, all circles and angles with strange writing and crosses scattered about, made him feel ill regardless of the angle from which he looked at them.

"I'm no expert but this sure looks like a book of spells to me," she said. At that point, the office door opened and Mike came in with a full coffee service on a tray. Behind him trailed Malachy in a bathrobe, sleepily adjusting his glasses.

"Oh that it is," Malachy said, plopping down in a chair. "With a name like '*The Book of the Secrets of the Devil*,' what else could it be? But aside from some superficial resemblances to the *Grimoire of Honorius* and several others I found in DeLaval's office, it's unlike anything I've ever seen. As you might well say, Bruno, it's damned weird shit. Here's what we've gotten before I went to bed. Sure didn't help me sleep any." He slid the notebook across the desk. "See for yourself, if you like.

"We made good headway with the introduction, which seems to have been composed later. The text itself is written in an archaic dialect of Church Latin with many peculiar technical terms. Hopefully, Bob will return soon with more dictionaries."

Blackstone picked up the notebook. "I guess we should try this now." She peered closely at Bruno. "While you were out, I tried to access your system. It was, um, interesting."

"Like a Hollywood exorcism, but without the green pea soup," Mike added laconically as he poured the coffee.

"Well, yes, it did get rather intense. We encountered a few of your dark alters which had been deliberately implanted. I won't lie: you have some pretty scary people in there, Bruno. But with the aid of some of the guardians, I believe we neutralized most of your more dangerous triggers, but to be sure, we need to see if you can handle this," she said.

His brother pulled out Bruno's .45 from the desk drawer and held it by the barrel. "It's not loaded; if you get out of line, I'll just have to hit you with it."

"Fair enough, I guess," Bruno said, hunkering down.

Hesitantly, Blackstone began to read the translation aloud. "'*In the Name of their Infernal Majesties, the most puissant Prince Lucifer, Lord of the Earth, King of Hell, Purifier of the Saints, Judge and Warden of the Damned, and His Lady Lilith, Queen of Hell, Mistress of Sorceries, Eternal Temptress and Whore of Babylon...*' Well, that's certainly explicit, I must say."

Bruno was hugging himself, rocking back and forth. "I'm still here, but please don't call up Old Nick just for my sake."

"I'm sorry, Bruno," she said sympathetically. "All your hard work getting ready to face this has really paid off. You did well." He nodded and reached for the coffee, hands trembling.

"That malevolent toadying is one of the sickest things about this evil book," Malachy said. "Oddly enough, most other grimoires take a commanding position over Satan based on the power and victory of Christ's Resurrection. However, this one's sanctimoniously subservient to the hierarchy of Hell."

Blackstone adjusted the lamp. "That opening part goes on for quite a bit," Mike commented. "The kicker's down in the last paragraphs." She flipped the page.

"Okay — '*Know then, that Hell is Heaven for those who Rule the Damned. Those who fail the Ordeal become the eternal Meat of Demons like ordinary Sinners, to be consumed forever in the Fires of Hell for the unending pleasure of Satan's Court and the holy satisfaction of all the Saints in Heaven.*'

"'*Those who succeed, the Dread Lord of Hades rewards by making them Friends of His Court, Infernal Saints of Hell and Princes of the Damned. They share in the torment of sinners with the Demons, and all that was forbidden them in this World is freely granted them that they may delight in their basest appetites without ceasing.*'

"Merciful heavens, Bruno, how horrible." She gazed at her client with a curious mixture of compassion and distaste.

"That explains it," Mike said flatly. "Those depraved imbeciles actually wanted to become possessed by devils, like they could escape punishment for their sins that way."

"There's more," Malachy said, reaching for the pad. Blackstone gladly handed it back.

"Here's what I thought you would find interesting," he said. "'*Book Five. On Choosing the Perfect Victim. This tells of the selection of Victims, for Sacrifice or as Candidates for Initiation into the*

Order from Families most afflicted by Sin and which Qualities are most desirable,' and so on.

"Now a note here in a different hand says '*Victimas Noviciis Comparerant*' and '*Victimas Immolerant*' referring to the final sections enumerating 'Victims Acquired as Novices' and 'Victims Sacrificed,'" he added grimly. "The latter seems to be a cryptic roll call of murder and fairly lengthy, I'm afraid. Most appear to be unidentifiable infants, but I believe an entry in DeLaval's hand lists 'Xaphon' — that is, Phil Wilson."

Malachy peered at Bruno with deep sorrow. "The former list, while much shorter, is even harder to figure out. But it has that cult name he gave you among them, I regret to say."

Bruno accepted the news silently.

"It's not just that name there, Bruno, but elaborate codes as well. They are labeled 'Keys'; triggers, no doubt," Blackstone explained. "While you were out, I used some to try to deactivate what I could find with the help of your inner children. I think we cleared out the most obvious bombs, at least."

"Bombs?"

"Booby-traps; deeply hidden programs to cause self-destruction if the host — or therapist — gets too near the truth or ceases being useful. Many unknown victims are lost that way and those around them just think it's an inexplicable suicide." She sighed. "Anyway, I couldn't be absolutely thorough and there was some heavy resistance. It will take time and hard work, but I think you're safe for the moment."

"This is preposterous," Bruno moaned. "Other people living in my head was awful enough; now I'm a walking bomb."

"Duh," Mike said sarcastically, and then softened. "Sorry, Buddy; some of us figured that part out quite a while ago."

"Anyway, the good news, Bruno, is that DeLaval should not be able to gain entrée to you again," Blackstone finished.

"Which means he was able to before," Bruno said dully. "How? I mean, I hate the guy. And I know I got away." He gazed up absently at the angels. "When he returned to Solitude, I once had to serve Mass for him. I worked it out with my friend Ralph that he would burst into the sacristy afterwards, and tell me some kids were stealing my bike so I couldn't stay."

He smiled slightly. "Worked like a charm. I was out of there before DeLaval could open his mouth. It was the happiest day of my life, because I thought I was free." He sighed. "I never again served Mass or called myself 'Eddie.' But I guess I wasn't as free as I thought, was I?"

"From what your kids said, I think he had your cult alter check in regularly by telephone, which is likely how he was able to set you up to attack your brother," Blackstone said.

"This might be the ticket to understanding the whole thing." Malachy interrupted, adjusting his thick glasses on the bridge of his blunt nose. "'*Book Six. On the Shattering of the Soul. Of the uses of Torment, Incantations, and Potions to break apart the Mirror of God. The method of Implantation of Spells and the Secret Words and Sigils of Power to gain absolute Mastery over the Shards of the Soul are shown.*'"

"If that doesn't sound like pure ritual abuse, I don't know what does," Blackstone exclaimed. "Breaking the soul into pieces is how some clients have described the effects of torture, rape, and drugs. These 'spells' and 'words of power' sound like what we might call 'hypnotic programming' and 'triggers.'"

"Sounds about right to me too," agreed Bruno, his face pinched and ashen. "But please, spare me any more details right now, okay? I'm still kinda woozy."

"Sorry, Bruno, but there's something more you all must hear," Malachy relentlessly bore on. "'*Book Seven. On Inhabitation by Devils. This book explains how Inhabitation differs from Fascination, Bewitchment, and Possession, being a perfect and agreeable form of Tenancy and Adoption by a Great Demon. Inhabitation rewards the Magus with the fell Powers of Blackest Magic in this life and the perfect Liberty of the Sons of God in the next. Why Blood Sacrifice must be freely offered by the Candidate to achieve this.*'"

"I guess I got out before that," Bruno said leadenly. "Maybe that's what would've have happened at that ceremony I avoided attending. The one I sent you to in my place, Mike. I'm so sorry, little brother, I'm so sorry." His eyes filled.

Mike appeared confused. "What — I never went to any ceremony, Bruno! At least, I don't think I did."

"He may be right, Bruno," Malachy said. "A week or so before Wilson was murdered, I stopped him from taking Mike somewhere one night." Bruno sat stunned, mouth agape.

"But even in my worst nightmare, I never imagined anything like this!" Malachy declared, firmly shutting the notebook. "I don't know what enrages me most; the horrible things these knaves have done, or their wicked arrogance in hiding this filth in the most sacred spot in the whole diocese."

"Maybe not just in La Victoria's chapel, either, Monsignor Malachy," Mike said softly. "They may have polluted every church, every shrine. How could we know?"

"You're absolutely right, Mike. Every building should be exorcised and re-consecrated." He took off his glasses to clean them. "And how can we know who all are involved? If this system actually functions like you say, Dr. Blackstone, wouldn't it give tremendous power to the top dogs? The entire outfit would be virtually enslaved by the leader."

"The consciously active members would also be bound by their common guilt," Blackstone said, "but their victims and slaves could conceivably be forced to participate without even knowing." She shivered. "Scary. Imagine a secret army, unable to disobey orders, and most likely not even aware of them. It would be the ultimate cult of assassins."

She gazed down at the *Codex*, and sighed. "The secrets are in here, not just for poor Bruno, but for who knows how many? We just need time to crack the mystery."

Bruno rubbed his face and stretched out on the couch. "It's all too much for me. I, I'm sorry, I just can't handle any more right now." As he closed his eyes, he mumbled, "Don't forget the new altar, Father Malachy. Some real bad things were done on it, too." Then he was fast asleep again.

Malachy paled. "Jesus, is there anything left untainted?"

Before Mike could reply, there came a sharp knocking on the door. Alarmed, he reached into the desk drawer for the Colt's ammunition clip.

But before he could reload the gun, the chancellor entered. Robert Cruz appeared as exhausted as the other men, and was burdened down by the weight of several large and dusty volumes. He dropped them loudly on the desk, but Bruno did not stir. "Here are the references we need, but I've been thinking," he said, carefully looking over his subordinates.

"I don't feel safe here with this, this thing. Once we're finished for the time being, I want it locked up in the secret archives." Sensing an impending explosion, "No, Sean; not to drop it into a black hole forever as it deserves, much as I'd like. But until we understand what this is all about, it's the only place around here with a lock that I can trust."

Mike said nothing.

CHAPTER FORTY-SIX

Tuesday, October 12

BRUNO stared dully at a gray history text, grimly trying to absorb it and failing again, when the ringing brought him instantly alert. He waited, somehow afraid to move. He heard his dejected announcement begin. "Hi, this is Bruno. What do you want?"

Then a deep, gravelly voice rumbled ominously. "Eddie, this is Father DeLaval. Eddie, be silent and listen! I call upon Kazideel! Awake, Kazideel, awake!" Bruno flinched, blood surging in horror.

"Your Master Baalberith commands! As soon as you finish hearing this message, erase —"

The hated voice was too much for Bruno to endure. He leaped upon the phone. "Hey! Eddie's not available to you anymore, you fat evil pervert. Nor is anybody else. What the hell do you want?"

There was a startled pause, then the monsignor chuckled, a deep, unpleasant sound like boulders grating together. "Well, well, well, this is quite a surprise. Good work, Eddie. Hardly anyone can truly awaken themselves. Phil was right — you did have potential."

"I'm not Eddie. I'm Bruno now, and always will be."

DeLaval chuckled. "Don't count on it, little man."

"Or what? You'll bugger me again? Put another damned spell on me?"

"Nothing so droll."

"You've lost, you know." Enraged, Bruno could not help crowing. "I found your damned book in the altar, turkey! And your stupid cross."

There was only the hissing of the line for a moment. "Unwise, Eddie, most unwise; I need them and will have them back, one way or another. I was going to have you fetch them for me anyway. So here's the deal: return my possessions voluntarily or what happens to your family will be upon your head, likewise if you tell anyone. I will give you an hour. Do not try your usual half-assed heroics." The line went dead.

Bruno sat there, breathing hard, until his fingers stopped trembling enough to punch in the number for Soledad.

Only the answering machine picked up. Bruno wavered as Mike's recorded voice recited the schedule of services, and then slammed down the phone. "Damn, why did I have to brag," he cursed as he dialed his former home.

It rang and rang on the other end; finally, just as he was ready to give up, his ex-wife cheerfully answered.

"Kathy! Where's Marie?"

"What? Why, she's not back from school yet. She should be still at the rectory with Mike, helping him box up the study. Buddy, what's wrong?"

"Holy Christ! When is she supposed to be home?"

"Heavens, not for another hour or so. She was going to stay late to help him get started packing up the old place after her tutoring session. What's happened?"

"Father DeLaval just called me and threatened my family. He was serious. I know this sounds crazy, but I think Marie's in danger, you, and even Mike, too."

"You haven't been drinking, by any chance, have you?"

Bruno bit his lip and counted to ten before speaking as calmly as he could. "Not for days," he snarled sarcastically but honestly, "and I'm not hallucinating, either. I'm dead sober and dead serious. I'm going over to the church. If you don't hear from me in an hour, call the cops."

"Is this necessary?"

"Just do it, for God's sake!" He slammed the phone down, knowing she would probably wait until long after her daughter did not come home. "Damn bitch never believes me," he muttered to himself. He redialed the rectory. Still no luck.

He was cursing himself that he had no gun when he heard a light tapping on the door. He grabbed a knife from the dish rack before approaching the door.

"Who is it?" he demanded.

"It's Cas," came a familiar voice.

"You alone?"

"Why, yes, of —" She didn't have time to finish. Bruno flung open the door, dragged her inside, and slammed it shut.

She saw the blade and froze. But Bruno sighed deeply and tossed it aside. "Oh baby, am I glad to see you," he said, enfolding her in his arms. She responded shyly at first.

He held her for a long moment then he pulled back, face grim. "There's trouble, big trouble. DeLaval just called, threatening me. I told him I found that damn book of his."

Despite her coat, he could feel her shudder. "Oh no, Bruno. What book? What are you going to do?"

Bruno disengaged and was already shrugging his black leather jacket on. "I'm going to kill the son of a bitch somehow, if I can find him. I'll explain on the way. First, I have to check Soledad." He looked about for a better weapon but he didn't have anything more formidable than that kitchen knife.

Cas twirled her hair nervously. "I'd like to help, Bruno, but you can't imagine how scared I am."

He stood close, gazing down into her anxious hazel eyes. "Yes, I do," he said simply, and she hugged him.

"I know," she said, voice muffled by his leathers. "That's why I came back. I've missed you, Bruno, so much. Nobody's ever understood us like you do, and still accepted me. I'm so sorry I doubted you."

He smiled sadly and she kissed him. "For luck," she said.

† † †

BY THE TIME they got downtown, it was fully dark and getting cold, an early fall storm threatening. Ragged clouds descending from the north had drowned the sun long before sunset.

Finding a parking spot was vexing in Plaza Vieja, the cramped, most touristy section of town, but Bruno did not dare risk the cathedral's own lot. Yet the narrow streets downtown were never intended for much more than two overladen burros at a time. Bumper to bumper with fat gringos in big cars, his progress was agonizingly slow.

Finally spying a hatchback being loaded, he held his ground and took the spot, to the vocal annoyance of those backed behind him.

Cas and Bruno cautiously approached the cathedral from a side street. A high construction fence topped with coils of razor wire already surrounded it. Only a filled-in hole by the front steps marked where her brother had died.

Pausing in the shadows across the street, they carefully surveyed the area. Bruno soon detected movement in the shadows of the trees near the darkened edifice's entrance, and cigarette smoke curled up into the light.

"There's our old friends, Laurel and Hardy," he whispered, discerning the dissimilar forms of the lurking men. "Something must be going on here. Come on."

Hand in hand, Bruno and Cas deliberately strolled across the plaza as leisurely as honeymooners to the other side where they could see into the parking lot. A clutch of vehicles was parked at the rear. "That's Mike's van, and I think that's Malachy's jalopy over there. Don't recognize any of the others."

The lights in the rectory past the school glowed invitingly as they walked along. Bruno stopped and glanced around. Then he rapidly crossed the street, pulling her along.

"Where are you going?" she asked as he scaled an adobe buttress by the back gate, but he gestured to her for quiet.

Moments later, the rickety wooden gate squeaked open, and Bruno let her into the back yard. "Why are we doing this?"

"I've got to get that book of DeLaval's," Bruno replied grimly. "Hopefully, Mike or Malachy stashed it somewhere."

"How are we going to get in?"

"Let's just hope they haven't remodeled back here too much," Bruno whispered. "Wilson showed me how to sneak out one night. Maybe we can get in the same way."

With that he broke off a dead branch of a nearby bare tree. He stretched upward, snaking his arm through a half-open window into a dark bedroom. A long moment of grunting and straining later and the security bars parted.

The hinges squealed loudly as he opened the grates but seemed not to attract anyone's attention, nor did opening the window itself. But it was quickly obvious that he would never fit. Cas took over and quickly slithered into the darkness.

There was another painful moment of waiting, but finally the kitchen door opened in a crack of light. Cas whispered, "I don't think anyone is here."

Bruno nodded and slipped in. They tiptoed into the front room and into a battle zone. The place had been violently turned out. The desk drawers spilled across the floor, volumes from the bookcases strewn everywhere. There were spots of blood on the carpet and on a chair. A quick check confirmed that the rest of the house had been similarly ransacked.

"Looks like the bastard beat us here," Bruno said grimly.

"Perhaps, but your Master has already failed," Cas said in a strangely exultant voice. Bruno spun around but was too late.

With a double-handed swing, she smashed a plaster statue of the Blessed Virgin over his head. As darkness closed in over Bruno, she bent over him, laughing. Her face was feral and sensual, a witchy green flame gleaming in her eyes as she smiled with lips red as blood. Her voice was low with baneful anticipation.

"And so have you, old fool. But Master Raume has been waiting for us. He will be most pleased."

✝

CHAPTER FORTY-SEVEN

The Feast of the Downfall of the Templars,
Wednesday, October 13

THE TORMENT in his twisted arms brought Bruno around, closely followed by the throbbing of his head, and then by the overall discomfort of his position. He found himself laying against a cold marble railing, hands bound tightly together through the fretwork.

He had to blink before he could focus on anything, and even then his vision was still not right. After some careful squinting, he decided it was due to his glasses being knocked out of shape rather than his cranium.

Bruno tried not to move much, but glance around discreetly in the dark. Peeking up, he saw the puny but gallant figure of the Blessed Virgin above the altar in the dim candlelight. He realized he was once again facing La Victoria.

"Holy Mother of God," he breathed.

"Amen to that, son," Malachy whispered hoarsely from the darkness beside him. Bruno craned his aching head around. The old priest, badly beaten, his swollen lower lip bleeding and without his mask-like glasses, was likewise trussed up next to him. Beyond him a motionless form that could only be Mike hung slumped forward, face down and limp.

"Is he —?"

"Keep it down," Malachy ordered. "No, he's not dead. Yet. They got the drop on us but he fought like a tiger. I've never seen that devil DeLaval rage like that. I feared they'd kill us right then and there."

Bruno twisted around. A dozen or so robed men, faces hidden by black hoods, scurried about silently readying the place. All wore the cross-and-snake emblem of the Black Order.

The sole light came from fat red candles, mounted seven apiece on several tall wrought-iron candelabrums that were being positioned on either side of the altar, with several other stands along the altar railing.

"Did they get it?"

Malachy shook his head. "The book? No, thank God, we told him nothing; he seemed to think you had it. He was awfully glad to get his old cross back, though. But Bruno, they also captured Marie. She was at the rectory when DeLaval and his gang burst in. I don't know what they've done with her."

Bruno began to feel nauseous. Groaning, he forced himself into a sitting position. From what he could see, the demise of the doomed chapel had already begun. Some of the pews had been unscrewed from the floor and shoved aside to make way for scaffolding in front of the stained glass windows.

La Victoria's altar had been stripped of its finery and draped with shiny black satin. A wooden throne and a lectern were being positioned to the left of it.

Suddenly a slender, petite woman in a long red gown slit to reveal more than it concealed walked past the railing behind him. "Cas!" he hissed. "Cassie, wake up!" She slowed, as if hearing a voice in the distance, but shrugged and continued.

A blow on the side of his face smashed Bruno's head against the cold stone, stunning him. DeLaval seized his chin, twisting his head back. "None of that, you little worm. You've done quite enough already to ruin my plans today."

He hit him hard in the stomach and then dragged him back up. "Eddie, you cretin, you have no idea what you've done! You've turned my precious Book over to my enemies. All you've accomplished in leading that bitch here is to ensure your death. Now I must contend for my rightful position and-it's-all-your-fault!" DeLaval emphasized the last words by bouncing Bruno's skull painfully off the rail in time to them.

DeLaval released his grip and ordered him gagged. "You ruined it for him too," he said, gazing at Mike, still unconscious. "Your poor, beautiful brother must now die too, I'm afraid." As one of the lackeys tightly fastened a cloth across Bruno's mouth, Hardy, the fat white stooge, whispered in DeLaval's ear. Still half-stunned, Bruno caught a glint of steel as DeLaval covertly accepted his own .45 from the minion.

Chuckling, DeLaval turned to Bruno, the whites of his gray eyes gleaming in the candlelight. "You're an ignorant chump, Eddie, and your intolerable interference will cost you everything. But even so, it shows initiative. A real take-charge spirit. The spirit I put there and nurtured," he boasted.

Pushing back his hood, he smiled coldly, and leaned forward just inches from Bruno's face. "How about it then?" he asked jeeringly. "The only way you're going to survive tonight is by surrendering to me. You could be useful calming the hysteria you've fomented. And in return, as I once told your brother," the deep voice became soft, "we could grant you — unimaginable delights." Bruno glared, straining at his ropes.

DeLaval beckoned and two men half-dragged, half-carried Marie into the sanctuary. The girl was trying to walk, but couldn't make her feet move fast enough. Clad only in a thin white shift, she seemed mercifully oblivious to everything.

The monks quickly laid her out on the altar, binding her ankles together. Leering wickedly at Bruno, DeLaval then roughly groped her for a moment. "Ah, still a virgin, after all? How sad for you, Eddie. Rest assured, however, that the Dread Lord will truly relish your donation of her sweet innocence."

He strode away chortling and licking his fingers.

Bruno's despair overwhelmed him. Only the measured pounding of a staff on the floor roused him again. One thump, pause, two thumps, longer pause, and then three more. A thin little man now stood to the left of the altar between the throne and the book stand. Garbed in red vestments with a black and gold embroidered cross and a curious horned hat, like a miter turned sideways, he leaned on a serpent-headed crozier.

"It is now midnight. The Chapter of the Order of St. Peter Martyr of the Province of Alvarado is hereby renewed and summoned for the five hundred and eighty-sixth anniversary celebration of the downfall of our enemies of old, the Knights Templar!" he declared in crisp English with an Italian accent. "I, Grand Master Abbadon, proclaim it! Let all aspirants attend! Seal the Chapel and prepare the place of working!"

From somewhere behind Bruno came a thurifier, befouling the air with a thick mixture of musky fumes from a huge censer. The smoke left Bruno light-headed but still in a lot of pain. There was a great deal of walking around widdershins, chanting, and mystical semaphoring in various directions.

"Let us offer obeisance to Our Dread Lord Lucifer and His Lady Lilith." Bruno desperately wished he could block his ears, as the group recited the Our Father backwards and the obscene parody of the Hail Mary, reverberating in his soul:

> *Hail, Mother of Darkness*
> *whom mortal men abhor.*
>
> *Death is within you*
> *whose power we adore.*
>
> *Black lust is your witness*
> *and terrible is your beauty*
> *that burns us like hellfire.*

> *Dread Lady,*
> *devourer of the Light,*
> *curse our foes with deadly fear*
> *now and forever*
> *with your might.*
>
> *Amen.*

Next to him, he heard Malachy whispering to the Blessed Mother against them. A nearby blackpriest did too, and savagely kicked him before gagging him also.

When all had been completed, the old man stated, "The Chapter is now open for the business of the Order." He thumped his snake-headed staff again and sat down.

There was a small disturbance behind Bruno. DeLaval strode into the sanctuary, bearing his black cross before him.

He knelt, humbly offering it to the Grand Master, who stood it in a slot at the back of the book stand. DeLaval kissed his lord's ring, rose, and turned slightly to face the sable-clad semicircle. "I, Master Baalberith, hereby claim the Magistracy of this Province once again. To justify my qualifications, I present the Cross of St. Peter Martyr. I bring two pure virgin Sacrifices, and a gift of an old enemy of our cause here." He bowed with a florid gesture at his captives. Only the Grand Master's scowl kept the cultists from applauding.

"Dare anyone dispute this Master's right to this office?"

"I do!" a confident voice echoed sibilantly from somewhere behind Bruno. "I demand that Frater Baalberith surrender all claims to this Province, and be deposed and tried at once for endangering the Discipline of the Secret," he declared, striding boldly into the sanctuary. He carried before him the black book, while Cas slinked a few steps behind.

The man knelt before his supreme master, presenting the *Codex*. The old man caressed it with a tender smile, and reverently placed it on the stand before the Cross.

The man rose, moving to the other side of the Grand Master, facing DeLaval. "I am Master Raume, and I too claim the Magistracy of this Province. I bring the Great Book of Art of Magister Azazael, a captured foe, and have the honor to present my now-tested candidate, Satrinya, for illumination and inhabitation as our new Black Madonna and High Priestess."

"That 'foe' belongs to me, and so does the *Codex*!"

"You abandoned —"

"Silence!" the Grand Master roared, thumping his staff. "Nothing belongs to either of you! Not even your minions. All are part of the treasured assets and heirlooms of this Order, to be bestowed as I, the Grand Master, see fit for our Order's benefit." He paused and said in a lower and even more sinister tone, "If you dare imagine otherwise, you are not brothers of this Order, but thieves to be numbered among our foes."

Master Raume pushed back his hood and bowed. Bruno realized with a shock that he knew that persuasive voice and that thick mustache. It was none other than Father Robert Cruz. He could tell from the jerking around and muffled curses coming from Malachy that he had recognized him, too.

"I thank you both, brothers, for your gifts." Abbadon seated himself regally on the ebony throne. "Especially I thank you for agreeing to resolve your differences in this Court, rather than with the fratricidal blood which once before drowned our liberty of operations in this Province.

"Nevertheless, this is a most grave dispute. Both your claims have merit. Master Baalberith, you have been accused with recklessly endangering the Order by a blatant and arrogant display of your faculties. Furthermore, having been publicly exposed, your usefulness to the Order has been greatly crippled. What do you have to say for yourself?"

Even Bruno could see the sweat start from DeLaval's forehead and he took a perverse satisfaction in it.

"Great lord, my brothers of the Order, it's true that these unfortunate scandals have undone many of our friends. But they came about during the long period when the Order was in abeyance here. For decades while it slept, I kept everything quiet and safe. If anyone's to blame, it's that worthless bishop.

"Yes, I demonstrated my skills by disposing of a toady turned dangerous. By then retiring, however, I've helped limit the scandals. Soon they will pass. After all, no criminal charges have been filed against anyone here. In the meantime, I've made important new allies, as you know, Luminence. And by the use of this oaf," he kicked Bruno's leg, "I regained vital evidence that would have doomed most in this room, which I fully shared with you, Master, as your loyal servant.

"As for Master Raume, it was his fumbling efforts to acquire the Book from me by deceit and treachery that has endangered our security more than anything I am accused of." His voice held an undertone of panic beneath its bravado.

The Grand Master gestured to Cruz, who bowed deferentially. "Luminence, Master Baalberith is too tainted to ever provide the public cover that is the primary duty of a Magister. He endangers us again as he has previously.

"Many years ago, Magister Azazael entrusted my master, the Master Xaphon, with the Book and Magus Baalberith with the Cross. This man then brought down my lord on the very same charges of which he now stands accused, by subverting one of Lord Xaphon's other novices. Likewise, the minion he so casually disposed of in that foolhardy attempt to kill me was one entrusted to him by our former Black Madonna, as Satrinya was to me, whose services he also sought to steal. Thus he has proved his vile contempt for all our traditions.

"His mad lust for power once before nearly exposed everything, so that the Order, once so vigorous here, had to be disbanded. He should never be entrusted again, but given up to the knife forthwith to ensure our safety!

"The Dread Lady delivered the *Codex* into my hands from his slave, and I am happy to say, as you desired, great Abbadon, that even now that buffoon of a bishop is paying for his error." He invitingly spread his hands. "Brothers, you may trust my stewardship. I call you back to the true and tested ways of the Devil that have given us the power of Hell on Earth. Help me rebuild the Order with sound demonology and restoration of discipline. Our might can grow unsuspected to ever-greater reaches. Some day we'll once again set our Grand Master on the Throne of Peter, to open wide forever the gates of Hades!" He bowed to the Grand Master with a flourish.

"And who should that Grand Master be?" DeLaval gibed.

"Enough! You Americans always talk like you're running for president." The old man stood up, leaning on his staff. "A pretty sermon, but this is not a popularity contest. All that matters is what you can do, now, with the keys of infernal power Our Dread Lord has granted us." He squeezed his hand into a fist, glaring about the room. A perturbation of terror emanated palpably through the smoky air and his underlings flinched.

The little man drew himself up in the flickering light. "Thus I have decided to put matters to the test. Let us see if you have truly mastered this ability you claim. Frater Baalberith, set your minion loose and allow him to sacrifice!"

The crowd shifted uncomfortably. "Luminence, are you sure that's wise?" Cruz said in a low voice to the Grand Master. "I am told that he has recently proven to be erratic and untrustworthy. Safer just to kill him and be done with it."

"I fear I must concur," DeLaval whispered. "He has become awake; I can no longer confidently vouch for him. He may go mad — or be taken by a spirit we cannot control."

There was excited murmuring among the members, several of whom snickered at Bruno. Cas laughed disdainfully too. "Masters, let me offer him to Our Dread Lord!" she implored. "Look at him — the fat imbecile! He thought he could save us, but he cannot save himself." Sneering down at Bruno, she leaned bewitchingly against her lord cousin's back.

"I demand silence!" the Grand Master bellowed. Cas cowered behind the blackpriest. But Abbadon then chuckled.

"Such eagerness!" the head of the Black Order said. "Fear not, little one; I remember you well. You'll get your turn." He smiled, not at all paternally, and nodded his approval at Cruz. "Well done, Frater — a worthy successor to her mother."

He looked disdainfully at his underlings and chided them scornfully. "Afraid, my little brothers?" His grin was pure malevolence. "Fear not, he will still be our scapegoat. I recall him, too — he did well back then; why not give him a chance also? He must face his Calvary, and you sometime as well, no? The will of a Magister must be of fire and steel. You must possess the courage to face the demons you summon. Or," he asked pleasantly, "need I try the Master Word, myself, on you?"

Both DeLaval and Cruz blanched, bowed and backed away. For several long minutes, DeLaval intently scrutinized the *Codex*, squinting closely and muttering. Finally, he straightened and with awful deliberation strode over to Bruno, who squirmed as the dark figure loomed over him. He shut his eyes momentarily and suddenly recalled the little nun who had given him the rosary in Denver. Opening them he gazed past DeLaval at the statuette of Mary and prayed with all his soul.

"Holy Lady," he thought despairingly, "I'm sorry if I had you confused with the bad one. Help me!"

But there was no salvation forthcoming. The blackpriest fell upon him. Bruno cringed but could not evade the old man's thick hands which gripped his skull. "Bruno, begone! Murmius awaken! Baalberith commands!" he rumbled, then bent over and whispered the Words of Power into Bruno's ear.

Bruno suddenly jerked violently and shook all over like a dog coming out of the water. DeLaval quickly stepped back. He signaled an underling to remove the gag.

"Who are you?" he demanded.

"I am Murmius. Why do you seek to command me, Master?" Bruno's voice was gutterally low and harsh.

"I do not command this time; I ask."

"Master?"

"This is your only chance, Murmius. Do you want to be the sole lord of the body?"

The creature that was no longer Bruno dropped his head limply and then raised it, unrecognizable. He curled his lips in a horrific grin, eyes burning under his furrowed brow, and cocked his head to one side. "What must I do, Master?"

With a grim smile. DeLaval gestured at the bound girl. "Take the blade and sacrifice."

†

CHAPTER FORTY-EIGHT

THE GRAND MASTER nodded and the blackpriests untied Bruno. They watched warily as he rose with animal grace into a crouch. He slunk to the book stand, hesitantly reached for the Cross of St. Peter Martyr, and lifted it upright high above his head.

"This is the Cross of Shame," he croaked and spun it around. He slid the longest arm off, revealing a slim, sharply-pointed blade, glistening evilly, upright in the candlelight. "Reverse it and it becomes the Blade of Power!"

Placing the scabbard carefully back down, he knelt and presented the dagger to the Grand Master, handle first. The old man laughed. "Behold," he commanded the others, accepting the blade, "how he observes the proper etiquette." He patted Bruno's bowed head paternally and casually nicked the man's outstretched hand before giving the knife back to him.

Bruno turned slowly towards the altar. For a long moment, he leaned over his helpless daughter bound there. The company of diabolists edged closer. He reached out and clumsily pawed her hair. Marie stirred, sleepily opening her eyes. "Daddy?" she groggily asked, and then began to scream.

Suddenly, Bruno shifted the dagger to his other hand, whirled, and stabbed the startled Grand Master. With an inhumanly ferocious grin, he drove the blade deep into old man's guts. Howling, Bruno then grabbed the knife with both hands, lifting Abbadon off the ground, throwing him off to the side. Robes fluttering, the Grand Master smashed into the wall and slipped slowly to the floor in a limp, bloody heap.

Bruno turned around and faced the shocked mob of lackeys. He did not seem quite human. His face was cruel and proud, lips set in a sensuous sneer, eyes shining with unholy joy. Flinging blood about, he mockingly roared in triumphant fury.

The coven stepped back with a collective gasp. But DeLaval and Cruz kept an eye on each other as well.

Bruno cackled darkly, sweeping the ensanguined dagger back and forth before him. "Is Murmius Grand Master now?"

DeLaval acted first, quickly reaching across the book stand to seize the *Codex*. As Bruno slashed at him, he drew the pistol and fired point-blank. Bruno fell, the dagger skittering noisily across the floor towards Malachy's feet.

Cruz leaped upon DeLaval. They wrestled recklessly, knocking over a candelabrum as they contended with all their might for the gun.

The toppling candlestick initiated a cascade of men and other fixtures falling about. A candelabrum landed on top of a fallen blackpriest, the spilling wax igniting his robes like a torch. He jumped up again screaming and ran blindly around.

Another candle rolled directly across the floor towards the scaffolding, coming to rest against some hanging plastic sheeting. It lit; the flames soon found several cans of industrial solvent and exploded with glee beneath the catwalk.

A stream of flaming fluid trickled across the floor towards the bound men. Malachy was struggling to reach the athamé with his feet when Bruno's hand fell upon its hilt. He dragged himself trailing blood over to Malachy and began sawing the ropes. "I'm back," he gasped. "Go, save Marie; I'll free Mike."

Malachy sprang to his feet, ripping off the gag. "Victoria!" he shouted like a conquistador. Striding over to the altar, he grabbed a candelabrum and brought it down hard upon Cruz' skull. The chancellor went down. The return stroke staggered DeLaval. He lost his grip on the Book, which spun across the floor under the burning pews to rest against the wall beneath the scaffolding, surrounded by flames but unharmed.

Cursing, DeLaval fired frantically at Malachy and missed. Then he ran to the metal framework and scrambled up it. Meanwhile, Bruno had finally freed Mike, and was desperately trying to rouse him when he beheld Cas across the room staring at the inferno in bewilderment. "Cas!" he yelled. "Whoever you are, be gone! Cas, return at once! Wake up, girl!"

Suddenly Cas woke herself from a bad dream into a living nightmare. She screamed piercingly and collapsed. By now the tumult was general, and the fire was spreading beneath the piled up pews. Black-robed men clawed the outside door open.

They scrambled out coughing, disappearing into the darkness, every blackpriest for himself. DeLaval, having reached the center of the wooden planks, dropped down to retrieve his precious Book. He set it on the catwalk, started to haul himself up, and found himself staring up into the pitiless eyes of Sean Malachy.

Malachy grabbed him and heaved him up with a great groan. "Now, you black-hearted fiend, it's finally time to pay for your sins!" He drew back his fist like the very wrath of God.

"You first," DeLaval growled and shot him in the stomach. Malachy looked surprised and crumpled at DeLaval's feet. Grinning, DeLaval contemptuously kicked him off the edge. "See you in hell."

He knelt and lovingly embraced the *Codex*. "Mine again, mine, all mine," he crooned. "Thank you, Dread Lord."

"You can do so in person," Bruno growled as he crawled through the fire onto the planks, clutching his bloody stomach.

"Murmius, be gone! Kazideel, come forth!" DeLaval commanded uselessly. "Eddie, stop! Please, Bruno!" The man hauled himself upright, dragging himself forward. There was no time to consult the Book.

DeLaval backed up and fired wildly but the man kept coming. The wizard was at the end of the scaffolding now, and could feel the fire lusting for him. Bruno grabbed the false priest, a satanic grin across his face.

He laughed horribly, mockingly. "Foolish creature, hoping to usurp the throne of God with your feeble magic. If Lucifer himself could not prevail, how dare you dream you ever could?" DeLaval gazed into the icy pits of Bruno's eyes and all hope and reason fled. The priest twisted in panic, slipped, and fell screaming into the flames, clutching the *Codex* to his heart.

Bruno stumbled back but the planks, now alight, collapsed as well. They threw him free of the blaze and a sudden silence ensued, soon filled by sirens nearing.

Mike arose uncertainly amidst the debris, dazed. His right arm was broken, nearly useless. He glanced around the smoke-filled chapel and heard coughing coming from the altar. Marie was there, insensible but gasping for breath in the increasingly foul air. Mike peered hopelessly up at La Victoria, knowing he couldn't save them both. "Forgive me, Blessed Mother."

Just then, Robert Cruz, coughing also, stumbled out of the smoke. "Bob, thank God you're here! Quick, help me." Their fingers fumbled at the knots binding Marie's limbs but finally succeeded. Still hacking, Cruz helped him lower the bewildered girl off the altar.

The chancellor kept looking around distractedly. "Save Our Lady," Mike yelled, as he clutched his niece. Cruz nodded. He climbed upon the altar and tore the statuette from its hidden brackets, setting off even more alarms.

Pandemonium ruled outside as firefighters sought to bring the hoses of several trucks to bear on the conflagration.

Mike stumbled out with Marie, surrendering her to the medics while Robert flopped down on the frosty grass, still holding the precious porcelain figurine.

Befuddled, Mike stood there coughing and gasping as rescue crews brought out Cas and Malachy, both unmoving.

The old priest was bleeding badly. A rescue worker ripped open Malachy's shirt while others ran for a stretcher.

Mike knelt beside him, tears leaving white channels down his sooty face. He was choking, too distraught to think clearly.

He took the old man's hand. "Are you sorry for all the sins you have committed?" Mike sobbed, remembering at last the rubrics for emergency confessions. The priest nodded.

The formula of forgiveness rose unbidden to his lips. "I absolve you —" he began, but Malachy opened his eyes and smiled weakly. "No, son; please, use the old words."

"Ego te absolvo," Mike wept, yet somehow the ancient phrases came out right, "ad omnibus censuris, et peccatis, in nomine Patris, et Filii, et Spiritus Sancti. Amen." Holding his right hand up with his left, he clumsily made the sign of the cross. Still smiling, the old man slowly closed his eyes. Mike gently kissed the top of his head, sobbing softly.

Still weeping, he rose then to seek out his brother. He found Bruno on a stretcher heading towards an ambulance.

"Don't worry about me, bro," Bruno said weakly through the oxygen mask. "I'm okay. We're free." He tried smiling and blood trickled into his beard. "Sorry for all the trouble."

Bruno coughed hard again and his breath was gurgling wetly as he gulped air in. From out of the darkness, Marie called. "Uncle Mike? Daddy? Where are you?"

"Over here," Mike shouted. Marie staggered over, nearly dropping the fireman's coat she was wrapped in.

"Oh Daddy, Daddy, please don't die," she sobbed, stroking Bruno's hair. He smiled slightly, eyes rolling as he slipped in and out of awareness. "Oh, good, sweetie, you're safe too," he mumbled. He raised his hand to her tear-stained face.

"Hold on, Bruno. We're nearly at the ambulance."

Bruno shook his head almost imperceptibly. "It doesn't matter," he whispered. "Everything's okay. We're all safe now. It's done."

His hand fell. Wailing like the sirens, Marie was dragged off her father as they loaded him inside the emergency vehicle, which quickly screamed off into the night.

Slowly, Mike pulled himself together as she clung to him, sobbing. He gazed around at the devastation as the pain from his own injuries began to demand attention.

The construction fences had been trampled down. The area around the burning basilica was a battlefield of fire hoses and running men. A soft wind carried sparks over to the adjacent flat roofs of the cathedral school and his rectory. Smoke was already rising from them also into the dark heavens.

He felt a soft, cold touch upon his cheek; unnoticed like some mysterious grace of God, it had begun to snow.

†

CHAPTER FORTY-NINE

1994: Sunday, April 17

THE CATHOLIC COMPLEX was a madhouse of activity this day a mere two weeks after Easter, when the Cathedral of Nuestra Señora de Victoria was to be officially dedicated. Most offices had been pressed into service as impromptu dressing rooms for the high members of the grand procession that would escort the statue to her new home.

Mike found the freshly consecrated bishop in his office, issuing last minute orders left and right as he vested. Robert Cruz' face lit up when he saw his old friend at the door.

"Mike! Come in! I didn't expect to see you — I thought you were already on your way to Ireland," he said warmly, shooing several scurrying deacons out the door and closing it firmly behind them. With a smile, Mike genuflected and formally kissed his superior's episcopal ring, then rose and hugged him.

"I should be, but I had to offer you my best wishes, Your Excellency. After all, your rescue of La Victoria from the fire, as well as the diocese from scandal, made this day possible."

"Thanks, my friend, I do appreciate it." The smile behind his mustache was as genuine as the sparkle in his eyes. "Delighted you could stop by. Now that the work of the Review Board is over, I've been wanting to ask you something. I'm going to have to reshuffle people anyway, so I thought I'd offer you the plum you deserve when you return. How about taking over St. Albert's?"

The bishop enthused, "As our newest West Side parish, it's growing fast. Lots of young families coming in as well as retired folks. You've been saying you wanted nothing more than to be a pastor, and we certainly need someone there who can remove the stench Olly left behind."

"Thanks, I'd like that," Mike responded but he didn't smile. "I wish I sounded more excited, but I'm so burnt out, my soul feels as blackened as the old cathedral. I'm not the priest I once was." He stared out the window towards the Espiritu Santos and sighed. "Yeah, I'll take it, but on one condition."

His glance at his superior was as sharp as his carefully stated words. "As Sean suggested, I want to formally exorcize every last church and consecrated space in this diocese."

"In God's Name, man, why? It's over."

"Everything could've been desecrated, not just the Lady Chapel. God knows how many other secret vaults there are, how many other altars defiled," Mike exclaimed, then forced himself to calm down.

"In any case," he concluded flatly, "all churches where children were raped have been polluted. Not just by the lewd acts but by the shedding of blood such crimes usually entail."

Cruz paled and flustered, "Not all our parishes, surely! Think what the media would say."

His subordinate shrugged. "You somehow managed to keep most of the disturbing details about the fire out of the news; this should be much easier. The purification can — and should — be done very circumspectly. No one need know other than the pastors. If I'm properly authorized, they might complain to you but they sure won't be able to stop me."

"They'll say it's a bloody witch hunt!"

Mike smiled grimly. "Perhaps we need one. I don't remember much of that night, but I'm sure there was a whole group of men involved. Those devils must still be around."

Cruz gazed at his old friend sadly. "You've definitely been working too hard. The sooner you get back to a normal parish life the better."

Mike smiled wanly. "You're right; I owed it to Sean to see the Board through — but I really need this sabbatical."

"Enjoy it well, my friend. Come back fully rested and refreshed: we need you here."

"I'll do my best." He checked his watch. "Well, we both have places to be. But I have one last question — something I've been wondering about ever since that night." He paused. "How is it you beat the fire trucks there?"

"Well, I called the rectory and there was no answer, so I drove over and saw the flames," Cruz said, frowning. "Why?"

"I recall so little; just still trying to fill in the blanks. In any case, it certainly was extremely lucky that you got into the cathedral so fast and were able to save La Victoria."

"Luck had nothing to do with it," the bishop said simply, with great sincerity. "I was supposed to be there."

"Of course," the priest replied mildly. He started to turn away, then paused. "You heard, by the way, that they finally found Chavez' body up in the mountains? Fell off a rock on the same day as the fire, the medical examiner said; dead even before the storm hit. Odd timing, don't you think?"

"Are you trying to somehow link the Ministers to all this?" Cruz demanded in surprise. Suddenly irritated, the bishop stalked over to the door. "Father Nolan, your vacation couldn't have come at a better time, I'm afraid. I grieve that these events have made you as skeptical as your brother," he said with a melancholy smile. "Have a good holiday, Mike. You need it." He made a perfunctory blessing.

"Take care of yourself, too, Excellency."

The bishop closed the door and stood there trembling with rage. Fingering a small key hung around his neck under his vestments, Cruz fought off a sudden urge to gloat over his priceless treasure and reassure himself that he had indeed won. He glanced at the closet door and sighed. No need — the photocopy he'd secretly made of the *Codex* the day before it was lost in the flames was doubtlessly safe, and he had more urgent concerns as the moment. He was glad Mike was going to be out of the country during the upcoming inaugural feasts. One less set of snooping eyes to worry about. But something would probably have to be done about his old friend, sooner or later.

He sighed again. There was an impatient tapping on the door. It was showtime. Putting a broad smile on his face, he opened the portal again to face his waiting assistants.

† † †

OUTSIDE, it was a warm morning for the season; only a few small clouds and several hot air balloons decorated the overarching blue sky. The trees in the valley below were already budding and blossoming, the sparkling river brimming with the spring runoff.

"I wonder what Father Malachy would have thought of all this," Kathy commented softly to her daughter. She gazed up past the smooth brown walls of the brand-new cathedral to its solitary bell tower crowned with a simple wooden cross. Already a landmark, Nuestra Señora de Victoria stood proudly as the centerpiece of the Catholic Complex on the bluffs of the Rio Espiritu overlooking the city, festively adorned with banners for today's grand occasion.

"Or Dad's goth girlfriend, the artist," Marie added. "Sorry, Mom, I shouldn't have mentioned her."

"It's okay, honey. I wasn't jealous then, certainly not now." Kathy hugged her daughter.

"Must we go in?" Marie didn't appear very eager but her mother had insisted they drop by the new basilica on the way to take Mike to the airport. The statue of La Victoria would be borne in full glory from its temporary quarters in the TV chapel in the chancery to its permanent display behind the high altar. It was time, Kathy had said, to face the past and let it go.

"Yeah, let's do it," she sighed. "But don't worry, we can't stay too long." She glanced at her daughter for confirmation. Marie had indeed recovered somewhat; still pale and thin, she seemed indefinably older than her age. Her vivacity was only beginning to bloom again after a long winter with Dr. Blackstone. But the psychiatrists had not been so successful with Casandra, still wandering lost amid the borderlands of madness. The other C.A.S.A. members had vanished like snow in sunshine as soon as their cases were settled.

"Come on, Mom, then," Marie said rather fatalistically, "let's get in there before they arrive." The Indian drumming in the distance had suddenly ceased and now the mariachis had struck up an energetic number.

Together they snuck through the happy crowds and the wide-open wooden doors, stopping in wonder just inside the spacious, shady interior. The adobe cathedral truly embodied the ideal traditional Southwestern church. Its gently-uneven earthen walls were painted white and tan within. Smooth, thick trunks of lofty ponderosa pines ascended to support the massive squared and carved wooden crossbeams and corbels holding up the patterned wooden slats of the ceiling. The choir loft, also housing the organ above the rear of the nave, was now full of eagerly waiting singers.

High, clear windows rather than stained glass provided light as well as a view of God's pure azure heavens and milk white clouds. Behind the altar, the tall stone altarpiece from the old chapel, with the soot removed and brightly repainted, glowed with fluorescent, almost psychedelic, intensity in the indirect radiance from the skylights concealed above the raised sanctuary.

Long and narrow, the nave was paved with polished dark-brown flagstones. The carved wooden pews were already half-filled with people waiting for the Mass to begin.

An usher handed Kathy a program booklet and they went to sit near the back at the end of one of the long burnished seats. "Since we have to leave soon, let's sit where your dad would," she whispered with a slight smile. "You bet," Marie agreed, "right near the exit."

Soon the church was filled to overflowing. Ushers packed the pews to keep the central aisle clear. But at last came the procession, and the congregation stirred.

It was quite a long pageant, led by a new master of ceremonies and an acolyte bearing a Pueblo bowl filled with sweet-burning sage and piñon. After them, the crucifer and several servers with candles preceded a vast double line of laymen, everyone from dignified Indians in velvet, silver, and turquoise, to the Knights of Columbus and other such orders with their plumed admiral's hats and cross-bearing capes.

Then the clergy entered, led by the tiny crop of six current seminarians, several platoons of deacons and priests, a squad of assorted bishops, and even a small flock of cardinals. Finally Bishop Robert Cruz, clad in ornate, shining vestments and miter with a brand-new crosier, made his entrance. He smiled widely at everyone, blessing the children as he passed. Indian dancers in their fanciest feathers and masked matachines surrounded the float behind him.

All rose when the bearers of the holy image of Our Lady of Victory paced in with great solemnity at last. Carried upon their shoulders, the indomitable queen swayed amid mounds of blooming lilies and roses, shaded by a white silk canopy. The mariachi band played zestily behind, bringing up the rear.

The line took some time to wind into the sanctuary and even longer for the statue to be installed in its niche with much ceremony and incense. Then Cruz briefly took the pulpit.

"Your Eminences, Excellencies, priests, deacons, Governor and Senators, Congressmen, Representatives, Mayors, and of course, People of God, greetings and welcome to our new house of worship," the Bishop of Alvarado pronounced grandiloquently. "¡Bienvenidos al nuevo hogar de Nuestra Señora!

"Today marks the end of one era here in our diocese and the beginning of another. Our faith in the Church has been tested with fire and it has been renewed.

"So today, before we begin this Mass of Dedication of this marvelous new cathedral, I just want to say thanks to you all. Muchas gracias for your support in the many kind letters and in the contributions that have kept our diocese afloat. The last lawsuits are being settled, and everyone injured by those unfortunate events of the past is being helped.

"Because of your continued faith in us, our Church is revived; those few bad apples from outside that corrupted our diocese have been eliminated, and strict screening for all our clergy is in place. Your children are safer than ever before."

He paused, smiling confidently. "So let this magnificent new home of Our Lady stand as a monument of our strength and endurance. Let its beauty renew us in our faith in Holy Church and Her Love for us all!" He spread his arms widely, in the prayerful, inclusive gesture so reminiscent of Chavez, reverently folded his hands and turned to begin the Mass.

The master of ceremonies could restrain himself no longer. He leaped up, declaring loudly, "¡Viva nuestro obispo nuevo! ¡Viva la iglesia santa! ¡Viva la fe católica!" There was enthusiastic and near-universal applause.

Kathy leaned over. "Can you feel it?" she whispered. "Christ, I mean. Do you feel His presence? I sure don't. This is all very grand and glorious, but it doesn't feel like Jesus is here at all. Maybe just because the place is so new, but even with all this pomp, it feels like a — a whitened sepulcher."

"It's empty somehow," Marie agreed. She shuddered slightly. "Mom, can we go now? All those priests up there make me nervous."

"Sure, honey. It's time, anyway." The two stood as one and quietly slipped out through the crowds. A couple leaning against the wall quickly snatched their vacated seats.

Outside it was still a warm, brilliantly sunny spring morning. Marie's eyes filled with tears. For a moment, the man leaning on the van across the street looked like her father. She waved, but it was only her uncle waiting for them. He waved back and she ran to him.

As the choir began to sing, her mother trudged slowly behind her, out of the shadow of the church into the bright light of day.

☦ ☦ ☦

ABOUT THE AUTHOR

JAY NELSON has been an unlucky altar boy, an impoverished artist and writer, an Independent Catholic priest, and an advocate on behalf of victims and survivors of clergy sexual and ritualistic abuse.

A native resident of the Land of Enchantment, he lives there much like a hermit, tolerated and amused by his cats.